THERE'S A BOND THAT DEFIES ALL REASON: A VLAD AND HIS CAR . . .

When Eric's treasured Fang the 'Stang takes on a life of its own, it turns out love is a two-way street.

The sight of a classic Mustang convertible parked on the street in front of me snapped me out of my reverie. Not just any Mustang, either—my Mustang. I love that car. Damn werewolves had wrecked it. It had cost me a fortune to have it put back together, but I just couldn't live without it.

"Try to start it again," Magbidion yelled over his shoulder to my mechanic, Carl. "I think we have his attention."

Carl climbed into the car and turned the key. "Nothing." He climbed back out. "I don't understand it."

"I do," Magbidion muttered. "Assuming his place of power really is his car, then it won't run unless we bring him back. We've got to make him mad."

My daughter, Greta, a blond Amazon, stood next to the car. "Shit, if Dad knew that Tabitha was shacking up with that bigwig up at the Highland Towers, we wouldn't need to—"

"She's shacking up with who, where?" I snarled.

The Mustang's engine roared.

ReVamped is also available as an eBook

Turn the page to read rave reviews of *Staked* by J. F. Lewis!

Praise for
STAKED
The gory, sexy, funny, fierce, and totally unforgettable
debut novel from

J. F. LEWIS

"*Staked* will probably appeal to most readers who like Jim Butcher's Harry Dresden but wish that Harry would stop being so damn nice all the time. Hugely entertaining—*Staked* is recommended reading."

—LoveVampires.com

"A pedal-to-the-metal demolition derby of sex and violence. Werewolves and vampires were never so much fun."

—Mario Acevedo , author of *X-Rated Bloodsuckers*

"A fast-paced story with a heady mixture of humor, violence, and sex."

—Library Journal

"Impressive. . . . The plot is reminiscent of the early, and best, of the Anita Blake novels."

—Don D'Ammassa

"From the start I could tell this book would be something special. By page 8, I was proclaiming it a winner to my friends. I'm happy to report that I was correct."

—BestFantasyStories.com

"Eric is the bloodsucking equivalent of a *Spinal Tap* song: he goes all the way to eleven. . . . An entertaining story that stands out from the more generic vampire fare. With a fast-paced plot, a variety of interesting characters, and a certain cheesy eagerness, *Staked* makes for great reading."

—Green Man Review

"Uncovering the mystery surrounding our rebel hero is a reward in itself, while the action scenes in this raucous, raunchy blood-opera make for a very satisfying crunch."

—Dark Realms magazine

"From the moment you step into Eric's world, you are rocketing from one high-tension situation to another. . . . The exciting conclusion will definitely leave you breathless and wanting more."

—RomanceJunkies.com

"Serious yet funny, gory yet tender, magical and still down-to-earth. . . . In other words, a must-read!

—A Book Worm's Diary

"Once you get caught up in the world of *Staked*, you're stuck in its thrall. . . . *Staked* walks a great balance between suspense and gore . . . a balance one rarely sees in first novels."

—Our Gaggle of Girls

Don't miss Eric's first hilarious adventure by J. F. Lewis . . .

STAKED

Available in bookstores everywhere

REVAMPED

J. F. Lewis

Pocket Books
New York   London   Toronto   Sydney

Pocket Books
A Division of Simon & Schuster, Inc.
1230 Avenue of the Americas
New York, NY 10020

First Pocket Books trade paperback edition March 2009

POCKET and colophon are registered trademarks of Simon & Schuster, Inc.

For information about special discounts for bulk purchases, please contact Simon & Schuster Special Sales at 1-800-456-6798 or business@simonandschuster.com

Manufactured in the United States of America

10 9 8 7 6 5 4 3 2 1

Library of Congress Cataloging-in-Publication Data

Lewis, J. F. (Jeremy F)
    ReVamped / J. F. Lewis.—1st Pocket Books trade pbk. ed.
        p. cm.
    1. Vampires—Fiction. I. Title.
    PS3612.E9648R48 2009
    813'.6—dc22
                                          2008039569

ISBN-13: 978-1-4391-0228-2
ISBN-10:   1-4391-0228-7

This book is dedicated to four very special guys:

My dad, Ferrell

My grandfather, C.M.

My friend & unpaid researcher, Rob

and

My good buddy, Rich

ACKNOWLEDGMENTS

Welcome back to the Void!

The author would like to acknowledge every single person who made this book possible, but he is quite certain (yet again) that he's left someone out. If it was you . . . oops . . . again.

First and foremost, my thanks go out to you, the reader. Whether you're here for a return visit to Void City or are a first time guest, I'm glad you came and I hope you enjoy your stay.

I owe a debt of gratitude to my writing group, the WTF (Write the Fantastic): Rob, Mary Ann, Dan, Karen, Janet, and Virginia. Literarily speaking, they are murderous bas tards yet they still manage to be good friends with enough mad baking skills between them that I am often the bearer of cookies at late night convention panels.

Thanks are also owed to Mom, Dad, Shea, Rich, Sandra, Rachel, Daniel, and the Lawleys (Jimmy, Linda, and Hunter) for support and friendship above and beyond the call of duty.

These acknowledgments would not be complete without mentioning two mighty women: my agent, Shawna McCarthy and my editor, Jennifer Heddle. Without them, you wouldn't be reading this. Plus, they both let me keep Fang, a character that I was (perhaps unreasonably) worried might not survive the editing process.

Thank you to Gene Mollica for the wonderful cover . . . I really like the way you incorporated Fang.

An additional "You rock" goes out to the many podcasters who happily agreed to run audio promos for the series, in particular: J. C. Hutchins, Mur Lafferty, Rick & Anne Stringer, Kimi, Michael R. Mennenga, Summer Brooks, and Shaun Farrell.

Last, but certainly not least, thank you to my wife and my sons . . . just because.

1

ERIC:

WELCOME BACK TO THE VOID

If you've never been blown up before, I can't recommend it. I suggest it even less if the perpetrators are using blessed shaped charges of C-4. Being atomized by that kind of firepower would have ended most vampires, but I'm not that lucky. I'm *special.*

In ice cream terms, vampires come in three flavors: chocolate, strawberry, and vanilla. I'm grape sherbet—hard to come by and much more likely to give you brain freeze. Technically there's one more type of vampire, Drones, but they're barely even immortal—the vampire equivalent of ice milk—and they certainly wouldn't have survived what happened to me.

My name is Eric Courtney and up until several minutes ago, I was a vampire. Now . . . ? Let's just say I'm working on it.

The only good thing about being explosively deconstructed was that the sensation was new and different, two essential requirements for keeping an immortal from getting too bored. Being blown up by my best friend, having my body destroyed, and seeing my strip club obliterated weren't what I would have chosen to shake things up, but I've learned to roll with the punches, even the sucker ones.

For the first few seconds I actually thought I might be really most sincerely dead. Ended. Gone for good. I hovered over the still blazing ruin of my strip club, a glowing blue specter wearing jeans and a *Welcome to the Void* T-shirt, unseen, unheard, and utterly unamused. The neon sign flared impressively before melting into slag. Shards of glass covered the street between the Demon Heart and the old Pollux Theater, where the *Casablanca* poster in the display began to wither under the intense heat, browning at the edges as it curled. I owned both buildings, having bought them inexpensively after, of all things, a fire.

Security alarms from the buildings on the block adjoining mine rang out into the night. I ran a hand over my spectral face.

How do I get my body back?

That was the first question. I'd been reduced to ashes before, but Talbot (my . . . bouncer) or one of my other employees had always been around to pour blood on my remains. Vampires run on blood, so blood plus vampire ashes meant poof—instant vampire, kind of like the instant Martians in those old Looney Tunes animated shorts. I had no idea how Talbot and the gang could bring me back this time, though. No ashes.

Being a ghost wasn't all bad, at least. As a ghost, my thoughts were clearer than they'd ever been, and the hunger for blood, that ever-present inner dark that had driven me to do most of the questionable things I'd done in my unlife, was gone. It was as if, for once, my brain worked like everybody else's; no memories seemed to hover just out of reach. Even my attitude had shifted. I'm an angry guy, but searching my feelings, I found my anger replaced by pain and more grief than I'd ever felt before, a sense of endless loss.

The world of the living was a faded watercolor painting seen through my noncorporeal eyes, blurry and surreal. Most of the Demon Heart's side of the street burned, flames devouring the place hungrily.

Firefighters and police showed up in time to save the Pollux. Distorted figures in half-recognized uniforms sprayed water on the ancient movie palace. It bothered me that I couldn't smell the smoke or feel the heat of the fire. Even with all the hustle and bustle, the heartbeats of the humans responding to the emergency did not echo in my ears. Instead, their voices were muted and far away.

I stared at the fire engine. They had parked it in the middle of the street, right over the spot where my former best friend Roger had been eaten by werewolves. I saw a flash of him in my mind's eye, reduced to a skeleton, still screaming as the Orchard Lake pack consumed him in his entirety. I felt a pang of guilt for siccing them on Roger, even though he'd betrayed me, but it was a brief pang. Intellectually, I knew he hadn't really been my friend.

For the last forty years Roger had plotted my downfall, but with my memory functioning properly, it was hard not to hear his screams echoing through my brain. Worse, though, were the memories of Marilyn, watching as the explosion ripped through her, seeing her die . . . Her death had been Roger's parting birthday present to me. What a pal.

At least Tabitha hadn't been at the club when it had happened. If there's a good time to ditch your boyfriend, I'd say right before he gets incinerated is a good pick. So, kudos to her for timing.

"It's all so eerily beautiful," said a voice. Marilyn was standing next to me. Young again, red hair hanging down past her shoulders, she sported the same leather jacket she'd worn in the photograph I'd carried in my wallet before it got torched with the rest of me. If Ann-Margret or Maureen O'Hara had been blessed with more attractive younger sisters, they might have looked almost as sensational as my Marilyn. She'd been the bait for the trap Roger had set for me. I had to give him high marks for effectiveness there. Picking the love of my life (if not the love of my death) to lure me to my final destruction was primo angst material.

"Like a Van Gogh painting," Marilyn continued. "*The Starry Night* or *The Café Terrace on the Place du Forum, Arles, at Night.*"

"'Starry, Starry Night' is an old Don McLean song right?"

Marilyn laughed. "That song's called 'Vincent,' but 'Starry Night' is in the chorus."

I was born in 1926 and Marilyn was a few years my senior. When I turned into a vampire, she stayed human, wouldn't let me turn her . . . so I'd watched her age for over forty years. I had missed her so much without even realizing it. The person she had become, the one who was old and sick and smoked too much, bore almost no resemblance to the Marilyn I remembered, the one who was here now.

"I'm sorry," she said softly. "I am so sorry, Eric."

Ghosts, as it turns out, can hug one another. I took her in my arms, crushed her to my chest. We probably looked like long-lost lovers in some old black-and-white movie, but given our ages, I guess that shouldn't have come as a big surprise. Her breasts pressed against me, without warmth. It didn't matter. I covered her with kisses and she laughed again, despite herself, before she pulled away.

"What is it?" I asked.

"I need to tell you something." I didn't need an orchestral cue to know it was bad news. Marilyn is not a timid woman. She could stare down an angry vampire, blow smoke in his face, and laugh when he snarled. I couldn't count the number of times she'd done exactly that . . . to me. I had never seen her so scared.

"Tell me," I said. "Look. It's okay. I mean, we may be forced to haunt the remains of a strip club for eternity, unless our bus is just late or something, but I don't see how this is your fault."

Shaking her head, she walked away from me, passing unthinkingly through a firefighter.

"I'm not staying," she said. "I can feel it"—she placed her hand over her bosom—"inside. I just . . . I have to tell you something before I . . . go."

Go? Going sounded like a bad idea. Marilyn walked back and put her arms around me. "I didn't know about it, I swear. When Roger told me, I was shocked and horrified, and when you rose, I knew that I couldn't go through with it. So he . . ."

A babbling Marilyn was an even bigger warning sign. My girl didn't babble. She didn't mince words, and she sure as hell didn't let her words trail off into nothingness.

"When I rose . . . as a vampire?"

As far as I knew, I'd died in a car wreck. Coming back as a vampire had surprised me as much as it had anyone else. When I rose, it was two weeks after the crash at two in the afternoon on the day Marilyn and I were supposed to have been wed. "Am I late for something?" I'd asked her before bursting into flames. The look in her ghostly eyes, there in the remains of my club, was the same as the look she'd had back then standing over my grave. And I was afraid of that look, that not-only-did-I-not-get-what-I-wanted-for-my-birthday-but-the-gifts-that-I-did-get-prove-no-one-really-understands-me-at-all look—full of hurt and disappointment and . . . fear.

I did not want to know. Call me King Avoidance. I have a sixth sense for things I don't want to know and her manner pegged this as top of the scale ignorance-is-bliss material. Her confession or revelation or whatever was best left unsaid, best taken into the grave and left there. All the bad ones are.

No one wants to hear that you never really loved them, that it was you who ran over their pet dog, that you forgot to pull out, or that you actually did nail your secretary that one time in New York when you claimed you were in separate rooms.

You've got to understand . . . being blown up was not the most traumatic thing that has happened to me lately. When it turned out Roger was behind all the attempts on my unlife, the one who set me up to fight the werewolves, the one who tried to spike my blood supply . . . I hadn't wanted to know that, either, would have given almost anything to change things so that he'd been smart enough to cover it all up without my ever knowing. That way I'd still have been able to think he was my friend. I'd have preferred the lie.

Marilyn's eyes told me I'd prefer a lie in her case, too. Any secret that had stayed buried that long didn't need exhuming. She opened her mouth to tell me, but I couldn't let her finish that sentence. I wasn't ready for her to move on, so I kissed her.

She kissed me back—not a passionate kiss, but the tender intimacy of two people who have grown old together and accepted the best and the worst in each other.

It might have been more romantic if that fat policeman hadn't stepped through us. A bed would have been nice, too. If we could touch, I was pretty sure we could do other things. For forty years I had craved her touch. To make love one last time would have been a kindness, but it didn't happen.

She ended the kiss and there was no second one.

Marilyn took my hand and led me over to a bench in the little glassed-in bus stop where my bouncers would leave guys who'd had one too many. "I missed you so much," I told her.

"I've been with you for half a century, Eric." She scowled.

"You know what I mean," I said sheepishly. I gestured to her body. "Not like this, not in the same way."

Her expression softened. "That ought to make me angry, but it doesn't. I always find it hard to be mad at you for long."

"Brain damage," I responded.

She almost laughed. It literally rose and fell dead in her throat. The laughter couldn't escape whatever was bothering her.

"Don't joke," she said sharply. "Don't be so much like your old self. It makes everything too hard."

"Good. Let it be too hard," I said briskly, rushing through the words, running them together. "If not telling me will keep you here with me, then don't tell me. I'd rather not know."

"You really need to know this, Eric. I'm sorry." She looked at me, expecting a response.

"No, you aren't," I told her. "You don't have to say anything, but if your mind's made up . . . I've never been able to unmake it."

"Do you remember what happened when you died?" she asked.

"I was driving Roger's car, the brakes went out, blah, blah, blah. What are you going to tell me, that you sabotaged the brakes because you didn't want to marry me?"

"Roger did," she spat out quickly.

I froze. If I'd been in a cartoon, the angel on my shoulder that represented my good nature would have just been gut shot by the devil representing my bad side.

"He wanted me to marry him," she continued. "Roger and I had been seeing each other for months, and I didn't know how to tell you—"

I got up and walked off toward the Pollux, leaving Marilyn still sitting on the bus stop bench. Two of the firemen pointed at the enclosure. Its rear window froze and shattered as I passed through it. I didn't know why it happened. I assumed it was part of whatever ghost powers I'd wound up with, but I didn't give a damn, not then.

"Eric," she called after me. "Wait! You need to hear this."

"Actually, I don't." My voice was calm, but I wasn't. "I was murdered by my best friend *and* my fiancée?" I scoffed. "Nope, didn't need to know that. What, then he got attacked by a vampire and voilà, sucks to be you?"

"No, Eric." She chased after me. I stopped just shy of the middle of the road, didn't turn to face her. "It wasn't like that. I had nothing to do with it. When they called me and told me you were dead . . . I called Roger and he already knew. I went over to his house and he told me what he had done to you and then he showed me what he had let someone do to him."

"He'd become a vampire," I said flatly.

"He said that it had happened three weeks earlier when he'd driven over to Chicago for that conference. He'd met a woman from Atlanta . . . a woman named Gabriella . . ."

"A woman who was really a vampire, and then she turned

him." I shook my head, rounding slowly toward Marilyn. "Well, that's just so fucking cute I could puke."

I felt a little tremor of rage, and when I did, I had a brief glimpse of Carl's garage, of my Mustang. I loved that car, an artifact from my living days, a 1964 ½ convertible. I'd wrecked it three days before, but Carl was doing a great job on the repairs. Why I saw it in my mind then, I couldn't say. It was weird.

"I told him to get away from me." Marilyn touched my shoulder, then pulled away as if she'd been stung. "I ran from the house, but he caught me. . . . He pushed himself inside my mind and touched my thoughts. He left something there. He smeared blood on my skin, willed it into a tattoo, a little frog. He said that if I wouldn't join him willingly then I would be his human slave, his thrall."

Thrall. I had one of those. Rachel, my ex-girlfriend's little sister, had damn near forced me to make her my thrall during the whole werewolf brouhaha. But as Marilyn described the process, it sounded pretty familiar, except I hadn't given Rachel any kind of tattoo, blood or otherwise, and Rachel sure as hell wasn't my slave. As far as I knew, thralldom granted the mortal participant protection from other vampires, marked them as protected. It also widened a vampire's senses, allowing them to detect the thralls of other vampires while simultaneously allowing the vampire to sense the location of their vampiric offspring.

"Why didn't you say anything?" I demanded, turning back to face her.

"He wouldn't let me. When you rose and you were stronger

than him, he wasn't sure what to do. He'd made me his thrall, and every time I tried to talk about it, the words just wouldn't come out. He'd specifically forbidden me to tell you."

I cursed aloud and saw another glimpse of my car. Ignoring the automotive strangeness, I grabbed the front of her jacket, the ghost leather creaking under my phantom fingers. "What the fuck good does this do me now? Did you tell me just to make yourself feel better? To drive me out of my freakin' mind so my crazy-ass ghost can haunt the Demon Heart?"

"He's been afraid of you for years, Eric, too afraid to kill you, and too afraid to really do anything to me when you were around."

"When I was around? What about when I wasn't around?" I yelled. "What then?"

"I think you already know the answer to that," she told me, resignation clear in her voice. And I guess she was right, at that.

"I'm so glad Willie and his werewolves ate that mother-fucker," I ranted.

"That's why I had to tell you," she sobbed. Marilyn tried to put her arms around me, but all the love-struck puppy had gone out of me and I pushed her away. She kept her balance, but I couldn't look at her. "Good! Be mad at me, Eric, as angry as you want, but you have to hear this. You may think you know how devious Roger was, but he's worse. I can't believe I ever thought about leaving you for him! He had some kind of plan to steal your power, to become whatever it is that you are. You're not a normal Vlad. At first Roger didn't believe it, but all the things he did to you, they were part of a test, to convince him, to prove what you were . . . are."

I looked back at her and she wasn't crying. The cadence of her words was increasing, trying to beat the clock. She sounded as if her time was running out, the commercial was almost over and she had to get the rest of her message out before she returned to regularly scheduled programming. "Last night, when I was tied to the chair, I heard them say that you are the rarest of the rare, a king of kings, an emperor."

"Emperor?" I scoffed.

"It has something to do with why your eyes are still blue, why you never went through postmortem syndrome. She said it's like your transformation stopped just before it was finished, and in that gray area, not alive, not dead, and yet not entirely undead, there is a lot of power to be had." In retrospect I should have asked her who the "she" in that sentence was, but I was too caught up in thoughts of Marilyn and Roger to think very clearly.

"Well, la de fucking dah, Marilyn." I tossed up my hands. "What the hell good does that do me now?"

"Because Roger had a backup plan. I don't know what it was, but he was working with . . ." She clawed at her throat, eyes ablaze with terror. "Oh, God . . ." She coughed. "It's coming for me . . ." I tried to help, but my hand passed through her shoulder.

"Marilyn!"

Her mouth opened wide in a silent scream, and then it grabbed her. I didn't know what it was, at first, and then my memories of El Segundo washed over me in a wave. I'd never been on fire so many times in one weekend. El Segundo was where I'd met Talbot, and where I'd met my first demon. Being in the presence of a demon had never bothered me when I'd been a vampire. Now that I was a ghost, its presence burned.

Fear ripped through me, tore at my ectoplasmic brain with tiny meat hooks. A swirling cloud of Marilyn screeched through the air toward its open mouth, her ghostly essence both compressed and stretched, converting her into an unrecognizable blue smoke funnel—a hellish *I Dream of Jeannie* moment. But this was a demon, not a bottle, and that was Marilyn, not Barbara Eden. Where Marilyn had seemed clear and precise to my spirit eyes, the demon was an outline, a hole of blackness in the air. Marilyn, what was left of her, vanished into that void.

The presence turned its attention to me. "Do I know you, revenant?" it asked.

"Give her back!" I charged the demon, certain that I might get sucked into the same vortex, but not giving a damn. Fighting is one thing I'm never afraid of. My hands passed through the creature with no effect. Ghosts can't harm demons, I guessed.

The demon let loose with a series of loud whinnies combined with the sound of a machine crushing ice. It could have been laughter. "Her soul was promised to me, angry one. It is my due for services rendered."

"Let her go."

"I have a contract." The demon moved closer. Supernatural panic forced me to my knees like a two-ton bouncer.

The power rolled over me, tried to pound me down onto my face, but I refused to go all the way down. A Mustang's engine roared to life somewhere far away. Beneath me frost formed on the asphalt.

Cops and firefighters screamed. I don't know if they saw me or the demon, but most of them ran. One of them was too close. His life called to me, not like blood, but warmth. The ground rushed up to meet him as his soul tore free and surged into me. The frost on the ground spiraled out from my phantom knees, crusting thickly on the man-made surface.

"Give her back!" Nourished by the firefighter's soul, I forced myself to my feet. His spirit coursed through me, the sensation not unlike the feeling of warmth and fullness I got when, as a vampire, I'd made a fresh kill. *Powers*, I thought to myself. *If I'm a ghost, then I have ghost powers, like freezing the window, breaking it. But will any of them kill a demon?*

"An arrangement might be reached," the demon purred. He sounded mildly impressed. If he was giving in, willing to deal, then it was likely I could hurt him. I just needed to figure out how. "An exchange," the demon continued. "You for her?"

"An old friend of mine warned me about deals like that," I growled. "He said that demons always cheat."

"No prevarication has ever taken place on my part, I assure you, but I do obey the letter of the agreement. It is true that many do not"—he paused—"think through contracts as carefully as they should.

"Marilyn made her deal. The agreement was reached under compulsion from her vampiric master, but the signature is hers. Her soul in exchange for an . . . interces-sion." The demon moved back, its edges bleeding into its surroundings. "I believe I have a viable substitute, however, and will be able to perform the ritual without using up Ms. Robinson's soul. I'll hang onto her for now, shall I? I hope we meet again, angry ghost. But having collected this lady's soul, I now have other duties to perform, including the inter-cession of which I spoke."

I lunged for him again, but when I crossed the white line in the middle of the road, I flew apart, my essence bursting into countless little particles of self, the world blurring even more than before. Everything went silent, then dark, until I re-formed, standing in the spot where the bomb had gone off. Nice! Not only was I a ghost, I was a ghost with a short leash.

2

TABITHA:

WATCHING IT HAPPEN

I was half a mile from the Highland Towers, suitcase in hand, when I heard the explosion. Two seconds later I felt Eric burning. He's my sire, the one who made me immortal. He was also the man I'd just dumped. When I walked away from him, I had expected him to chase me, but he hadn't, not yet, and now I didn't know if he'd ever have the chance. I'd walked out on him in the middle of a crisis, one I'd thought he could handle.

I was wrong.

Eric's scream cut through my head, the scent of charred flesh and smoke hit me hard, dropping me to my knees on the sidewalk. The suitcase fell from my hands and my scream matched Eric's. We shouted, not in pain, but in anguish. We shouted a name. It wasn't mine. It was hers. "Marilyn!"

Other vampires screamed the same name. A flash of contact linked us all for a single heartbeat and I saw them—Eric's other ex-girlfriends, the vampires he'd made and discarded, even Greta, his pretend daughter. The connection wavered, and my viewpoint withdrew, arcing up and back from the wrecked remains of the Demon Heart.

Nearby, I thought I saw my sister's face looking out of the doorway of the Pollux, but it wasn't her; it couldn't be. Rachel was dead. It had to be the witch, the one who looked like my sister. A small gold padlock hung from a choker around her neck, glittering in the firelight. She wore the same tight black hip-huggers and midriff top she'd been wearing when I ran into her at the Demon Heart, when she'd been with Roger. The red and blond highlights in her hair echoed the colors in the flames. She smirked and walked back inside the Pollux, removing a jade bracelet from her left wrist as she went, and the vision faded.

My sense of Eric was gone. He was dead. I closed my eyes and blinked back bloody tears.

"Damn it!" My voice was swallowed up by the empty street. Cars passed in the night. In Void City, you don't stop to check on people. You mind your own business, even if the damsel in distress is wearing a low-cut blue dress and filling it well. *I can still go to Phillip*, I told myself. *He'll know what to do.*

I didn't hear the car stop, but when the car door opened, the music snapped me out of it. Rob Zombie's voice rang out, singing strains of the chorus to "Living Dead Girl," and I laughed. When Rachel had died, I'd gorged on chocolate, but that option was lost to me now. The heartbeats of the men in the car hammered in my ears. I was angry, lost— my whole unlife plan had revolved around Eric, making him love me—no, making him realize that he loved me—and it was all gone. Ruined.

"Hey, lady. You okay?" Alcohol-tainted breath singed my nostrils even from ten feet away. I stood up, and there were catcalls. Four men, three in the car, and one on the sidewalk. The car smelled of blood and sweat and fear. A metallic tang mixed with gunpowder and I knew that at least one of them had a gun.

"We don't have time for this," the blond in the backseat muttered under his breath. A wedge of blond bangs hung down over his right eye. "We have what Mistress wants."

"Fuck you," snarled the driver. "We made a big score tonight. Might as well celebrate."

"Look at the tits on that bitch," whispered the other man in the backseat, next to the blond. "Are we going to—?"

"She's a vampire, you idiots," the blond muttered even more quietly, anger glinting in his eyes. "And she's a Queen, at that."

The man on the sidewalk wore a *Void City Howlers* jersey and jeans. He wiped his nose with one hand and stared at me with bloodshot eyes. "You need a ride, lady? We can give you one." He looked back at the car and stifled a laugh. "We can all bunch up."

"Do you have a gun?" I asked.

"Maybe." Mr. Bloodshot Eyes went still and serious.

"Want to get it out?"

He took a step back toward the car, as if he subconsciously sensed the danger. I came forward, stepping under the streetlight. When he saw the blood running from my eyes, the tears of a vampire, he took a breath. "Shit."

The blond stepped out of the car, gun drawn from a shoulder holster under his jacket. He aimed it at the driver. "Pop the trunk."

"What the hell are you doing, Esteban?" Esteban was gorgeous. He wore black slacks, a white dress shirt with an open collar, and a black suit coat. The way he moved made it clear he was used to custom-made suits. Esteban pulled the trigger without blinking, firing through the open window. The driver's brains exploded across the steering wheel.

Mr. Bloodshot Eyes spun on Esteban, drawing a gun from the back of his pants. It snagged in his jersey and I charged him. Vampire speed is one of the best parts of being undead. My fingernails extended into claws, a vague stinging in my fingertips as they grew. I flayed open Mr. Bloodshot's back and ran my tongue along the wound as he screamed. He fired the pistol in his hand reflexively and I sank my fangs into his throat, the brief painful tearing as my fangs pierced my gums completely erased by the sudden infusion of warm fresh blood in my mouth.

"Holy shit!" the man in the backseat screamed. He had olive skin and wore a ratty T-shirt. "Holy shit!" He glanced back and forth between me and Esteban as if he didn't know who to run from. There was a switchblade in his hand. Esteban rolled his eyes. I bent Mr. Bloodshot's neck at an angle so I could watch them both without taking my mouth from his throat.

"Esteban, what the hell are you doing, man?" None of the four men looked older than midtwenties, but the last one in the car looked youngest of all. "We went to school together, man."

"That's why I didn't kill you." Esteban opened the driver's-side door, reaching down to pop the trunk.

A yellow pickup passed by us in the other lane; the wind from its passing ruffled Esteban's hair and the headlights illuminated his dark-blue eyes. Another car swung wide around the stopped car, edging into the other lane.

Esteban reached into the trunk and pulled out a heavy leather satchel, then dropped it on the asphalt. It sounded like the bag was filled with chains or links of metal, but the sides of the bag squirmed as if the contents were alive. I dropped my snack's cooling corpse to the ground.

"What's in the bag?"

"The Infernal Chains of Sarno Rayus, Majesty." Esteban swapped the gun to his left hand. He slipped his right arm out of the suit coat, letting it hang loose as he swapped gun hands again before ripping the sleeve of his shirt at the seam to show me a rose tattoo. "I am Esteban, thrall to Lady Gabriella. I offer you my apology for interrupting your evening, the life of my companion, the vehicle, and its contents, excepting only the chains for which I was sent. In exchange, I ask only your leave to depart this area and deliver to my mistress that which she has requested."

Hunger gone, my fangs and claws retracted. I looked at the vehicle, the dead driver, and I didn't want anything to do with it or the would-be rapist inside. It wasn't that he'd done or said anything overtly threatening, but his scent, a mixture of arousal and aggression, gave him away.

"He was going to . . ." I hadn't even gotten all the words out when Esteban shot the man with the switchblade, the bullet shattering the rear window of the car. Esteban holstered his gun and slid his arm back into the jacket.

"Shit!" I blinked. "You went to school with that guy."

Esteban nodded. "And then his presence offended you, Highness."

"What are you again?"

"Thrall to the Lady Gabriella." He bowed once, looking up at me with a movie star's smile before he straightened. "May I have permission to approach?"

"Sure."

His eyes never left mine as he walked across the concrete. It was reassuring, and I realized that it was meant to be. Eye contact was all I needed to assault his mind and he knew it. Esteban bit his lip.

"Your makeup is running," he said, touching the blood on my cheek. He drew a small plastic pack of wet wipes out of his jacket pocket. "May I?"

"Yeah . . ."

Tenderly, as if I were a sacred object, Esteban wiped away my bloody tears. Using a second wipe, he cleaned the blood spatter from my chin, neck, the swell of my breast . . . all the while watching me closely for the slightest sign of displeasure.

"That's better." Esteban carefully folded the used wipes and put them in his pocket. "I do hope you won't hold any ill will toward Lady Gabriella?"

"No," I whispered.

"Then, if I may?" He gestured to the car and I nodded.

"Just make sure Gabriella takes care of any Fang Fees," I added belatedly. Fang Fees are the vampires' equivalent of parking tickets, but much more expensive. If the VCPD has to cover something up, they find out which supernatural citizen did the deed and submit a bill. Since I hadn't been a vampire for long, I'd yet to be billed for one, and I didn't want to start now.

"Of course."

I picked up my suitcase and looked past Esteban at the people he and I had slaughtered, then walked away, trying to ignore the nausea rising in my stomach. They weren't real people, I repeated in my head, they were just food. Just food. I almost believed myself.

In the distance I heard sirens. Half a block away I watched Esteban light a cigarette, the flash of the lighter revealing a mischievous smirk. Then he walked back to the car and shut the trunk. Seeing him there, standing amongst the bodies as if they weren't bothersome at all, he reminded me of Eric.

"Eric . . ." His name felt good on my lips, but the thought of him brought warmth to my eyes and the tears started again. Most vampires cry blood, but now that I'd fed, there was no blood in my tears, just water, saline . . . whatever tears are made of. That's part of my gift. Unlike all the other vampires I know, I can seem to be human; I can cry, breathe, and even eat. I haven't managed to actually taste anything yet, which makes the actual eating less cool, but I'm working on it.

Talbot tells me that it's not really life, but it feels real enough to me. When I turn it on full blast, I even show up in mirrors. It damps my other vampiric abilities—a lot—but it's worth it to be able to do my own makeup. I couldn't help but think how impressed Eric would have been if I'd simply shown him. *Eric, what am I going to do without you?*

3

ERIC:

BETTER OFF DEAD

The Demon Heart was a lonely place to be. It wasn't completely gone. During the fire, I'd been sure there'd be nothing left, but the central runway, though charred and smoking, still stood. Part of the bar lay on its side across the front sidewalk. I stared down at the twisted remains of the break room refrigerator, watching the mass of melted plasma bags mix with the blood that had once been contained therein. Decades of blood, breasts, and bad art design were gone. The surprise? I didn't really miss it. I couldn't bear looking at it, either, though, so I spent a lot of time watching the Pollux across the street, waiting for the cavalry.

Greta was still out at Orchard Lake, and it was unlikely

that she could get back here until morning. Talbot would come waltzing back eventually. He always does. I thought of Tabitha. No . . . Tabitha wouldn't come back to me on her own. If I wanted her, I'd have to chase her. I still wasn't certain if I wanted to do that. Most of the time folks I care about are better off far away from me. I offer my recently blown up and soulnapped former fiancée as Exhibit Ow. Which left me with Rachel, my thrall. . . .

I had half an idea that she'd run off to find Talbot or get some other sort of help. Maybe one of her friends at the Irons Club, the local thrall hangout, knew something about putting explodicated vampires back together again. When the headlights pulled up, I'd convinced myself that it was her until I saw the Void City Department of Public Works logo on the side of the van.

In Void City, most humans don't know about the supernatural. I'm not sure how it all works, but I know there is an enchantment in place that keeps them from remembering all the spooky crap that goes on unless they're into the whole scene. The spell replaces the memory of actual events with mundane occurrences which can explain it all away. The magic isn't always very thorough in the way it creates the new memories, though, so a lot of us hire magicians to do touch-up work. I use a local guy named Magbidion. He's not a member of the guild because he got his powers by selling his soul. Apparently the high-born magical families frown on that sort of thing, so he's an outcast. It also means that he works cheaper than a guild mage and doesn't ask as many questions.

I also use Magbidion when my victims stick around after they die and try to haunt me. He moves them along, no fuss, no muss. The city can't use him, though; they have to pay guild rates. Half of the money taxpayers call graft and corruption is actually money that gets paid out to the guild. In exchange, the guild provides memory alteration service, ghost removal, and whatever else they do, at a reduced rate.

Ghost removal . . . I think not.

The van parked in front of the Demon Heart, and a portly looking goofball with brown hair and a disarming grin stepped out of the driver's side. He wore the same blue jumpsuit that the sanitation workers do. The name tag on his left breast pocket said *Melvin*. He tugged a portable two-way radio out of his right pocket and spoke into it.

"Big Top, this is Mother Goose. I see him. He's a mean mammer jammer, too. You should feel the noncorporeal manifestants he's putting out. Are you sure we want to contain him, not just send him to the great beyond?"

A male voice responded. "This is Alpha-One, Mother Goose. Big Top advises to continue with containment."

Melvin sighed. "Okay, but this is going to cost extra. He's a full-blown revenant."

"Is there a difference?"

"Is there a difference?" Melvin sounded as indignant as a Trekkie who'd just been asked if Spock is the one with the funny ears. "Revenants are an earthbound manifestation of anger and rage. They're capable of class five contact with the natural world: drastic temperature alteration, applied telekinetics . . . These bad boys can suck the soul right out of you. A ghost is just spam mail compared to one of these guys!"

"Just capture it!" shouted Alpha-One.

I floated over to Melvin, and the windows on his van fogged up. "Can my code name be Yosemite Sam?"

He jogged around the van and stood on the other side of the white line in the middle of the road, still talking on the two-way. "I sense a secondary presence as well. Nobody said anything about two. Guild regulations require one mage per ghost present."

"If you were doing this on the books then you could whine to the guild about it, but you aren't. Just capture the damn thing and get it back here!"

Melvin pulled a picture out of his breast pocket and gave it the once-over. He showed me the picture. It was me, Roger, and Marilyn standing in front of my classic Mustang convertible, back when we'd all been alive. My face had been circled with a black Sharpie. "Nice car," Melvin said. "Do you still have it? My uncle had an old '67 Mustang. What kind of mileage do you get on her?"

I let it distract me. His fingers danced in tortuous knots. Words that hummed like wasps in my head cut through me. Never underestimate a mage. A lambent purple coffin-size box snapped shut with me inside. Numbness flowed up my ghostly extremities where I braced against the sides of the glowing prison.

He shouldn't have underestimated me, either. "You ain't dealing with the Stay Puft Marshmallow Man here, you Dan Aykroyd–looking motherfucker!" The cage held for about three minutes, with me pounding on it as hard as I could. I treated it like a workout, punching it over and over again, locking in on the wall of the box closest to Melvin, focusing my rage.

I smelled the sickly sweet mixture of cigarettes and machine oil from Carl's garage. The lights in the garage were turned off; the only illumination came from the high beams on my car. For three seconds I could see the interior as clearly as if I'd been sitting at the wheel. Then multicolored shards of energy flew in all directions as the walls surrounding me gave way.

My vision cleared. Melvin picked himself up off the ground and grabbed his radio. "Alpha-One, this is Mother Goose." His voice contained equal parts excitement and respect, but he wasn't afraid. "Nope! Can't contain him. He tore through Hamnard's Holding Cell like he was opening the fridge to grab a beer. You'll have to pay for a high-end soul prison if you want to snare this bad boy."

"For Christ sake!" Alpha-One sounded irritated. "I thought you were the big man on campus when it comes to ghost crap."

"Tell him to come down here himself if he doesn't like it," I snarled. Tendrils of ice raced along the pavement from my feet to the vehicle. Frost formed on the public-works van.

"Did you copy that, Alpha-One?" Melvin asked. "Subject suggests you come down in person."

"My ass," the radio crackled. "How much for the soul prison?"

Melvin frowned, working it out in his head. "Well, you'd have to call Jimmy over at the local and get official clearance. I can't just do something like that freelance. There's no way I could slip magic of that caliber under the radar with Sheila on monitor duty. If you want to do it next month, when McGibbons is up on the rotation—"

"Forget it," the voice snapped angrily. "Just get the hell out of there. We'll pay you for the site visit, but that's it."

"Not what we agreed on, but okay. Sounds fair to me." Melvin put the radio back into the pocket of his jumpsuit and looked directly at me. His smile was open, honest and indescribably childlike. "I'm done. Would it be okay if I got back into my van now?"

I stepped back, and he climbed in through the passenger's side. The driver's door was frozen shut. He cranked the van and rolled down the window. "I gotta tell ya. I've never seen anything like that before. You had to be approaching a class six physical interaction there when you laid the smackdown on my containment spell. Very impressive. You're the most powerful revenant I've ever seen . . . in fact, I'm not even sure that's all you are."

"Thanks," I said in confusion.

"When they come at you next, they'll try the soul prison route, but I can guarantee you they'll get nonguild labor to put it together. It'll look like a big cat's-eye marble—more than one, maybe. They're wicked powerful, but they'll shatter like glass if you hit them with a rock." He gave me a thumbs-up. "Good luck."

I watched him drive away. Melvin seemed like a good guy. I made a mental note to look him up if I ever got my body back and my own mage wasn't available. He might frown on the whole vampire thing, but aside from the supernatural powers angle, I was betting Melvin wouldn't see much difference in working for a bloodsucking undead monster than for a politician.

Melvin stopped at the street corner and began cordoning off the area. Normal people would see the sign he was putting out as whichever public warning sign they were most likely to heed: *Road Closed, Police Line—Do Not Cross,* or whatever. He blocked off one end of the street, drove back by, and finished up on the other side before speeding off into the night, leaving me alone again.

Or was I? What was it Melvin had said about a secondary presence?

"Hello?" I called out tentatively toward the Pollux. The response was immediate and it came from behind me.

"If you're done fornicatin', consortin' with demons, and chewin' the fat with the locals, son, I'd like a word." The country drawl reminded me of my granddad, a syrupy cocktail of John Wayne and Clint Eastwood. Sparkling in the rising sun, a single-action Colt revolver lay beneath the remains of the Demon Heart's runway.

The gun caught my eye when I turned toward the sound. Gun smoke rose from the barrel as I recognized *El Alma Perdida.* In English, the gun's name translates as "The Lost Soul." It had been used by one of my ancestors, John Paul Courtney, in some crazy crusade against werewolves. I'd been shot with it the night before and it'd been stuffed down the back of my pants when I'd blown up.

Manifesting in the smoke like a cowboy stepping through

the hazy dawn, a man with my blue eyes and a face a lot like my dad's puffed on the stub of a spectral cigar. Red mud caked his boots and pants, running halfway up his thighs. The buckle of his gun belt displayed a cross. He took a drag on the cigar, smoke billowing out through a multitude of bullet wounds in his upper torso, curling back in as he blew the smoke out through his nostrils. Old blood had turned the red-and-white checkered shirt he wore to a uniform shade of brown, the pattern only emerging at his shoulders.

I guessed this was the ghost of John Paul Courtney, the gun's original owner. His brown leather duster flapped in an unseen breeze. His head lolled from side to side as he walked toward me, like his neck had been broken. He steadied his head with both hands, snapping it into place with a sickening crack, and took another long draw off of the cigar. The end flared brightly, but the cigar didn't burn down, stuck forever with an eternal puff or two left in it.

"Great, it's the Ghost of Fuck-Ups Past," I said. I wondered if that made me the Ghost of Fuck-Ups Present or the Ghost of Fuck-Ups Yet to Come. The way the morning was going, it could have been either or both.

"Figures you'd talk like some no-account heathen." He ran "no" and "account" together like it was just one word and the way he said "heathen" included an "r" near the end that wasn't supposed to be there. In short, he sounded like I might've if Mom hadn't been from Michigan.

"If I'm a ghost, do I have to have a bad Southern accent, too?" The ghost of John Paul Courtney didn't respond to my question.

Just what I needed, a stick-in-the-mud ghost of some ancestor I didn't give a shit about. Another person might have wanted to ask him questions or hoped he was there to help, but I don't think that way.

"What do you want?" I asked.

"I want Judgement Day to come so I can change my shirt." He stopped a half step too close to me, nearly nose to nose, or rather, nose to lip since he had a couple of inches on me. "I want to see Jesus and find out if I done enough good to keep myself outta Hell, boy."

"Fine." All I wanted was my thrall to come back and fix things, but did I get that? No. I got Hillbilly Roy the Gospel Cowboy. *Where the hell are you, Rachel?* I thought. I closed my eyes. Since Rachel was my thrall, I was supposed to be able to feel her presence if I concentrated, but I couldn't. Whether that was due to a lack of concentration or because I was a damn ghost was anybody's guess. I wanted to know why Rachel wasn't out here doing her job. She knew more about vampire mystic bullshit than I did. Maybe she could get me out of this. I hoped that she hadn't taken off after the explosion. I opened my eyes again and the cowboy was still there. "You wait over on your side of the burned-out strip club and I'll wait on mine," I told J. P.

"I can help you, not that you deserve it." His cigar bounced up and down with the motion of his lips.

"You can help me get my body back? You know that it blew up, right?"

"Your body? This ain't about your body, son. This is about your soul, about your destiny."

"I'd rather have a body, thanks." I tried to re-form myself, rematerialize, coalesce, whatever you want to call it. I reasoned, if I tried hard enough . . . Nothing. I glimpsed my car again and stopped pushing. I didn't need my car; I needed my frickin' body back. "Damn!" I cut my eyes over to the ghost. "Are you in it?"

"Am I in what?" He drew back and cocked his head to one side; something gave, and his head fell over, cheek flush with his shoulder.

"This destiny of mine that you're talking about."

He straightened his head again, forcing it back into position. "I am."

"Then, no offense, but fuck that. I'm not going through the rest of eternity with a cowboy bobblehead bitching and moaning at me about Jesus." If Rachel didn't show up, I knew Greta would come resurrect my happy ass. She's my daughter, vampirically speaking, but it's more than that. To her, I'm Daddy with a capital _D_.

His laughter came from all directions, surrounding me, disorienting. "Suit yourself. You've got the Courtney temper, boy, yes sirree. Like a young stallion with a brood mare's scent in his nostrils. You'll get that pounded out of you soon enough."

"What the hell are you talking about?" I stepped closer.

"Oh, no!" He shied me away with his hat. "You git on, young buck. You need time to simmer down." Smoke curled up from his chest, obscuring his expression. He cleared it with a wave of his hat. "I was just like you in my day, boy. I mean it. Just like you."

Really? He was a screwed-up vampire who got reamed by his best friend, framed for murder, and blown up over a lame-ass real estate deal? 'Cause that's what happened to me yesterday and I doubted he could say the same. "Just tell me what you were going to tell me." I sighed.

"Go ask your demon friend or that fat magician for answers." He spat the cigar out of his mouth. It vanished when it struck the ground, coming apart like smoke. "Just like me," he said. "You'll go to Hell and back before you'll be of any use."

I waited for him to swirl back down into *El Alma Perdida*, like a genie in a bottle. Instead, he flashed, burning brightly with an inner light, and then he was gone.

4

TABITHA:

IN THE PRESENCE OF EVIL

I sobbed, fumbling with my crystal glass as I sat in Phillip's suite at the Highland Towers. Blood wine sloshed up the side. A human wouldn't have noticed, but as the wine ran down the side of the glass, it moved more slowly than real wine would have. A thin residue clung to the surface for a fraction of a second until something, maybe magic, maybe gravity, pulled it down.

"I . . . I'm sorry." I cursed myself for crying, but I knew Phillip didn't mind. Phillip's an old vampire, or so he says. He feels younger when I sense him, but he says that's because he's used magic to make himself more powerful over the years and since he basically rules Void City, I believe him. He probably thought my crying real tears was sexy, miraculous, interesting—any number of things. Once you've been a vampire as long as Phillip has, anything different is good. I'm different.

I reached to put my glass down on a little half-moon table, but missed the edge. The long tapered crystal tumbled and I froze, unable to react with sufficient speed. My vampiric abilities don't work well when I'm seeming human and I had turned my abilities all the way on (heartbeat, body heat . . . the works) to impress Phillip. He righted the glass as it toppled, moved it closer to the center of the little table, and returned to his chair so quickly that I barely saw a blur.

"I just didn't know what to do . . . where to go . . . so I came here, because . . ."

He didn't smile. I was so thankful that he didn't smile. I don't know why, but if I had looked at him and seen happiness, I think I would have exploded, or died, or shattered . . . something. He patted my hand and crossed the room to stoke a small fire. His small wood-burning stove was putting out a lot of heat. I didn't remember having seen it before.

"Tell me everything," Phillip commanded gently.

"Eric died," I whined. My voice was high-pitched and sobbing. I hated myself for it. Trying to stop just made it worse. "I broke up with him out at Orchard Lake . . . He went there because the werewolves were trying to kill him and he wanted it to stop, but they seemed so much like normal people . . . there were teenagers and little kids and old ladies. One of them looked like my grandma. I couldn't deal with it. I told him that there had to be another way, but . . ."

"But he disagreed." Phillip touched my hand, his fingers warm and comforting, his cheeks rosy, like he'd just fed.

"Yes, and then I told him that I hated him." I smiled weakly at Phillip, fighting back the tears. Phillip was being so sweet to me. He leaned forward and I got a glimpse past him at the last person who'd made Phillip really angry. His name is Percy. Phillip keeps him, staked and immobilized, but conscious, in a glass display case at the center of his living room. There is a plaque underneath that I'd read before: *My dear Percy, who serves as a remembrance to all that I do not bluff, I do not make empty threats, and there are indeed worse fates than death.*

Wiping the tears from my eyes, I picked up the glass, staring down into it before drinking. In the sparkle of blood wine, I could see the Demon Heart, my ex's strip club, burning to the ground. I hadn't mentioned that part yet.

"Anyway, I . . ." I could have saved Eric, come to his rescue, and instead I ran off to the Highland Towers to make a point, to make him chase me? I didn't think Lord Phillip would appreciate being chosen as a convenient jealousy device.

"I don't know why I even came here, it's just that you're the only other vampire I know and I thought you wouldn't mind."

"You were right to come here," Phillip crooned. He leaned in closer, the firelight glinting in his pale colorless eyes. In another frame of mind that predatory look might have frightened me, but I didn't give it much thought. "But what, if you don't mind my asking, makes you think Eric has been ended?"

"I felt him burning."

Something about my glass must have bugged him, because he stalked purposefully over to the table, grabbed the glass, and pitched it toward the woodstove, following it quickly with his own. The metal door on the stove opened all on its own, accepting each glass like a hungry pet gobbling down treats.

"I'm tired of the 1301," Phillip explained, "aren't you?" He looked at the bottle and hurled it into the stove. "It said 'Catherine' on the label." He shrugged. "I don't even recall a . . ." Lit with inner mischief, Phillip's eyes widened in recognition. "Oh, yes, now I remember." Looking back at the stove, he smiled. "Fitting end, I suppose."

I nodded noncommittally and wondered what would happen when Phillip lost his fascination with someone. Would a guest be so quickly discarded? Would I? He flipped through a small ledger, his wine list, he called it, and I felt a sudden chill. Not seeing what he wanted, he dropped the wine list onto his chair and, laughing, clasped his hands together. That same impish light seemed to shine behind his eyes as he walked toward me. "Should we be naughty?" he asked.

"In what way?" Phillip scared me when he asked questions like that. His ceaseless good humor and his generosity were treacherous. With him, all of the terrible things seemed distant and avoidable. The past became fuzzy and unimportant, like a movie so bad you could only like it if you watched it with a friend. He muted everything else, overwhelming it with his own presence. For a short, bald, fat man, he managed the Dracula vibe effortlessly.

"We could play the game . . . No, no, we've no time for that now . . . I had almost forgotten." He returned to his chair. "You were telling me about Eric, about feeling him burn. Tell me exactly what happened."

"I was on my way here. The car had broken down and I was walking down the sidewalk when I felt him . . . Eric . . . die. He burned. I can't explain it any other way."

"Fire, you say?" Phillip chuckled in a nasty sort of way. "Burning unto destruction? No. No. No, my dear." He touched my hand. It was so reassuring, I wondered if I ought to sleep with him, you know, out of gratitude, which sounds twisted, but it's how he was making me feel.

"But I felt him die."

Phillip giggled. "Did you?" He stood up. "Well, then, I suppose you had best be on your way, hadn't you?"

"On my way?"

"Back to the Demon Heart," he explained. "That's where I would start."

"Start?" I asked in confusion.

He pulled me to my feet. "Start looking, my beautiful, wondrous, precious creature. Looking. If I know our good little maniac Roger, I assure you that he has no true understanding of the game in which he's become entangled. Even if he does, I can without fear of error tell you that he does not know how to kill the one you love, your sire, the oft-enraged Eric of Void City."

My heart beat twice in my chest. "Eric's alive?"

"Insomuch as a vampire lives, yes, yes. *Vivat imperator* and so forth." He danced in a circle as he talked, his excitement mirroring my sense of relief. I almost forgot how mad I'd been at Eric.

"That's . . . I mean. Are you . . . Would you tell me how you know?"

"I was quite the mage in my day, you know—alchemical experiments, terrible firestorms, creating new life . . . It was all immeasurably childish, I assure you, but I remember it fondly," Phillip said, sounding pleased with himself. "To see the modern magi of today still puttering about with the same problems I solved in my youth . . ." He clucked his tongue disapprovingly. "Ah, well . . . *dum spiro, spero*, eh? Not that I do, of course, but the sentiment is the same. Surely they'll learn their collective lessons in the end. We all do."

"Huh?"

Phillip's smiled broadened until I was afraid his face might tear at the corners. "Let's call it wizard's intuition. I know of Roger and I am aware of his methods. To burn a vampire in the vampire's own lair is exactly the sort of melodrama that a neophyte like Roger would devise. If I know your sire as well as I ought to know him, I find it hard to believe that mere burning could destroy him for very long. Oh, I'm sure there's something that would destroy him, there's always something, but not fire, not even magical fire. I am an expert on killing other vampires, my dear, and death by burning is far too mundane for your sire."

He scoffed. "You yourself would likely survive a mundane fire. All you would require is blood. Or time."

"What about Eric?" I asked.

"Blood or time," he repeated. "Either will do, but blood is much more expedient."

The wall phone buzzed and Phillip answered it. It was Dennis, the current leader in Phillip's personal game of *Who Wants To Be a Vampire Millionaire.*

"On the other matter, milord," Dennis said warily. "I have done as you requested." Vampires and their servants learn to be very circumspect on the phone. One of the benefits of enhanced vampire senses is that when a vampire can hear one side of the conversation, they can usually hear the other, too.

"Very good, Dennis," Phillip replied. "I've one more favor to ask for the moment; do you have time?"

"I am always at your service, milord."

"Round up one of those little sprayers—like the exterminators use. Clean it out and fill it with a few bottles of whatever I have . . . the 1250s if you want; I'm bored with the whole decade."

He continued giving instructions and I continued to listen, but in the back of my mind something was bothering me. Phillip had said *as well as I ought to know him* when he referred to Eric, but the first time we'd met, he had acted as if he didn't know who Eric was. Why had he done that? So he knew about Eric . . . But why the lie?

"Give it to Lady Tabitha when it is prepared and then drive her out to the Demon Heart, or, rather, the remains thereof," he continued. "She needs to revive her sire and I want to be sure she doesn't spend all night trying to figure out which pile of ashes is his."

"Within the hour, milord," Dennis replied.

"What if I don't want to revive him?" I asked softly.

"Not revive him?" Phillip arched an eyebrow.

"If he's going to be okay . . . I mean, if he's not 'dead' dead . . . then I'm still mad at him."

Phillip encircled my waist with his arm. "I knew you'd be interesting the instant I first sensed you." His eyes sparkled with delight. "Why don't you stay here at the Towers?"

5

TABITHA:

LAP OF LUXURY

Talbot stopped by a week after Eric blew up. I'd wondered how long it would be before one of Eric's little resurrection squad came to check on me. He was dressed, as always, in a smart black suit and a tie that matched the warm rich brown of his eyes. I wanted to reach out and run my hands along the dark skin of his cheek, but he didn't seem to be in the mood.

"I haven't seen you down at the Demon Heart," he said, stepping through as I opened the door.

"Hello to you, too." They were all on Eric's side. The whole group of them, probably . . . all his former employees and friends running around, trying different spells, and spraying blood everywhere . . . It wasn't working. I couldn't bring myself to care why, yet even Phillip continued to ask about Eric.

Why did it matter how long it took him to re-form? He gets so much more waking time than the rest of us, me in particular. Eric is a corpse for a few hours a night, four at the most. Me, I'm dead from an hour before dawn until an hour after sunset. Let him feel what it's like to know that people are running around enjoying immortality while he's stuck, for a change. Even if he lost a whole year, it would serve him right.

I watched Talbot take in our surroundings. The Gryphon Suite had belonged to Roger, but Lord Phillip said that it now belonged to me. Nobody was going to argue with Void City's vampire overlord even if Roger did manage to find his way back from Hell.

"I've redecorated since you were here last," I said, gesturing at the room in general. "What do you think?"

Talbot's eyes took in the decor with a casual flick from side to side. I was proud of it. I knew I wouldn't miss a scrap of the extremely retro office furniture I'd had removed along with Roger's late girlfriend Froggy's awful choice of bedding, an obviously secondhand smoke-scented sofa, and all the rest of Roger's stuff. A week's worth of shopping with Lord Phillip's credit card had given the suite a little long-overdue pizzazz. Dennis promised that an interior designer was coming soon to redo the exterior waiting room. If I was going to be receiving guests, I couldn't very well have them staring at Roger's severe lack of decorating flair.

"I don't think Eric's going to like it," he said brusquely, "but it's very—you."

"Why does everyone care what Eric thinks?" I slammed the door too hard and flinched when one of my decorative plates fell off the wall. Talbot caught it smoothly with his usual catlike reflexes and hung it back in place.

"I'm uncertain what you mean by everyone, but you have a vested interest in making sure that you're on good terms with him if you plan on living in Void City."

"And why is that?" I asked, crossing my arms under my breasts to better show my assets. Since I hadn't been expecting company, I was only wearing a pair of shorts and a tank top. Being undead meant that I no longer needed a bra for support. A vampire's skin and muscles tighten after death, leaving us looking thinner and more toned than we did in life. As big as I am up top, it still does the trick, so for me bras are strictly a "for effect" clothing option. Talbot was normally immune to this type of flirting, but I knew I was an exception to the rule.

"Don't flirt with me unless you mean it," he snarled, eyes glowing green. I'd seen them go slit-pupil and feline, but I'd never seen them glow before. I took it as a sign that I still revved his engine. "Or you might find yourself engaged in the act against your will."

"Maybe that's what I want," I told him. "Maybe I miss you."

"Maybe." He winked. "I think it more likely that you've found out firsthand what a freak Lord Phillip is between the sheets and you don't like it. Has he tried to share you yet?"

"No," I lied. I think Talbot could tell, though. I'd only

slept with Phillip once and it had been a mistake. Sex with him was an exercise in the pain-pleasure threshold. He was always biting, pinching, or prodding things that didn't need or want it. It worked out for both of us, because regardless of his deficiencies, he's good with his tongue, but his suggestion for the next night had involved more partners than I was comfortable with. I mean, I'm not a fucking power strip! Since then I'd gone out with him a few times, but other than a little heavy petting, I'd cut him off.

Talbot closed the gap between us, taking up my personal space. "He will."

"Stop," I whispered.

He slipped his arms around me. "Or maybe corpulent little sadists are your thing?"

"What does 'corpulent' mean?"

His fingers slid over my butt, just below the butterfly tattoo, his claws catching slightly against the fabric of my shorts. He brushed my ear with his lips as he answered. "Fat."

"Oh."

"Aren't you going to tell me to stop again?"

"No." I pouted at him. "I need you, I want you. Take me now." My delivery was less deadpan than I'd meant it to be, but he wilted anyway, pulling away from me.

"Fine. Now you are being a tease." He sighed.

"We can do that in a minute," I told him. His fangs came out in his smile when I said that. "First, you should tell me what you came here to tell me."

He sat on the edge of my new daybed and fiddled with

the lace coverlet. "I've gotten calls from three of Eric's other children, all on the outs with him. They each called to see if they needed to come back and help."

"So?"

He began taking off his tie. Talbot is built like a bull, all muscled and firm. He caught me watching and bared his fangs. He's not a vampire and he's not a lycanthrope, but I don't know what he actually is. I do know that dominance games turn him on . . . and so do cats.

"He's tried to kill all of them in the past, but they know how this works. Even though they escaped him and even though they'd rather do anything than come to his aid, they know that if he gets pissed about their not helping, then when he does re-form he might take out his frustrations on them."

"Oh, please, what's he going to do? Kill me?"

"Probably not." Talbot strung the tie on the side of the daybed. "But he might take this away from you."

"This? What do you mean?"

"This place. It's yours, right?"

"Yes."

"Then, as your sire, it is also his. Anything you have is his if he wants to claim it. Technically, so are you."

He slid off his jacket and hung it on the bed knob.

"I am not!" I shouted.

"Technically, you are." He unbuttoned the first button on his dress shirt. I wasn't paying much attention, so he stopped. "What?"

"I'm not property."

"You are until you become strong enough to prove you're not."

"Phillip could protect me." I tried to bite it back, but the response was out and there was nothing I could do but stick with it.

"I'm sure he could," Talbot laughed, "and if *One Hundred and Twenty Days of Sodom* is your idea of a good time, then go right ahead."

"One hundred and twenty days of Saddam?" I asked.

"It's a book by the Marquis de Sade; you wouldn't like it. Your horizons are broad, but not that broad."

"You don't know me." I looked away.

"Have you ever met Lady Gabriella?" He ran one claw along the bedsheets.

"I've sensed her. She's got a really cute thrall named Esteban . . . and I know she doesn't get along with Phillip very well."

"Do you know why?" Talbot asked. "Phillip seduced her while she was still a virgin, but not before he turned her."

"So you mean?"

"For her, every time is like the first time." Talbot picked up his jacket and slid it back on.

"That's sick." I winced thinking about it. I thought back to Esteban's manicured nails and the tender way he'd wiped the blood from my skin. No wonder he's so gentle with vampires. "Why would Phillip do that?"

Talbot smiled, showing too much of his teeth. "According to Esteban, Phillip told Gabriella that it would make her his eternal love, always fresh, always new, his immortal virgin, but really, he did it because he was curious and because he knew that in time it would deepen her hatred of him."

"You're lying." He went to put his tie back on, but I stopped him with a touch.

"What?" he asked. "That turned you on?"

"No." I ran my hands across his shoulders, dug into him with my claws. "You turned me on. The story just made me not want to be alone."

6

TABITHA:

THE CAT CAME BACK

I deserved a night on the town. I'd been cooped up in the Highland Towers for over a week. Talbot had kept me from being too lonely, but he wasn't around every night. When he did show up, I'd smell the smoke and ash of the Demon Heart clinging to his skin. Tonight, I was dressed up and waiting for him.

He opened the door and stopped, his eyes raking my body. I'd broken out my little black dress, a tight slinky number with a plunging back that showed off the butterfly tattoo at the base of my spine. The front of the dress showed ample cleavage and if I shifted wrong (or right depending on your point of view), I knew he'd catch a flash of nipple. I'd cut my hair short and the new look surprised him. I waved a pair of six-inch heels at him.

"You're taking me out." I bent over, slipping on first one shoe, then the other, and his eyes stayed right where I wanted them.

"Tabitha," he started.

"If you want me, then we're going out." I slid my hand along his crotch and felt the rigid warmth of him.

Talbot bowed his head, giving in. *Easier than I thought.*

"I don't mind taking you out," Talbot said. He stepped closer, cupping my ass with his free hand. His musky wild scent, not quite human, not quite animal, filled my nostrils as he brushed his lips along my neck. "But it's a bad idea."

"Why?"

"Because I'm a mouser, and though the High Society vamps tolerate my kind, they are never pleased to see us mingle with vampires." His tongue darted along my jawline in a delicate lick, not wet and slobbery like a human tongue, but rough, warm, and grasping. I wanted to feel that touch lower down. My free hand found the back of his head and I pushed him lower without thinking or meaning to and he laughed—the low chuff of a predator.

"And to think you get mad if I do that." Talbot slid a claw across my back, not breaking the skin, tantalizing me. A slight scratch from Talbot would send curls of smoke wafting up from my skin. Done right, it felt erotic, more pleasure than pain, and Talbot always did it right.

"Let me taste you," I said, fangs extended. "Just a little bit."

"No." He shoved me away from him, one hand on my abdomen, and I stumbled, catching myself with the door.

"Why?"

"My blood isn't good for vampires."

"Why not?"

"I've told you before. My claws and fangs are sacred weapons." I rolled my eyes as he spoke. "It's true," he said, showing me his claws. "If I scratched you with these, really scratched you, not sensuous scratches, the wounds would burn. And my blood? The mingled essence of deities flows through my veins. If you took my blood internally . . . ?" He clucked his tongue.

"Ouch?" I wrinkled my nose at him.

"Ouch," he agreed.

"You're so full of yourself." I hit him playfully in the shoulder. He bit back a comment, but I saw it in his eyes. I didn't know exactly what he'd been going to say, but it had been vulgar and very male. "You better be glad you left that unsaid."

"Where do you want to go?"

"Somewhere I've never been . . . someplace high class with dinner and dancing."

"I know a place."

"A vampire place?"

"No," Talbot admitted.

"Then let's ask the concierge."

We took the elevator down to the lobby and I spotted Dennis by the front desk talking with Esteban. Dennis wore a standard suit and tie, while Esteban wore a tailored gray suit, open collared as it had been when I first met him. The shoulder holster was barely noticeable.

"Good evening, Lady Tabitha," Dennis greeted me with a polite incline of the head.

Esteban bowed low, eyes on mine as he moved, forever smiling. "Lady Bathory," he said using the more archaic address for a female Vlad. The satchel from our previous encounter was by Esteban's feet, near the desk behind which Dennis stood.

"Haven't you delivered that already?" I asked.

"My mistress wishes to have it delivered to the Lovett Building." He gestured to Dennis. "And Dennis was kind enough to call me a cab."

"You don't drive?" I asked.

"I'm not allowed to drive at the moment." He shrugged, but a look of genuine regret touched his features. "I was . . . insensitive."

He took the satchel and left when his taxi arrived. The bag jerked toward Talbot as Esteban passed, and Talbot raised an eyebrow in response to the metallic clinking within.

"Sorry about that, Talbot," Esteban called over his shoulder.

Talbot stared after him but didn't say anything.

"He actually said your name." Most people at the Highland Towers acted as if Talbot wasn't in the room and refused to speak directly to him.

"He's not a vampire yet," Talbot murmured. "It pays to be polite when you can't protect yourself." He slapped his hand down on the desk in front of Dennis with a loud slap. "How are you doing tonight, Dennis?"

"I'm doing quite well . . . Highness." Dennis choked on the word, but he got it out.

"Highness?" I asked.

Talbot offered no explanation and neither did Dennis.

"My date wants to go somewhere exclusive and fun." He leaned over the counter, nose to nose with Dennis. "I think she wants to pick a place that will cause a stir, create a scene . . . She wants to get noticed."

"But . . . Highness."

Talbot patted Dennis gently on the cheek. On the first pat, Talbot's hand was human, but with the second pat it transformed. A white glow washed along his skin leaving a covering of thick sable fur in its wake. Each digit on the altered hand terminated in a metallic silver claw.

"I'll make the reservations right away," Dennis stammered. "There is an exclusive engagement at the Iversonian club tonight. Lord Phillip was invited, but his sleep schedule is at its most erratic this evening, and it seems as if he might sleep straight through. I'm certain he wouldn't mind . . ."

"Sounds perfect." Talbot removed his hand from Dennis's cheek and I held it up to mine, rubbing the fur along my skin.

"It's so soft." I felt a warm tingle. "Does it . . . ?"

"Cover everything?" Talbot completed my question. "Yes, but I'm not sure you'd be up for the . . . full Talbot."

"Why not?"

"Mousers have a lot in common with domestic cats and cats require stimulation to ovulate," Talbot said carefully.

"Huh?"

"During sex, a female cat only produces eggs after the male cat withdraws and the . . . spines scratch the walls on the way out."

"Spines?" *Ow.*

"Barbs might be a better word."

"Barbs?" *Double ow.*

"I'll show you later," he promised as he led me to the car.

7

TABITHA:

LASTING IMPRESSIONS

Talbot drove us to Northside, past the trendy shops and the office buildings, into the portion of Void City with an average of one specialty coffee shop per block—occasionally two. We passed Jimmy Chew's where Eric had taken me to dinner for my last pre-vampire birthday.

I didn't need vampiric supersenses to tell that Talbot was stressed out. I just didn't know what was bothering him. His threat to Dennis had been out of character, but even after that, he'd opened up, given me info (even if it had been icky info) about being a mouser. That wasn't like him at all.

Spotlights cut through the night sky, highlighting the garish white walls of the Iversonian on the block ahead of us. Cars lined the street and their occupants weren't human, their heartbeats wrong or absent altogether.

I'd asked for exclusive. Talbot had delivered. He cut around the other cars, forcing his way into the front of the line. The valet didn't even want to let us park. He glared at the two of us through beady-black doll's eyes, gnashing his razor-sharp teeth, the blood-slick cap on his head leaking a tiny stream of wetness into his hair.

"You aren't Lord Phillip."

Talbot lashed out with his claws, leaving streaks of raw burnt flesh on the valet's face. Screaming, the valet fell away from the car.

"And you aren't getting a tip." Talbot had his seat belt undone and the car door cracked open before the valet could respond.

"Park where you want," the valet cried, crab-walking away from the car. "Park wherever you want."

Talbot slammed the door and peeled out into the parking lot. He kicked the Jag into a slide and came to a halt straddling two parking spaces. My door was opening, his hand on the handle before I could blink. Angry masculine scents poured off his skin and he pulled me to him, nuzzling my face with his like a cat.

"You want attention, right?"

"What's gotten into you?" I asked. "You could have maimed that . . . valet guy . . . thing."

"He's a redcap. They eat people." He sniffed me then shook his head. "You really want to make an impression?"

"I want excitement."

"If we go inside," he spun me around and began licking my hair, grooming me between words, "you'll get it."

"What's going on, Talbot?"

"You have to show fey who's boss up front," he said between licks, his voice deep and resonating.

"Stop." I pushed at him, but he tightened his grasp, forcing me against the car with his weight. I felt his teeth on my neck as he growled in my ear and grew. Light from his transformation washed over me and I was being straddled by a leonine beast with soft black fur. A low pounding drum beat against my back, the rhythm of his heart, and then he was off of me, diminishing.

"That should do it."

"What the hell, Talbot?" I whirled on him, claws out, but there was no need. He held out his hand to me, humanoid once more.

"You need to smell like me if I'm going to protect you." I took his hand as he spoke. "There are more than just vampires here."

"I'm a Vlad," I protested. "I can take care of myself."

"Vampires can be destroyed, Tabitha."

"What, and mousers can't?"

"We can, but it's harder to keep us that way. And anyone outright killing me would have to answer to my mother."

"Your mother?"

"You wouldn't know her."

"Talbot," I said plaintively.

"It won't mean anything to you anyway, Tabitha."

"Just tell me her name." I cupped his face and kissed him. "Please?"

"Sekhmet."

"That's an . . . interesting name."

Talbot chuffed. "It's Egyptian. You should hear my given name."

"It isn't Talbot?"

"No," he said patiently, "I just like *The Wolf Man*. C'mon."

We walked across the wide parking lot toward the club. Tiers of neon spelled out the name of the club in staggered wedges: IVER SON IAN descended from the roof, hanging like daggers over an open oval through which alternating bursts of red, green, yellow, and blue light pulsed, casting twisted shadows of the two suit-clad heavies manning the door against the white-layered facing.

"Unlike us, the owner of this club, Iver Richardson, is a true immortal. He can't be slain in the normal sense of the word. They call him 'The Iversonian,'" Talbot whispered in my ear.

"Why?"

We set foot on the sidewalk leading up to the main doors, and the concrete beneath us lit up, pinpoints of warm light marking the surface below our feet. A line wound around the building, but Talbot and I headed for the doors.

"It's a pun. He likes to collect things and the joke is that once something winds up in his collection, he never lets it go—like the Smithsonian."

"What sort of things does he collect?"

Talbot bared his fangs at the two doormen, flashing them

our invitation. Up close, their knotted green skin was dry, but shiny like a snake's.

"What are they," I asked, "trolls?"

"As a matter of fact, they are," Talbot answered out of the side of his mouth. The trolls parted, displeasure clear on their gnarled faces.

The music hit us, a wave of bass, shaking my body as it thumped. Men and women, or rather, males and females of varying stripes, moved about the medieval decor, doing high energy versions of classic ballroom dances, but to a punishing techno beat. Creatures I didn't recognize flittered on gauzy wings about the old-fashioned candlelit chandeliers. A fully transformed werewolf with a disco ball hanging from his collar did a hyperfast waltz with a thin-limbed androgynous creature that shimmered, opaque one beat and translucent the next.

I sensed a Master vampire, newly risen and clad in leather bondage gear, having sex in the bathroom with something squat and toadlike—an image I could have done without—but the other vampires gave me no reading at all, meaning they were all Soldiers or lower.

My ears slowly adjusted to the volume of the music, but the scents hurt my sinuses. A bald man in a pinstripe suit, which looked like it had been custom made on Saville Row, cut through the crowd toward us. His overlarge eyes bulged under bushy brown eyebrows that reminded me of the wizard from "The Sorcerer's Apprentice" in *Fantasia*. He stood six foot nothing, and he was not smiling.

"You wanted to make an impression," Talbot reminded me, gesturing at the oncoming person. "Here's your chance."

"He looks angry."

"That's because we don't get along."

"Why?" Talbot's muscles tensed under my fingers.

"That's the Iversonian. He's always wanted to own me and he's always wanted to own a Living Doll."

"*What?*"

"That impression?" Talbot straightened his tie as the Iversonian closed with us. "You're about to make it."

"Talbot!" A crocodile grin flittered across the Iversonian's lips and stuck as if it were trapped there more by habit than a conscious effort. "How nice of you to come uninvited."

The Iversonian's hand jutted out in an offered handshake, which Talbot spurned. "This is Tabitha."

"And she is quite beautiful," the immortal replied, adding a brief bow (or maybe he was just staring down my top) before continuing, "but what makes you think you would be welcome with or without a lovely companion?"

"Two reasons." Talbot held up two fingers. "The first? She's Lord Phillip's newest . . . special friend . . . and she's here using the invitation that you sent to him. It allows a guest. I'm hers and therefore his."

"And the second reason?"

"She's an extremely rare type of vampire, a Living Doll, and I know how much you've always wanted to meet one."

"You wanted to flaunt her in front of me, is that it?" The Iversonian closed his eyes and the hair on the back of my

neck stood up. An electric hum rose from his body, only dis-
cernable over the music because it was more a feeling than
a sound. A short utilitarian sword coalesced in his hand as if
the metal were being formed of smoke rising directly from
his skin, held together by sparks of lightning.

"A gladius?" Talbot mocked. "Are we in a Ridley Scott
movie now?"

"I am not in any sort of movie, Talbot. I haven't attacked
you yet, I'm merely preparing to defend myself."

I touched Talbot's arm. "What's going on? I said I wanted
to go somewhere for dinner and dancing."

"My bad," Talbot growled, upper and lower fangs extended. "I thought you said you wanted to go where there
was dinner and dancing." He indicated the long wooden bar
at the back with a toss of his head. The inhabitants ate dishes
I didn't recognize, some of them odd colors and others just
plain odd. "You can get both here."

"I will not attack first," the Iversonian interrupted.

"Wrong," Talbot spat. "We had a deal. You were to keep
the Chains in your collection."

"I never said that." The Iversonian held his sword at the
ready. "I only ever said that I wouldn't use them against
you."

"Iver, do you honestly expect me to believe that you, Iver
Richardson, the immortal who never gets rid of anything,
sold the Infernal Chains of Sarno Rayus, a unique artifact for
which, I might add, you spent centuries searching, because
you didn't want them anymore?" Talbot leaned in close, his
lips brushed the immortal's earlobe as he spoke. "Or is it

more likely that you sold them because you wanted to get back at me for picking a new person?"

"I was good to you." The Iversonian blurted the words in a whispered rush.

"It's been eighty years, Iver," Talbot said, his eyes pitying the immortal. "You got clingy. You thought I was your pet. But I keep telling people, mousers don't have owners. We pick people who interest us and we hang out. That's it. No guarantees."

Have you ever had one of those moments at a party where you're speaking really loudly, close to shouting, so you can be heard over the noise, and then there's a sudden quiet and you embarrass yourself? That's what happened when I said, "Maybe we should go?"

The music died. Half of the dancers were confused, but the other half, the vampires and the fey, were staring at Talbot, the Iversonian, and me. A finger snap broke the silence and we were fighting.

Talbot seized the Iversonian's wrist, bones crunching as he squeezed. The gladius fell from the immortal's hand and Talbot caught it, impaling the immortal in one smooth motion. Metal flashed in the club's lights as the blade drove straight through Iver's sternum and broke the skin on the other side. He went down and Talbot kept pushing, pinning him to the dance floor, the hilt of the gladius protruding from the immortal's chest like the head of an eccentrically fashioned nail.

"Stay put," Talbot snarled at the downed immortal, then tossed me a savage grin. "Impression time!"

I kicked in the speed, but the fey were faster. Three elves, pointy-eared Orlando Bloom wannabes, with street clothes modded out to look like they'd been made by the costume designers from that movie about a magic ring, charged me, drawing swords from underneath their jackets like the guys in those immortal movies. They left long thin gashes in my shoulders and across my belly, whirling about me in overlapping circles.

More cuts appeared, but they were in the wrong places, not inflicted to do damage so much as to look bad, to hurt. They twinged when I moved, but it wasn't anything I couldn't handle.

Talbot had already gutted two Soldier-level vamps, dust trailing from his claws where he'd ripped out their hearts. "You've got to admit this is better than dinner and dancing."

"I do not. Ow!" One of the elves flayed my cheek with his blade and I caught his wrist with my claws, pulling him to me. He rammed the blade into my chest with a sound like ripping fabric. A stab of explosive pain flared and died in my chest as I tore out the swordsman's throat with my fangs. Mouth open in a silent scream, the elf went down as blood gushed from the wound. I expected the blood to taste different, but it was the same. I spat out the meaty flesh on the floor as one of his friends ran me through.

The one on the left drew his sword out, going for a decapitation, but I pulled the sword out of my chest and parried, forcing his blade into his fellow elf instead. It only worked because I was stronger than he expected and the whole pulling-the-sword-out-of-my-own-chest thing had really caught him off guard.

Quicker than all of us, popping from opponent to opponent like popcorn in an old-style popper, Talbot danced in and out of other fights, one moment rending a troll into flaming green chunks, the next hurling a wailing faun through the ceiling tiles overhead.

Once I orked the third elf, Talbot and I worked as a team. My wounds healed as we fought and by the time the last of the immortal's minions fell, I was sweating blood and glaring balefully at my escort.

"Dinner and dancing," I said.

He shrugged. "Maybe next time."

Noncombatants, human and nonhuman, fled the club as sirens blared. The VCPD rounded up the humans and took them down to the station to have their memories altered "just in case."

"I'd hate to see the size of the Fang Fee for this one," Talbot said.

"Sir?" One of the police officers came over, pad in hand. "Are you Talbot?"

He nodded.

"Then Captain Stacey says this is for you." The officer handed the ticket to Talbot. Crumpling the paper into a ball, Talbot walked over to the Iversonian, who was still stuck to the floor.

"If you pay half the Fang Fee," Talbot offered, "I'll pull the sword out."

8

ERIC:

FANG

Dawn rose over the ruins of the Demon Heart, casting everything into the brilliant light of day. It was the first dawn I'd been able to really watch for over forty years. The sun doesn't take kindly to vampires.

Even though my eyes were only spectral approximations, I was determined to enjoy it. In ghost vision, the sun twirled and danced as if rendered by an invisible painter constantly forced to repaint it in oils of yellow, orange, and burnt umber as it moved across the sky.

Each change was distinct, unique, a succession of masterpieces, each surviving for less than an instant. I'm not a big painting guy, but the scene mesmerized me. The sun vaulted over the Pollux, rumbling through the sky and crashing down on the other side of the Demon Heart in a splash of red, pink, and violet. The canvas changed from day to night—stars, planets, and constellations swirling through the air. Each star pattern I recognized burst into greater focus, writhing and dancing in the night. All too quickly the cycle began anew. Sunrise, sunset, night, disrupted only by the weather, circled in the air with increasing swiftness. Soon the sun zoomed through the air in a smear of color.

Time was passing. Obviously I was out of it, or I would have done something, moved, blinked. Maybe it was the shock of being dead and bodiless. I think that's the real reason angry ghosts can go so long without outbursts. Things start to run together; one hour bleeds into the next. One day. One month. I lost count.

When you're alive, time flies when you're having fun. In death, time flies if you don't grab it with both hands and hang on tight. During my reverie, things changed. People came and left. The remains of the Demon Heart were covered in a light dusting of snow. We don't get snow often in Void City. A half inch of snow on the ground means no school, closed roads, and thousands of tiny snowmen flecked with grass and dirt.

It was the snow that snapped me out of it, that and the sight of a classic Mustang convertible parked on the street in front of me. Not just any Mustang, either—my Mustang. I love that car. Damn werewolves had wrecked it, trying to get at me over what was really Roger trouble. It had cost me a fortune to have it put back together, but I just couldn't live without it.

My daughter Greta, a blond Amazon, stood next to the car. She had my mechanic, Carl, with her. My Mustang was hooked to the back of his wrecker. He'd finished the repairs beautifully; with ghost-vision, I couldn't tell it'd been wrecked. Between the two of them stood my hired mage, Magbidion, a crazy little magician who was always hitting me up for protection.

Magbidion's hands were cupped over his right eye. He twisted and turned them like a photographer focusing his camera. "Try to start it again," Magbidion yelled over his shoulder. "I think we have his attention."

Carl climbed into the car and turned the key. "Nothing." He climbed back out. "I don't understand it."

"I do," Magbidion muttered. "Assuming his place of power really is his car, then it won't run unless we bring him back. Conversely, if we can manage to start the engine and keep it running, then he'll re-form. He's tied to it—linked. Goddess, but he must love this car." An idea lit up behind Magbidion's eyes, and I watched him dismiss it out of hand. "We've tried everything else. If this doesn't work, then we're going to have to rebuild the whole Demon Heart."

Magbidion is a smart magician, even if he is a little needy. He got his powers from a demon in exchange for his soul. Now that he's getting near his expiration date, Mags wants a little muscle on his side to try to renegotiate the contract. I don't know how many times I've turned him down. If he could get my body back for me, though, then he might have a deal. Heck, I might even make him my thrall.

"We've got to make him mad."

"Shit," said Greta, "if Dad knew that Tabitha was shacking up with that bigwig up at the Highland Towers, we wouldn't need to—"

The Mustang's engine roared.

"I see him," Magbidion shouted.

"She's shacking up with who, where?" I snarled.

Greta ran forward. "You can see him? Can he hear me? Daddy?"

She ran right past me. Some vampires have to be in one of their animal forms to detect ghosts. Others can't see them at all. Greta is ghostblind. I wish I was.

"We're missing something," Magbidion yelled as the engine died. "I don't know why I was wasting my time on the Pollux. You were right, Greta, he's definitely invested in the car, but we're missing something. What am I forgetting?"

"Answer my question, Mags!" I shouted. "Tabitha broke up with me, what, a day ago, and she's already shacking up with some asshole?"

"Just try to stay mad and give me a few minutes." Mags closed his eyes and sat down on the curb. "The body creation ritual didn't work with the Pollux, because the car is really his place of power . . . But the ritual didn't work with the car, either." He gestured with his hands while he spoke. "Why not? Something must be different about the car. What's different? What is the fundamental difference between a car and a building?"

"Cars have wheels," Greta answered.

"Cars move around," Carl suggested. "You drive them, steer them."

Right on cue, as if she timed it that way, I saw Rachel. I don't know if it was because she was my thrall, but she looked brighter to me, the red of her lips more red, the very essence of what red means. Her smell, a mixture of cinnamon and sex, wrapped itself around me and didn't let go, the first scent I'd experienced as a ghost. She wore hip-hugger jeans, a white crop top, and a black leather jacket. The cold accentuated her bralessness. In her hand she carried a red gas can.

"Cars eat," she said. "Cars run on gas. Vampires have different needs, but they still require fuel." Rachel paused and shook the gas can as she spoke, blood sloshing up the side and seeping back down. "Eric runs on blood. Feed the car what Eric needs and you nourish Eric through their connection." She gestured at me, then at the Mustang. "Nourish Eric and he can rebuild his body. He does it every time he changes into an animal and back, but he needs blood to fuel the transformation."

Magbidion wiped sweat from his forehead with a cotton handkerchief. "I put blood in the car! All over the backseat."

"You put *what* all over the backseat of my car?" I shouted. Staying mad was not a problem.

"But you didn't feed it." Rachel wrinkled her nose at Mags and he stood up quickly, backpedaling. "You don't put the gas in the backseat, you put it in the tank."

"I'm not sure what that would do," he stammered. "Let me clean the car, modify the ritual. There's too much magic wrapped up in the body-creation spell to continue safely. And we'll need human blood, not—"

"It is human blood." Greta, Rachel, and I all spoke at once. I could feel it through the can. I wanted it, needed it, which meant something they were doing was working. If anyone ever asks you what vampires really are, tell them I told you we're a bunch of worthless junkies, eternally jonesing for our next fix. The hunger hadn't been there after the explosion, but it was back now.

"Where'd you get it?" Mags asked.

"Sweetheart Row," Rachel answered.

It was a lie. My spectral eyes saw phantom blood on her hands. She'd washed it away, but the stain remained. She hadn't gotten the blood from Sweetheart Row. Think of The Row as a red-light district just for vampires. For the right price, the girls of Sweetheart Row would give blood, sex, or both at the same time, but the phantom blood on Rachel's hands felt more like murder than a business transaction. More things I didn't want to know.

All the anger about Tabitha subsided. I missed her, but there was no sense beating myself up about it. If she wasn't my girlfriend anymore, why did I give a rat's ass who she fucked? And to be honest, I was sleeping with her younger sister. Rachel is the kind of little sister all boyfriends dream about.

"We're losing him," Mags shouted. "Someone piss him off again. Pour some of that blood on him."

Ignoring his orders, Rachel started pouring blood into the gas tank of the Mustang. Greta snatched the gas can away, the force of her action spinning Rachel around and knocking her to the asphalt. "What do you think you're doing?"

"The car is a place of power for him. He loves it. He had sex with the woman he was going to marry in it. When the car got wrecked, he was as pissed off about losing it as he might have been about losing a child. He has no body. I've sprayed blood all over this damn wreck of a strip club, and none of these ashes are his." Rachel pulled herself up off the ground.

"Whoever planned this," she continued, "completely obliterated Eric's remains. So he can only re-form in his strongest place of power. I went along with you guys on the whole movie theater idea. I told you it wouldn't work and it didn't. The Pollux is just too damn big to be a *memento mori*."

I may not speak many other languages, but Latin I remember from school. *Memento mori*, in English: remember your death.

"A what?" Mags asked.

Rachel's finger pointed at Magbidion, but her eyes looked directly into Greta's. "You had your shot! Now let me try this. If it doesn't work, then we can always go get more blood for the next big idea."

Reluctantly, Greta emptied the rest of the blood into the car.

"Carl's just going to have to drain the gas tank," I said. "You guys are all fucked in the head. This is never going to work."

"Just give it a second, Eric," Magbidion said. At least *he* could hear me.

"Now what?" Greta asked softly.

"We piss him off." Rachel beamed. "We make him want to have hands so that he can strangle us with them. Where is he?"

Magbidion pointed me out to her, but I really thought she'd seen me all along. Hadn't she pointed at me or had I imagined that? I stood in the midst of the rubble where *El Alma Perdida* had been. It was gone. Maybe the Lone Stranger had better things to do and had taken the gun with him. Fine with me.

Magbidion resorted to the equivalent of "yo' mama" jokes, and Greta didn't fare much better, but Rachel knew just how to piss me off. She pulled a sharpened piece of wood out of her purse and jammed it through Greta's heart from behind.

I'm very protective of Greta. I'd brave daylight for her; I've done it more than once. Greta, like me, is one of those lucky vamps who is only immobilized by a stake through the heart, not actually destroyed by it. I knew she'd be fine, but I got mad anyway.

Getting angry doesn't usually hurt, but I felt like a po- tato being peeled. The Mustang's engine revved. My heart beat once. Beginning with the center of my field of vision, the world unraveled and rewove itself into normalcy. Gone was the surreal vision; in its place, colors and clarity reigned supreme.

"It's working," Rachel shouted.

"Something's wrong," Magbidion said slowly, drawing out the words so that wrong took two syllables. "I told you to let me cleanse the vehicle. The magic is interacting with another spell."

When Greta was a kid, I used to buy her little pellet toys that expanded in warm water, getting bigger and bigger until you could tell what kind of vehicle they really were.

That's what it felt like. I've re-formed from ashes before and it doesn't happen the way this did. A piercing scream escaped my re-formed mouth. The Mustang's horn honked wildly and all four tires spun in impossible directions.

Suddenly I was sitting behind the wheel of my beloved Mustang. Carl's rusty-ass tow truck was a sight for sore eyes . . . and I do mean literally sore. My heart was beating again, while air ripped in and out of my lungs. I wasn't just back amongst the undead; I was really alive!

"Oh, shit!" Magbidion cursed. "Everyone get away from the car!"

Then I was reliving the worst wreck I'd ever been in. I had been coming around the sharp turn on Duggan Road out near Marilyn's house, driving Roger's car, but in this memory, I was driving my Mustang. The warning sign says to take the turn at fifteen miles per hour, but, being speed-limit-sign dyslexic, I always took it at fifty-one. When I died the first time, it had been because Roger tampered with the brakes, and I found out firsthand that if you crash through the guardrail on that turn and have enough speed going, you have an amazing view of the quarry.

This time it was different. When I get extremely mad and black out, I turn into a large coal-skinned creature with leathery bat wings and glowing purple eyes. Now that I have a thrall, I can turn into it pretty much at will. In the new memory, the uber vamp sat in the passenger's seat, smoke trailing off of his skin as it popped and hissed in the sunlight.

"It's about fucking time," the uber vamp said. It grabbed the wheel, stomped its clawed foot over my own, jammed the gas pedal to the floor, and purposefully steered us through the guardrail and over the cliff. As we soared through the air, the paint job changed from black to red, then the uber vamp faded, leaving me alone to face the sudden stop at the end.

When I hit bottom, I flashed back to the present, but the damage to my car was real. The steering wheel had broken in half, and the steering column was shoved up and partially into my chest. My Mustang had re-enacted the wreck all over the street between the Pollux and the Demon Heart. My legs were crushed in a mass of accordioned metal. Lacerations from the windshield glass covered my face and upper body . . . *Memento mori.* Remember my death. Fuck Latin!

When it was finally over, Maghidion ran for the car and tried to pull me out, so he was up close and personal for what happened next. Later he'd tell me that I was dead for over a minute, but I never lost consciousness. I remember the steering column pulling back, the collapsed roof straightening, every dent and ding popping out smoothly as the whole car essentially fixed itself. My heart shuddered, then stopped, my skin cooled, and I was a vampire again . . . undamaged except for the whole undead angle.

Other than the paint job changing from black to red, my Mustang seemed to be none the worse for wear. I stepped out of the car, and Rachel jumped into my arms, pulling my head toward her neck. I drank; the hunger subsided, and Rachel sagged against me.

"I've missed you," she whispered.

"I don't get it," I said.

Magbidion laughed. "You weren't made in the traditional way, Eric. What happened just now . . . when we resurrected you . . . is that you came back as a human. There is a slim chance with the ritual we used that such a thing can happen, but then another spell intervened."

"What kind of spell?"

"It's so complex, so powerful, that I couldn't tell you. I think it was some kind of curse—very primal and old— probably two hundred years at least."

"And it gave me a supernatural bitch-slap back into the realm of the undead?"

"That's not how I would have put it, but yeah."

I unstaked Greta, kept her from killing Rachel (which wasn't hard once she realized why Rachel had staked her) and sat with the group of them on the snow-covered sidewalk.

"So . . . I wasn't embraced or turned or whatever by an-other vampire, but by some kind of curse."

Magbidion nodded.

"So I don't have a sire?"

"Yes and no," the mage sighed. His hands twisted around his eye again, but the circle through which he looked was smaller than before. "If I focus, I can usually tell who sired a vampire. When I look at you that way, there is an indistinct figure and I get the impression this person is a vampire. It's as if the curse made you his or her offspring."

"Can you tell who cursed me?"

"No." He focused even more tightly. There was a loud pop, a spark, and Magbidion fell over backward. "Ow." Smoke trailed away from his fingers and he rubbed his eye. "Do you remember tastes?"

I nodded.

"You know how people say that x or y tastes like chicken, but it isn't chicken? It's really duck or alligator or snake?"

"Yeah."

"It isn't magic. It tastes like magic, but it isn't magic. It's cleaner, purer. Maybe it is just a kind of magic I've never encountered before."

"One more question: Why is my car red?"

"It could be a side effect." Magbidion shrugged. "The car was subjected to a great deal of magic, conventional and otherwise. The curse touched it, too, re-creating the accident in which you died. . . ."

He put a hand on the hood. It revved its engine at him, screeched into reverse, and backed across the street. Magbidion hit the asphalt in front of the Mustang and it flicked on its high beams.

"Mags, do not tell me that my car—"

"That's so cool, Dad!" Greta shouted. "You have a vampire car! I always wanted a vampire car! Can we name it Fang?"

"Fang the 'Stang," I grumbled. "Somebody shoot me."

9

ERIC:
PROBLEM NUMBER TWO

Nobody seemed to know what would happen to Fang if the sun hit it, so I parked in the old Bateman's Department Store deck next to Magbidion's RV, where the sun couldn't get at my 'Stang and where Mags could keep an eye on it. Bateman's burned back in the seventies, and I bought their deck since it adjoined the Pollux anyway.

Green, red, blue, and yellow lights dotted the outside of the Pollux and the interior railings. I always decorated for Christmas, and in my absence, someone had done it for me. Usually I would close the Demon Heart and all the girls would come over for a bit of nonworking Yuletide revelry. Yeah, Christmas. I guess my ghostly eyes had stared at the sun for four whole months. I could have stared at it for another eight.

My flocked white Christmas tree stood proud and tall in the center of the lobby, decked in the same bubble lights I used every year. The star, a silver contraption made of tinfoil and popsicle sticks, waited on the edge of the concession counter where Greta put it every year. Whether we were on good or bad terms, there was always Christmas.

Greta's my biggest failure and one of my greatest loves. She made the star for me on our first Christmas together, back when she was still alive. A ten-year-old girl and a sixty-year-old vampire don't have much in common, but we did have Christmas. I don't remember exactly what happened anymore, what her foster parents had done, but I remember that it had been bad and that I'd taken care of it. Afterward it had seemed natural that she stay with me. If I'd stuck to my guns and kept her human, she'd be in her thirties now . . . I think . . . but I hadn't lasted much more than a decade before giving in.

I turned into a bat, grabbed the star with my feet, and dropped it into place (which is exactly as hard as it sounds) before flying upstairs. Rachel followed me up, but I wasn't in the mood for sex and I certainly wasn't in the mood for Rachel. I wanted Marilyn, but she was gone. She was gone and there was something I was supposed to do about it . . . something important. A nagging thought haunted the cobwebbed corridors of my bat brain. It darted between thoughts about what or who Tabitha was doing and hid behind filing cabinets when I tried to look straight at it. I was forgetting something. I'm always forgetting something.

Abruptly, I dropped out of my bat form, landing on my feet, fully dressed. Some vampires can take their clothes with them when they change shapes. I'm one of the lucky ones who can and the process leaves my clothes clean with a fresh-out-of-the-dryer warmth that makes me smile. I snapped my fingers. "Presents," I said softly. "Shit, I've got to get everybody presents."

"Money might be an issue," Rachel interrupted. "Someone closed your accounts."

"Excuse me?"

"Your alias, Eric Jones, was declared legally dead. You left everything to Marilyn, she left everything to you . . . To make a long story short, the city tried to claim your assets. Greta bought the Pollux, the Demon Heart property, and the parking deck with her savings, but now she's tapped out. She wouldn't say anything to you about it, I'm sure, but . . ."

Rachel looked shorter all of a sudden. She took two steps back. And now I'd changed into my uber vamp form without realizing it and I hadn't lost control.

Marilyn would be impressed.

"Marilyn." Screw Christmas. Screw the money. I'd forgotten Marilyn. A demon had her soul. A demon that was waiting for me to contact him. How could I have pushed that to the back of my ghostly brain, gotten caught up in the sight of the sun, for months? I hoped he was still waiting. The tangy scent of cinnamon hit me hard enough to make my eyes water, or bleed, as the case is with vampires. I wiped it away with hands that were black as pitch and ended in claws.

Ever since I met Rachel, I've smelled cinnamon whenever she's trying to calm me down, convince me to do what she wants, or seduce me. I don't know if it's magic or something all thralls can do, but it annoyed me that she'd done it in an effort to keep my mind off Marilyn.

"A demon has Marilyn's soul." My voice was deeper, threatening.

"I'm sorry," Rachel told me. She cautiously ran a finger along my bare chest. "Do you know which demon?"

"No . . . a smarmy-sounding one."

Rachel ran her hand much farther south. "You're such a big boy in this form."

"It's hard to concentrate when you do that."

"Then don't concentrate." She stripped out of her top, rubbed her breasts against me. "I don't know any demons, but I know a vampire who would know."

"Not the guy from the Highland Towers," I said churlishly.

It was a moment before Rachel could answer. "No, not that guy. Another guy. We'll go to see Winter." She slipped out of her pants. No underwear there, either. "I've heard that he's very on top of things." As she said "on top" she pushed me back and I sprawled out on the floor. The wings made things awkward; but, like most guys, I could have been lying on a lit cigarette and it wouldn't have bothered me at that moment.

Despite her comment about size, Rachel had little trouble when she climbed on top of me. The way she worked sex into any situation reminded me of a succubus Talbot had saved me from in El Segundo. Rachel wasn't a demon, but she certainly acted like one. Succubi feed on sex, get power from it. Rachel just seemed to get off on screwing vamps.

As we moved together, she kissed me on the top of my head, then again between the eyes, then on my throat. Her soft, wet kisses made my skin tingle, flush with warmth, and feel alive. She placed a fourth on the middle of my chest over my heart and it began to beat. We both climaxed, her left hand resting on my solar plexus, her right hand at the base of my crotch. She guided my fangs to her neck again and I drank. Her blood was rich and full; it had body and flavor, burning my tongue like Tabasco.

Once before, I'd felt little messages broadcasting from Rachel when we were close. Thoughts had danced through my head, pretending to be mine. I heard them again as she lay panting against my chest. "Trust Rachel. Need Rachel. Love Rachel. Be still of form. Be bound of form. Be mine. Be mine."

Cinnamon, the smell of it, the taste of it, surrounded me, just as surely as Rachel's flesh enfolded mine. My heart beat and my lungs drew breath of their own accord. Heat built at my core and my body temperature soared. Blood flowed through my veins as I climaxed again, painfully, and Rachel's eyes rolled up in her head, her legs clamping around me as best she could, her hands pulling at my ass.

"Fuck, yes," she hissed. "Keep going, baby. Come on."

Pushing myself up with my wings, I rolled us over and kept thrusting, my hands on her shoulders, holding her in place. I expected my erection to subside, but it didn't. Purple light from my glowing eyes cast strange shadows on the floor and made her eyes seem to glow a matching violet. As the orgasm hit her, my heart beat faster, and I climaxed a third time, which is pretty much unheard of for me, let alone most men. Maybe it was a thrall thing, some sort of mystic Viagra for vampires.

Every time I asked her about one of her little skills, she said it was a thrall thing. I was going to need a second opinion. Again, I had the feeling I was forgetting something. Something important. I rolled off of her and quickly returned to my normal self, dressed in jeans, a belt, sneakers, and a black *Welcome to the Void* T-shirt.

"I wish I could do that," Rachel laughed as she struggled back into her jeans.

"Do what?"

"The instant clothes changing thing."

"It *is* a perk." As I picked up her top and threw it to her, I remembered. "We're supposed to be doing something."

"We just did," she teased.

"No." I smacked the floor. "I was talking about it right before. What was it?"

"I don't remember."

She remembered. I knew she did. I grabbed one of her nipple rings gently, but firmly. "Don't lie to me."

"I thought you were joking."

More little voices danced in my head. They were harder to hear now, but they were there. *Trust. Trust. Trust.*

"I wasn't."

"We're supposed to go see Ebon Winter at his club, the Artiste Unknown. You wanted to find the demon that took that old woman Marilyn's soul."

I pulled her close and kissed her. She had a hard time returning the kiss in the beginning, mad that I'd accused her of lying, but she covered it up. I'm the kind of guy who would rather not know if all my friends really hate me. If my girlfriend is sleeping around, I'd like her to have the decency to be smart enough about it that I never find out.

"You'll need a tux if you want to talk to Winter," Rachel blurted.

"Does everyone dress like that at Winter's club?"

"No." She fluttered her eyelashes at me. "But we will. If you want to meet Winter, you have to make an impression."

"I don't own a tux anymore. It blew up. Where's Talbot?"

"I haven't seen him."

"He wanders off sometimes." I sighed. "Like a damn cat. He'll be back eventually. In the meantime, I guess you'll have to go rent me one. Do you have the right kind of dress?"

"I still have the green one you bought me, but you'll need to come with me to get your tux."

"Why is that?"

"Because if you're going to make an impression on Winter, it will need to fit well."

An impression? The impression I usually make on most High Society vamps is my boot print on their asses. Now I had to charm some jackass to get information? Shit.

✦ 10 ✦

ERIC:

THE ARTISTE UNKNOWN

For a man who'd just risen from the dead (again), I looked good in the rented tux. Rachel had suggested that I buy one, but I didn't want to eat up the rest of Greta's savings. I felt guilty enough about renting the limo with Greta's credit card, but Rachel said that entrances were important and an undead Mustang did not say elegance. It was her first ride in a limo and I think the only thing that kept her in that strapless green gown was a desire to impress Ebon Winter.

The driver, an oni named Tiko, didn't need to be getting any ideas anyway. Oni are Japanese ogres that eat people. He was big, green, and had a single black horn protruding from his forehead. In Void City, Tiko and his brothers perform public services for the supernatural folks who can afford it and don't want to pay off the cops. They are also the reason that a lot of disappearances go unsolved, thereby avoiding a costly Fang Fee for the supernatural perpetrator. If there's no body, then there's no crime, and, like the werewolves who'd eaten Roger, Tiko and his brothers don't tend to leave any leftovers lying about.

The Artiste Unknown was in a much nicer neighborhood than my club. It looked bigger, more expensive, and in all ways superior to the Demon Heart, except that I could tell just from looking at it that there would be no naked girls inside. Even if there were naked girls inside, they wouldn't be dancing the way my girls had. They'd be covered in silver body paint or disguised as trees or something. Even so, it was quite impressive, a modernistic palace of glass and light and style. I hated it.

As we walked up, a smooth-looking vampire with blond highlights joined the one watching the door. They had a quick discussion and I could tell that the newcomer was not pleased. From the sound of it, the guy at the door really worked security and had just pummeled a prospective guest. I supposed he was used to a far more straightforward job description than being a doorman at this club required.

"I'm sorry, Mr. Andre," the stand-in said. "Klaus said he would just be a minute and that guy wouldn't wait."

The human in question was standing off to one side and his vampire girlfriend was gazing into his eyes with a concerned look on her face. When Andre looked her way, she bared her fangs. "That cretin almost killed Ken."

I stepped forward with Rachel and the female vamp bared her fangs at me. I bared mine in response and "announced" myself.

Vampire society classifies vampires by how powerful they are and any known weaknesses they have, dividing them into Drones, Soldiers, Masters, and Vlads. It has nothing to do with bloodline, but everything to do with personality, the strength of the individual's character. I've always thought of it as a supernatural Rorschach test. I guess being a Vlad is like getting the perfect score. That makes being an Emperor like getting college credit for the course or something. All I know is that I have all the powers in the book and I tend to come back from just about anything, like Dracula.

The lower down the food chain you are, the more your betters can fuck with you. Vlads and Masters can detect each other. We get a mental image, a sense of age from those nearby, and if we want, we can push an awareness of ourselves into a Drone or a Soldier, kind of a big *don't fuck with me* bulletin. That was what I did when I "announced" myself to the three vampires at the door. From their reactions, the girl and the stand-in were both Drones, but Andre was a Soldier. He kept his cool pretty well. I almost liked him.

"Might I be of assistance?" I offered. Social interaction with most vampires is like a damn dance. I knew a few of the beginner steps, but if we started to cha-cha I was going to be out of my league. I'd probably have to start putting undead back in their graves.

I missed Roger, even though he had killed me twice. Roger had been much better at this crap. He'd enjoyed it. He'd liked hanging out at the Artiste Unknown.

There was a reason I'd let him handle all of this stuff before I found out what a murderous little backstabbing power whore he was. God, he'd been good at it, even if he had always been a little sloppy. If you pushed him around, he developed a stratagem and set plans into motion. By the time the last domino fell and you finally saw what was going on, you were already screwed to the wall and crying for mama. When I get pushed around, I push back. I can't help it; it just happens. I had a feeling that killing off this Winter guy's employees wasn't going to help my situation.

Andre looked into my eyes and smiled. His eyes didn't, but his mouth did; it made me like him a little less. "No, thank you, sir. Everything is well in hand. Go right in, Lord . . ."

"Eric," I told him. "Just Eric. Kind of like Sting, but not."

I offered Rachel my arm and Andre held the door for us as we walked in. The music and the lights hit me all at once, but that wasn't what made me pause. I sensed twelve Master vampires and two Vlads. I couldn't sort them all out, but I thought I recognized one of the Vlads. It was Ebon Winter; it had to be. The second thing that hit me was the people. Over five hundred hearts pushed a few thousand quarts of blood. Most of them were dancing; the varying scents and perfumes, the heightened states of excitement . . . after the calm of being a ghost, it was just too much. I pulled Rachel tight to my chest and buried my face against her neck.

"Shhh . . . ," she said soothingly. Her fingers traced small circles on my back underneath my jacket. "Focus on me. One heartbeat, all yours. One blood, all yours. One body, all yours."

My hands clenched and I grabbed my own forearms, afraid that if I grabbed her, I might break her. Rachel blew softly on my neck, cooing to me as if I were a child, whispering little nonsense words. I smelled the cinnamon that was perpetually on her breath and knew she was up to something. The background noise began to fade; the scents, the blood, my intense desire all slowly abated. Concentrating on Rachel helped. Another thirty seconds and I was able to pull slowly away from her. Her scent was confusing. She seemed excited, afraid, and relieved, all at once.

"Works like a charm," Rachel said mischievously. "Are you okay, baby? I thought I was going to lose you there for a sec."

I nodded.

"How did you do that? Was that more thrall stuff?" I asked.

"I have my ways," she teased. "The principle is similar to what some parents in England did during World War II. Children were having trouble sleeping because of the war, the air raids, all of that, so they learned that if they put the child to bed with a piece of bread, then the kid could sleep at night because at the very least they knew what they were going to have for breakfast."

"I remember that."

"Same thing," she said as we worked our way through dancing couples, some human, some vampire, and most mixed. "It doesn't matter how much blood is out there or how many women, because . . ." She guided my hand to her left breast. "You've already got your prey right here."

I didn't want to think about that, so I changed the subject.

"This Winter guy . . . How would you describe him?" I removed my hand from her breast and took her by the arm. I could smell the alcohol from the bar across the room. More surprising was the aroma of food. The tang of various fried, grilled, and broiled things made my mouth water. The thought of watching Rachel eat was appetizing; there was also the possibility she might actually be hungry. We headed that way.

While I maneuvered us toward the bar through the crowd, Rachel answered me, "He's . . . well, beautiful, like a piece of art or something. Really metrosexual."

I stumbled over the word for a moment, before I realized I'd heard Tabitha use it before. If I remembered correctly, it meant a straight man who had the style and fashion sense of a gay man. That sounded like him. The image in my mind had shown him to be physically in his early twenties. He had carefully ruffled blond hair that reminded me of David Bowie, but younger and more attractive.

Outward appearances can be very deceiving amongst the undead, but from the feeling I'd gotten when I sensed him, Ebon Winter couldn't have been more than a decade old. He felt like the last performance of "Candle in the Wind" or Johnny Colt and Marc Ford's last show with The Black Crowes . . . very late nineties.

"He's younger than I expected." I wasn't used to sensing a large group, but I got the same feel from the others in the room. They were all young as far as vampires go, only ten or fifteen years undead at the most.

We made our way through the club. A circular glass stage moved up and down in the center of the room on a sleek column. Large screens of various sizes showed the action onstage. The two biggest screens had to be fifty feet high and ran the entire length of the walls they were on. A band was onstage—modern alternative, but good. Raw talent was propping them up until they got a little more experience under their belts. If I'd been a talent scout, I would have signed them in a heartbeat.

"He was supposedly turned on his twentieth birthday eleven or twelve years ago," Rachel told me. "I hear it pissed off a lot of people when he was made instead of the competition."

"Competition?"

"His sire is some really ancient Vlad from way back and he only turns two vampires every ten years, a male and a female. I don't know exactly how it works, but apparently the potential vampires have to compete against each other for the privilege. There's supposed to be a lot of money involved, too." The music changed, and Rachel, recognizing the tune, laughed and let go of my hand. She moved in amongst the dancers and joined them. She belonged there, dancing with them to the techno beat. I didn't. Dancing is something I watch others do. The hunger and the presence of so many people began to close in on me again. I gave her a warning look and she stuck her tongue out at me in reply, but came back to my side.

"A lady doesn't leave her escort," I said, quoting Sinatra at her.

She pointed up at one of the walls that didn't sport an enormous video screen, indicating a series of terraced box seats. "Winter is probably in one of those when he isn't on-stage. Or he could be in the lower level under this floor. There is a whole second club down there just for his highest paying patrons and their guests. It's called The Velvet."

"Winter? He goes by his last name?"

"Yes." She rolled her eyes at me. "Everyone knows that."

Everyone but me. "Okay, okay. So if we can get down to The Velvet and they let us in, we have a better chance at getting to meet him. How do we do that?"

"I don't know everything." She smiled. "But we'll think of something."

That didn't sound good.

✦ 11 ✦

ERIC:
DOMINANCE TRAINING

For the next few hours we killed time waiting to be noticed. Rachel and I danced half a dozen times. I know, I know. I don't dance. Don't get me started.

We got seats at one of the little glass-on-metal tables near the bar and Rachel ordered an appetizer. The chairs looked—and felt—like they'd been bought for appearance over comfort.

The bartender kept trying to sell me blood. I wasn't buying. I make it a practice never to accept bottled blood from strangers. Not since El Segundo. Instead, I watched Rachel eat.

I don't know why it surprised me, but she had gotten a lot better at entertaining vampires. Little things, like talking through the choice of the next bite of food mean a lot. A good dining companion for a vampire knows how to keep up a dialogue. The façade lets dining instructions be couched within phrases that could pass as normal dinner conversation. "Oh this is all so good, I can hardly decide what to eat next" was code for "What do you want me to eat?" Responding to subtle commands like "that looks like a juicy one" or "have you tried mixing x with y" gives vampires a little control over the meal without making us feel like total freaks.

The appetizer she had ordered was fried mushrooms. The mushrooms were bite-size, but she cut each one in half as she ate and she alternated between using a fork and her fingers. As she bit into each piece, she lingered over the morsel, leaving her lips parted until her teeth actually touched one another. She chewed slowly, savoring the food, letting the expressions accompanying each taste show on her face. Her eyes would half close with pleasure if a bite of mushroom was just right. After the first few she called the waiter over and asked if he could get any horseradish sauce. He did.

When he brought the sauce, she took turns slightly dipping a piece of fried mushroom into it and eating daintily and immersing the entire piece in the horseradish, carefully licking off the excess before it could drip on the table.

There were mistakes. She hurried through a few of the pieces too quickly and she ate more of the mushrooms than she should have before asking if I'd like her to order something else, but I could tell that she had practiced since I'd watched her eat breakfast some four months before.

She must have given it serious thought, studied the voyeuristic nature of vampires in detail. It was as if while I'd been out of the picture for four months, she'd taken a class. I pictured a room full of thralls practicing how to eat for voyeuristic purposes. She would have been at the top of the intermediate class, a real A+ student.

I wasn't the only one who noticed. She was drawing attention. Some of the vamps looked on with the same vicarious pleasure that I did, but a few looked hungry and more than a few of the human escorts looked envious and angry.

"What do we want next?" she asked, looking over the menu. Even with the phrasing of her question, she showed a subtle understanding. Tabitha would have asked, "What do you want to watch me eat next?" That spoiled part of it, but Rachel understood: she asked for advice, not directions. It was perfectly clear that whatever I suggested was what she would order, but doing it this way sustained an important part of the illusion. It allowed an abnormal act to retain a semblance of normalcy.

"I want to get in to see this Ebon Winter guy and then I want to take you out to dinner. Real dinner. Do you like steak?"

Before she could answer my question, another vampire spoke up. "Eat another mushroom."

Rachel shrugged, picked up the fork and looked at me.

I shook my head.

"Make the bitch eat another mushroom."

There was really no way he could have known how touchy I am about how other people treat my companions, particularly my women. The little I did know about vampire High Society told me that an insult to her was an insult to me. That I felt possessive of Rachel even though I knew she had a hidden agenda bothered me, but I tabled that shouting match to myself until I'd dealt with the new moron.

The way I see it, my women take good care of me; they give what I need, blood or otherwise, and they don't make me feel like a monster or a freak. For the most part, I try to take care of them. When I ran the Demon Heart, I paid for their college, and more. I paid my strippers an annual salary between fifty and seventy-five grand, before tips. They had health insurance with dental and vision. When they left, they knew they could still call on me if they ran into trouble and they knew that I wouldn't call on them unless they'd said it was okay.

Some of them had already called to ask when I was reopening the club. But now that the club was gone . . . I didn't know how I felt about a new one. I don't want to say that I've ever felt like the club objectified women or abused them, because I've always gone out of my way to make sure that the Demon Heart helped rather than hindered the girls who danced in it, but now that I didn't have to worry about filling a rotation . . .

"I don't know," I said, thinking out loud more about the idea of reopening the club, than the asshole hassling us.

Rachel seemed concerned. "Why don't I just have another mushroom, Eric?"

As I turned to her, I could feel my eyes light up inside. "Do you want another mushroom?"

"N-no," she stammered, "but what's the harm?" I think Rachel was a little surprised at my reaction. She must have been worried that I would go all black skin and leather wings. I was mad, but not that mad. She still had a few things to learn about me.

The vampire with a malnourished heroin addict on his arm had more to learn about me than Rachel did, but he probably wouldn't live long enough. I went from sitting to standing in one pulse of the club's multicolored lights. In the next flash I was next to him. By the third, he was already on the floor with my foot on his throat. I love it when my powers work well. They can be finicky, but they hadn't really misfired since I'd re-formed.

He was much slower than me. "Did you say something?" I asked.

Gurgling at me, he tried to push my leg up and lift my foot.

He was weaker than me, too. I looked at his date. "Would you like a mushroom?"

Happy Boy popped his claws and I broke his neck. "If you cut my tux, I'll end you," I said. "It's a rental." He pulled his claws back in.

His date started to cry. "Please, don't hurt him. He's sorry. Aren't you sorry, Irwin? We'll leave; we won't come back. We'll hang at the park or something."

She was defending him. It made me sick. It always makes me sick to see someone beg. A human pleading for the life of a vampire is even worse. I lifted my foot a fraction, just enough for him to slide out from under it.

"What's your problem, man?" he said, popping his neck into place. "She's just a human. What do you care?"

I grabbed him by the throat and cut him off before he got himself dead for real. Why I cared, I can't tell you. I just did. "The reason you will understand is this: She is mine and I don't share well. I never have. It's a childhood malady. Maybe I had too many brothers and sisters and I have a deep need to indisputably demonstrate my ownership of things."

Anger started building up inside me again and I could feel myself starting to go. Fang's engine roared in my ears, echoing my anger. I wondered if anyone else could hear it or if this was another symptom of the strange bond we shared. If I lost control in a place like this, with so many people around, there was no telling how many might be killed.

Maybe Rachel was right to be worried. There were probably enough Masters and Vlads to take me down, but not before I caused a lot of damage. Irwin's girlfriend looked into my eyes and panicked. "Look at his eyes, oh my God!"

Fang hauled ass out of the parking deck back at the Pollux, heading for me. *It's okay*, I tried thinking at him, *I've got it*. I think he understood because it felt like he was heading back to the deck.

I snapped out of it, as though calling off Fang had taken some of the steam out of my anger. All the same, I was sure my eyes were glowing purple. "Want to see something really scary?" I asked, but Irwin was already dragging his date out of the club. I turned back to Rachel. She was afraid, too . . . far too afraid for someone who'd fucked an uber vamp. She'd almost peed herself. *Why?*

"They're purple, right?"

Rachel got up. "I have to go to the ladies' room."

Biting back a vulgar remark, I walked her to the ladies' room and waited outside the door. While I waited, security headed my way. People watched out of the corners of their eyes. They glanced away when I turned to look at them, but I could feel the eyes upon me. A female vamp came out of the bathroom and I smiled at her. "Is there a no-fighting rule here?"

"No fighting, no killing, no maiming, no threatening of any kind. It's a civilized club," she scoffed.

I glanced around me. Sure enough, there were little signs posted in obvious places that said pretty much what she had told me. The signs were more ornate and so was the wording, but she'd been dead-on. No wonder Roger had never asked me to come here.

I waited for security and made fun of their little plastic armbands in my head. Andre came out of nowhere and joined the goons sashaying in my direction.

"Winter," Andre told me when he arrived, "wishes to thank you for enabling him to win the wager he placed upon your entering the club. As he suggested, you managed to last an entire hour before breaking any of the rules that would cause you to be ejected from the club. As thanks, he would like to invite you and your guest to join him for a pre-ejection drink in The Velvet where he hopes you will be able to restrain yourself amongst those who are your equals, if not your betters."

"Well, fuck you very much," I replied.

Andre was so taken aback that he physically took a backward step.

"He means we'd be delighted," Rachel said as she exited the bathroom behind me. Andre looked at me for confirmation and I shrugged. That was one way to interpret what I'd said.

As he led us toward an elevator, Rachel whispered in my ear, "How many brothers and sisters did you have?"

"None." I smiled. "I'm an only child." *I think.*

12

ERIC:

FIRST IMPRESSIONS

I liked The Velvet. It reminded me a lot of the Pollux's decor. Crimson velvet wallpaper and lamps in brass-backed sconces lined the walls. The sconces' circular rear plates had little snowflakes etched into them. In the Pollux, pentacles had been similarly etched. A collection of intimate booths and vintage-era tables were spread out around a small stage. Dark carpet covered the floors. Wooden railings separated the seating area from the small dance area. There was no bar.

The club could have held around sixty people, but there were only eighteen vampires in it now, each with a human date. Twelve of them were the Master vampires I'd sensed earlier. They were dressed in an array of styles ranging from mob chic to the same metrosexual look Winter sported and they had arranged themselves so that Winter was the center of their attention. One vampire had even pulled his chair around at an odd angle as if he was afraid that showing Winter his back would be disrespectful.

Onstage, Ebon Winter changed songs as I entered. He went into an a capella version of "Love Her Madly" by The Doors and though I disliked him, his voice was like nothing I had ever heard. In comparison, Sinatra's voice had no character and Bowie sounded bland and safe. Wearing matching white leather jumpsuits, the other Vlad and her date sat at a corner booth. Their motorcycle helmets sat on the floor next to them. I stifled a laugh and let Andre lead Rachel and me to a booth a little apart from the rest of them. It was probably a slight of some kind. Maybe it was supposed to give me a message about not belonging. Either way, I was still edgy from the confrontation upstairs and glad of the distance. The only ways I knew to take the edge off involved killing or screwing and neither seemed a likely option here.

Two of the vampires reoriented their attention on me, only to be silently rebuffed by the other vampires. Winter didn't miss a beat, but a flick of his eyes made it clear that the two offenders would have to answer for the momentary lapse in loyalty later. Stupid High Society bullshit.

Each couple was served by their own steward, and apparently there were several chefs hard at work beyond one of the sets of double doors, because delicious smells wafted in from the kitchen. Our server's name was Chad, and I was only mildly surprised when he brought a steak dinner to the table. He brought with it a red merlot for Rachel, which even I could appreciate in terms of color and bouquet. For me he brought a draft beer in a frosted mug. He even set it in front of me as if I wasn't going to have to watch Rachel drink it for me. "Compliments," he informed us, "of the house." I'd had some blood booze once. It had tasted like crap, but I almost asked if he could order me some before I remembered that it had been very expensive and I was on a tight budget.

Winter winked at us from the stage. If he'd been a girl, I would have cherished that wink. Since he wasn't, it made me uncomfortable.

Rachel ate for me and herself at the same time. She did even better than before, and despite the improvement, the show was just for me this time. The other vamps and their dates were too busy watching Winter. I listened to him off and on. I like music to be loud and angry. Skill isn't the most important aspect of it for me. Again, he was great, the best I'd ever heard, but for me, the radio would have been fine. He switched styles effortlessly, making everything work without instruments, going old school with "Lightnin' Strikes" as well as music that was either original or too new to have entered my playlist.

"Are you even listening to him anymore?" Rachel admonished gently. "You'll make him angry."

"I'm edgy. Maybe it's all the not killing people. I'm not used to it."

Before she could comment, the current song ended and soft applause came from the other tables. Rachel clapped, and I joined in halfheartedly. I knew what my problem was.

I wanted to get the information I needed from this Winter guy and get the hell out.

Winter flitted over to our booth and beamed at us. "So, how are we doing over here in the rowdy section?" he asked.

"Not bad," I admitted. "My compliments to your chef."

Winter gestured for Rachel to move over and he sat down once she had scooted enough to make room for him. This elicited some shocked looks from the other vamps and some hasty reorienting on their part, as if they wanted to make sure I knew they were focusing on Winter rather than me. Winter was apparently doing us a favor by crowding our booth. "Emil is wonderful, isn't he? Your escort has unique talents, too, wouldn't you say? I almost stopped singing to watch her eat." His eyes flashed red right through the blue contacts he was wearing and then faded, revealing a conspiratorial lightheartedness that rang false to me. I wondered why the light hadn't turned purple when it flashed through the contacts. "What did you think of the performance?"

"It was good. I liked it. I tend to like heavier stuff, though, so I can't really judge . . ."

"Good?" he asked carefully. "Liked?"

"He's not very careful with his words, Winter," Rachel butted in. "I hope you'll excuse him."

"Roger was much better at this sort of thing than I am," I added. "I'm not trying to be an ass."

Winter eyed me carefully and then eyed Rachel. "I suppose we can let it go this once . . . if you'll tell me how you do it?"

"Do what?" I asked.

"Your eyes." As he spoke, he reached up and pulled out a contact, revealing a washed-out-looking iris, a typical vampire eye. I knew immediately what he meant, and it wasn't the funky purple glow I'd sported earlier in the evening. My eyes have always been blue. They were blue in life and according to Marilyn, they are the same color they've always been. "They're blue, really blue. Is it a dye? Some type of implant?"

You'd think he'd have been more interested in what had frightened the folks upstairs when I had started to go off on Irwin, but I gave him the spiel, knowing that, like most, he wouldn't believe it. "If I knew why I still have human-looking eyes, I would tell you, but they've always been that way. To be honest, I didn't even know that they had stayed blue until Roger pointed it out to me some time in the seventies. I haven't done a whole lot of mirror gazing since I became a vampire."

He scoffed at me and rolled his eyes. "Fine, if you won't tell me, then I have nothing further to discuss with you. Andre," he called, "see this plebeian out."

"Wait a minute!" I snarled. "That's it? I wasted three hours and got all dressed up in this monkey suit just so you could throw me out for not knowing how to give you a pair of bright happy blue eyes? I don't think so!"

I put my hand through the mahogany table and Winter flinched. When I tried to grab Winter himself, my hand passed through him. He looked solid, but his body had changed to mist. Movie vampires turn to mist all the time, but I'd never met a vampire who could do it, much less one with control like that. I locked eyes with him instead and was stunned to find myself almost drowning in his mind. I withdrew and he tried to chase after me into my head, but I snarled, announcing myself again, pushing him out. The Master vampires started to casually saunter my way and I turned on them with my eyes aglow.

"I came here for information, not to be deliberately provoked in your club and used as a source of amusement! Why did you bet on me, anyway?"

The Vlad in the Elvis jumpsuit stepped forward. "Everyone knows about the blue-eyed vampire named Eric. We all know that you're supposed to be some kind of badass who's not to be messed with. One of the first things my sire told me was to stay far away from the Demon Heart and farther away from you."

"Mine told me that you killed other vampires for sport," said one of the Master vampires, a short little guy with a shaved head and a Vandyke.

One of the female vamps, an Asian girl with a red wig, stood up. "Mine said you didn't drink human blood. He told me you only drank from your own get. He said that you had special rooms underneath your club where you kept them."

"We were curious," explained Winter. "You sounded monstrous."

"And this made you want to meet me and play mind games?"

As Winter laughed, small curls of vapor poured out of his mouth and around the sides of his face, flowing back into him. He smiled as if reading my mind. "There is beauty in monstrosity, wonder in diversity, and to these simple truths even the gods must confess."

"And we do," the others said as one.

"We are the new gods and you are a titan," Winter explained. "You are powerful, but your ways are the old ways and we are far more powerful together than you are alone."

These guys were nuts! They thought this was a grand adventure, a game to amuse themselves. They could form a great big circle jerk in the parking lot for all I cared, but they could not fuck with me. I turned back to Winter.

"Look, you pansy little fuck! I came here for some information and I'll be damned if I leave here without it. Now I know that you're used to dealing with Roger and other High Society fangs and maybe they buy into this vampires as Greek gods bullshit you've been blowing up your own asses, but here's reality! You're all overgrown corpses that drink the blood of the living to survive. You're not gods! God doesn't want you. If he did, then crosses, Bibles, and holy water wouldn't burn the shit out of you. You can't go out in daytime or the sun will burn you to ash. A stake through the heart will still immobilize you.

"What you are is a bunch of namby-pamby, pretending-drinking-blood-is-like-drinking-ambrosia motherfuckers that haven't come to grips with what sad sacks of shit we all really are! You think being a vampire makes you Tom Cruise in that damned movie, but it fucking doesn't, okay? It just makes you poor dead bastards that can't even eat Doritos anymore without puking blood on the kitchen floor. Now, if fucking with me makes you feel all high and mighty, then bring it, but you better get ready to reap the whirlwind, 'cause I guarantee that the first Lost Boys wannabe that lays a corporeal finger on me or mine will not survive the experience. Now, I want some answers. Either you have them or you don't, but if you do have them, you better give 'em up or I'll fuck you up. Am I crystal fucking clear?"

They clapped. They actually fucking clapped.

"Okay," I began. Closing my eyes, I massaged my temples for a moment. "What the hell are you doing now?"

"I won again," Winter said cheerfully. "You are every bit as amusing as I thought you might be. What was it you wanted to know?"

Rachel looked as confused as I did for once, and since Little Miss Know-It-All was taken by surprise, I felt a lot better about it, too. "Before I tell you," I said, "are there any other bets?"

"That would be telling." Winter chuckled as the others applauded. "I win again."

I laughed in spite of myself. God, I hate vampires.

13

TABITHA:

BUMPING INTO PEOPLE

Pulling up in front of the Artiste Unknown reminded me why dating Phillip was so much fun. This would not be like the fiasco at the Iversonian. Vampires and their human escorts wrapped around the club, a band of wannabes waiting to be told no. Two vampires dressed in suits were stationed at the door at the head of an area cordoned off by red velvet ropes on brass stands, extending all the way to the sidewalk as if one were approaching an award show in Hollywood rather than a nightclub in Void City. Dennis rode next to me, and I leaned close to him, not because I craved his touch or because I wanted him, but to soak up the heat.

"Thank you for coming with me, Dennis," I said as the limo came to a stop. Even though I was pouting, I was glad Phillip had decided to stay in. I could have flaunted my ability to seem alive with Phillip along to protect me, but the more I got to know him, the more he changed from mysterious and cool to short, fat, annoying, and just plain sick.

"Of course, Lady Tabitha. Lord Phillip explained the difficulties making an appearance with Mister Talbot might cause."

"Winter's policy says human escort, not just living escort," I said with a shrug. Dennis's eyes dipped involuntarily to my cleavage, brightening my mood. My dress was tight, black, and sleeveless, cut to make the most of my assets. The diamond necklace Phillip had given me hung around my neck, throwing little dots of rainbow color on the walls. My shoes had an extra inch on the heel that I'd only been able to wear comfortably since becoming a vampire.

One of the vamps, a smooth, casually attractive man in a sharp gray suit, left his station to open my door. This was the side of dating Phillip that I enjoyed, the glitz, the glam, the not having to dance in some stupid art deco strip club.

Dennis climbed out after me and took my arm just quickly enough to steady me when I sensed Eric. When Eric and I were together, I didn't get a strong sense off of him, maybe because he sired me. Now, though, he felt powerful and strong, way more powerful than I am . . . which shouldn't have been possible since we're both Vlads. His "announcement" made Phillip seem small and not just in a wow-that-thing-is-tiny way.

Eric stepped out the front door and I froze. God, he looked gorgeous! I'd never seen him with his natural hair color before. He had always dyed it black, but tonight it was blond. Maybe he hadn't noticed yet. When had he come back? Why hadn't I felt it? The tux he wore looked like it had been tailor-made for him. I'd forgotten about those true-blue eyes, but they pierced me briefly before taking in Dennis. Eric weighed Dennis with that gaze and found him wanting. I looked away, embarrassed.

Eric glanced over his shoulder and said, "C'mon" to someone behind him. A woman stepped out of the doorway wearing a smirk I'd seen a thousand times. *The witch!*

"It's customary for a man to open the door for a lady," she bantered in my dead sister's voice.

"I was distracted." He nodded in my direction and the woman who wore Rachel's body looked over at me with the exact same glint of mischievousness in her eyes Rachel'd had when I caught her making out with Martin Coleberg in the bleachers at my senior prom. Martin had been my date.

"Hi, slut," she teased. "Where you been?"

Those were the same words she'd used at prom. It was impossible. This woman could not be my little sister. I'd discounted it ever since I'd seen her for the first time at the Demon Heart, but suddenly, seeing her standing with Eric, the innate possessiveness she showed, I knew. It was her, but it couldn't be.

Rachel was dead. She'd died of cancer, wasting away to nothing, and she had not been brave. She'd been angry, hateful, and mad at the world. At her funeral I'd watched

Dad, Uncle Tommy, her boyfriend Paul, and three of Mom's friends from church carry her coffin to the family plot, watched as the funeral-home people lowered her into the ground and buried her next to Grandma.

"I don't want a scene." Eric sounded bored with the exchange before it had even really started. "You broke up with me, remember?"

"But—"

"Did he really tell you that you were a moist warm tightness?" Rachel taunted. "I'm his thrall now. He doesn't need your cold dead cunt anymore."

"His what?" I was at a loss, still not wanting to believe that it was really my sister Rachel, still wanting, needing, it to be a trick, an illusion. "He what?"

"Leave her alone," Eric interrupted. "She's still your sister."

Words that I wanted to say, questions that I needed to ask, ran through my mind and bounced off, overcome by the same thought over and over again. *It can't be her. It can't be her. It can't be her.* "You're dead!" is all that I could get out.

Rachel deliberately misunderstood me. "You'd kill your own sister?"

I looked to Eric, pleading with him to understand what I wanted to say. Our eyes met and his mind touched mine. *Shut the fuck up, before you make an even bigger ass out of yourself, Tabitha.* My mouth snapped shut. Eric was my sire, the one vampire whose mental compulsion I could not resist. "Go inside with Toy Boy there . . . What's your name?" he asked my escort without breaking eye contact with me.

"It's Dennis, Lord Eric, but I'm not—"

"If I want to hear more from you, I'll ask you another question. Now shut your yapper."

Only Eric would say "yapper."

"Yes, milord."

"Tabitha here may not be my girlfriend anymore, but she's my spawn, get . . ."

"Offspring," Dennis inserted.

"Thanks. Offspring, and she hasn't tried to kill me yet, so if anything bad happens to her, I'll find you and . . . you're not somebody's thrall, are you?"

"Not at this point in the competition, milord."

"Good. Then I'll find you and kill you. You savvy?"

"I savvy, milord."

Savvy? Eric had been watching too many pirate movies.

"Now. Tabitha, go inside with Dennis and have your fun." His hand touched my cheek. "I've got to go get Marilyn's soul back from some demon. Swing by on Christmas Eve if you want. I'll have something for you." He pulled away. "I'm not mad at you. Now, go."

He's more powerful than me and he's my sire. I had to obey, would always have to obey, even though I didn't want to go into the club anymore. I wanted to ask how my sister was alive. How she'd come back. Had she really gone to Hell like she'd claimed before, when I'd thought her nothing more than a doppelganger? I wanted to know if I could help with the Marilyn thing. She'd never approved of me, but she'd stuck up for me once when no one had any reason to. I felt like I owed her one, but thanks to Eric's compulsion, I had to walk into the club, let Dennis escort me to a booth, and sit down before my mouth would open.

Eric announced himself three more times before I felt him drive away—the final time, all of the other vampires in the Artiste Unknown winced.

"What was that?" Dennis asked.

"Eric was roaring. He does that when he gets angry or overprotective. It's a man thing. You wouldn't understand." A waiter brought us blood wine without being asked, muttered something about compliments of the management, and fluttered away. "When we first started dating, I went to see my parents for a few days without telling him, and he went ballistic. God, how he shouted at me."

"Sounds a little overprotective," Dennis observed.

I wasn't sure anymore. Maybe Eric had just understood the dangers of the world better than I had. Maybe he still did.

"Was that really your sister?"

I wanted to answer him, but Eric's compulsion kept me from talking about it. I was supposed to be having the fun that I'd come to the Artiste Unknown for, before I'd known Eric was here with Rachel. Hell, I had more fun than this at the Iversonian with Talbot, fight notwithstanding. But after a dance and a few drinks, the compulsion eased up enough for me to ask Dennis a question.

"How is it possible?" I asked.

Dennis stared without comprehension. "Lady Tabitha?"

"Rachel was dead, really dead. She died over a year ago. How could she have come back?"

"Maybe it isn't her." A server had brought him a sampler platter of hors d'oeuvres. He'd been eating them slowly for the last ten minutes. He seemed to be really tasting each bite, and it was pissing me off. "It could be a shape-shifter."

"If you take another bite of that food in front of me," I snapped, "I swear to God I'm going to break your fucking neck!" Dennis dropped his fork the way one might drop a poisonous snake. He accidentally tossed it too far to the side and it clattered to the floor.

"I'm sorry, Lady Tabitha," he stammered. "Most vampires find my talent for eating quite enjoyable."

Most vampires aren't stuck being able to eat food, but not taste it, I thought. That subtle cruelty went along with my ability to seem alive. It emphasized the fact that it wasn't real life, just a very clever approximation.

"Just don't," I said. "I don't like it and she's not a shape-shifter. That's what I thought at first, that it was some kind of spell, but—"

"It could have been a construct, a simulacrum summoned to act like your sister."

"Simulacrum?"

"A fake duplicate of a person," Dennis offered.

"Oh."

Maybe. Which would be worse, to have my sister back from the dead and despising me, or to have a weird creature wearing her face?

"No, it was her." Or did I just want her back? Yeah. I did. Even though we hadn't really been friends since puberty . . .

I wanted her back. She was . . . is my sister and family is family. "Could it be her?"

"Well, it depends on how badly she wanted to be alive, milady, and how concerned she was about what happened to her soul. Did she know that she was dying?"

I couldn't think about that part too hard. My emotions were too raw. The food I could eat but not taste was still on the table. The music was too loud. Too many hearts were beating all around me. And my mind was filled with lurid images of Eric and Rachel together in bed and on other flat surfaces. "Yes."

The funniest thing of all was that I wasn't mad at Eric for being with her. I knew Rachel. She had gone after him. He wouldn't have pursued her. Eric isn't a go out and get 'em guy. He lets women come to him. What did she want from him? If she could sell her soul, then she might be capable of anything. This was the same Rachel that had dated three different guys at the same time in high school so that she could make one pay for her lunch every day. What would she be capable of now that she'd wrapped herself around Eric's . . . um . . .

"Dennis?" I wished I'd shown Eric that I could seem alive or that instead of walking out on him at Orchard Lake when he went to kill the werewolves, I'd just waited in the car for him. Didn't Eric realize that the only reason I became a vampire in the first place was so that we could always be together?

"Yes?" Dennis looked at me across the table, bored but polite, and I wondered what he thought when he looked at me. Did he see a beautiful woman or did he just think of me as a vampire? Worse than that, maybe he viewed me as little more than an errand—a chore. Was that how Eric looked at me now?

"Why do you want to be a vampire?" I asked.

"I'm not certain I understand the question, Lady Tabitha."

"I mean," I began, "I've always thought vampires were cool. You get to live forever and you get the powers, but now that I have them . . . I don't regret anything, really, there isn't much point to regretting, but it isn't really . . . I didn't expect it to be like it is."

He was nervous. His heart sped up when I asked him the question, but his eyes didn't give anything away. What must it be like to be a human looking at Phillip or Eric, or me, for that matter? Was it like the spider and the fly?

It hadn't been like that with Eric and me. Actually, it felt more like that after I was a vampire than it had before he turned me. He didn't need me now as much as he did then. I was no longer a source of food and warmth. Life with me had lost its vicarious thrill. Not for long. As a Living Doll, I could eventually provide him almost everything he wanted.

If I hadn't dumped him, that is. God, was I that weak? Was seeing him again enough to make me ache for him even when it was so obvious he'd moved on? He wasn't supposed to be able to move on! He was the one who was supposed to be craving me, not the other way around.

"Power," Dennis answered finally. "Influence. Money. All of those things. Immortality is nothing to sneeze at, but you can still die. You need the money, the wealth, the political influence, and all of the powers just to survive the immortality side of it."

"But, I mean, I don't know. Isn't it . . ."

"A high price to pay?" he asked.

"I guess that's where I was going with that."

He put his hand in mine and the warmth teased my fangs out of their hiding places in my gums. It stung when they cut through the tender tissue, but I didn't wince. Dennis smiled. "Look. I'm a power guy. I've always wanted it, needed it, really, and I've always been willing to do whatever it took to get it. Right now that means that I go through Lord Phillip's glorified hazing, which is fine with me. I do my time as an intern and then I get adopted by the most influential vampire in the city, someone who just happens to be one of the oldest vampires in the world."

I didn't believe him; I guess he could tell by the look on my face.

"Come on, Lady Tabitha. Surely you realize Lord Phillip is more than he appears." When he said Phillip's name he sounded worshipful. "The man is a god. He's still rising, sure, but he is definitely ascendant. He's totally incapable of deficit spending. He owns the police, the fire department, you name it, and the beauty of it is that most of them don't even realize that they've been bought."

Could the same be said of me? Did Dennis think of me as someone Phillip had purchased? Sure, he did, and worse, I thought so, too.

"Are there rules against biting your date in a club like this?" I asked.

"No, milady, but Lord Phillip—"

"Lord Phillip said that I could do what I wanted with you."

His heart sped up again and a bead of sweat rolled down his cheek. "That's true, Lady Tabitha. If something I said offended you . . ."

"Just crawl under the table and lick my shoes," I ordered. "I'll tell you if I want you to go higher." Dennis crawled under the table with a resigned look on his face. How gross. Eric would have told me to kiss his ass. Talbot would have told me off. "Go higher," I commanded absentmindedly. He did. I missed Eric.

✦ 14 ✦

ERIC:

THE DEMON

We rode to the Pollux in silence and that suited me fine. I'd had enough social interaction for one evening. It had left me tired and frustrated. The last thing I'd needed was to see Tabitha with her dinner or toy or whatever he was. Rachel scooted closer to me in the backseat of the limo, but I ignored her. Talking to Winter and then seeing Tabitha made me want to hit something, break it, smash it on the concrete, and grind it with my foot.

After I turned Tabitha, I'd treated her like crap, because it's what I always do. It's a little like when Humphrey Bogart asked Lauren Bacall to marry him. He told her that she had to decide whether she wanted to be a famous actress or be his wife.

He told her that if she wanted to be a famous actress, he'd do everything in his power to help her, but if she wanted to be his wife, then she had to be willing to be with him, travel with him, even if it meant that she had to turn down good roles because they conflicted with his shooting schedule.

Seeing Tabitha again made me realize how much I wished I'd thought to make her the same kind of offer. You can be with me or you can be a vampire. What would she have said if I'd laid it all out for her like that? Instead, I gave her what she wanted and then pushed her away so that we couldn't hurt each other.

Because that's what happens with vampires. Sometimes it happens to the woman first and other times it's me, but one or both parties always wind up betrayed and angry when a young attractive living human comes between them. The warmth is too much of an aphrodisiac and it isn't like Tabitha could have both warmth and immortality. It doesn't work that way.

I shook my head vigorously, trying to wipe thoughts of her and her human boy toy out of my head, but visions of her, the boy toy, and a faceless male vampire clung to my brain like a porno decoupage. In the absence of her vampire fuck buddy's true appearance, Winter filled in.

Winter. Thinking of him brought me back to the task at hand—finding the asshole demon holding Marilyn's soul. Winter obviously knew more than he'd given me, but even Rachel had been surprised when he'd offered me not just a name, but contact information. "His name is J'iliol'lth. He maintains an office at the Lovett Building. Demons adore the Lovett Building." Winter had handed me a business card with a number printed on it.

"Dig a little deeper, darling," he'd told me. "Do your research and by all means, keep your eyes on the demon. They're tricky and you should know that he isn't working alone. Most important, you should know that I had nothing to do with it."

"Nothing to do with what?" I'd asked.

"Exactly." He had laughed in a way that reminded me of golden raindrops falling on my brain. I think I was supposed to be charmed. Instead, I'd been irritated, especially when he'd added, "Now, run along."

Outside the window, Void City blurred past. Seeing me with Rachel had shaken Tabitha. I almost had Tiko turn around, but I didn't know what else I could do. The reasons we couldn't be together were still valid and she'd obviously moved on. If I went back it would just start another scene. Maybe she really was happy with those High Society leeches. It occurred to me that I wanted her to be happy. I rolled that thought around in my brain for a while.

It didn't take as long as I thought it would for us to get back to the Pollux, or maybe I was just too distracted. Rachel's pulse beat too fast. *Nervous or guilty?* I asked myself. She smelled excited, ready for sex, but I didn't trust the scent. Around her that odor was as constant as the cinnamon smell and the little thoughts that weren't quite mine. I didn't want to think about that, either. I hoped she'd just pull whatever scam she was trying to pull without me figuring it out. Ignorance is still bliss.

I felt the Pollux before I saw it, like recognizing an old girlfriend's footsteps in the mall. Certain things felt more real to me since Magbidion and Rachel had brought me back. I felt Fang, too. He wanted to be driven, to hunt.

When we got there, Rachel followed me upstairs to the office. Greta was sitting in my desk chair, typing on the computer. She hadn't been able to keep all of the furniture in the rest of the building when the state had come for my assets, but my office was intact.

"I just reclaimed your e-mail address. I meant to have that done already, but . . ." She shrugged. Vampires get a weird waxy smell when they haven't fed and they're hungry. It takes a few days for me to get to that point, but Greta gets hungry fast. She smelled already. Never turn a human with an eating disorder. You'd think the change would cure the disorder, because you can't gain weight, but it doesn't. It's either famine or feast with that girl and stress makes it worse.

"You haven't fed," I said.

"I wanted to make sure you got back okay."

"You didn't smell like this when the resurrection thing happened, so you can't have gone more than a day. Go eat."

She hugged me. "I missed you, Dad."

"I missed you, too," I said as I returned the hug. "Go eat, but only one person and don't kill them; you can't afford to pay Magbidion right now." I glanced around the room and listened hard. "Where is Mags anyway?"

"He said he wanted to get a buddy of his to pull the info on whoever filed to have Eric Jones declared dead. I told him it was okay if he kept parking in the deck."

She bounded out of my office.

"Take Fang," I called after her. "Run over a cat or something. It'll cheer you up."

"Okay. Cool," she called back.

I picked up the phone, an old-style handset, while Rachel flipped through the CDs stacked on my desk.

"Iron Maiden. Metallica. The Rolling Stones. Are any of these still around?" she asked.

"They are." I pulled the business card Winter had given me out of my wallet and started to dial. Rachel hung up the phone with her finger and leaned over my desk so that the silver rings in her nipples peeked out at me from beneath her dress. "What?" I asked.

"This demon you're supposed to meet, J'iliol'lth? Winter said he was a power broker, but that's not the part you need to worry about. He's a demon, a scary one, I've . . . um . . . heard people talk about him at the Irons Club before."

I was tired of hearing about the damn Irons Club. I moved her hand away from the phone and dialed the number for J'iliol'lth. Rachel wrinkled her nose at me and stuck out her tongue. She slid past me, grinding against my crotch on her way to the computer.

"Samhain Industries." The voice on the phone was reminiscent of Ebon Winter, curiously androgynous with a dash of civilized disdain. Samhain Industries? Cute, a funny demon.

"How can you help me?" I asked flatly.

"Excuse me, sir?"

"You're supposed to ask how you can help me or how you can direct my call."

"Excuse me, sir?"

"Just let me talk to the demon."

"Excuse me, sir?"

Rachel pulled up a picture of a beautiful girl with lines of piercings laced like a corset up her sides.

"Do you like it?" Rachel asked. "I was thinking about getting one."

I held my hand over the receiver. "It looks painful."

"Sir?" called the voice on the phone.

"Sorry. Look. I need to speak to Jill E. Olth or however you say his name. He may be expecting my call."

"Vampire, human, demon, or other, sir?"

"Vampire."

"Is this issue soul related, ascension based, or other?"

"Soul related." Jesus, she sounded like she was reading from a script.

"Yours or another person's, sir?"

"My aunt Trudy's! Just get the demon on the fucking phone!"

"I don't have to listen to that kind of language, sir."

"You know what? You're in the Lovett Building, right? Why don't I just come down there? I'm sure you've got all kinds of cool wards, but my car recently became undead and I think I ought to see if I can just drive it into the lobby. Then, I think I'll turn into a giant uber vamp and start tearing the place apart. Ooh, or better yet, I'll turn into a revenant and start sucking people's souls out. That would be fun." I don't know why I said that. Turning into a revenant had to be near the absolute bottom of my to-do list. Then again . . . I wondered. *Could I change back and forth if I wanted?*

"Hold on a sec."

I turned into a revenant. Done on purpose, it felt as if I were expanding and contracting at the same time, my body bursting and then drawing into the center of my spectral self as my skin went even colder than usual. The receiver fell through my hand to the top of the desk and I changed back quickly, afraid that I might get stuck again. That answered my question, though. I could do it if I needed to do it.

The voice laughed at me.

"You must be the being for whom we're holding Marilyn Robinson's soul." It wasn't the same voice, but it sounded like the same person. He now spoke with a polished, educated accent, almost British.

"Yeah, that's me."

"Then it's my great regret to inform you that you've been speaking to a very talented, but quite mischievous answering imp." The voice changed again. Now it was nasal and annoying. "Call the master's human secretary at the following number." I scribbled the number down, hung up, and closed my eyes for a minute.

Rachel was afraid again. Her body pressed into the left side of the chair.

"Problem?" I asked.

"How are you doing that?" she blurted.

"Doing what?"

She looked stricken, biting her lip rather than answering. I held up my hand in front of my face. Purple light illuminated my palm. With a little effort, I changed the light from purple to red.

"I'm not that mad. I don't know what makes my eyes glow purple."

"But how . . . never mind."

How can I still lose my temper with you doing whatever it is you're doing to try to control me? I thought to myself. Good question.

"Get the piercing," I told her. "Why don't you go get it now, tonight? I want to see it tomorrow."

"It's awfully late."

"I'm sure you can find someone to do it."

"Okay." She sounded cheerful again, but her heart was pounding. She was pissed, but hiding it. If she was a good little thrall, she'd have to go, wouldn't she? But was she a good little thrall? Based on what Marilyn told me, I could order her to do it and she'd have to obey. Something rose up in the hindmost part of my brain . . . something quirky about frogs, or maybe tattoos, then it was gone.

I dialed the number. Someone answered before it even rang. "Yes?"

Rachel moved past me without the grinding.

"I want to set up a meeting with the demon."

"Lord Eric." The speaker sounded like she'd never been happier to speak with anyone in her entire life. "I'm so pleased you called. Lord J'iliol'lth has been waiting to talk to you."

"How soon can he meet me?" And how'd he know my name? I guess he'd had four months in which to do some digging.

"Perhaps this evening around eight?" the voice offered.

The clock on the wall said it was after midnight, almost one o'clock. "No, I want to meet him now . . . this morning, before dawn."

"I'm sorry." Her tone told me everything I needed to know; she thought my request was absurd. "Lord J'iliol'lth has already retired for the evening. We can't all be nocturnal. If you didn't suffer from your condition, of course, then he would be happy to meet with you at his offices in town as early as seven o'clock this morning."

I could hear Rachel changing out of her prom dress in my bedroom down the hall. "Fucking Emperor," she mumbled under her breath. I heard her fingers touch her lips as if she were covering her mouth, having spoken out loud by mistake.

"Where are his offices again?"

"Suite 603 in the Lovett Building."

I scrawled that on my notepad. Everyone in Void City knew the Lovett Building. It was the skyscraper downtown with the big golden dome on top. Rumors said that all kinds of satanic rituals took place there late at night. Obviously, the rumors were wrong. The satanic rituals took place early in the morning. It just goes to show that you can't trust rumors. "What's the window situation?"

"Sir?"

Rachel stopped in the doorway wearing jeans and a T-shirt. She smiled at me and I motioned for her to wait. "The window situation," I said more slowly. "What is it like? Does he have windows in his office?"

"Yes, of course."

"Do they have blinds?"

"Well, yes, sir, of course they do. They were designed by Lady Gh'st'na'kzi herself. They are quite stunning."

"Tell him I'll see him at seven, then, and he'd better be prompt. My assistant Rachel will be with me as well. Is that an issue?" Rachel raised an eyebrow at that, but I held a finger to my lips to keep her from asking any questions.

"No, sir. But if you don't mind my asking . . . won't you be asleep, sir?"

I laughed. "Just confirm the appointment, lady, and make sure he has the damn blinds closed."

She did so and I hung up. It felt good to have a plan. Smiling at Rachel, I put my arms around her and kissed her full on the lips. She returned the kiss passionately before disengaging herself. "Do you mind telling me what I just volunteered for?"

"In five hours I need you to run an errand for me."

"I don't take much sleep, Eric, but even I have to get three or four hours. Otherwise, I'm useless," she complained. "That's the only reason I was worried about getting the piercing tonight."

Sure, that was the reason. I would have believed her if the office didn't smell like a whorehouse running a special on cinnamon-scented panties.

"I think you've told me that before." I walked around behind her, pushed her facedown onto the desk, and helped her off with her jeans.

Later, as she slept, I spooned with her, feeling the faint

reverberation of her beating heart against my skin, wallowing in her warmth, in the unconscious rise and fall of her chest as I held her. My fingers traced the intersection of flesh and metal at her nipples. Asleep, there was no cinnamon, no little not-my-thoughts.

"You're making it awfully hard to ignore whatever it is you're doing," I whispered. She gave me a sleeper's sigh in response.

What had been up with the piercing anyway? Why offer to get it if she didn't want it? If I'd been turned on by the piercing, would she have gotten it? I had no doubt that she would have done so gladly, but why? Because it would have enhanced the sex, the attraction? That felt like the right answer. Everything was tied up in that. I disentangled myself and she stirred, reaching back unconsciously not for my hand, but lower. I climbed out of bed. A frown, brief but present, touched her lips before she settled back into her normal circadian rhythm.

I took my clothes with me and changed into them out in the hall, not sure where I was going until I was already in the parking deck near Magbidion's RV. I pounded on the door and was answered by a bleary-eyed Mags wearing nothing but a poorly tied bathrobe.

"What is it?" He clearly wasn't awake yet. "Where's the car?"

"Don't worry about the car," I told him, "and cover up."

He drew the robe tighter, the light of intelligence behind his eyes growing brighter as he fought his way free of the sleep toxins I no longer possessed. "You look intense this morning."

"Yeah. Sorry to wake you. Look, I need to ask you a question."

"As long as it's nothing too complicated." He leaned against the door, not inviting me in. Not that I needed an invitation. Vampires don't.

"What do you know about vampire thralls and sex magic?"

"So you've been thinking it, too?" He smiled.

"Thinking what?"

"That your girlfriend Rachel is a tantric witch."

"Yeah," I lied. "I was thinking something like that."

"Come on in." He stepped clear of the door. "If you don't mind, can you tell me exactly what you did, step by step, when you made Rachel your thrall?"

I told him everything that I remembered, and then he told me how it was supposed to work and I had him write it all down. We ran some tests. Could I sense my vampiric offspring if I concentrated? Yes. Could they tell I was sensing them? Yes. Even if I focused on hiding from them? Yep. Could I sense Rachel? No, or not always. Could I see through her eyes? No.

"It's called the dark tantra," Magbidion said finally. He clarified before I even asked. "Normal tantric magic is about healing energy, divine union. It's healthy and positive, but what Rachel is doing sounds like what succubi use: sex of power, by power, and for power."

"That doesn't sound too bad."

Magbidion balked at that. "She's a human using magic that's meant for demons, very specific demons that suck your soul out through your privates or use sex to control you."

"Is she sucking my soul out?"

"No, or I don't think so. Hold on." Magbidion made a circle with the thumb and forefinger on his right hand, then looked through it at me. "It doesn't look like it, but I can see why she might want to."

"Why is it that? Do I have a really cool soul or something?"

"Um, well, okay, yes, sort of, but I don't think you understand how rare this is. It's like the core of your being exists in a state of grace. There's something else weaving through it, too, a curse or an enchantment. You—"

"Now you're sounding like Talbot." I covered Magbidion's hands with mine, blocking his view. "So I have the York peppermint pattie aura. Whoopee. I don't want to hear anything else unless it has to do with Rachel."

"The short version?" Magbidion said.

I nodded.

"My best guess is that she's trying to control you, but at your power level, I don't know how effective she'd be . . . maybe she could influence your emotions, put thoughts in your head, but very little direct control. She could even leech power off of you, but I don't think it's something you'd miss. I'm talking little dribs and drabs."

"Tell me how it works."

By the time Greta pulled back in with Fang, I felt like I might be ahead of the game.

15

ERIC:

EVERYBODY LOATHES JILL

Rachel approached the Lovett Building a little before seven o'clock. She was dressed in a smart-looking red business suit that showed just a little too much cleavage and way too much leg to be appropriate for the workplace (well, this particular workplace, anyway). The lenses of her sunglasses were also tinted red and the heels of her shoes were three or four inches high.

As many times as Rachel had carried mouse-me in her purse, she should have known to bring a bigger one. I knew she had at least one purse big enough—she'd carried both me and Greta in it after one of our big werewolf fights. While I wrestled her lipsticks, her wallet, her keys, a compact, a pencil, two pens, some Kleenex, a tiny sewing kit, some Band-Aids, a Tylenol bottle, several individually pack-aged wet wipes, and God only knows what else, I seriously considered throwing out everything that wasn't me. Better not to leave a trail, I decided.

Rachel walked up to the front door and pulled it open. Once inside, her footsteps started to echo. It sounded like the room was big and the floor was tile or marble. It was hard for me to tell. I smelled coffee, donuts, and other breakfast-y kinds of things in the distance. Food court, probably. If I strained, I could make out the sounds of people talking in another large space. There was even a fountain or a waterfall, I couldn't tell which, but I could hear the water.

"Can I help you, ma'am?"

The voice was male and the speaker was taller than Ra-chel. I guessed it was a security guard from the tone he'd used. He sounded at once willing to help, friendly, and mildly suspicious. Pulling off all three at once as well as he did made me suspect he'd been doing this awhile.

"I'm here to see J'iliol'lth," Rachel told him. "I'm an assis-tant to Lord Eric. He's expected."

"Is he here now?"

Someone was watching me. I couldn't see them, but as he asked that question, I felt a presence sweeping through the lobby. It was a low but constant pressure on my senses. It brushed the edges of my mind, began to push inward. Nobody had mentioned anything about any psychic check-points or mental searches, so I felt no need to cooperate. Using the same technique I used when controlling lesser vamps, I pushed back hard.

The pressure went away, but the presence was still there, flitting about like a gnat, too small to squash but still an annoyance. It was probably that obnoxious imp I'd talked to on the phone.

"Yes, he is with me now. Could you please show us to J'iliol'Ith's office or a waiting area with no sunlight?"

"Let me call on up and see."

The guard and Rachel both started walking and I was once again assaulted by the contents of her purse. A zipper tab came out of nowhere and tried to go where no one had gone before. I was halfway out of her purse before I saw daylight and slid back down, landing on top of a compact. I made a mental note to put some kind of thrall compulsion on Rachel and make her only buy really big purses from now on.

By the time we got to J'iliol'Ith's office I had discovered a small leather pouch inside a little zippered pocket sewn into the lining of her purse. It smelled like spices and old bones. I couldn't tell exactly what was in it, but I wanted Magbidion to take a look at it. If his suspicions about Rachel were correct, it might be important.

"Greetings, ma'am. Please tell your master he may now appear. The shades are secured. I assure you, the room is quite safe for him."

Rachel turned around and opened the bag carefully. I would have liked to do something impressive—turn into a revenant and try to make it look like I was coming out of her mouth, but for all I knew, I might have eaten her soul by accident. Instead, I leapt off of the top of her purse and landed in my human shape. Both of us turned to face J'iliol'Ith.

I was still wearing jeans, tennis shoes, my *Welcome to the Void* T-shirt, and a black leather belt, but I'd added a pair of sunglasses and a leather jacket. The sunglasses would keep our pal "Jill" from noticing the strangeness of my eyes if they went purple again. They were still doing the black-with-purple business off and on unpredictably. I was sure I'd have been able to control my eyes if Rachel would just stop screwing around with me. With her tantric magic or whatever it was.

J'iliol'lth was an ugly son of a bitch. He wasn't red, like I'd expected, and he didn't have little horns or a pitchfork. I always expect demons to look like that, although I've never met one that did. I guess it's some kind of nonhuman prejudice. The confounding thing was how familiar he looked. I couldn't place it.

J'iliol'lth had black skin with small brackish-brown sores that oozed dark green pus. Patches of gray moss covered his skin in an odd approximation of hair and his beady little eyes were transparent except for cloudy brown irises and stark white pupils. Even so, he wore an expensive suit. I guess he thought it would make him look more businesslike. In his case, it didn't help much.

He also had a smell. It wasn't so bad, a touch of mint and a little wintergreen, but he was colder than room temperature and his heart, if he had one, was silent. I try not to trust anyone who doesn't have a heartbeat.

The office itself looked normal except for the window treatments. The blinds were ghastly metal creations covered with a surreal paint job. They were bolted to the wall, drawn

closed with a set of chains, and locked tight with a small
padlock. Someone was trying to make sure I felt comfortable
and safe. Just like a demon . . .

"Ah, Mr. Jones," he began. "How good of you to come,
and at such an inconvenient time, too."

"Yeah, whatever," I said, dropping down into one of the
two available chairs opposite his desk. Rachel gracefully
lowered herself into the other. I stared at one of the mo-
tivational posters he had hanging on the wall. It was about
leadership and had a picture of a lion. This demon was really
going all out to make sure he fit in. "Nice poster," I said sar-
castically.

"Thank you, Mr. Jones."

"Eric," I corrected. "No one calls me mister anything. Of
course, some people call me asshole or bastard or mother-
fucker, but I usually kill them. You should probably just stick
with Eric."

Rachel gave me a wide-eyed look of warning, but I ignored it. It's what I tend to do with all the good advice I'm
given. J'iliol'lth smiled politely. I couldn't tell if he was getting angry yet or not, but my guess was that I could get him
there.

J'iliol'lth opened his mouth to speak, but I interrupted him.
"So Jill . . . Can I call you Jill? I want Marilyn's soul back and I
want it now. I know you want something for it and I'm happy
to work with you there, but do you think you could cut all
the posturing bullshit and just spell out what you want?"

The moss on the demon's head whitened and the mint
smell grew stronger. As he clasped his hands together, they

made a slightly disgusting squishy sound. "Eric, please, let's both do our best to be cordial here. I've held on to Miss Robinson's spirit in good faith and I'm quite certain—"

I took off my sunglasses and "Jill" stopped speaking. I caught Rachel staring at my eyes, too. I guess she hadn't seen enough of the purple glow, yet . . . Either that or with her influencing my emotions toward calm, it scared her that I could still get this angry. According to Magbidion, Rachel was using no small amount of mojo to keep me from being able to black out, to force me to stay in control. The only things Mags and I couldn't figure out was why.

"Jill" looked questioningly at Rachel as if he expected her to do something. Maybe it was because we'd told him she was my assistant, but it seemed like more than that. I made a mental note of it and decided to press my advantage, if it truly was an advantage. I popped my fangs.

"Look, Jill, I've been having some anger management issues lately. What's four-month-old news for some folks is two days ago to me, so let's not mince words, okay? Because even though I haven't eaten today, you don't look very appetizing and I don't want to be picking demon out of my teeth. What the fuck do you want in exchange for Marilyn?"

J'iliol'lth regained his composure instantaneously and smiled a toothy white smile. "So you have no problem with the associated costs?"

"I'm not signing anything. I'm not shaking hands and you can't have my soul, what there is of it, in exchange."

He managed to look crestfallen at that and I wondered how much of it was an act and how much was real.

"I'm afraid it is not just a matter of the cost. I'm certain that she's special to you, but Miss Robinson was likely already hell bound. She had long since ceased believing in any sort of deity—"

"Good, then I should be able to buy her off you cheap."

"Normally, yes, in any other circumstance, by all means I would have given her to you as a sign of good faith, but the purpose for which she was intended has rather exacting parameters. To retain her soul as a courtesy to you, I was forced to use the next most compatible soul in my possession, a soul which was a bit more"—he paused midsentence and his eyes flashed—"costly."

Shit. I crossed my arms. "How costly?"

"You see, the ritual in question required a willing sacrifice, a soul who was aware that he or she was sacrificing themselves for another." He was positively giddy just describing it. "Self-sacrifice, especially the sacrifice of one's soul for another, even if the sacrificial soul is already hell bound, is quite rare. The next most comparable soul I had was a Catholic priest from oh . . . ten years or so ago, give or take . . . He gave his soul to save one of his parishioners who'd bargained theirs away to me. I'd been saving him for a special occasion."

"Fu-uck me," I cursed. "What the hell kind of ritual was it?"

"Normally I charge for this sort of information, but for you . . . consider it a gift to the vampire who killed my brother, J'hon'byg'butte."

El Segundo was about to bite me on the ass. I killed a lot of demons in El Segundo. Okay, to be fair, Talbot killed most of them, but he ostensibly worked for me and in the demon world, as in the vampire world, that made it all my fault.

"Eric." The demon stood up and walked around his desk as he spoke. "My dear, dear, Eric, I'm afraid your friend, Mr. Malcolm . . . Roger . . . came to me for an enhancement."

"God, you must be loving this," I said. "What sort of enhancement?"

J'iliol'lth leaned against his desk and looked down at me. I stared up at him and tried to make my eyes glow red. They didn't. Instead, two little color-changing dots hit the demon in the pupils and he turned away quickly. He didn't have eyelids, so he couldn't blink. Interesting.

"Sorry," I said casually, putting my sunglasses back on. "Anger management. I'm sure I mentioned it. What kind of enhancement?"

"He wanted me to make him a Vlad, like you," he said, walking back behind his desk. The mint smell went sour, replaced by a rotten citrus odor. Was that what demon fear smelled like? I could sense that Rachel was afraid, too. Both of them probably knew more about my anger management issues than I did, but I wondered if they knew that I wasn't quite as ignorant as they thought I was. I leaned back in my chair.

"How?"

"He was going to capture you and bring you to me. We were going to use your essence to 'promote' him to Vlad-hood." He opened his desk drawer. "You undid his plot and defeated him when you had your lupine friends devour him; you should be very happy."

"Yeah, I'm thrilled all right. What does all of this have to do with Marilyn?"

"We worked out a contingency, an intercession." Just as the final word passed his lips, the chair I was sitting in sprouted scaly orange hands that grabbed my arms. Rachel's scream told me hers had done the same. Smoothly, in one motion, J'iliol'lth drew a gun I recognized from his desk drawer: *El Alma Perdida.*

"You've gotta be kidding me." Bang. The shot rang out. A familiar burning sensation spread through my chest. Silver licks of flame poured out of the wound. J'iliol'lth dropped the gun with a howl, his hand sizzling where he'd touched the butt of the gun.

"Shoulda staked me," I roared. *El Alma Perdida* was made to hunt werewolves. The bullets are magic. If a werewolf gets shot with one of them, the bullet steals its soul. A bullet from *El Alma Perdida* also shape-locks any supernatural creature it hits. As long as the bullet stays inside them, they can't change shape. A vampire can't pop his claws, can't even pop his fangs. Unfortunately for J'iliol'lth, my fangs were already out.

J'iliol'lth said a word I didn't understand and the chains on the curtain vanished, dropping the padlock to the floor where it transformed into a tiny demon with little red horns and a pitchfork—the imp.

Another orange-scaled hand rose up from between my legs. This one had a sharpened wooden stake in its grasp. It stabbed at my heart, J'iliol'lth opened the curtains, and I kicked off of the floor with both feet as hard as I could. My demon chair flipped up and over, but its grip didn't loosen at all. The stake plunged into my chest and bounced off my sternum. I sank my teeth into the only knuckle I could reach and the creature yowled.

"How's it going, son?" John Paul Courtney's voice drawled inside my brain. My mouth was full, but there were plenty of things I felt like saying. "Still fornicatin' and consortin' with demons, I see," the ghost of the gun added. "You could have at least woke up when the demon sent some of his boys to collect the gun. But no, you was jest starin' off inta space."

The back of my head hit the floor and the chair rocked over on its side. Both the demon and I let out "oofs." Sunlight poured into the room and my ankles caught fire between my socks and the jeans. The demon chair's orange scales ignited as the silver flame from my bullet wound touched them. The hand holding the stake at my chest recoiled. I tucked my burning shins up under the demon chair and it howled.

"Fire sucks, don't it?" I snarled. The demon chair let go. "Flame on!"

You've got to question the wisdom of using a nonfireproof demon to restrain a vampire and then opening the curtains. I think J'iliol'lth had intended for me to be staked by the time I caught fire. No such luck. I may be stupid, but I'm not slow. Flame engulfed my entire body as I stood. I raised both hands over my head, clasped them together, and brought them down on the floor. Go, go, vampire strength.

"Someone stop him!" J'iliol'lth shouted.

Fire, pain . . . it causes some vamps to freeze up, roll around on the ground. I catch fire on a semiregular basis. It comes with having a poor time sense and a bad memory. I'm not immune to fire; I'm bored with it.

"But he's on fire!"

"Why didn't you stake him?"

"He caught fire!"

Blinded by flames, I couldn't see anything, but vampire hearing is very good. Somewhere nearby a toilet flushed. Water moved through the pipes. Water was just what I needed.

The floor gave out on my third strike, dropping me to the next level. I ran toward the sound of the moving water, smacked into a wall and punched my way through it, still following the sound. People screamed, cried, and ran, but I ignored them in my pursuit of the water. Another toilet flushed and I burst through the wall and into the ladies' room.

Grabbing the bowl of the nearest sink with both hands, I tore it free of the wall. Water sprayed out of the shorn pipe, dousing the flames. Behind me, a woman backed away, screaming. I needed blood quickly, more than she could spare.

But there was one thing I needed more. I grabbed her throat. "If you can help me get the bullet out of my chest, I won't eat you." She swallowed hard and nodded.

Her waterlogged purse lay on the floor nearby. When I released her, she snatched it up, rummaging through it purposefully. "I . . . I think I have a pair of tweezers."

For me, the healing hurts worse than the burn itself. Vampire nerves stop registering pain after the initial injury.

My entire body had been charred. With a sound like two vinyl records melted together and being pulled apart, my skin began to regenerate.

Three dog-headed demons burst into the women's restroom. One of them had an ax decorated with fancy filigree. The second wielded a frost-covered sword. Demon number three just came with claws and a mouth full of sharp pointy teeth. I threw a sink at them to buy time. Everything slowed to a crawl, rivulets of water drifted through the air in lazy streams, and I realized my vampire speed had kicked in. I've never been good at controlling it, but I was glad it had decided to show up.

The contents of the woman's purse fell slowly toward the tile. I spotted the pair of tweezers flipping through the air. I snatched them up with a grin. Some demons have the speed thing, too. These guys didn't. By the time they made it halfway across the room, I had the bullet out.

Can you say uber vamp? I knew you could.

◆ 16 ◆

ERIC:

RENEGOTIATIONS

I walked back into Jill's office in uber vamp mode, holding the frost-covered sword in my right hand and the heads of his three dog demons in my left. Seven other demons stood around the room, not counting the two funky-looking chair demons. Sunlight began its slow sizzle on the ebony skin of my uber vamp form. It stung. I had no idea how long it would take for me to catch fire this way, but it undoubtedly made me seem like a badass.

Jill closed the shades. "If everyone would excuse us, please?"

Rachel ran over to me when the chair let her go, skirting the big hole I'd put in the floor. She moved to embrace me, but I pushed her away. Hunger can do strange things to a vampire, alter perceptions. I couldn't see Rachel's skin anymore, just the veins and the blood coursing through them. My color differentiation faded as well, rendering the world in shades of monochromatic red. I knew if I stayed hungry long enough the perception changes could become permanent.

"I'm too hungry," I explained. "If I feed on you, you'll die."

"I'll order in," J'iliol'lth said casually. He pushed a button on his desk. "Julia?"

"Yes, Master?" the speaker on his desk crackled.

"Could you send a couple of girls up here, please?"

"Right away, Master."

I broke my rule about accepting blood from strangers. Both of the women looked like supermodels. They came willingly, apparently resigned to death. I didn't want to know why a demon like J'iliol'lth kept beauties like this on tap or what he held over their heads. Did he own their souls? How can you tell if someone's soul is in hock anyway? I knew Magbidion's was owed out but it's never been something that I could smell.

After I'd eaten, colors bled back into my vision, but everything still had a tinge of red to it. If I'd drained the girls dry, it might have cleared up immediately, but since there were two of them, I didn't have to kill either of them. The girls were unconscious and I had my unwanted color tint, but I hoped we'd all be fine in a night or two. I also felt more mellow, artificially so, sleepy, too. "Okay, what was in the blood?"

"Nothing that will harm you, I give you my word." His tone made that sound important, believable. "Just a little enchantment to calm you so that we might speak on more friendly terms."

"I don't like being drugged."

"You have my apologies, Eric," J'iliol'lth said with debatable sincerity. "Shall we move to an interior room?"

"As long as it isn't a trap." You have to expect deceit from demons. I'd forgotten, and now I was drugged. I decided I was going to get one hell of a discount on Marilyn, or Jill was going to be on the tooth and claw end of my anger stick. "And I'll want my gun back," I added, pointing the sword tip at him.

He handed *El Alma Perdida* to me and I changed back to my human form, tucking it into the back of my jeans. I pulled the sixth bullet out of the mouth of one of the dead dog demons (where I'd stowed it) and dropped it into my pocket.

"It isn't a trap, Eric. You have my word. I can put it in writing if you like."

"So long as it's nothing that I have to sign and I'm not agreeing to anything." *Bullshit. With demons, it's always a trap. Why else would he have given me my gun back if not to lure me into a false sense of security?*

"Touché," he laughed. "Touché."

Twenty minutes later we were in a plush conference room with leather chairs and a plasma screen television someone had obligingly set to the sports channel. Rachel and I sat down, but not before I sliced into each seat with the frost sword just to be sure.

"What the hell were we talking about?" I asked.

"Miss Robinson's soul?"

"Something else, too." I racked my brain and, very unusually for me, I remembered. "The contingency you worked up with Roger."

J'iliol'lth's mossy covering turned blue. "A vampire can be restored to unlife after destruction once and only once through the willing sacrifice of a human soul." I threw the long sword through the television. It didn't explode like they do in the movies.

"I had his happy ass eaten by a pack of werewolves and you brought him back?" J'iliol'lth stared at the smoke drifting up from the television. "Don't look at the damn TV. Look at me!"

"You're a very expensive guest."

"Get over it, peckerwood. You tried to kill me."

"And you killed my brother."

"Your brother fucked with me while I was on vacation and he got dead. He had a dumb fucking name anyway. Johnny something. Besides, don't you guys come in clutches or something, like flies? You must have a few hundred brothers."

"Eric," Rachel cautioned.

"Give me Marilyn's soul back, right now, for free, or I'm going to tear this building down around your ears."

"That's not going to happen. If you damaged the building enough that I had to leave, I'd drag Miss Robinson's soul with me. You can banish me, but my death would be far from permanent. You are not the only being that is insufferably hard to exterminate. You don't have your mouser here, Eric. You have no leverage."

"Like I give a shit. People try to kill me, unmake me, and screw up my junk all the time . . . or haven't you been paying attention?"

"I assure you, Mr. Jones. No, let us dispense with such foolish pretenses. We both know your true name, don't we, Mr. Courtney? I know that you are the great-great-grandson of John Paul Courtney, just as surely as I know that you do, as you so quaintly put it, give a shit. You care for humans. Your family always has.

"True, yours is a sporadic and capricious morality, but you have one. You're a Courtney. You care. You mean well. You make an effort. That is where we differ." He put his hands on the table between us and leaned toward me. "Go to war with me and you will find that I understand you all too well, where to hurt you, how to make you cry at night. I'm a demon, Mr. Courtney, it's what I do, but," he made a placating wave, "I have no wish to fight with you. As you say, I have many siblings."

He attempted to snap his fingers, succeeding on the third try, and a glowing purple cube rose up out of the table. "She's in there." I reached for the box, but my hand passed through it.

"What gives?"

"I will send her with you, as a good faith gesture, an advance payment for the services you will render. I want you to obtain the Stone of Aeternum for me in exchange."

I jerked the sword out of the TV. "I don't work for demons, Jill. Come on, Rachel. We're leaving." Rachel peeled herself out of her chair and we started for the door. "Thanks for your time, Jill. It's been real fun. I'll be back with my mouser. If it doesn't work out, you make sure to tell Marilyn that I tried."

"Are you sure you aren't even the teensiest bit interested in being able to eat food again? Bask in the sun? Enjoy the sound of your own eternal heartbeat?"

I stopped. "What the hell are you talking about?"

"It's quite simple, actually," the demon said. "Without a contingency, I'm uncertain that your friend Roger is willing to work with me. He's used his last get out of jail free card and, for him, there are no other routes back to this world if he is destroyed again. Any being may come back once through supernatural means . . . being turned into a vampire, zombie, et cetera." His eyes cut to Rachel for less than an eyeblink and I nearly missed it. "To come back one other time requires the expenditure of a soul, a willing sacrifice."

"And a thrall qualifies?" I asked. "I thought you said she was forced."

"Normally true as well, but it's all a matter of intent." He licked his lips. "Roger didn't force her to sign the contract using his power as her master, he forced her to sign it by threatening you."

Fang's engine roared in my head and the red tinge to my vision went purple.

"He's dead," I said in a whisper. "He just doesn't know it yet." I turned to leave.

"But, Mr. Courtney," Jill said. "You haven't heard my offer."

"What are you talking about, the stuff you promised

Roger, the wanting to be a Vlad thing? I am a Vlad . . . you have no leverage," I mocked. "I'm going to go kill Roger and then I'm coming back here for Marilyn."

"A Vlad? Please, Mr. Courtney. I thought we were being honest with each other. We both know that you are not a Vlad, just as we know I can't make you a more powerful vampire than you already are. But I can make you something better, or at least, better as far as you are likely to be concerned."

He stood up. He was taller than me, but from his posture, the extra height didn't reassure him any. "I'm not interested," I said. You can't trust demons.

"Are you sure?" he asked. "I could make you an immortal, Eric, a true immortal. Living, breathing, yet undying, untouched by death, disease, or the ravages of time. You wouldn't be able to change shape anymore, true, but—"

Before he could finish his sentence, Jill was up in the air with my hand around his throat. "You'd better not be lying to me, Jill. You won't like what I'll do to you if you're blowing smoke up my ass."

"I assure you, it is possible. It will only work for you. You are different. For one like you, it will work."

I set him down.

Different. Sometimes I felt different. It wasn't just the eyes. I'd never been a typical vampire. It sounded . . . possible. I struggled to remember something that ghost-Marilyn had said, but it was gone. "Tell me more."

"Indulge me for a moment first," J'iliol'lth said. "What do you remember about how you died?"

"*Memento mori,*" I murmured.

"What?" J'iliol'lth's eyes widened and he drew back. "I assure you I would never ask—"

"Remember your death," I translated. "That's what you want, right? Me to remember it? Well, I do and pretty well, since I just relived it a little while ago. Why do you want to know?" I asked suspiciously. J'iliol'lth walked back over to his seat and lifted a small glass paperweight with a scorpion carapace preserved inside. He held it up so that I could see it.

"Why do I have this?" he asked. "Curiosity. I like to look at it. I like scorpions. We have things like them where I'm from, but they are intelligent and quite dangerous. Here, they are not so dangerous, but look exactly the same. I like having it. It amuses me."

"So?"

"So I want to know because I don't know and because it would amuse me to know."

Sounded very Hannibal Lecter to me. Rachel and I both sat back down. "I was driving Roger's car," I told him. "The brakes went out and it went down into a quarry. When I woke up, I was a vampire."

"So you never knew your sire?" J'iliol'lth asked eagerly.

"No, I always assumed it happened in the hospital or in the ambulance or something."

He put down the paperweight and crossed the room to stand in front of the TV. "And the next evening you rose as a vampire."

I decided not to tell him anything about what had happened when Magbidion brought me back, about the curse, or about Fang. "No, I was dead for a while. Marilyn always said I rose after the funeral."

Rachel looked like a bee had stung her on the butt, but she didn't say anything. Her breathing picked up, her pulse started to race, and I could smell the sweat. There was something very important about all of this and I had no clue what it was, but I wondered if it had something to do with the curse.

"So you rose on the seventh night and—"

"Day," I corrected. "It was in the afternoon. Two weeks later."

J'iliol'lth turned to face me; his eyes glowed a burnt copper color. "By any chance, were you embalmed?"

"I think so," I said. "Why? Is that important?"

J'iliol'lth smiled again. He was always smiling, frowning, and then smiling again. Maybe it was a hobby. "Embalming a person who is going to rise as a vampire stops the process. They die without rising, but you did not die, and in that gray area, between life and unlife, there is much power to be had. You are a Child of Wrath . . . a person who rose as a vampire second and as something else first."

"Horse puckey." John Paul Courtney chuckled in my head. "He's pulling the wool over your eyes, boy. Child of Wrath. Huh, sounds like one of those so-called music groups you listen to."

I should have listened to old J. P., but something about what Jill was saying sounded familiar . . . I'd heard it before from someone I trusted. Hadn't Marilyn said something like that?

I smelled mint again as J'iliol'lth continued, "I think it is very likely that you were murdered, Eric."

"Yeah, I know that," I told him. "It was Roger. He was screwing Marilyn behind my back."

"Even better," Jill crowed. "I think you rose as a revenant, but some unique circumstance caused you to rise as a vampire as well. Sometimes it's a family curse, or it could have been something as simple as a vampire having fed on you in the ER. It's very rare and it makes you exceedingly unique. I've only heard of it happening once or twice every few millennia."

Family curse. I knew Jill made a living by capitalizing on things that sounded right, but it was the little bits that weren't exactly true, the lies of omission, that he used to turn a profit. The thought of being alive again, living in the sunshine forever, made it hard to walk away, even though I still had the feeling a smart man would have done just that.

"What else does it do?" I asked. "I can see why I would want it, but what do you want with this thing . . . the um . . ."

"The Stone of Aeternum," Rachel inserted.

"Right," I continued, "this Stone of Aeternum, what do you want with it?"

J'iliol'lth pretended to consider it, but he already had an answer planned out. The way he spoke, the subtle motions he made as he crossed the room or answered a question, it all had the feeling of something rehearsed, a script or a speech. He knew what I was going to ask him. I had fallen right into the role he wanted me to play. It wasn't a feeling I enjoyed.

"It will only work once per century, but it can grant certain desires of the supernatural. It is within the Stone of Aeternum's capabilities to, under the correct circumstances, elevate a Master vampire into a Vlad or change a normal lycanthrope into an Alpha. Its transmutative properties are substantial," he said with unfeigned avarice. "If one were to possess such an item, the profit would be equally substantial. One could even raise the dead, and not just the newly dead like a Zaomancer can, but the long dead—if the stars were right and the ritual done properly. But, silly me, we're getting ahead of ourselves."

He walked away from the television to put a placating hand on my shoulder and I gave him a look that made him wince. Removing the offending hand, he turned away from me. "Get me the Stone of Aeternum and not only can you have Marilyn Robinson's soul as previously discussed, but I will make you immortal as I have described. You will have enhanced senses, strength, and speed, you will no longer need to sleep, eat, or drink, but will be fully capable of enjoying all three. You can even have children, if you want. You get to retain your soul and you will not gain any hidden weaknesses."

"And all I have to do is bring you the . . . ah . . ."

"Stone of Aeternum," Rachel provided again.

"Right . . ." I stared at Rachel and then continued. "I don't suppose somebody can just buy one?"

"Of course not," J'iliol'lth answered. "I would have purchased it myself long ago, if such were possible. No, the Stone is something that can only be freely given or taken by force. The current owner might be persuaded to surrender it, but most likely you would be required to take it.

"Even so," he continued with a dismissive wave of his

hands, "the current owner is a vampire and we all know you have no qualms about killing them."

"Why haven't you tried to take it by force yourself?"

"Because, Mr. Courtney, I must still function in this city. If I sent a force of demons to assault the Stone's owner, it would be bad for business, but if I send you . . . Well, let's say it would be very simple to claim that I had nothing to do with that. You are an unknown quantity."

I stood up. "Who is he and where do I find him?"

"His name is Phillipus and he lives at the Highland Towers."

I nodded. Highland Towers. According to Talbot, that place was a real bitch to get into. I'd have to be creative. But, on the other hand, that was where Tabitha was shacking up with some guy, so I wanted to go there anyway, find out who he was, knock him around.

"One last thing," I said before Rachel and I left. "Someone had my human ID declared legally dead, you wouldn't know anything about that, would you?"

The demon shook his head. "Not specifically, but Roger did strike me as the kind of person who would have taken steps to avenge his own death."

I started toward the door and Jill held out his hand. "The sword, please?"

"Sorry," I said. "This bad boy's mine. Magic sword. Magic gun. I'm starting a collection. All I need now is a spear and magic helmet."

"Fine," the demon purred. "Take the cube, too." He picked it up, a casual arrogance in his demeanor as he tossed it to me. I caught it in my off hand. It felt solid enough this time, cold to the touch. "My secretary will even give you a canvas bag in which to transport . . . everything. But remember this, Eric. I want to work with you. I've gone out of my way to be as reasonable as possible. Working with me on this is a win-win scenario."

I looked at Rachel's tiny purse and bit back my usual obnoxious retort. "I'll take you up on that bag."

I was so on the ball that I even remembered the sun was out. We headed for home, with me squashed in Rachel's purse jouncing alongside a canvas bag (with the Lovett Building's name and logo on the side) containing a glowing purple cube and a magic six-shooter. The sword wouldn't fit, so she had to carry it separately.

Rachel had a hard time hailing a cab while holding the longsword, but not too hard a time. After all, this is Void City.

✦ 17 ✦

TABITHA:
WINTERRIFIC

A single claw sensuously pricked the skin above my sternum before wending its way down my torso, across my belly, and lower. Talbot's touch was masterful, scratching the skin without breaking it. It was a wake-up call that I'd enjoyed yesterday. I glared at the clock. Exactly one hour after sundown. What had everyone else been doing in that lost hour of wakefulness? What . . . no, who had Eric been doing in that hour? It irked me.

"Get off." I slapped Talbot's hand away.

He rolled off the edge of the bed. "What?"

"I'm not in the mood," I said, heading for the shower.

Hi, slut. Where you been? Rachel's voiced echoed in my head. I twisted the shower knob to hot before staring at myself in the mirror. No reflection. I willed myself to appear in the glass.

He doesn't need your cold dead cunt anymore.

"Damn it!" I couldn't concentrate enough to make my image appear.

Talbot poked his head into the bathroom. "You okay?"

"Tell me that I'm beautiful."

"Why?"

"Just tell me!"

He smirked. "No."

My fangs and claws extended of their own accord. Talbot's heartbeat echoed in my ears, but the heat of him was dulled by the shower. "Tell me!" Red light from my eyes cast odd shadows on the wall.

"No," he repeated.

I slammed the door in his face and stepped into the shower. Too cold. My speed kicked in instinctively as I tried to avoid the water. Each frigid droplet stung as it bounced off my skin, then froze, suspended in midair as the universe slowed down. Sometimes the speed is a blessing and sometimes, like when you're standing on a wet surface, it's a curse. My feet went out from under me, sending me backward into the glass shower door.

Shards of broken glass fell toward me in slow motion like little knives. The superspeed was gone before I hit the ground. Talbot threw open the door, scooped me up, and carried me back into the bedroom, leaving a thin trail of blood across the nice white carpet.

"Ow."

"I've never heard of a clumsy vampire," Talbot said. He pulled a large hunk of glass out of my left breast, leaving a jagged stretching tear that was quickly replaced by the tender tingle of regenerating flesh.

"Shut up," I hissed. "It isn't funny."

Did he really call you a moist warm tightness?

Someone knocked on the door and both of us nearly jumped out of our skins. Talbot sprouted claws and fangs as he sniffed the air. A vision of a man leapt into my brain and announced that he was young, not as young as me, but certainly every bit as powerful. He wore clothes that had been made just for him, in shades of blue and white. I normally don't like blonds, but Eric and now this guy were the exceptions that proved the rule.

"I never knock twice," he whispered through the image of himself, "and I'm the last person you want to offend."

"It's Ebon Winter," I whispered to Talbot.

Talbot dumped clean towels over the glass on the bathroom floor and sat me down on the toilet. "Get cleaned up."

"Just a minute," I called. "I'm in the shower."

Five minutes later I opened the door wearing a T-shirt and shorts. I could have prettied up, but I didn't feel like it. Besides, he was on my territory and I didn't want to be ogled tonight, not by him. Winter looked me up and down in an odd, appraising sort of way before gliding past me into the room.

Over one shoulder he was carrying a black garment bag, which he hung from a hook on the back of the door. Every movement seemed calculated. He was the most exquisite being I had ever laid eyes on, but instead of attraction I felt an instant . . . wariness of him. He rotated on his heel in a complete circle, frowned, and glared at me.

"It is important that you understand something." He held up both arms and gestured to the room around him. "This entire room is offensive and I absolutely will not redecorate for you. I loathe it all."

Crooking a finger, he pointed it at Talbot. "Especially that mouser." He shuddered theatrically. "Hideous things, like rats, they really ought to be exterminated."

"Hey!" I began.

The vampire put a finger to my lips. "Do not raise your voice to me, Elizabeth Tabitha Sims," he said pleasantly. "I am enjoyed best as an ally, not an enemy, and I abhor shouting. No harm will come to your . . . servant as long as he behaves himself. As long in the tooth as he is, I'm confident he knows his place."

Talbot leaned idly against one wall, out of the way, and tried to look nonthreatening. It was precisely the same way he acted in Phillip's presence. After our adventure at the Iversonian, I knew why.

My tongue stumbled around my mouth for a second before finally managing to ask, "You're Ebon Winter, from the Artiste Unknown, right?"

"I am Ebon Winter, but you must call me Winter. It's the *nom de guerre* I prefer and I will not answer otherwise. As your sire might say: call me Winter, just Winter. You know, like Madonna but with a dick."

Winter winked when he said the last sentence as if he'd made a clever little jest. I came close to laughing despite myself except that the joke wasn't really very funny, he only wanted it to be funny. What scared me was that that had almost been enough.

"I hope I didn't interrupt you in the middle of anything kinky," he added mischievously. "You must have very broad horizons to take that into your bed." He indicated Talbot when he said "that."

"What? Who the—who the hell do you think you are?" I asked, flabbergasted. How dare he judge me? He'd insulted my decor, my lover, and me personally. I had half a mind to throw him out.

"Although," he caressed my cheek, "you are lovely. Your breasts are a bit large for me, but lovely all the same."

"Who the hell do you think you are?" I repeated.

"I've already introduced myself, darling. Please attempt to focus and I truly will not remind you again about the volume. Let's recap." He placed a hand on my shoulder and steered me toward the front door. "I came in through there. This apartment is hideous. My sire Phillip—I believe you know him biblically—asked me to redecorate your entryway, but you offend me, so I won't be doing so. I'll send Andre around when I can spare him. Keep your pet away from me and put on the clothes I brought you."

"What clothes?" I asked, still bewildered.

"The clothes in the garment bag, dear," he said casually. "Do you honestly believe that I flit willy-nilly about town with luggage in hand?"

"No, I suppose not, but—," I began.

He unzipped the bag and began sorting clothes. He set

out a black leather skirt, stiletto heels, hose, and a green silk blouse, leaving the most incredible blue dress I'd ever seen still in the bag. It was sexy yet casual, and I could tell just by looking at it that it had been made with me in mind. He zipped the bag back up and gestured to the rest.

"While you were doing whatever it is you were doing, others were making things happen, love. Now do be a dear and put on some nice clothes. You're making my eyes bleed. They'll look quite fetching—the clothes I mean—and you must promise to take proper care of them. The dress is dry-clean only, and I'll be quite angry if I hear you've been leaving it lying about on the floor. Mommie Dearest has nothing on me and don't you dare put it on a wire hanger, either. I call the dress Isabella. She's an original Winter. Do you like her?"

"I . . . yes," I stammered. "It's . . . I've never seen a dress as beautiful as that—" His eyes narrowed and I quickly changed what I was going to say, ". . . as Isabella."

Still suspicious, I started climbing into the clothes he had laid out. They smelled normal and I hoped Talbot would warn me if I were in danger. They fit perfectly and were utterly flattering. I doubted even Eric would complain. What surprised me the most was the blouse; made for a vampire who didn't have to wear a bra, it gripped and lifted just enough but hung normally.

"Always make sure your tailor has an enchanter on the payroll, darling. They're worth it," Winter told me.

I was a true believer.

Winter walked around me in a circle and shook his head. "No, not *vert* . . . The blouse is the wrong color." He clucked his tongue and lightly touched my shoulder. "Crimson, *s'il vous plais.*" Colors blended across the blouse from my breasts outward and it changed from green to a deep bright crimson. "Darker, *s'il vous plais* . . . a little more blue, not purple and not red . . ." Responding to his commands, the fabric darkened by fractions until at last he said, *"Merci."*

Circling me once more, he made much more appreciative noises. "Excellent, that's much better. Yes, definitely your color. Of course, that may change as your eyes continue to fade, but contacts can take care of that. Do you have a good picture of your eyes?"

I shook my head.

"I thought not." Winter pulled a photo from his pocket and handed it to me. In the picture, Rachel and I were kids, standing in front of the sign for a roller coaster. Behind Rachel, the *You Must Be This Tall* sign indicated that at last Rachel was indeed "this tall."

"They were a very nice shade . . . a green . . . three on my color scale. I have a fey who makes my contacts; he could probably work you in."

"Where did you get this?"

He laughed. I thought that laugh could take hold of a person and screw them to the wall. If it had been a melody, it would have stuck in my head forever.

"I can get anything."

"Thank you," I said belatedly. "Does the dress change color, too?"

Winter tossed back his head, revealing perfect whiter-than-white teeth as he chortled once more. "It had better, or Melvin will certainly have some explaining to do, now, won't he?"

"Melvin?"

"My enchanter," he crooned. "Have you ever noticed most magically inclined mortals in this city have an M-name? He's a dear little thrall. Most people think that since he does Guild work, he's his own man, but in truth, he's all mine."

None of this made any sense. Why would Ebon Winter come out of nowhere and shower me with gifts? The necklace Phillip had given me, the suite of rooms, I understood, but the clothes from Winter were totally unexpected.

"Why didn't I sense you before you were at the door?" I asked.

"Perhaps your exertions left you too preoccupied to detect me? That's one of the reasons I've given up sex. It's vulgar and distracting. Ah, and a word of advice: never use your vampiric speed on a slick surface. Well, perhaps not never, but certainly not until your skills improve."

I know I didn't blink, but he vanished anyway, reappearing beside me, his hands adjusting the way the skirt clung to my body. "Incidentally, given our kind's enhanced senses, you really must remember to use an air freshener. Change your sheets twice a day. Your mouser's scent is all over the room."

"You're avoiding the question," I observed. "Why didn't I sense you earlier?"

Tilting his head to the left, Winter frowned. "Perhaps I am, at that. Though I think it's more a case of you not liking my answer than a refusal on my part to give one. Haven't you ever tried to change the subject when you didn't want to give a straight answer?" He sported a very savage grin. "I'm sorry, did you say you didn't want the clothes?"

"No!" I said more emphatically than I intended. "I mean . . . I would like to keep them. Please. And thank you."

He clapped his hands and kissed me on the cheek. "My, my. You are quite the whore, aren't you?" Winter's eyes sparkled as he spoke. My hand passed through his cheek when I tried to slap him; an intense cold spun up my arm. He could turn to mist! The only vampire I'd met that could do it was Phillip and even he couldn't hold his shape at the same time.

"I'm not a fighter, Tabitha. I never ever fight unless it's utterly unavoidable and then I never fight fair. Fair fights are for professional pugilists and the mentally deficient." He touched my cheek, peering directly into my eyes, his lips a hairsbreadth from a kiss. "I kill. I murder. Remember that and don't be so prudish; everyone is a whore to a certain degree. We all have our price. Mine was immortality."

Words fired effortlessly from his lips, tickling my ears. In an episode of *Charmed*, they'd had a creature called a siren that lured people to their deaths with her song. Winter's voice was like that . . . mesmerizing. "Even so, I have no intent of enjoying your . . . ah . . . girlish charms. I simply wish a favor of you."

"Which is?" I asked carefully.

"I like to make wagers," he said with a smile. "It's a hobby. I like to predict outcomes and I am always right, unless someone . . . How shall I put it so that you will understand?" The charming look vanished and anger, terrible and beautiful, showed on his chiseled face. "Unless someone fucks things up!" His eyes flashed blue as he spoke, his finger lancing in my direction as if he intended to spear me with it. "You, dearest, have fucked things up for me. Quite unknowingly, you have caused me to lose a bet." And the anger was gone and he was calm again as if he had never displayed it at all.

An incredulous look crossed my face and I eyed Talbot for guidance. "And for this you give me gifts?"

"No," he said. There was something in his eyes then, not anger, but the potential for its return. "No, the gifts are either an apology or an inducement. Do me a small favor." He pointed at Talbot. "Send that thing back to its master."

"He's not mine. I can't just tell him to go somewhere and expect him to—"

"Oh, he would go if you told him that his precious Eric had returned."

"What?" Talbot demanded. "I was just over there three days ago. I thought they weren't having any luck."

"Didn't I tell you?" I asked, attempting to sound casual about it.

Talbot shook his head, then kissed my forehead on his way to the door. "I kept you safe until he came back, but now I gotta go."

"What? You're running back to him? Just like that? What about us?"

Talbot frowned. "There is no us. You keep expecting me to act human, but I'm not. I never have been. I'm sorry if that hurts your feelings." He scooted carefully past Winter.

Why is it that the only man who was honest and up front with me is the vampire I broke up with?

"What kind of bet did you have?" I asked Winter.

Winter smirked and turned to mist, letting his outer edges blur into wispy trails of vapor. "That would be telling. Besides, I ought not bend *all* the rules. I already had to use a loophole to set things straight. Do you know how hard it is to convince a priest to give up his soul? Fortunately, I'm an exceptional parishioner." He laughed. "The words just bounce right off of your forehead, don't they?" He tapped his own lightly. "My apologies. Enjoy the clothes."

His entire body dissipated as if he had been nothing more than a cloud or a puff of smoke. I picked up the phone and dialed the front desk.

"How may I be of assistance?" Dennis answered.

"I need someone to clean my room and fix my shower."

"I'll send someone immediately," he said cheerfully. "And, milady?"

"What?"

"Lord Phillip asked me to send you to his room when you awoke. He has another visitor that he'd like—"

I didn't let him finish the rest of the sentence. "You tell Lord Phillip that he's a fat, balding, demented little freak and he can go fuck himself." I slammed the phone down hard enough to spider-web the glass-topped end table. That was stupid, but stupid felt really, really good.

◆ 18 ◆

ERIC:

AT THE MOVIES

Inside the projection booth at the Pollux, modern equipment sat side by side with the original reel-to-reel technology. My *Casablanca* print was gone and so was *Singin' in the Rain*. *The Court Jester* was still there, but only because someone had spilled Coke on the film when they'd inventoried the canisters. Greta pointed at the newfangled digital projector, rambling on about picture quality and noise ratio.

"Does it work like a DVD player?" I interrupted.

"Basically."

"Then it's great. Thanks."

"I got you a selection." Greta opened a filing cabinet. The films inside were all classics, and I saw my two favorites tucked right in front.

"I don't deserve you," I said.

"Yes, you do, Dad." Greta hugged me. "You saved me. I know you don't like to talk about it, but do you remember . . ." She sagged as her words trailed off. My face must have given me away. I felt like a turd for not wanting to listen. She has highs and lows. At her low ebbs, she always wants to talk about our time together when she was human, how much I remember. The truth is, I don't always remember or sometimes I get it mixed up. When we talk, she can tell. It's a bad situation.

"Do you miss Kyle?" She bit her lip when she asked, turned her face away.

"Kyle who?" I wonder if there is a vampire equivalent of Alzheimer's.

"Nothing. Nothing. It's okay, Dad. You just watch your movies." Greta kissed me on the forehead and hugged me again, so tightly that I worried she wasn't going to let go. She pressed a remote into my hand. "I . . . couldn't afford to have the sensor put in professionally, so just point it at the center of the mezzanine and try to ignore the wire."

"Uh-huh."

She opened the door to leave.

"Greta," I called after her. "I really do appreciate all that you've done to hang on to the Pollux for me. I'll pay you back."

Her smile could've made a dead man happy . . . which I guess it did, if you think about it. "It's not an issue, Dad. Just glad to help. I'm gonna go eat again." The door fell closed with a heavy thud after her exit, which left me alone with

Marilyn. I loaded *Casablanca* into the glorified DVD player and scooped up the glowing purple cube with Marilyn's soul inside.

Thirty-two minutes into my second run through *Casablanca*, as Ingrid Bergman's face loomed above me on the big screen, I knew what to do. If you haven't seen the movie, I highly recommend it. I always watch it when I have to make big decisions . . . if I have the time. I know people say that *Citizen Kane* is the greatest movie ever made, but they're wrong. I don't care about an old rich guy who dies longing for more innocent times. I live that every night.

Marilyn's cube sat on my left in the front row. *El Alma Perdida* rested in the seat on my right. Pointing the remote control over my head at the mezzanine, I stopped the movie. Blue light from the projection default screen cast the theater in an eerie underwater light.

"I have some options, Marilyn," I told the cube. Who knew if she could hear me, but I hoped that she could. "I can try to bring you back to life. I don't know if you'd be mortal or immortal or undead, but there has got to be a way. If I do that, though, you still won't be in love with me. You'll pity me like you always have, even when you were screwing Roger behind my back and planning to go through with our marriage anyway."

I climbed out of my seat. The Pollux no longer smelled like stale popcorn. Whoever had put it up for auction must have had a cleaning crew come in and do a real once-over on the place. Magbidion's failed rituals on the stage had left an odor of blood, a scent that mixed badly with that of the disinfectant. I considered burning some microwave popcorn to see if it would help, but it was all avoidance.

I knew what I needed to do and didn't like it. My fingers drummed on the wooden stage of their own accord. I couldn't look at the cube. If I could release Marilyn before giving Jill his magic rock, then it meant one of two things: either I was stronger than demon magic (doubtful) or it meant that Jill wanted that rock so badly he would be willing to do or say anything to get his claws on it.

I hit play. Ilsa begged Sam to play "As Time Goes By" and he did. I stopped the movie again. I was wasting time. Roger was out there plotting against me and I was watching old movies. All I had to do, if I believed Jill, was to run on over to the Highland Towers and pick up a magic rock that could make me immortal . . . and I was watching old movies.

"Even if you did come back to life," I told the glowing cube, "even if you did still love me, it wouldn't be the same. Knowing what I know. I mean, I might forget in time. It's . . ."

I seized the cube. It felt warm in my hand. I held it long enough for the warmth to work its way through my fingers and seep into my palm, pretending that I was holding Marilyn's hand, not just her soul in a box.

"I had to save you from the demon, Marilyn." I turned the cube over and over in my hand, the purple light mixing with the blue from the projector and coming out red, which should have been impossible, but you can never tell with magic. "But you're still dead. I talked to Magbidion and he says that's really you in there. He can't tell where you're going to go when I let you out, though. I'll avenge you or whatever, but I can't just keep you here in this cube. I suppose what I'm saying is: I hope you don't burn in Hell, but if you do—it's on you.

"You make your decisions in life, in my case, unlife, and you hope you do the right thing. We never had Paris, but we'll always have . . ." *What? The backseat of a Mustang? Roger? A stolen moment on the sidewalk as cold dead ghosts?* "Aw, fuck it." Marilyn's cube shattered in my hand with less pressure than it takes to crush a soda can.

She hovered before me, bathed in conflicting colors, purple, blue, red, orange. Where the colors touched they disobeyed the color wheel. The blood magic all over the stage didn't mysteriously bring her back to life. She didn't smile at me and float up into the sky with a choir of angels. She didn't even get to haunt the Pollux like I'd secretly hoped.

She screamed, wreathed in spectral flame, and I knew which direction she was headed.

I couldn't watch. The walk back up the stairs to the projection booth took under a second. My speed, activated by the stress, put me into fast-forward, prolonging the moment. Ages passed while I waited for the player to eject *Casablanca*. Marilyn dwindled by fractions while I swapped movies. By the time *Singin' in the Rain* had loaded and begun to play, Marilyn was gone. I sat down in the dark and watched the movie. What else could I do?

I'd gotten to Cosmo's "Make 'em laugh" routine when one of the theater doors opened. It was the wrong time for Talbot to saunter in smelling like Tabitha.

"Hi, slut," I quoted Rachel. "Where you been?"

"You're angry," he said neutrally.

"What gave me away? The eyes?" I pointed to the purple glow. "Yeah, they used to go red more often than purple. I think it's the whole sex kitten mind control thing screwing it all up, but I haven't asked Rachel yet."

"Where is Rachel?" he asked.

"Asleep," I answered. "Humans do that."

"So do most vampires." Talbot advanced down the aisle. Smell is a powerful agent of memory. I smelled fluids on him that Tabitha shouldn't have had anymore. "How long has it been since you slept? Even you need one or two hours of dead time—"

"You smell like Tabitha." I picked up *El Alma Perdida*.

"I've been keeping an eye on her." He tried to shrug it off. "Welcome—"

"And a cock in her," I spat.

"—back." He winced. "She's not your girlfriend anymore."

My anger simmered. "What happened with Tabitha?" A whisper would have been loud in comparison, I spoke so softly.

He didn't answer right away, taking time instead to look around and survey the theater, making sure no one else could hear. "I fucked up, man." The words leapt desperately from his lips and I was just as curious as he was to see how I was going to react to them. "She can turn into a cat, like you can, but when she does it, her heart beats, her body temp rises, and she breathes, okay? She moves like a cat, the whole deal. It's obviously a favored form thing or something like it. The first time it happened, she came on to me . . . It may have been postmortem stress—I didn't think it was, but from the way she tore up my car later, it easily could have been."

"Was she a cat or a human when you did it?" I asked.

Letting his eyes close, he let out a long sigh. Booming, thundering heartbeats resounded in his chest and blood rushed through his veins like it needed to go as fast as it could because in a few moments it was going to stop forever.

"Which time?"

"I don't have to kill you, you know," I said acidly.

"Eric, you're sleeping with her sister." His tone made it clear that he was hoping I'd just let it go. "It's not like you were pining after her."

I walked down the aisle toward him. "That's why I'm not mad at *her*. She can do whatever she wants. Did you know Marilyn's soul got stolen by a demon?"

"No, but I'm sure we can get it back."

"Did that. Broke the containment cube about an hour ago. Watched her get sucked into Hell."

"That's harsh, but what happened to her soul is not your fault."

I cocked the gun. "I know. Did you know that Roger came back from the dead again? That a demon brought him back?" I aimed the gun.

"Shit. I suppose you could've used my help with that." He took off his sunglasses. "Look. Just do whatever you're going to do." He braced himself to accept his punishment. I had no idea what I was going to do. It's not like I was ever really going to shoot him.

"What is that thing anyway?" asked the voice of John Paul Courtney. "Is it a werecat, one of them rakshasa things, or what?" Thank God for interruptions.

I could tell that Talbot saw him, too, the ghostly cowboy sitting front and center in the mezzanine, looking down on Talbot and me.

"He's a mouser," I answered.

"Where I come from, that's just another name for a cat," Courtney drawled.

"Shut the hell up!" I snarled up at him. "They didn't even have penicillin when you were alive. What the fuck do you know about anything?"

"I know a lot about werewolves." He took my ranting in stride. Like before, the more angry I became, the greater the sense of bemusement I got from the ghost. He disappeared between sentences, reappearing on my left. His sidelong glance was ruined when his head lolled over again, but he kept talking. "And I know this. You've got a good soul. It's why your eyes are still so blue." He straightened his head and jammed it back into place, taking a hard, close look at Talbot. "Never seen anythin' like it in all my born days. So since I don't know anythin', why don't you be the one to educate me? What is a mouser?"

In any other situation, I wouldn't have blown Talbot's secret, but I was angry. "Okay, you're right. He's a cat."

"You let a glorified house cat steal your sweetheart?" Courtney jeered.

"Okay, Statler. Not one more fucking word out of you or you're going to be one dead muppet."

"What's a muppet?" Courtney asked. I lost it. Vampires can't touch ghosts, but I'm not just a vampire. Color leached from my skin as the blue glow rushed in when my solidity left me. *El Alma Perdida* was still in my hand.

Talbot went wide to the far aisle, steering clear of me. "Eric, what the hell?"

I didn't answer him. Instead, I popped off a shot at John Paul Courtney and wondered if the bullet would hurt a ghost since ghosts could touch it. The bullet sailed through his stomach and embedded in the ceiling.

"It cain't suck up my soul, boy," Courtney assailed with a laugh. "I ain't no werewolf. You can club me with the barrel, though. Any Courtney can touch *El Alma Perdida* no matter what form they're in. It belongs to the family."

I drifted up as he spoke, my desire to reach him, to wipe the smile off his face, enough to send me into the air. A parody of the song from Disney's *Peter Pan* went through my head: *Just think of a terrible thought. Any evil little thought.*

Ghostflight didn't work like winged flight. I sailed right past John Paul and plunged intangibly through the seats, losing my grip on *El Alma Perdida* in the process. It landed in one of the seats through which I'd passed. Leaving the gun where it was, I tried for Courtney again, again sailing right past him, coming up short of phasing through the ceiling. I rotated in the air to face him.

"You don't want to fight me, son," John Paul said. "I've been tied to that gun and this family for a lotta years. I've fought my share of ghosts along the way and—"

He let out an "oof" as I soared into him, arms wide in a tackle.

We plunged through the mezzanine and into the lower seats.

"You cain't kill me again, Eric." Courtney slammed a knee into my stomach and it hurt; the pain was real. I smiled. It had been forty years since being injured hurt properly. Vampiric nerve endings don't register pain beyond the initial injuries. Cut us and it hurts, but the wound doesn't continue to ache unless you tear it open again.

"I cain't rest until the curse has run its course." He punched me twice in the back of the head and I let go with a snarl.

"What curse?" I backed away from him, waiting for my head to clear.

"The one I cain't tell you about."

"Can you guys hold on while I go get some popcorn?" Talbot called.

John Paul Courtney glared at Talbot in shock. "You can really see me? Ain't nobody hardly ever able to see me."

Talbot opened his mouth to reply but didn't bother. I hit JPC square on the jaw, knocking his head back over his shoulders, where it dangled loosely at his back. My knuckles didn't hurt as badly as they should have, but I chalked that one up to John Paul's Nearly Headless Nick syndrome.

"Dude," Talbot exclaimed, partially covering his eyes with his fingers, "that's not right."

Hammering Courtney's stomach with blow after blow, I forced him back through the wall and into the lobby. We stood under the lights in front of the empty concession stand. "Well, what can you tell me, Hopalong, because you popping up to heckle me is getting pretty damn tiresome."

He held up his hand and I waited while he snapped his

neck back into place. "I can tell you this." He stomped down
on my foot, following it up with a right cross that sent me
toward the ticket booth inside the foyer.

"I appeared to you for a few reasons, one of which was
this: When you fought the werewolves of Orchard Lake, you
didn't use *El Alma Perdida* on them—you showed discretion.
They weren't evil. They were God-fearin' folk, skinchangers
or no. Later, when you used my gun against Roger, you fired
it at evil in defense of the righteous."

He held his arm out to his side and *El Alma Perdida* material-
ized in his outstretched hand. "That made your business my
business," he said as he holstered the gun. "You put yourself on
the right path and seeing as how you're Courtney blood, that
means I can help you, but it don't mean that I have to."

"I don't want your help," I snarled.

"Then you don't get my gun."

"Fine." I resumed my material form, eyes glowing red.
Even the warmth of my newly re-formed clothes didn't take
the edge off of my anger. "Keep the damn thing, but don't
bother me, either."

"Son," Courtney tipped back his hat and looked down at
the marble tile, "this doesn't have to be hard. You know the
demon's lying to ya. You know he's up to no good. All I want
you to do is take yer foot outta the dern bear trap. Turn aside
from the demon's offer and—"

"You don't know me very well, J. P." Talbot walked through
the theater doors and we both stared at him.

"You two keep on fighting," Talbot told us, hands up in a
placating gesture. "I'm just watching."

"When I see a bear trap, when I know that everybody around me thinks I don't see it, I don't walk around it." I took three steps forward. "I don't skirt the danger. I ram my foot down harder just to spite them. And you know what, John?"

"What?"

"Nine times out of ten, the bear trap loses."

Courtney smiled. "Courtney through and through. I'll be watching, Eric."

"What?" I asked. "You can just be around?"

"I can manifest near anybody that's fired *El Alma Perdida* and to anyone of Courtney blood. I got you both ways, boy." He faded away in the same burst of light as before.

"Guess I'm stuck with him," I told Talbot.

"Yep," came an echoing reply from the disembodied ghost.

El Alma Perdida appeared on the concession counter and I picked it up. "I thought you were taking this?"

"I can't go too far with it anyway," Courtney admitted in a disconsolate tone.

"I like him," Talbot said, grinning.

It was either take a swing at Talbot, too, shoot him, or cut my losses and get on with my bear trap. Since I didn't want to start in on him again about the Tabitha thing, I stepped toward the front doors, stopping with my hand on the glass.

"I'm supposed to go get something from the Highland Towers for a demon," I said. "I'm going to go over there and beat the shit out of people until I remember what it was." I looked at Talbot. "You coming?"

He didn't answer so I moved on.

"Wait. We're doing what?" Talbot burst out of the door behind me. And just like that, I was forgiven for being an ass. I wonder what Talbot sees in me.

"We're taking your car."

"Why?"

"It'll be light out in a few hours. Mine might catch on fire."

"Wait," Talbot asked again, "it might what?"

I opened the front door of the Pollux and sensed Tabitha. "Jesus, I just can't get a break tonight." The click clack of her heels on the sidewalk was the loudest sound. She crossed the street as I sat down on the bench in front of the Pollux. The pad of cat feet softly disappeared toward the back of the theater. Obviously, Talbot didn't want anything to do with whatever happened next. "Coward," I mumbled.

◆ 19 ◆

TABITHA:

IN HIS ARMS

Snow doesn't last long in Void City. During the day it had mostly melted away, but a small patch was clinging to its icy state in the shadow of the bench, close to the base of the Pollux. Eric didn't seem to notice or care. I'd parked the Lotus Phillip had given me next to the police signs warning that the street was closed. Eric still hadn't redyed his hair. God, my thoughts were jumbled just looking at him. Phillip, Winter, they didn't act like people anymore . . . even Dennis, in his quest to become a vampire, was already so fake. But Eric . . . Eric was still Eric and he always would be. He wasn't perfect, but he was real and without him . . . I could see myself becoming just like the vampires at the Highland Towers, a caricature of me.

"Hi," I said lamely.

"What?" Eric asked.

"Did Talbot—" I stumbled over my words, "make it back okay?" *What do I say to you, Eric? Can we just talk, please?*

"If it's pussy you want, go to a pet store and get your own. Leave mine alone," Eric said.

"What are you even talking about? No. I was just . . ." *El Alma Perdida* rested on his lap. He put a defensive hand on it when he caught me looking. "Why are you carrying that around?"

"Because my magic ice sword is in the closet."

"No, seriously."

"Because if I leave it unattended, someone always finds it and shoots me with it. I need to get a holster." His nostrils flared. "Why do you smell like you?"

I stepped closer. "Who else would I smell like?" *Can we talk please? I think I made a mistake and I don't know how to tell you. I never should have left.*

Eric seized my wrist and jerked me forward, pulling me off balance. He buried his nose in my crotch. Too shocked to act like a vampire, I struggled ineffectively. "What the fuck? Eric, let me go!"

"Every woman has a unique smell. It goes away when you die. You still smell like you. It's . . . nice."

His grip relaxed and I slapped his face. He caught my hand and held it against his cheek. "How'd you get so warm just from feeding?"

My vampire speed wouldn't kick in. I'd been practicing seeming human in the car on the way over and it still had me sluggish. I'd gone full out, heartbeat, saliva, warmth, breath. I'd even eaten a breath mint. My heart beat a few times, little skips as it slowed down. Eric heard it as clearly as I felt it, I could see the surprise in his eyes. I knew I should have waited in the car for twenty more minutes.

"Your heart just beat." Eric put his hand on my breast and my heart beat again. He stood, letting *El Alma Perdida* tumble toward the ground. "I felt it." He caught the gun with his left hand.

"Get off of me!" I shoved him hard, used to having vampire strength, but that wasn't back yet, either. I stumbled backward.

"You did something to yourself. When a vampire feeds, the bones stay cold. You're warm to the core."

"Eric, stop it."

"You smell like more fluids than blood." It was an accusation. He kissed me and I responded. "Even your tongue is warm. You taste alive."

I turned it all back on, body heat, saliva, the works.

"What are you doing?" he asked. "And how?"

"It's my talent. I can be nearly alive." He watched the pinkness creeping back into my complexion. I forced blood back into my veins, made it flow like it was supposed to. Pins and needles ran along my arms and legs. "There's pain in the beginning when I go this lifelike, but it's worth it." I took a compact out of my handbag and showed Eric my reflection. "Do you like?"

"No."

"Yes, you do." I ran my warm hands along his cold shoulders, across his chest, and he shuddered. His skin was like ice, but I didn't mind. I'd warm him.

"This is a bad idea." Eric sighed.

I kissed him tenderly, working my hands under his T-shirt, against his skin. His mouth was warmer, like he'd been inside long enough for the heat to seep in and the cold had yet to leach it out.

No, it isn't. "We're good at bad ideas, you and me." I undid his belt buckle, pulling him toward the lobby of the Pollux. Resistance sparked in his eyes, but he didn't stop me.

"Why are you doing this, Tabitha?" he asked me. I gave up on taking him inside, pulled his T-shirt off over his head. Both sides of the street were blocked off so it wasn't like anyone was around, but I still got a giddy little thrill at the thought of being with Eric out in the open. It felt like the first time I'd stepped out onstage at the Demon Heart. I smiled lasciviously and he took it the wrong way. "What do you want this time? You're already a vampire. I'm broke."

"I've got money."

I kissed him again, painful hungry kisses because even in human guise, as excited as I was, my fangs poked out of my gums a fraction of an inch, peeking through the pink.

"I don't want your money," I said between kisses.

"I do."

His zipper stuck, the metal tab trapped against the upper seam. Eric's fangs grazed my tongue as we kissed. That only ever happens when he's really aroused.

"Something I learned in vampire society. I'm your creation, everything I have is yours, even my body."

"That's bullshit," he said acidly, pushing me away. He
stomped toward the Pollux doors, his hands touching the
glass before he stopped and looked back. "I don't own you
and I don't own any of your crap." He took a few steps
back to me. "If that's what you're worried about, you can
tell everybody I said you're free or released or whatever the
High Society pricks call it."

I shook my head. "But I don't want to talk to them. I hate
them. They're all freaks. They don't even act like people
anymore. They're not like you." I took his hand in mine. "It's
you I want."

"This won't work out," Eric said under his breath.

"Yes, it will." I shrugged out of the magic dress I was wearing; I'd changed into Isabella before driving over, wanting to
look my best in a dress Eric hadn't even noticed or cared the
least bit about. He cared about what was under the dress.
He cared about me. I snapped a fingernail, but the zipper
surrendered. Eric wasn't wearing any underwear. The same
was almost true for me.

I pressed my breasts against his chest, felt his hands on
my ass, his right hand lingering over the butterfly tattoo he'd
designed just for me. He didn't need chains, whips, or party
favors. Eric just needed me. *I love you.*

"You're not like Phillip at all." *Did I say that out loud?*

I slid my lips over him, like only a woman who doesn't
need oxygen can do, but he turned off. He's the only man I'd
ever been with who could do that, go from ready to not in

seconds when he's angry, sending the blood from one head to the other, tinting the whites of eyes with aggressive red swirls.

"Who the fuck is Phillip?"

I knelt outside the Pollux, only the priceless fabric of Isabella, my Winter original, between me and the pavement. *Why did I say that?*

"Nobody. He . . . I . . . Nobody, baby."

"Baby? Just like that we're back together?" He didn't trust it, shaking his head in a silent *no*. "Look, I won't say that I haven't missed you, that I haven't thought about you. I have, and you doing the warm thing, that's very attractive, but . . ." He reached for his pants.

How do I stop him? "Do you want us to be?"

"Do I want us to be what?" Eric froze in the middle of pulling up his pants.

"Back together."

"Um . . ."

The door to the Pollux opened wide, releasing the pent-up odor of freshly baked cinnamon rolls. In the doorway, wearing a bright red thong and a *Vampires Do It Upside Down* T-shirt, Rachel stared at me with eyes full of hate and a face that was all smiles. "Mind if I cut in?"

"She . . ." Words caught in my throat. The cinnamon made it hard to think, difficult to form words even in my head.

"We could have a three-way, if you want, Tabitha." Rachel's nails, the same bright red as her thong, flickered in the multicolored rays shining down from the Christmas lights. "I don't mind sharing."

"You bitch!" It was a thought, but it came out of my mouth, too. Of their own accord, my fingernails elongated into claws; my fangs slid into place. Goose bumps rose on her skin. She stepped out onto the concrete holding a sharpened stake.

"Bitch? You're the one trying to fellate my master in the street."

"I'm a vampire, Rachel. Don't make me hurt you." The thoughts rushed out of my mouth and it didn't quite feel like they were mine.

"I'm not afraid of you, Tabitha." We moved toward each other. Eric interposed himself between, one hand out to restrain each of us. His right hand touched my breast and his left touched Rachel's.

He squeezed softly, his eyes rolling up, then closing as he announced, "I am now officially going to Hell. I hope you're both very happy."

Rachel giggled.

"How are you even alive, Rachel?" I shouted around Eric. My pulse raced. Being this close to alive came with more drawbacks than I realized. Being a vampire really does take the edge off. No adrenaline to make you freak out. Vampires have something similar, but it doesn't have the kick of the true-blue homegrown chemical nature provides. Eric was old enough to ignore the difference. Going back and forth between states, I lived the difference.

"I didn't want to be a vampire, Tabitha," she snarled. "Not every woman needs to deprive their man of the warmth, the blood, the sex he needs. I'm his thrall. I'm happy to be his thrall."

"That's not what I mean and you know it!" I shouted. "Eric, you've got to know this. She—"

"Hush," Eric ordered, looking me dead in the eye. "Both of you just zip it—for a minute or two. I can't think with you shouting back and forth at each other. It's like a verbal demolition derby, for Christ's sake."

His command sent me right back to mind-control land, so I physically held my hand over my mouth, the rest of my sentence: *was dead and she came back somehow and now she's a witch or a demon,* stuck in my mental queue, unable to be spoken. Rachel winked and touched her nose with her tongue. Eric's hand left my breast. He checked the time on his wristwatch.

"It's four forty-one in the morning," he said. "Rachel, go back to bed. You can crash in one of the dressing rooms backstage. See if Talbot can find you a sleeping bag or a cot. There used to be a couple of rollaways back there, but for all I know they've been sold."

"But, Eric—"

"You're supposed to be my fucking thrall, right? So do it." He cut her off with an angry wave. "Tabitha is one of those early-to-bed, late-to-rise vamps, I want to talk to her before that happens."

Rachel nodded before kissing him, hard and urgently. "Okay, *Master.*" She grinned at me when she said it. "But for every time you fuck her, you have to screw me twice."

"Go inside before something freezes and falls off." Eric rolled his eyes, looking to me like I was his buddy. "She's a pistol. I've gotta . . . tell . . . ya. Right."

We stood in the cold under the flickering Christmas lights on the Pollux marquis, listening to the sound of Rachel's bare feet moving deeper into the Pollux, followed by her talking to Talbot, settling in. Eric motioned me inside and I followed him like a lovesick puppy, my priceless dress in my hand. I followed him upstairs. His bedroom smelled like cinnamon, too, and like Rachel.

"Eric—"

"I don't want to talk about Rachel, Tabitha."

"But—" I began, but he narrowed his eyes and it became a command. I couldn't talk about Rachel, not a word. Maybe tomorrow the compulsion would fade . . .

"I can't explain anything and I can't toss her out. She's my thrall, or she sort of is, if what Magbidion told me about how you make a thrall was right."

But she was dead. She's my sister and I saw her buried. I visited her grave and I . . . I searched for a safe reply, one his compulsion would allow. "Okay. If you won't ask about the guys I was with, then I won't ask about your . . . girls."

"I don't know if we can be together, Tabitha. I'm still the same guy you left."

"And that's exactly why I'm back," I told him.

Eric narrowed his eyebrows. "What? Absence made the heart grow senile?"

"Let's talk about it tomorrow." I nodded at the clock next to his bed. "We're running out of time." I helped him back out of his jeans. We rolled around on the bed for an hour and I did my best to replace Rachel's scent with my own. Just before dawn, as I felt the day catching up with me, we climaxed one more time. Eric panted on top of me and it felt like home. "Are you really going to make love to her twice for every time we did?" I asked.

He opened his mouth, but I never heard the answer. Not every vampire walks the daytime. It hits me hard and fast. My sense of the world went away and I lay cold and dead like the living corpse I'd begged to become.

❖ 20 ❖

ERIC:

AFTERTHOUGHTS

I found Greta asleep in my office, curled up under my desk with a blanket. A half-intact rag doll was clutched tightly in her arms, nestled between her breasts. Greta's long blond hair spilled over the edge of the sofa cushion she was using for a pillow. Clumps of semidried blood matted her hair. She'd fallen asleep without cleaning up, which wasn't unusual for my little girl.

"Not so little anymore," I whispered. The memory of the first time I saw her stabbed into my brain. I don't like to remember it. My eyes squeezed shut. After I banged my head into the door frame a few times, the memory faded. I went back to my bedroom for a washcloth and towel. The water in the Pollux gets hot very quickly. It warmed up my hands, which made the rest of me feel colder. I let the water soak into the washcloth, then wrung it out so that it wouldn't drip.

Cleaning Greta's hair took three trips back and forth to the sink. Trip number four got the blood off of her face and neck. Her shirt was a goner, so I tore it off. Greta could sleep through the Apocalypse. Her limbs go rigid, too, rigor mortis for the undead, which made getting a clean shirt back on her something of an ordeal. At least there were no dead animals in her pockets this time. I carried her into the bedroom, tucked her in next to Tabitha.

Tabitha.

Hadn't I wanted to turn back around yesterday evening and go back to her? Now here she was and all the reasons that things couldn't work blared loudly in my brain. Rachel could make me feel alive, but I didn't have to have that. If my partner was warm, then that was enough. And now Tabitha could pretend to be human, could wake her body back up. That changed things, but whether it changed them enough to make us work, I couldn't say. Thinking about my love life made me tired. When was the last time I'd slept? Another answer I didn't have.

"Boss?" Talbot called from the doorway. "Eric? I heard you moving around and came on up."

Turning away from my girls, I only slid the door open a crack. I didn't want Talbot seeing Tabitha naked and uncovered on the bed. God, I'm a sap. For all I knew, what we'd just had was nothing more than really good breakup sex, despite Tabitha's words to the contrary. "What is it?"

"Rachel's gone. I don't know when she left, I was catching a few z's. I thought you should know."

"Shit." On a whim, I checked the closet. The magic ice sword was still there where I'd left it, leaving condensation rings on the floor. I should get a better hiding place for it, like maybe a freezer. "What time is it?"

"A quarter to nine."

"Is Magbidion still parked out in the deck?"

"I think so."

"Good. Just a sec." I closed the door. Tabitha's breasts rose gently up and down, each time more slowly than the last. The warmth radiating off of her was three or four degrees lower than a live woman. Watching Tabitha cool down was infinitely more entertaining than what I was going to be doing. Maybe we could work it out, Tabitha and me. I covered her up before I reopened the door. "Can you keep an eye on Greta and Tabitha? I have to go out."

"It's daytime." Talbot put his hand on my shoulder.

"So?"

"The sun?"

"What about it?"

Talbot's quirky smile lit up his entire face. "You'll catch fire."

"Not like I haven't done that before. You worried?"

Talbot doesn't need me. If he did, he'd resent me enough not to care what happened to me. It's a hazard of dealing with mousers. They think like cats. "Just be careful, man," he said, "you look beat."

"You haven't been looking at my aura again, have you?"

"No."

I popped my claws and grabbed his important bits. "This stuff with you and Tabitha is total mouser bullshit, Talbot. You know that, right?"

Talbot shrugged, but I caught the twitch of a grin at the corner of his mouth.

"What the fuck really happened with Tabitha? Was it really just a screwup or was it on purpose?"

"You're not going to hurt me, Eric." The grin was unrestrained now.

I tightened my grip but let go when I realized that it was turning Talbot on.

"Shit, man."

Talbot laughed, long and clear. "Sorry, Eric, but you know how it is."

"Seriously, Talbot. No bullshit this time. Did you string her along on purpose, let her see how inhuman the supernatural crowd really is, just so that she'd come running back to me?"

He didn't answer right away, taking time instead to look around and survey the area, making sure no one else could hear. Who did he think might be listening? "I fucked up, man. I know I already said this, but when she's a cat, even when she's not, the way she acts, the way she moves, it's like she's one of my people. It had been a long time for me, okay?"

Inside my head, it felt like a door opened, just a fraction, and anger that had been hidden away, restrained, flooded forward and Talbot stood illuminated by the red light in my eyes. I seized him by the collar and his grin vanished.

"If you ever touch my girlfriend again to do anything other than extinguish her flaming body, if you ever have any form of sexual relations with her, I will make you a eunuch, chain you to the wall, and pay the oni to eat you like a tortured animal cracker. Do you understand me?"

He took a deep sniff, smelling me, then nodded. I let him go.

"Okay, now don't get mad, but can I ask you something?" Talbot panted.

"Sure."

"A tortured animal cracker?"

I flipped him off. "Feetfirst, asshole. If you want to torture an animal cracker you eat it feetfirst. Everybody knows that."

Suppressing a smile, Talbot coughed. "Why would you want to torture an animal cracker?"

Walking down the stairs, I turned my back to him. "Shut up. Just shut up. Obviously it's a human thing. Just—"

"I don't think it's a human thing, Eric, I think it's more of—"

I stopped at the front entrance and didn't bother to turn around. "Balls ripped off and stuffed in your mouth while you're eaten alive by oni. Don't mess with me today, Talbot. Are you going to keep an eye on my girls or not?"

"I'll keep them safe, Eric." He gestured grandly. "I'll keep the whole place safe."

"Thanks." I stepped out into the sun and darted around the corner. Smoke trailing behind me, I rolled into the protective darkness of the deck. I should put in a sunlight-safe connection between the two, some kind of underground walkway, but I've never gotten around to it.

Mag's RV was still parked where I hoped it would be. *For the luv of God! Sumbudy wash me!* was written in the grime on the side of the RV, but other than that it looked roughly the same as it had the last time I'd come knocking.

The side door on the RV hung open. Eggs and pork chops were cooking on the stove. I rapped on the door with my knuckles. "Mags?"

"Come in, Eric," Magbidion called in an obscenely cheerful voice. In the RV's tiny kitchen, Magbidion wore hemp pants, a white T-shirt, and a black apron. On the front of the apron a mystic design I'd never seen before glimmered brightly. The symbol looked a little like a floppy pentacle. "I'm just cooking myself some breakfast. If there is anything you want me to eat for you, speak up now."

"How do you eat your eggs?"

"Over easy."

"Fried pork chops and eggs?"

"It's my favorite breakfast," he answered. "And I'm in a good mood this morning. Someone tried to blow up my home."

He was showered and shaved. The inside of the RV was spotless, if cluttered. All of the ashtrays had been emptied; there was no porn to be seen. The bed had been made. Even the funky smell was gone, replaced by something lemon scented.

"And this made you happy?"

"Of course. I've known for days that someone was going to try to kill me. The signs and portents were all there. I just couldn't tell if it was the demon who gave me my powers or not."

"It wasn't, huh?"

"No, I think it was that Rachel of yours." Mags flipped hot grease over the top of the eggs with his spatula. I eyed the two chops he had sitting on a paper towel to soak up the excess grease. Even if Jill's deal was bullshit, I was going to give it a shot. He knew just how to tempt me. One quickie ritual with his Stone of whatever and I could be eating breakfast just like Magbidion. Hell, I could eat pizza. "She's as powerful as I thought, but not as experienced, I think," Mags continued.

"What happened?"

"Just a minute and I'll tell you." Magbidion slipped the eggs onto his plate, then forked both pork chops next to them. He sat the plate of food on a little built-in table. "Damn it. I forgot to cook the hash browns."

"I'll do it," I said. "Where are your potatoes?"

"In the freezer."

"What kind of a jackass keeps potatoes in the . . ." my voice trailed off when I opened the freezer. Frozen hash-browns? "This frozen crap?" I held up the plastic bag.

He laughed. "You vampires are all such food snobs. I'll microwave them."

"No." I shook my head. "I'll cook your damn potatoes. Eat your eggs before they get cold and if you put ketchup on them, I'm going to kill you."

He frowned. "Is salt and pepper okay?"

"It's fine. Tell me what happened."

I read the directions on the back of the package. Microwave instructions? Nope, don't think so. I was a bachelor in the 1940s. I don't need a microwave.

Some vamps like to nuke their blood, but I can't drink that crap. Literally can't. I have to warm blood bags up in a pot of water on the stove, or just drink them cold. The microwave changes it, my body rejects it—the result is very messy.

"About an hour ago, maybe forty-five minutes, I don't know. My spell barrier was tripped by a fire spell cast with tantric energy."

"Tantric? As in that the sex magic you talked about before?" I rubbed a little butter on the bottom of one of Magbidion's skillets, sprinkled in a dash of salt and dumped a serving or so of the potatoes into it. I love hash browns, not as much as I love pizza, but breakfast, God, there is just so much good food that you can eat at breakfast: link sausage, biscuits and gravy, pancakes . . .

"Yes." Magbidion tucked into his eggs. I like eggs, too. He broke the yolk with the fork. Rich and yellow, it ran out over the plate against a pork chop. It's dangerous for any vamp to watch a human eat when they haven't fed yet. Double dangerous for me. I wondered if I bit into Magbidion, would he taste like eggs, pork, and sizzling potatoes? If smell really makes up a large percentage of taste, then maybe.

"Eric?"

I retracted my fangs. "Just tell me what happened."

"My barrier enchantment has a quick wake-up spell keyed to it. When one is tripped, the second goes off, Like dominoes. It's a good spell. I learned it from a technomancer down in Orlando who works for one of the big theme parks. It's the equivalent of five double shots of espresso and two energy drinks. You're so awake your eyes vibrate." He picked up the pork chop with his fingers and slopped it around in the runny egg yolk. Breading, a perfect golden brown, flaked away to land on his plate.

"I must not eat Magbidion. I must not eat Magbidion. I must not eat Magbidion," I whispered softly.

"Did you say something, Eric?" Magbidion said with a mouthful of food. "Are the hash browns done yet?"

Close enough. I pushed them onto his plate with a spatula. "I need to eat."

"Ah, the short version, then." He slid away from his food, reaching casually under the table. I heard the rough calluses of his fingers rasp against wood. "Fire from her. Counterspell from me. She's very sneaky. I couldn't confirm that it was her, but I think it was. How can I help you?"

"I can't feel her. I was going to track her down, but I can't tell where she is."

"Like I said before, if you had made her into a full thrall, if you'd finished the job, given her the blood tattoo, you would be able to sense her all the time. Tell me how you made Rachel again. Exactly what happened."

"It involved blood, sex, kissing, and me pushing my mind into hers, which hurt. There was nothing about a tattoo or a bunch of words."

"Then you may have formed a connection with her, but it wasn't a bona fide thrall connection and I don't know for certain, but it sounds like it might have given her more power over you than it gave you over her. Of course, you could make me your thrall. Then, you'd know for sure what it feels like. And I'd have protection from the demon in return."

Like I said, Magbidion isn't a natural-born mage. He'd signed his soul away in exchange for his magic and his contract was coming due soon. He'd been after me for years to protect him from the demon in exchange for his services. He was going into his whole spiel, but I barely heard him. "That's just great. All my girls are gone. My club is gone." The hunger roared inside my head; I could hear his heart beating. "I don't remember ever being this hungry, Mags."

"She may have been suppressing your appetite; a proficient thrall could do that. A tantric witch could also do that. I once knew a vamp who was fed illusionary blood for a few days. It took care of all the usual problems, except for the"—I heard his hands tighten around the wooden object, a stake—"hunger." My vision ran to red. His flesh dropped away, becoming a mass of veins. Bump-bump. Bump-bump.

The nearest other living person was Talbot. Tabitha registered, too, and something else . . . cold blood, human blood in Magbidion's fridge. I opened the refrigerator door, grabbed a bowl of human blood covered in plastic wrap. "This is human."

"I was saving that for my next obscuration ritual, Eric. You can't drink that."

"Okay, then," I turned on him, fangs bared, "I'll try not to take too much from you." I moved toward him. He thrust the stake at me; a stake through the heart would only immobilize me, but it still made me mad and I tore the stake away in a flash. Why does the speed always work when I need it not to? Why was I so angry, so hungry? The same feeling that I'd gotten a few minutes earlier, when I'd gone all red-eyed at Talbot, throbbed through my skull like someone had turned on the anger valve in a steady flow.

Fortunately, the speed kicked off again, allowing Magbidion time to do some fast-talking, "Drink the blood in the bowl. You're welcome to it. Be my guest. I can get more. I'll just find another blood whore. Sweetheart Row's full of 'em."

The blood flew out of the bowl and into my mouth, in one long thin stream, defying gravity. Magbidion tried to step back, but there isn't that much room in an RV. "How did you do that? I've only seen that flying-blood trick in Asian vampires."

"I don't know." I was still hungry, but it was enough to rein myself in. "I'm going to go outside."

"Think over the whole thrall proposition thing . . . a magic-using thrall can come in handy," he called after me. "If I were your thrall, you wouldn't have to pay me."

I stepped out into the deck. Fang was parked nearby, his paint job black again, as it apparently was every day from sunup to sundown. Fang unlocked the door for me. I climbed behind the wheel and instantly felt calmer, more in control of myself, too calm . . . as if that faucet of anger had been turned completely off.

Falling asleep in a parked car is a bad idea for a human. It's a worse idea for a vampire who has a lot of people out to get him, but it's what I did. Somehow, I knew I'd be safe with

Fang. Twelve hours later I woke up to the sounds of "Second Hand Kiss" playing on the radio. Fang was parked on the upper deck with the roof down and the engine running. My car did a donut on the concrete. The engine revved twice of its own accord.

"I'm happy to see you, too, pal." Okay, I guess I liked the damn undead car. "Let's go hunting and then I've got business to take care of." Fang tore out, leaving a layer of rubber on the deck, screeching toward the lower exit. Heading out into the night with the wind in my hair, I felt more normal than I'd felt in twenty years. When Fang ran over a possum and it didn't come out the other side, I actually laughed. When I'd told Greta to go out and run over some small animals, I'd been kidding.

✦ 21 ✦

ERIC:

FUN WITH FANG

My undeath is punctuated by things I should be doing. I should have been figuring out where Rachel went. I should have walked over to the Pollux to check on Greta, but she'd done fine for four months without me. She'd really grown up while I wasn't looking. True, she still didn't know how to clean up after herself, but that wasn't a trait she needed for survival.

Tabitha. I should have gone to see Tabitha, listened to her explanations. Did she expect us to be back together and if so, why the fuck did she want me? Fang and I cruised Void City looking for victims and answers. No answers leapt out, but we did wind up on Forty-third Street, locally known as Sweetheart Row. The strip between Third and Fourth Avenues is vampire groupie central, but not the nice, pretty ones like Tabitha or Rachel; the real bottom of the barrel. It's where old groupies that never get their golden ticket on the undeath train go to lie to themselves that they still have a shot.

"Hey, baby. Want a fuck and suck?" A grandma in her late sixties wearing less than was decent or attractive waved at me as Fang and I drove past. Fang slowed and the blood whores began to gather. Either Fang knew what I was thinking, or maybe I'd stepped on the brake. He steered toward the curb, ready to hop it and mow them down, but I veered back onto the road and stopped. Up and to my left in the Bitemore Hotel, the sounds of eight or nine working girls were clear to my trained supernatural ear. The Bitemore was as long-standing a tradition as Sweetheart Row. It used to have a different name, but now *Bitemore* was on the actual sign.

"Hi, honey." The woman speaking to me now was in her forties, but the bloom wasn't entirely off of the rose yet. Someone must have broken her self-esteem in a serious way to drive her so far so fast. "Want a date?"

"What's your name?"

"You can call me anything you want, baby."

"Don't play games with me." I stepped out of Fang. What the fuck was I doing? I had no clue, running on instinct. Maybe Magbidion's mention of blood whores had started me thinking about them. Now that I was looking at Sweetheart Row and the women who worked there, I knew it was wrong and I wanted to fix it, stop it, break it. It's the same feeling I get whenever I step into another man's strip club. Did the

401(k) I'd offered at mine, the health coverage, and the college tuition really make me any better? I liked to think so.

"It's Cheryl."

"Hi, Cheryl. I'm Eric. I'm the crazy asshole who used to
run the Demon Heart before it got blown up."

Her heart sped up and I smelled her fear. It was a brief
burst of scent and she locked it down fast. Smart girl. Fear
makes a vampire want to attack. I closed my eyes, concentrated on the transformation, certain I could go uber vamp
on purpose. I grew taller, black as the night sky overhead.
The street noises stopped. I announced myself, sent out my
vampiric will into the surrounding area. The noises from the
Bitemore stopped, too.

"What are you going to do?" Cheryl asked. Her voice
sounded tired, beaten.

I didn't know. My actions were becoming more unpredictable lately. Was this a nervous breakdown? Had postmortem syndrome come at last? Maybe it was some kind of
aftereffect from the drugs J'iliol'lth had slipped me. No, none
of that. If I concentrated, I could feel the valve on my anger
tightening as I strained at it. Rachel was doing this, screwing
with my head. Which is fine, it's what women like her do
even if they don't have magic powers and I think I knew that
from the beginning. What I wanted to know was, why?

Gently, with my taloned forefinger I wiped the smeared
lipstick from Cheryl's lips. "I think I'm going to kill a lot of
vampires," I said in that deep otherworldly voice that my
uber form has. Her eyes sparked, an instant of real interest
and I think I got a glimpse of the woman she used to be.

She'd been strong and brave. I liked that woman, wanted to bring her back, let her have a life again. "Do you have a boss? I think I'll kill him first."

"Why?" she whispered. There was no fear in her now, only something else. I can't describe it, but I think in those few seconds, she'd begun to hope.

"Because I don't like what they've done to you. I'm hungry, and they're already dead, just like me. Who runs Sweetheart Row these days?"

"Are you going to hurt me?"

"Not tonight." Her green eyes caught the light from the streetlamp. "I've been thinking. The other vampires in this city used to understand the whole stay-out-of-my-way thing. When I was in El Segundo, some of them took turns looking after the Demon Heart so that it wouldn't be all fucked up when I got back, so that I wouldn't go ape shit.

"I think they used to self-regulate, keep out of my portion of the city. But lately they've forgotten who I am. They thought Roger had actually ended me. If I was dead and gone, then it was fine for them to let my shit get sold off to the city, but I'm still around, and so is Roger.

"I've decided not to look for him. I'm going to make them bring him to me on a silver fucking platter and if they don't, then things will get worse. If they hurt my people in retaliation, I'll just up the ante. It'll be fun, the vampire equivalent of mutually assured destruction, but to be honest . . . I think I'm a higher tonnage weapon."

"They'll band together," she said breathlessly. "They'll kill you."

I laughed, a deep croaking noise in the uber vamp's body. "I really don't care. That's the difference between us. Who runs Sweetheart Row nowadays?"

"Petey and the gang."

"Is Petey a vampire, demon, or a human?" Jeez, I sounded like the damn answering imp.

"Vampire."

"And where can I find Petey?" I asked. She pointed.

Petey was right behind me. I'd expected a Master vamp, one that I would sense when he walked up. Soldiers like Petey don't even show up on the radar. He rammed a stake into my back, splintering it on my ebony uber vamp skin. Nice safety feature. Petey raked two sets of claws down my back, tearing angry rents in my flesh. Somebody else's blood—my dinner—seeped out of the wounds. Too bad the safety feature that makes stakes splinter on my uber vamp skin doesn't apply to claws.

One of the girls shouted, "Kill him, Petey!" Others joined the chorus, but not Cheryl.

Cheryl mouthed, "There are eight of them," turned, and ran. It wasn't fear that made her run, either, it was prudence.

In stuttering flashes I touched the same level of speed that other vampires get to use all of the time. Petey glared at me. He was a kid. I'd never seen him before; I would have remembered. In his whole gang, nobody looked like they'd been embraced at older than ten. If they hadn't been dressed in modern clothes, I'd have thought I was fighting the Little Rascals.

The fat one stepped in front of Fang, which was a mistake. Darting forward, Fang knocked him flat and rolled over the front of his legs. Fat Boy screamed. Fang's engine revved and the vampire began to slide under the car like he was being pulled in by a strong current.

"Help me!"

The rest of the gang didn't give him a second glance. Only Petey had a set of claws; the others carried switchblades. "You guys are freaking me out," I told them.

A little girl vampire in a pink dress, her hair done up in ribbons and curls, sprinted up my chest and stabbed me in the eye.

"Leave our bitches alone, fucko," she snarled. *Fucko?* Petey clawed at my stomach and two differently weighted kids hit either shoulder, sinking their fangs in deep. The one on the right bit into my shoulder blade and fell off of me, screaming and clutching his mouth. A piece of one of his fangs still protruded from my shoulder. I guess he hit bone.

Dancing in and out of range, they stabbed and bit in tiny microbursts, like piranhas. I snagged Petey by the throat with claws of my own. Two of the kids drummed on Fang with their fists, but I lost sight of what was going on with the car. I had my own rugrats to deal with. Pretty-in-Pink went after my other eye, hacking into my cheek instead. Flipping backward like a ninja, she would have evaded my grasp if the speed hadn't kicked in for a brief second. I caught her by the ankles and ripped her apart.

It was a blow to morale for the little bastards. Petey stopped fighting to cry, tears of blood running down his cheeks and soaking his shirt. One of the kids fighting Fang reeled back in horror, clutching a stump. Fang had chomped him with a well-timed hood slam. Three of the ladies of negotiable volume shielded him as if he really were a helpless nine-year-old boy, not a bloodsucking undead thing. Two more of the gang tried to get away, but the vamp speed had worked up a head of steam and I was firing on all eight cylinders at last. At full speed, I've never seen any creature faster than me as an uber vamp.

Short and thin, a child vampire wearing a hoodie ran right up the side of the Bitemore Hotel. It's not a trick I know, but I do know the "throw a discarded switchblade into the little fucker's spine" trick, so it worked out. It never even occurred to me to fly after him. He fell into my waiting clutches and I beaned another one of the vampire delinquents with the dismembered head of his buddy, still wrapped in the hood. That made four for me. I popped off their heads and ripped out their hearts, just to be sure. Petey still knelt in the middle of the road, bawling his eyes out.

"How many did you get?" I asked Fang. Like he could answer me. He popped his trunk and I walked around back. Inside were the bones of ten or fifteen small animals, and two fanged children. I don't want to know how that works. Fang's dings and scratches were gone, and polished chrome gleamed on his bumpers.

Why couldn't the prostitution ring have been run by a bunch of evil-looking guys with swastikas tattooed on their foreheads? How come I never get attacked by things like that? It's always Bible-thumping werewolves or vampire babies. Okay, and the occasional demons.

A crowd of the bravest ladies of the evening was forming around me. In uber vamp mode, I could clearly see the thin golden veil blocking off both ends of the alley, steering most mortals unconsciously around the street from Third to Fourth Avenue. Petey must have been pretty well connected. He knew who to pay and how much to pay them.

"He killed Darla!" No way that tyke's name had really been Darla. Vision, cloudy, but getting better by the second, returned to my left eye.

"Who provides the spells you use to shield Sweetheart Row?"

"None ya," Petey shouted at me.

"Who is Nunya?" I asked stupidly.

"None ya business!" Without warning he charged, swinging this time not like a vampire, but like an angry kid, pounding on my legs with his fists. "You killed Darla!"

I read somewhere that your emotional development freezes when you become addicted to drugs. Petey made me wonder if the same thing wasn't true of vampires. If you turned a nine-year-old, was he really forever stuck with the emotional maturity he'd had in life? I'd never done drugs and I've lived past thirty, what was my excuse? Was I stuck in some eternal midlife crisis?

A shard of the stake Petey had used to try to kill me lay in a puddle of blood at the edge of the sidewalk. I picked it up, took its measure in my hand, and ended Petey. When he died, the prostitutes screamed in unison. On one of them I saw a tattoo with the words *Petey's bitch* glow brightly and then fade.

The girls of Sweetheart Row were all thralls?

A scraggly looking vamp in an army surplus jacket stumbled out of the hotel. Fresh blood trailed down his chin, dripping on the jacket. "You killed them. The little guys. Why did you do that?"

You know, I can only feel so much guilt for killing a pack of little pimps.

"They were fucking vampires," I shouted. "Maybe you don't get it. Maybe you never got the memo. They were fucking monsters. I'm a fucking monster! You're a fucking monster! The question you should be asking yourself is why should I even feel the teeniest bit guilty about it?"

"Chill out, man." He held his hand out in a gesture that meant *calm down and lower your voice.* "We're all friends here."

"No, we're not." I dropped back down to humanoid, the splintered bit of a stake I'd used to kill Petey still clutched in my hand. "I only have four or five friends: two women, a mage, a cat, and maybe . . . just maybe, one freaky little tantric witch." Fang honked and I added, "And one heck of a car. Nowhere on my list does 'sad little poser in a green jacket' appear." Speed control still with me, I spiked his chest with the stake and watched him explode into a cloud of dust. I love it when that happens. It's so much tidier than the bubbling puddle of rot you get most of the time. "Does anyone know where Petey and the gang kept their cash?"

I turned around. Of the eighteen girls on the street, nine of them had turned to ash.

"What the hell?" I hadn't thought about what might happen to a thrall if the vampire who owned them died. I spun quickly, looking at the other girls. Three others were rapidly going from old to decrepit. Then I understood. Time was catching up to them. But how? Marilyn had been Roger's thrall and she'd grown old and Roger was a Master. Petey and his gang had been Soldiers. Shouldn't Roger's ability to keep his thralls young have been stronger?

The other five girls looked like they might be okay, and Cheryl appeared to be completely unaffected. She walked back, her demeanor much more confident.

"What now?" she asked me. "You got what you wanted. I'm sure some people will be pissed off. Even if we don't stay here, I'm sure I'm not the only girl who has regulars that are a little bit obsessed. They'll track us down. We're going to need some protection. I don't want to be snapped up by the next sadist who comes along just because Petey was pimping me out on Sweetheart Row."

And that, my friends, is exactly why when I eat out, I tend to kill the donor. If she's dead, it's harder for her to stick around and whine. "Hold that thought." More vampires stared at me from the Bitemore, peeking out windows or from the fire escape. Three big vamps in suits that shouted *hired muscle* walked out through the front doors. I don't know if they worked for the hotel or the vampires I'd just killed, but it didn't matter to me. If I was going to send a message, why not send a fucking message, you know? I transformed into the uber vamp again. Two of the muscle-bound morons showed me fang-filled grins. They didn't grin for long.

22

TABITHA:

LOOK WHAT THE GANDER DRAGGED IN

The accommodations at the Pollux made me miss the Highland Towers. There was a shower behind the stage near the dressing rooms, but the water smelled funny and no one offered to bring me a bottle of blood wine, mulled or otherwise. Industrial strength cleaner mingled with a background stench of disinfectant.

At least the shampoo from Eric's office was recent. He didn't seem to need or understand the uses for conditioner. I guessed he'd picked the shampoo himself, because it had no strong scent, smelling like soap rather than any herbal concoction or perfume.

After the shower, I put on the magic skirt and top Winter had given me. Even though I had them change color—a blue top, a black skirt—so that no one would notice I'd already worn them once this week, I kept wishing that I'd packed something else. Magic or not, wearing the same clothes is just icky. Rubbing my hair dry with a towel, I nosed around the dressing rooms hoping to find something else to wear. Greta emerged from the one at the far end of the hall, looking hunted. I didn't sense her until I saw her, making her the second vampire I'd met who could do that with their mystic presence. She closed the door behind her too quickly for me to see any specifics, but it looked as though a whole apartment's worth of furniture had been crammed into the small dressing room. Her hands slid across the door protectively.

"This is my room and my stuff." Her fangs glistened as she spoke.

"I don't want any of your junk."

"You want my dad."

"Maybe," I told her truthfully. "I guess I do. I'm really not sure."

"Cut off your head, stuff your mouth with garlic, stake you through the heart with any kind of hard wood, then bury your head and your body in two different plots on consecrated ground. That's all it would take."

"What?"

"You're so unimaginative. I know vampire hunters who would try that method first thing and then you'd be gone forever."

My fingernails stretched into claws. "Is that a threat?"

"No." Greta vanished. The floor rose up to hit me in the face, bloodying my nose, bringing tears of blood to my eyes.

Her weight was heavy on my back, grinding me into the cold tiles. Fangs touched my neck and my arms bent backward, broken at the elbows. "This is." She knelt in front of me, head canted at a curious angle. "Hurt my daddy and I'll kill you."

"How did you . . . ow, God!" My elbows reknitted, shifting into their original orientation. The pain was remarkable. It felt . . . it felt . . . like having your elbows broken and then having them jammed back into place. I'd like to compare it to something witty, but it's a unique sensation.

"How did I beat you up?"

I nodded. "I'm pretty fast. I should have seen that coming, at least."

"Daddy is made for strength and hitting him is like punching a brick. You're made for speed and you can do the whole lifelike thing, which is cool; Daddy deserves that. I could feel your body heat from the office last night, hear your heart beat, the rhythm of the two of you. It rocked me to sleep."

Okay, now that was disturbing . . . I wondered if we could get some kind of mystic soundproofing.

"Daddy can do so many things and he has the angry eyes and the uber mode, oh, and the ghost mode, but me, I'm made for killing and I'm hungry all the time. When we're fighting together, Daddy and me, I always make sure to let him look the best, because, you know, he's Dad. It's like when you used to fake an orgasm. You didn't want Daddy to feel bad. I get that. That's why I hope we can be friends."

"Wow." I gushed insincerity. "I totally get that." Our gazes met. My mind darted into Greta's, but her mind was a vacant room, literally. I was standing in a living room. Ozone, tinged with burnt carpet, dominated the room's scent. An undercurrent of blood, sweat, and sex drifted in from elsewhere in the house. The salty tang of the ocean crept in through a broken window. I'd dominated another vampire's mind before. This was nothing like that. Greta had no walls to keep things out, no nice neat ordered core. Walking down a set of stairs came a pretty blond girl, not more than ten, wearing an oversize T-shirt that read: *Daddy's Girl.*

Blood trickled down her left leg. Bruises mottled the side of her face along the jawline. "Greta?" I asked.

"Daddy isn't here right now," she said softly. "Are you my new mommy?"

"What happened?"

"Bad things." Her face was expressionless, but a single tear streaked her cheek. "Daddy made it stop. New Daddy Old Daddy is upstairs." The girl set her jaw. "You aren't one of Old Daddy's friends are you?"

"No!" I assured her. "No, I'm with Eric."

"Then you must be my new mommy." Little Greta rushed to embrace me, holding me like an anchor, a temple, a safe haven. My God . . .

"Sure. Sure. Okay." I returned the hug, patting her back absentmindedly. "Mommy's here." What the hell had happened to her?

"I'm sorry I hurt you, Mommy."

"It's okay," I muttered. "It's okay. Your father will be home soon."

"I feel him," Greta answered in the physical world. Breaking the contact, I discovered that Greta and I were sitting on

the floor of the corridor, hugging each other. Greta pulled
me to my feet. Eric's presence brushed mine. Human heartbeats pounded around him. Five of them. "He brought pets,
or maybe snacks!" Greta bubbled. "Let's see which!"

Long blond locks of hair bounced against her back echoing the excitement in her voice. In the rush to get downstairs,
she left me forgotten in the hall. I followed more slowly,
pausing to straighten my clothes. I'd noticed Eric changing
into different sets of clothes without even realizing it, but I
couldn't manage that trick yet. I end up wearing whatever
I'd been wearing before I transformed or the black dress I'd
worn the first time I tried shape-shifting.

"Honey," Eric bellowed from the box office. "You'll never
believe what followed me home today."

"Dad," Greta laughed from upstairs. "Don't you already
have enough pets? What will Mom say?"

"I was going to tell her they were yours."

"Dad!"

Women crowded around Eric in the foyer, wearing worn
lingerie, latex, and Lycra. The smell was disgusting, like
sex in a slaughterhouse. Eric introduced them to Greta, his
words evading me completely.

"They're hookers!" I blurted.

"Blood whores," Eric corrected.

"We prefer women of negotiable volume," the youngest
among them said. She was maybe forty, but she still had
spirit in her, the others were older, broken and empty-eyed.
"But you can say whore if it means we don't get eaten."

"Where are we?" asked the most senior.

"We're in the Pollux, Gladys," the youngest one told her. "You've got to re-enthrall her." She pushed her finger into Eric's chest. "Gladys has been a thrall as long as any of us can remember. Petey wasn't even her first master. She hasn't got much time left." The older woman sagged physically, her breasts drooping visibly, the curvature of her spine becoming more pronounced as if on cue.

"Can she hang on for another twenty minutes, Cheryl?" Eric asked.

Cheryl sighed. "You don't know how to do it, do you?"

"Just . . . What? Yes, I know how to do it," Eric scoffed.

"Then do it."

Eric held up a finger. "Just fucking wait." He put his hand on Greta's shoulder. "Watch these ladies for me, okay?"

"Sure, Dad."

"Did Rachel show back up?"

"No, Dad."

"I'll be right back." Eric glanced my way for the first time. "Tabitha, just, I'm sorry, just . . ."

"Hi," Greta told the girls. "I'm Greta. I think if you're bad, I get to eat you." She pointed in the direction of the front doors as Eric passed through them. "Anybody want to watch a movie?"

She led the women into the theater, a demented troop leader herding her Hooker Scouts out of the foyer and into the dark. Nope, nothing like this ever happened at the Highland Towers.

✦ 23 ✦

ERIC:

MAGBIDION'S BARE BUTT

Okay, so I lied. I didn't know how to make a real thrall. Mags had given me a few pages of notes that he'd scribbled down, but I'd never made a real thrall and for some stupid reason, I wanted to get it right this time. I didn't need anyone else to have the same sort of power over me that Rachel had—one was enough.

The concept was simple. Like everything with vampires, making a thrall involved blood. All I had to do was tattoo Mags with my blood . . . somehow push my mind into his to forge the link, then say the "magic words" to seal the deal and claim him. I'm not sure why he had to be naked.

I hadn't noticed it before, but in Magbidion's RV, the bed, when it was unfolded, pretty much dominated the available space, which may have exacerbated the discomfort that I sensed from Magbidion as he removed his clothes. Mags isn't gay, nor does he seem to be interested in women in an actual bumping uglies sort of way. There has to be a term for it, but I tended to think of him as solosexual: a self-sufficient sexual entity having no real need for human contact outside of himself. A vampire can tell these things. Plus, with his shirt off, anyone could tell that his left bicep was bigger than his right and Mags seemed to be a lefty in everything else, too.

Knowing that neither of us was homosexual did very little to relieve my discomfort, either. When Tabitha walked in, I was still hovering over Magbidion's ass trying to copy the butterfly off of the sketch I'd done for Tabitha. Try explaining to your girlfriend that you are copying a tattoo you made just for her onto the lower back of a naked sweaty man . . . It doesn't matter what excuse you use or how reasonable it sounds inside your head or how true it may be, you cannot win. The butterfly had seemed like a good idea. When he mentioned the need for a tattoo, something unique to me, it's what I thought of first. I already had the sketch—I'd designed it. I was pressed for time. . . . Yeah, *embarrassment* is too weak a word.

"Holy shit!" she said when she opened the door. I turned to explain, but she had already closed the door again and retreated.

I went back to what I was doing. "That's just fucking great!" I grumbled.

"You want to go after her?" Mags offered.

"And tell her what?" I asked in exasperation. "It's not what you think. I'm not fucking the naked guy; I'm making him my eternal slave?"

"Slave? My friend, I will not be your slave, so much as a companion, a confidant . . ."

I guess Mags had illusions of freedom. "Who has to do what he is ordered and is bound by an eternal unbreakable mystic link unless his master releases him? Should I go on?"

"Okay, okay. Slave is technically correct, but I still like to think of our arrangement as something special, more an alliance than—"

Definite denial. "And don't say companion. For anyone but Doctor Who, that word has different connotations, especially when nudity is involved. Let me put it this way: Do you want to fight the demon yourself, Mags? Because if I have to listen to much more of your hedging, I'll just try it on one of the Golden Girls in the Pollux and be done with it." He shivered and it really wasn't something I wanted to see from behind. Magbidion naked was something I already hadn't wanted to see, but watching his sphincter tighten reflexively was too much. "Okay, I'm out," I said as I headed for the door. "I am not doing this. Too much naked-man ass for me."

"No, please, Eric," he began.

I turned. He turned. Tabitha opened the door again.

"All right," she started, "I have to ask."

"Please, Eric," Magbidion continued. "You must do it. I need you!" He sounded frantic and afraid. He also sounded like he was begging for something else.

Tabitha put a hand over her mouth. "Oh. My. God."

"This is not happening," I said as I covered my eyes with

my palm. Even if Tabitha and I weren't getting back together, this was not the image I wanted her walking away with.

"I'll just leave you boys alone then, shall I?"

"That would be nice," Mags said.

"Okay." I put a hand on Tabitha's shoulder. "Everybody just stop. Magbidion," I pointed to him, "turn around. Nobody here wants to see your twig and berries. Looking at your pale little ass is bad enough." I wasn't looking, but it sounded like he did as I asked. "Tabitha, you've got superhearing. Did you hear what we were talking about or not?"

She giggled and kissed me on the cheek. "That's why I turned back around. Is it mean to have a little fun?"

"Does this mean you two are getting back together?" Mags asked as I uncovered my eyes. He also turned around to face us again. "I don't want to keep you from your . . . festivities. Eric and I were just prepping for the blood whores."

"You are so not helping." I looked Magbidion in the eyes and gave him the universal gesture for *turn around*. He seemed to deflate a moment, but he resumed the position.

"I wouldn't be standing this way if he would hurry up. What's taking you so long anyway? All you have to do is put blood where you want the mark and then picture it in your head. Indecision is one thing, but—"

"Picture it in my head?" I interrupted.

"Yes."

I smeared the blood around on his lower back. "You didn't tell me that. I thought I had to draw it. Tabitha, show me your tattoo."

She obligingly lifted the back of her blouse. It took a few seconds for me to focus, but once I could concentrate properly, the blood on Magbidion's back pooled and sank into his skin. Line by line, the butterfly tattoo on Tabitha's back was replicated on Magbidion's. Red lines slowly changed to the appropriate colors and when it was completed, the entire tattoo flashed brightly one time.

"I mark thee and bind thee," I incanted. "Master to servant. Servant to master. You are mine until I set you free. You are mine. So mote it be."

Of course there was more pain. Why I had thought there wouldn't be, I can't say, but it felt like molten lead had been poured on an open wound and unfortunately, I do know what that feels like. Pretty much the same as having molten lead poured onto healthy skin, just a little more vicious. I bit through my tongue, severing the tip nicely. "Fuck! Damn! Son of a bitch!" I cursed, falling to my knees. And I was fixing to do this shit five more times in a row—lovely.

Magbidion joined the menagerie of people in my mind's eye, only now the vision was clearer, more distinct. Greta was watching *The Goonies* with the survivors of Sweetheart Row. Tabitha felt guilty about screwing Talbot and some fat ass named Phillip, but she did love me. It would have been nice if I could decide whether or not I loved her back. I've been in love before and what I felt for her wasn't the same. Was it close enough? That was the real question.

Rachel, I still couldn't get a fix on, but I could sense her, which was progress. She felt like she was still in the city, but where was anyone's guess. Outside, in the neighboring streets, I felt eight thralls belonging to other vampires. Two of them belonged to Winter, three to a female vamp I didn't recognize, another to a short fat vampire, and the last two to a vamp I'd seen around town but couldn't name. I guess the stunt I'd pulled out at the Bitemore has gotten folks' attention. Either that or I was a very popular person to spy on.

If you added it all together, it was more proof that Rachel had lied to me. It was possible that she was just wrong, that she had, like her sister, read too many books about vampires and had good info mixed with the bad, but Magbidion seemed to think she was too powerful a witch to be so wrong about something so simple. Then again, I had been a vampire for decades and her version had sounded reasonable to me. If it turned out that she was an unwitting pawn in all this, then so much the better, but—not likely.

I felt like I was playing Texas Hold'em with only three cards. I could still win, but everything counted on the flop going my way.

Tabitha knelt next to me and cradled my head against her bosom. Another vampire's scent was there, too, on the diamond necklace. It was a few days old, but the scent infuriated me all over again. What the fuck had she been up to? I couldn't lose my temper about it. Getting mad felt like the right thing to do, but it wasn't going to help me. Instead, I reached down to hand Magbidion his clothes and even though I tried to do it at vampire speed, he beat me to it. "Great!" I hissed.

"What is it?" asked Tabitha.

"Nothing," I told her, "just more of my shit not working right. Mags, get the fuck out of here. Go set up an early-warning system or something. Like the one you have for your RV, but for the whole Pollux."

"But that will take forever," he complained.

"Good," I snarled, "'cause that's how long you belong to me for."

He headed for the door and I beat him to it. The speed kicked in that time and I had no idea why. Mags looked like he wanted to get dressed first, but my expression told him that this was no time to argue. He stepped naked onto the parking deck and I slammed the door.

I spoke, still facing the door. "Go take a shower."

"I just took a shower." She didn't even look hurt. Instead, she smiled at me and got to her feet. "But if you want to join me?"

"Then wash the necklace." I sighed. "It smells like some other guy."

"If you're going to start in on me, remember our deal." She crossed her arms. "You bring up what happened with me and I—"

"Just do it, please."

Smiling the entire time, Tabitha took off her necklace, set it on the dresser, stripped off her clothes, and went into Mags's bathroom. My girls always seemed to leave their clothes lying about on the floor. I've never minded picking up after them. I remember liking that sort of thing even as a human, to have a woman's clothes and underwear just lying about my bedroom. It made normal women seem so brazen. Her panties lay on top of her blouse. I picked them up and sniffed them before hiking over to the Pollux. Yep, it was nice to have her scent back.

✦ 24 ✦

ERIC:

NEW RECRUITS

Talbot stood next to the stage in front of the wooden elevator that would have raised the old Wurlitzer organ up and down, except that it wasn't there anymore. It had been sold in the auction along with tons of stuff I would never miss. Talbot missed the thing. He and Marilyn had always harbored a hope that I'd play the organ again one day, but I won't. Music aids memory and I don't want the help.

Five women lay on the stage with their tops rolled up to expose their backs . . . except for Gladys who insisted on being completely nude. I went down the line, smearing blood on each of them, willing it into the form of a butterfly tattoo, and this time around I thought to make the mental

connection before saying the words again, having been ad-
vised by Magbidion that it would ease the pain.

"I mark thee and bind thee," I began. The pain started
and with it my range expanded further until I could sense
one more thrall, in service to a vampire I didn't know, a vampire with golden-rimmed glasses. "Master to servant." As I
chanted, Gladys began to moan and change. Her skin drew
taught, the muscles in her calves and buttocks clenching.
"Servant to master."

"You're so good, baby," she said between clenched teeth
as her hair went from gray to a rich auburn.

"You are mine until I set you free." The others sighed
then, in unison, and I realized that it wasn't painful for them.
The process was pleasurable. Their breaths came in quick
rapid pants. Gladys rubbed her thighs together, rolling her
head to one side so she could look at me through those timeless bedroom eyes.

"You are mine," I continued, ignoring my own arousal.
Gladys rose up slightly, revealing the curve of her full
breasts, a hint of nipple. "So mote it be." They climaxed in
unison and Tabitha thumped me in the back of the head
but didn't say anything. They were mine, the former girls of
Sweetheart Row. My pain built to a crescendo, five distinct
spikes of agony and I hit a knee onstage.

They moved for me, as one, but I waved them off. "Wait
down there for a second." I gestured at the front-row seats.
"Except you, Gladys." She paused and I looked up at her
only to find myself eye level with her belly button, the scent
of her filling my nostrils.

"Yes, Master." Her fingers curled through my hair and I shuddered as it eased the pain. Note to self: a good thrall is twice as effective and fast acting as aspirin . . . not that I can take aspirin.

"You get some clothes on first and don't call me master."

"Tease," she said with a wink. Her hand left my head and the pain returned. Wait . . . so I was going to have the rest of the girls stand around smelling like sex? What was I thinking?

"Get cleaned up," I called as she headed for the seats. "All of you." I put my head down on the cold wood, ignoring the scent of sex. Red tinged my vision again and the waxy smell in my nostrils was coming from me. After making them, I was running on empty. The magic had used up too much blood.

"Eric?" said Talbot, a note of concern in his voice.

Talbot smelled appetizing, but feeding from mousers is a bad idea as a general rule. "Hungry," I said. Magbidion rolled up onto the stage and shoved his wrist at my mouth.

"It'll be fine, Eric," he said. "Just be careful."

I sank my teeth into his veins and he stifled a hiss. It doesn't feel good when I bite. I'd thought, now that he was my thrall, there might be a flavor to his blood, like with Rachel's. There wasn't, but it did the trick anyway.

When I'd taken enough, I pushed him away from me and closed my eyes, head still pounding. Note to self: when making thralls, do them one at a time. An hour later I opened my eyes. My six new thralls sat in the front row looking a century or two younger between them. Even Magbidion looked younger and healthier, despite the snack service.

Turns out Soldiers slow the aging process when they make thralls, Masters freeze it, and Vlads—or Emperors—can turn back the clock. Gladys in particular was bright eyed and bushy tailed, ready to please. It had been decades since she was a cute young thing, she had probably been around longer than I had, but her beauty was timeless. I could see why each successive pimp running Sweetheart Row had kept her around. She looked like a redheaded version of Marilyn Monroe or Brigitte Bardot, but she was willing to do anything with anyone as long as it was okay with "her daddy." Like I needed another grown woman calling me Daddy.

Magbidion had summoned them all up a set of fresh clothes that he warned would only last twenty-one hours. Talbot had had him burn the others. Greta had supervised showers for the girls and aside from a lack of hair spray, they looked better and smelled better than I was willing to guess they had in the last ten years. My army: five ex-hookers, a glorified house cat, one crazy female Vlad, a greasy magician, my car, and my ex-ex-girlfriend.

I caught Tabitha smirking at me in the back row and flipped her off.

"Okay, here's the deal. Who here knows the trick—" Gladys raised her hand.

"Yes?" I asked.

"I know the trick."

"I haven't even said which trick I'm talking about."

Gladys laughed. "Oh, you might know it by another name, honey, but trust me, I know the trick." Everyone laughed, including me. She was a breath of fresh air.

"Simmer down, ladies," I said affably. Gladys looked over her shoulder. "Yes, I mean you," I added before she could comment.

She winked at me. "Go ahead, sugar. I won't interrupt no more."

"Who here knows the trick where you regenerate blood quickly, so that a vampire can feed off of you multiple nights in a row?"

Four hands went up. Sally, a brunette, laughed out loud. "Gladys can go all night on three Slim-Fasts and eight hours of sleep. I can take three drinkers, more if they just want a taste near the end."

Erin, one of the two blondes, held up two fingers. I'd yet to hear her speak and she wouldn't meet my eyes. Jodi, the other blonde, put her arm around Erin. "She doesn't talk any, but she can give blood a couple times a night. Petey was kinda hard on her, but if you work with her, you might get her numbers up. She's a real good girl and the johns like her 'cause she's quiet. I can do three."

Cheryl was the only one of the gals who hadn't raised her hand. She'd gotten rid of the wig she'd been wearing. Beneath it, her hair was short-cropped and brown. I looked at her and she stared back at me. The other girls were all sexually excited, but not Cheryl. Cheryl smelled angry.

"What?" I asked.

"Nothing."

"Tell me."

"I—" She cut her eyes at the other girls. "I just thought it would be different. You seemed different."

"I am different. Let me explain something to you, Cheryl." I hopped down off of the stage. "This is my theater and that"—I pointed in the direction of the land where the Demon Heart had once stood—"was my club. The women who danced there were my girls. I looked after them. I paid them an excellent salary. I paid for their health insurance. I even put them through college. I didn't do that because I'm a nice man. I did that because it is a fair reward for what I expect from my girls. I expected them to dance their asses off for me for three to five years. They shook their boobs and showed their crotches, but that's only part of it."

"You had your own whores." Cheryl sighed. "I get it. Just tell me who to fuck, Master. Tell me what to charge and I'll do it."

My eyes glowed blue and as I looked into her eyes, she stared back at me defiantly. "You want to leave? I'll let you go right now. No strings attached. No questions asked." She grew still and quiet; I could feel her panic. She was like me, even as a thrall she needed to be in control. "If I wanted you to be my whore," I told her, "I'd throw you on the ground and bang you like a beast and there wouldn't be a thing you could do to stop me." She squirmed uncomfortably in the seat. Gladys's excitement was growing. She wanted me.

"Keep it in your pants, Eric," I muttered to myself.

"Why don't you do whatever you want to with it?" Gladys said. Maybe there is some sort of pheromone I give off . . . an airborne brass monkey or Spanish fly. Whatever it was, it didn't affect Cheryl.

I bared my fangs at her. "I'm a vampire."

"No shit," Cheryl said.

"I don't want to have sex with you." Gladys and the others looked crestfallen, but I kept talking. "I have a girlfriend . . . possibly . . . and I'm really trying to work on keeping it down to me and her, but that's not what this is about." I rubbed my eyes.

Cheryl stood up. "So, you want us to be strippers?"

"No," I said sulkily. "I'm not building another strip club. I built that in the seventies and now that it's gone . . . I don't know . . . I was thinking a bowling alley, maybe. I like bowling."

"Anything, so long as it has balls," Gladys chimed in.

"So all you want is our blood, right?" Jodi spoke up.

I nodded. "Basically."

"Do you have to drink it straight from the source?" asked Erin. "And what vein do you like? Because I don't really like anybody feeding near my nethers. I'm always afraid they're going to bite something that don't need bitin'." Everyone stared at her.

"Well, I *am*." She blushed. Anybody broken just loves me. Maybe like attracts like? The others girls crowded in around her, hugging and smiling, thrilled that she was speaking again. Cheryl asked a question and despite my hearing, I couldn't make it out in the din and excitement, but I heard her reply.

"'Cause he's got a real nice aura," Erin said shyly. Her eyes widened. "I've never seen such."

"You and me both," Talbot whispered.

When everyone had settled back down, I continued, "When I ran the club, all my dancers owed me one unit of whole blood—that's not quite a pint—every fifty-six days. Some of them gave it via the needle and I stored it in the

fridge. Others liked to have me take it in person . . . maybe
they were into the pain or it fulfilled some creepy vampire fe-
tish. A few did it because they knew I like it better that way.

"Some of my girls voluntarily gave more than is healthy
and became anemic; they weren't thralls and they didn't
know any tricks. I usually kept around twenty eligible female employees and ate out a few nights a week. If things
are going well, I only have to consume about a cup of blood
per night. Which doesn't mean that's all I want, but it is all
I need. With your unique talents," I smiled at my group, "I
might not have to eat out anymore."

I stood and nobody flinched, but, then again, these were
professionals. They knew more about the needs of vampires
as a whole than I did and Erin's trust in me seemed to work
wonders for their morale. I should have shut up, but I went
on anyway, to fill the silence. "On the other hand, when
the shit is hitting the fan and everyone is out to get me, I
require more nourishment. Usually, I get it by killing someone and draining them dry. Even if everything is fine, I still
wind up hunting eight to ten nights a month. On most of
those hunts, my victim dies. I never feed on Thanksgiving,
Christmas, New Year's Eve, or Halloween. I even take my
turn protecting folks during the Void City Music Festival.
And just so you know who you'll be working for . . ."

I was into the same spiel I gave prospective strippers. From
a certain perverse perspective, anything that happened to
them if they chose to stay was their own fault. They'd have
been warned. "Because of what I am, I murder, on average,
roughly one hundred and thirty people a year. I've been doing

it for over four decades. The first twenty years I killed someone almost every single night. Sometimes I killed more than
that, because I was learning my limits. Overall, I suppose I
have been responsible for the deaths of over ten thousand
human beings. Charles Manson can kiss my ass. He has no
comprehension.

"Most vampires I know haven't killed a third of the people
I have. They either don't have my control problems or they
make do with animal blood. And yes, if you're wondering, I
have tried animal blood. It didn't work. For me, it has to be
human or I just get hungrier. I don't like what I am, but I'm
too selfish to let anyone kill me. Any questions?"

Gladys raised her hand and I nodded. She bit her bottom lip, gave Cheryl a sidelong glance, before saying, "Then
could you fuck me, like, right now?"

Maybe it was an act, but she knew how to keep things
from getting too dark.

"Talk to her about it." I pointed up the row at Tabitha.
"I think if we stay together she's going to want things to be
mostly exclusive unless it happens on a hunt."

Tabitha raised an eyebrow.

"Things happen when you hunt sometimes," I explained.
By her expression, I could tell she understood. I wished that
she hadn't. It made her one more woman that I'd turned into
a monster.

"What else do we have to do?" Sally asked.

"If I open something across the street, you have to work
in it. You'll be paid, I'll put you through college if you want
to go, you'll get health care with vision and dental, and you'll

feed me. Since you're all thralls, shall we say, experienced with blood regeneration, we'll work up a rotation. I'm sure I'll still hunt some, but this will minimize the damage I do."

"Can I give you mine via blood bag?" Cheryl asked.

"Yes."

"Then you can drink it straight if you want." Her expression softened. "I'm not saying you're all that different," her eyes flicked to Erin, "but I'll give it a try."

"Why are you so nice to them?" Magbidion grumbled. "You hardly know them! Me, you call your slave."

"Because you know I'm kidding," I told him. "They've been slaves too long for me to be sure they know the difference."

"Oh." The mage slunk down in his seat.

"In the morning Talbot will take you shopping for new clothes, linens, makeup, and whatever. Go backstage, pick out a dressing room each . . . any room but Greta's."

"*Talbot* will?" Talbot perked up.

"Yep." I flashed my fangs. "You've got money squirreled away for a rainy day. I'm sure of it . . . and it'll get you off my shit list."

"Okay. Done." Talbot nodded.

"Pick up some bedding, too, sleeping bags and cots or something. Those dressing rooms are small."

"What about me?" Magbidion asked. "Should I just keep working on the early-warning system? I'm going to need blood, oni claws—"

"The girls can help you with the blood, but you'll have to buy the other stuff."

"With what?" He ran his thumb along the other fingers on

his right hand. "I have some money, but not what I'd need for a spell that big. To do the whole building I'll need a whole claw, not just a piece of it, and a very expensive ruby—a huge one. Oni are happy to sell their clippings, but ripping out one of their own claws by the roots? For the RV, I used a small ruby, full of flaws, but to do more, I need better materials. On the RV, little gaps are less noticeable, on the Pollux, the gaps would be large enough to walk through."

"I'll work on the money side of things, then. Table the spell until I get back to you. For now, I want you to do a little research. Have you ever heard of . . . Damn. What was it called? The Rock of, no, the Stone of Eternity? I'm supposed to get it from some guy named Phil."

"Phillip?" Tabitha coughed. "Do you mean the Stone of Aeternum?"

I snapped my fingers. "That! The Stone of Aeternum."

"I think a vampire can use it to become more powerful, steal another vampire's power," Magbidion answered.

"You ever hear of it making someone immortal?"

"No. Well, wait. Maybe. I remember a few years ago there was a big brouhaha in the immortal community. One of my friends, Shelley, said that the Council of Elders wanted to locate it."

"Immortal community," I scoffed.

"Oh, yes, they are much more structured and regimented than the vampire hierarchy. They've divided the world into fiefdoms. It's very intricate."

"I don't care about that, just tell me if you think it's possible that the Stone could be used for that."

"I suppose it's possible," Mags admitted.

"Then I'll go get it."

"Eric," Talbot and Tabitha spoke up in unison. An exchange of glances, a silent agreement between them, sent a spike of jealously up my spine, raising the hairs on the back of my neck. Tabitha closed her mouth, letting Talbot continue.

"Lord Phillip is the vampire who owns the Highland Towers, where Roger lived." He did his best to look straight at me, but Talbot's eyes kept straying toward Tabitha. When it happened a third time, he took up a position directly in front of me with his back to her.

"He showed Tabitha a bunch of artifacts he used to elevate himself through the levels of vampiric power. He claims to have been a human wizard who made himself into a vampire to gain immortality. He didn't realize that it would make him a Drone. Since then, he says he has found ways to make himself more powerful. He's a Vlad now."

"Not bad," I said. Suddenly I remembered having heard Tabitha mention this guy. She'd said he was nobody. He didn't sound like a nobody to me. "Did he fuck her?" Why do I even ask questions like that? It's not like I really want to know.

Greta put a hand to her mouth, but said nothing. I caught Tabitha shaking her head in disbelief. I wasn't supposed to bring up her guys, I know, but like I really wasn't going to catch hell from her over Rachel sooner or later?

"Eric," Talbot began.

"She was fucking a vampire up at the Highland Towers, the vampire I smelled on her diamond necklace. Is this Phillip asshole the one who fucked her?" I repeated. "It shouldn't be a hard question unless so many people screwed her while she was with you that you lost count!"

"Yeah, Eric. He fucked her," Talbot told me. "And before you ask, there was no one else, just me and Phillip."

"Holy shit, Talbot!" interrupted Greta. "You fooled around with Mom? What does she have that I don't have?"

"Catlike reflexes," I answered, "and warm fuzzy feline genitalia, apparently."

Greta's eyes widened and she glanced over at Tabitha. "You guys did it as cats? And I thought Dad was kinky!"

"Greta, please," Talbot pleaded. "No, we didn't. It has to do with the way she moves, feline grace . . . Let it go, okay. I'll tell you anything you want to know about it later."

"No, he won't," I said abruptly. "That warning I gave you earlier—"

"The thing with the balls ripping off and the tortured animal cracker imagery?"

"Yes," I said. "It now applies to Greta, too."

"Understood," he said quickly. Greta mouthed the words "tortured animal crackers" and shook her head. Was I the only one in the world who had ever eaten an animal cracker feetfirst because it would theoretically hurt more?

"So, this Phillip, he's got the magic rock I need," I continued. Then I couldn't help but ask Tabitha, "Why'd you leave him?"

"God! He was a freak, okay? He's rich and powerful, but he's twisted. Everything is like a game to him, even people. He wanted to show me off to his special guests in ways even you would never have asked, so I told him to fuck himself. He'd already tried to get me to be the guest of honor in a Victorian-style gangbang. Not that you should even be asking."

I turned Talbot around. "So I should pretty much kill him."

"He runs the city, Eric," Tabitha blurted. "You can't just waltz into the Highland Towers and kill him. He's got magic wards and security."

"Is he awake during the day?" I asked.

"Sometimes," Tabitha answered.

"How hard is he to wake?"

"Pretty hard. Why?"

"That's all I needed to know." I nodded to Talbot. "How long will it take to get there?"

"About twenty minutes," he answered.

"Is there a parking deck or anything? You know what? I have a better idea. I'll head over there in the early afternoon. Are there any good pet-supply stores around here?"

✦ 25 ✦

ERIC:

PARKING

We pulled up outside the Highland Towers in Talbot's Jaguar. I trusted the shade in his car enough to just peek my mousey whiskers out of Talbot's shirt pocket. The building was impressive in a monumental Gothic sort of way. Very West Side, but I had to admit that I liked it more than the buildings around it. It wasn't the tallest, but it had a certain architectural extravagance with which I identified.

Talbot pulled into the parking deck. I didn't ask about the key card he used to get us in. I figured that Tabitha had one, too, and I didn't want to think about it any harder than I already was. Despite its normal appearance from the outside, the deck was very vampire friendly. The subtle

angling of the exterior wall maximized shade on the exterior parking spots. An interior divide granted access to
a second parking area, completely sealed off from the sun,
and a covered walkway connected the deck and the main
complex.

My little detour to the pet-supply shop had run us later
than intended, so Talbot pulled into the covered area. Each
parking spot was labeled by suite name. Talbot parked in
one of the four marked *Reserved—Gryphon Suite.*

"I wonder how much it set these rich assholes back to
outfit this deck?" I asked, crawling out of Talbot's shirt pocket
and returning to human size.

"Are you sure you won't let me just go inside and get you
in?" Talbot asked again. "Tabitha was given Roger's old suite
as a gift. I should be able to get Dennis to let you in past the
wards and then you could talk to Lord Phillip."

I picked up the shopping bag from Void City Pets. Inside was a roll-around ball for hamsters and gerbils. I'd spray
painted it black. My plan was more fun than Talbot's. Talbot
would shut me in the ball in mouse form and then point me
toward the Highland Towers. In my new sun-proof plastic
ball, I'd roll right up to the wards, go uber vamp, and . . .

"You suck all the joy out of life." I pulled the plastic contraption out of the bag. "The SunRunner Five Thousand,
man. It's a cool idea." *Just not a practical idea,* I completed the
thought mentally.

"You named the plastic pet ball?"

I sighed. "I *could* just use the walkway."

"You could."

"But busting in through the front door just sounds like fun, Talbot."

"If you say so."

"Okay, you win." I tossed the SunRunner Five Thousand back into the car and stomped toward the interior corridor.

Unlike most parking decks, there was no trash in the stairwell, no stains on the floor or on the walls. Everything was very well kept and the lighting was good. Sand-colored walls were painted with little coral patterns and the floor was a rich brown. The door into the walkway opened easily into a small receiving area. It was carpeted in thick burgundy carpet and the walls were light brown. It was supposed to look welcoming, I guess. Instead, it reminded me of an Italian restaurant I'd taken the living, breathing Tabitha to six months before.

That was when I felt the other vamps. Most of them were sleeping, but a few of them weren't. Fifteen Masters lived here. Their faces blurred in my mind's eye. Some of them were old, others were new, but none of them seemed important. I never get much data off of any vampire, so it didn't surprise me.

It did come as a shock when one of female vamps stood out. She felt familiar. I'd seen her face before, in the minds of some of the thralls spying on the Pollux. This was their owner, the one who made them thralls. She was asleep. Concentrating on her face made her appear more clearly. She was sleeping soundly, though I recognized one of her thralls moving around in the room. I deliberately reached for more information, a name, anything, and, for once, I got it. The vampire's name was Gabriella, and she was old, far older than me.

Her eyes opened and she screamed. Her panic ripped through the connection and I heard a ramble of thoughts: *Not during the day. He wasn't supposed to be here yet. Good Lord, what if he knows?* before she regained control of herself.

What if I knew what?

Let me in, I thought at her.

Roger is not here, she thought back. *I will have him send Rachel back to you. Please, leave in peace!*

Roger? Huh? I was here for the stupid stone thingy, not Roger. Of course, if he just happened to be in the building . . .

Our contact was severed when I sensed the Vlads. There were seven of them. I wondered which one was Phillip and in response, a balding little man, not a midget but still pretty damn short, swam to the front of my mind. He slept in a huge canopy bed with three humans lying on or next to him for warmth. Two of them were chatting while the third just lay there trying to sleep.

Even after decades of being a vampire, I felt like there was an instruction booklet that everyone else had and that people were purposefully keeping away from me. Previously, when I'd sensed other vampires, I'd known whether they were Masters or Vlads or whatever, and what they looked like. I'd never gotten such good, clear information before.

I heard the sound of Talbot's footsteps on concrete and then he came running down the stairs and into the reception area. "Why did you kick in the superspeed?" he asked. "Are we in a race?"

"I didn't know that I had."

"Let me go in, see if I can find Dennis, and get you permission to come inside," Talbot told me. "Just wait out here. It should only take a minute."

A minute passed, followed by five. I looked at my watch, walked up to the door. There was something there that made the hair on my arms stand up and the back of my neck grow cold.

Reaching out with my left hand, I could feel it, a barrier. It was invisible, but very real. A presence touched my thoughts and then retreated. The double doors ahead of me swung open and the barrier seemed to part like a curtain.

"You are expected," a voice whispered in my mind.

Talbot came around the corner. "Dennis is asleep." A young woman with bleary eyes followed him. "Hannah says she can add you to the system, though. She'll need a drop of your blood."

Hannah held out a golden needle with a crystal at one end. "It's for the security systems," she said and yawned. "That's all. I promise."

"Fools rush in," I cursed under my breath.

She pricked my finger. The crystal turned red, then purple. Her eyes widened and when she spoke next, the words tumbled out too fast. "That's all. Will you be requiring anything else, milord?"

"No, thanks," I told her. "I've got Talbot here to show me around."

Hannah hesitated, but she did comply, wandering off into the complex toward her appointed task.

"Where to first?" Talbot asked.

"You're going back to the Pollux," I told him.

"Why?"

"Call it a hunch. I want you watching over my girls."

Talbot shrugged. "Do you need anything before I go?"

"Leave the SunRunner Five Thousand in the parking place," I told him. "I might need it."

He turned to leave.

"Hey, Talbot. One question."

He looked back at me, waiting.

"Is there something important I'm supposed to know about a female Master named Gabriella? She freaked out when we sensed each other."

"She's Roger's sire?" Talbot said, his answer a question itself.

"So?"

"I know you don't care about the whole who-belongs-to-who thing, but she's a Society vamp and she doesn't know you well. What she does know is that her offspring messed with you and technically, if you wanted to, you could take it out on her for not keeping him in line."

"Thanks." I watched him go, then charged into the bowels of High Society. There is a sickly sweet feeling you get in your chest, a burst of adrenaline right before you jump off of a cliff or stick your hand into a hornet's nest. It's the thrill of the moment, the challenge. I knew suddenly that I wasn't about to walk over to the front desk or find an elevator, grab a house phone and call the concierge, or even go talk to Phillip. I was going to go find Gabriella and make her tell me everything she knew about Roger and Rachel.

"I'm about to whip somebody's ass," I sang under my breath like a little boy. I love those moments of enlightened "I don't give a fuck." If you survive them, later, you even get to look back and laugh. If you're really lucky, you get to do it with all four limbs intact.

✦ 26 ✦

ERIC:

LE DÉMON COEUR

Long ornate hallways and well-furnished sitting rooms took up the bulk of the interior at Highland Towers. Young men and women in bellhop garb manned old-fashioned elevators; each one slid the doors shut moments before I reached them. Talbot's scent had vanished when I crossed the threshold, but I did smell Rachel. I even smelled Roger. It was all quite irksome.

Stained glass windows portrayed mythological scenes at regular intervals along exterior walls. At the end of one huge hallway was an image that grasped my full attention. It depicted an army of vampires marching on a church. The sky was thick with bats and only one knight stood before a hulking black thing that was a pretty good likeness for what my uber vampire form must look like, except this one had breasts.

At the top of the larger tableau, bats were shown to part for rays of sun to shine down on the monstrous vampire. As I studied the scene, the shards of stained glass began to move. Words I recognized as French danced across a scroll at the bottom of the window, narrating the events above. Slowly, the colors all faded to gray and then a title appeared on the scroll: *Le Démon Coeur.*

Seen from the beginning, the dog and pony show was much more impressive. Under the cover of darkness, a lone knight rode in on an injured steed and left his horse dying on the steps up to the chapel. He hesitated, tore off his helmet, and cowered before an immense cross above the door. Baring small fangs, the vampire knight gathered his courage and charged into the church.

Time passed. A stylized sun rose over the church and the white clouds transformed into a churning horde of black bats, blocking out the sun. A female vampire dressed in medieval finery flew into the image from the left-hand side. Thirty vampires on horseback followed her on the ground. She landed before the steps of the great stone church and dialogue in some foreign language flew past on the scroll. Maybe it was French, too, but the font made it hard to read at all. Periodically the stained-glass figure's lips parted and she seemed to laugh.

My guess was that the fancy pants vampire was taunting the one who had fled to the church. A priest in brown robes came out of the church. He held a golden cross before him in both hands. There was more dialogue. Fancy Pants didn't seem pleased by it, whatever it was, and became the winged black beast with which I was familiar.

The vampire knight emerged from the church, snatched the cross away from the priest, and pushed him back inside. Flames engulfed the knight's gauntlets around the base of the large crucifix. The knight walked toward the uber vamp, stopped at the center of the steps, and fell to his knees. His head slowly lifted up to the heavens and more dialogue went by on the scroll. I recognized some of it as Latin.

All of the vampires cast their eyes upward and gold-lettered text went by on the scroll, even I recognized the Lord's Prayer. The knight held up his cross defiantly. Two angels with fiery swords parted the horde of bats. All of the vampires, the knight included, were bathed in the light of the sun. Wisps of gray smoke began to drift up off Fancy Pants, but the thirty vampires with her exploded, and their horses along with them. Fancy Pants had a few words to say and even though I couldn't read them, the posturing led me to believe it was something indignant and threatening— very Wicked Witch of the West.

She exited stage-left in a huff and the knight collapsed in the sun but did not burn. His skin became less pale and he sat up, touching his chest, his teeth. I was betting that he had been given a free trip back to the land of the living— lucky bastard.

More golden text slipped by and the priest came back out of the church, looked at the knight, and fell to his knees in prayer. Miracles will do that to a padre, I suppose. Everything went gray again, the picture returned to the initial image of the knight opposing the uber vamp and her posse. The cross was gone and the knight held a sword in its place, but I just took that as poetic license.

I didn't smell Ebony until she put her hand on my shoulder. She used to work in my club, before it exploded. Lady Gabriella's face was momentarily overlaid on Ebony's own when I looked up at her. "Take this one to refresh yourself," Gabriella's image said.

"Is this the vamp equivalent of offering the guest a Coke?" I asked as I turned.

She was dressed in white lingerie, the kind that showed a lot of leg but didn't really give anything away. She and the outfit both looked expensive. Unfortunately for me, the nose knows. Ebony could give me all the come-hither looks she wanted to and I would still have smelled fear where excitement should have been. In the right mood, it might not have mattered. Sometimes it seems like Little Eric has more say in matters than I do, but not today. She was a distraction and nothing more.

"So Rachel works for Gabriella?" I asked, feigning anger. I would have been mad if I could have been mad. Maybe those drugs of J'iliol'lth's were time-release or it could have just been run-of-the-mill mind alteration, courtesy of my would-be thrall, Rachel. I decided to fake it. "How does that work?"

"I don't know." Panic rose in her voice. She'd seen the club burned to ashes, knew that I'd come back when others couldn't. Here I was, without a scratch and wearing the same damn tennis shoes. She knew what I could turn into if I lost my temper and as far as she knew, she was making me angry. Worse, she knew what I could do just out of spite.

Her eyes told me what they've always told me, that Ebony understood what vampires are. We are one of man's natural predators. We hunt. We kill. We breed. Resignation had its place in her eyes as well. She'd known what she was getting into. Swimming with the sharks is dangerous business. It had been her choice. "The Lady Gabriella didn't tell me. She said to get dressed and come find you, so I came. I'm to tell you that I belong to you now. You can do with me what you will."

"Well, that must make you feel real special." With a big sigh, I patted Ebony on the shoulder. She flinched. "How do I send you back without getting you in trouble?"

"Please, I am for you. Enjoy me." Her hand slid up my chest.

"Get off," I shouted too loudly, spraying her with spittle. Vampire spittle is a little gross if you aren't used to it. Like all of the rest of our fluids, it's basically blood. Little flecks of it dotted her jaw and the front of her outfit. To punctuate it all, my eyes had gone purple. Two telltale violet dots of light appeared on her face.

Ebony's eyes darted to the right and her head tilted involuntarily as if she heard a voice that I couldn't. Her eyes closed and she bit her bottom lip so hard it drew blood. Her heart pumped madly, thundering in my ears. It was so loud and the scent of terror was so great that I nearly missed it when she mouthed, "God, no."

Tiny footsteps came toward us down the hall. There were two of them and I knew without looking that Lady Gabriella had just upped the ante. She'd sent out the mother and now she was sending out the children.

"We're for you now, mister," said a little girl in a white sundress. She was the spitting image of her mother. The boy was dressed in a little suit. Neither one of them was older than six. They weren't thralls, either, just conditioned to obey their mother's mistress. Talbot had been right when he said Gabriella didn't know me. I have a thing about hurting kids. You don't do it. The gang back on Sweetheart Row hadn't been children anymore. In my opinion, I'd done them a favor. These two, however, were still human.

My skin crackled like frying bacon, trying to change into the uber vamp. I fought it. *Don't turn into the uber vamp, you moron*, I told myself, *you'll scare the damn kids.*

I met their gazes, the two little babes, and pushed my mind at theirs. "Sleep," I told them and they both fell into a doze standing up. They wobbled for a moment then collapsed. I caught them, each child by the shoulder, and eased them to the floor. "Makes you feel really important, doesn't it, Ebony? I may have had you dance naked onstage, but I paid you good money, and I never treated you like this, like a whore.

"Your children . . . She sent me your children all dressed up like snack food." Disbelief had replaced the anger in my voice. "What the fuck, Ebony?"

"She's not normally like this, Eric. She's a little demanding, but she's usually so good to the kids and she gives them things that I never could. When their daddy got turned, I didn't know what to do. I couldn't come to you for help because you were . . ."

"Blown up at the time," I completed for her.

"He kept coming over, threatening to turn them, to make them his little forever children, Eric. What could I do? She offered to take care of us, to protect them. I would do anything for my kids!"

Real tears poured down her cheeks. She was on the verge of collapse and the mixture of emotions that was coursing through her sent a nauseating array of smells at my sensitive nostrils.

"One more thing, Ebony," I said harshly.

"What?" she answered, blinking up at me through her tears. I caught her face between my hands and made her look at me. I had no idea whether I could do it or not, but I wanted Gabriella out of her head. I touched Ebony's mind with mine and felt Lady Gabriella in there with us. I ignored her, stuck my thumb in my mouth and wiped the blood onto Ebony's shoulder. Her eyes widened conveniently and I reached for Lady Gabriella's mind. I couldn't leave Ebony tied to the kind of undead thing that would discard her this way and send her children out to pay the butcher's bill.

Pain, merciless and blinding, filled my head, but I kept on pushing. Ebony screamed. High on her left breast, the rose tattoo flashed brightly before it faded. An echoing scream came from farther down the hallway. My pain was gone and Ebony was sweating through her clothes. My blood formed a tiny butterfly tattoo on her shoulder. Ebony went limp in my arms and as I lowered her to the floor, I said the magic words. "I mark thee and bind thee. Master to servant. Servant to master. You are mine until I set you free. You are mine. So mote it be."

Propping Ebony in a convenient armchair and tucking her sleeping kids into her arms, I announced myself to the whole building. "If anybody touches these three, I'll find you, wherever you are, wherever you run. I'll ram a stake through your heart and then we'll get to be all experimental and find out what it takes to actually make you stay dead! Do you hear that?" Without a clue whether anyone actually heard me, I sat down, stared at the kids and their mom, and wondered what the hell to do about them.

About two minutes later it became clear that someone in the building had gotten my message and taken it very seriously. Elevator doors opened to reveal a young blond man. "I'll be happy to look after them, Lord Eric," he said cheerfully. There were bags under his eyes and he looked like he had gotten dressed in a hurry. It was the same little prick I'd seen at the Artiste Unknown with Tabitha.

"I'm Dennis, personal assistant to Lord Phillip. I assure you they'll be quite safe," he said, and either he was the world's best liar or he was telling the truth. "I'm dreadfully sorry for the inconvenience. Had you called ahead, I should have been quite happy to meet you at the door. Hannah should have awakened me upon your arrival. I'd like to extend my master's regrets as well. His sleeping schedule has become quite erratic over the years and is now completely unpredictable. He's slumbering now; otherwise I am quite certain that he would have come to meet you in person."

"If he's asleep, how did you know that I was here?" I asked.

"Sir Hollingsworth and Lord Giarmo were awake playing Go and when they sensed your ire, they contacted me at once," he explained. "Lord Phillip owns this building and since I am his personal assistant, many of the tenants are used to coming to me with their problems rather than disturbing Lord Phillip himself. Now . . . regarding the young ones and their mother, if you've no objection, I'll just take them up to Lady Tabitha's rooms and have guest services send up a nice nutritious meal."

I nodded numbly, said, "Thanks," and helped him carry them into the elevator. The doors to the elevator closed and then reopened.

"Oh, and one more thing, Lord Eric," he said convivially. "Lady Gabriella is in the Rose Suite. It's down the hall and on the right. You can't miss it."

The doors closed again and I turned to look down the hallway. Somebody had just been sold out by the management and it sure as hell wasn't me.

27

ERIC:

GETTING TO GABRIELLA

The Rose Suite was hard to miss. A transition from carpet to rose-colored marble began in the middle of the hallway and continued on into a side passage that opened onto an interior courtyard. Gabriella's waiting area was large, maybe twenty feet wide and twenty-five feet deep, not that I'm Mister Fix-it or anything. It was tasteful, in that same extravagant way in which other vampires seemed to approach everything.

Several squares of grass broke up the marble floor and gave the impression of a small yard or patio rather than a reception room. A white wrought-iron table and three matching chairs had been tastefully arranged in the center of each square. Parked at a decorator's angle on the right near the gate was a small tea cart.

Looking up revealed a glass ceiling about a foot below a skillfully painted mural designed to replicate the sky outside. I was willing to bet that the lighting changed to match the time of day, even the time of night. Puffy white clouds slowly drifted across the ceiling . . . definitely magic.

At the back of the courtyard, separated from the front by a gated white picket fence, there was a private stair constructed of the same rose-colored marble. It led up to a doorway, set into a wall that looked like the outside of an old plantation home, windows and all.

So many vampires seemed to spend so much time and money pretending that things are as normal as they were before they became living dead things. In my experience, it just makes things worse. If crying about what you've lost in the middle of the night sounds like fun to you, then be my guest, but this kind of make-believe only makes things worse for me. I'd tried it, more than once. It's nice for a few months, but it sucks every time the happy little house of cards comes down and reminds me that I'm just a bloodsucking undead monster that kills to live.

Gabriella would eventually learn that lesson the hard way: all vampires do, providing they survive long enough. Whether or not Gabriella survived really depended on what I found inside her place and what she had to say about Roger and Rachel and why the hell they were together. It was nice to know that my antics earlier were good for something. Taking out Sweetheart Row and the Bitemore must have been enough to rattle Gabby's cage.

The fence wasn't locked, so I reached over and opened

the gate before marching up the stairs. One flight up, the stairs opened up onto a wide platform. On either side of an ornate wooden door were potted plants that went three-quarters of the way up the door, roughly even with the sliding view slot.

A crimson cord with tassels on the end hung next to the door. There was also a gold-plated knocker in the shape of an opening rosebud. I ignored them both and knocked "shave and a haircut" on the door. It's a habit.

Gabriella's rooms must have had excellent soundproofing, because I could barely hear inside. There was movement and a muffled conversation and then the view slot slid open to reveal two blue-gray eyes. A human? My thrall-sense went off like an alarm.

"I am quite sorry, sir," spoke a soft feminine voice. Whoever she was, she wasn't Lady Gabriella, but she did belong to her. Her voice was very pleasant, with a lilting accent. French, maybe? "Lady Gabriella is not at home to visitors this early in the day. Perhaps you could come back after sundown? If you would like, I would be happy to schedule a visit with the Lady Gabriella for another time? For you, sir, I believe that she could be available as early as Friday. To others, of course, her schedule is quite full, but the Lady is always happy to make exceptions for important persons such as yourself."

"No, that won't be necessary. She knows what I want to know and she knows that she'd better tell me. She just sent one thrall and two children to me as some kind of freaky-ass peace offering and now she's got you up here acting like that didn't just happen. Does she think I'm an idiot?"

"Bien sur que non, monsieur!" I could barely hear her pulse, but it was racing. "Excuse me, what I mean to say is, of course not, sir. The Lady Gabriella did awaken briefly, overcome as she was by your grand presence, sir, and she immediately dispatched Ebony and her little ones to you as a token of her respect. It is regrettable that she is a very heavy sleeper, however, and lapsed back into the slumber of the immortals shortly after confirming that you had received her tokens of esteem."

She paused and I heard someone faintly whispering in the distance. It could have been Gabriella, but there was no way to be sure. Mystical soundproofing. When the voice resumed, it was shaking. "I have been instructed that should the Lady's offerings be displeasing to you, I am to offer you myself if my demeanor and appearance would be more acceptable."

"What's your name?" I asked softly.

"Beatrice, sir," she answered.

"How would I know if I find your appearance more pleasing if I can't see all of you, Beatrice?"

"I would be happy to reveal myself to you, sir, but I am instructed to make certain that milord is aware of the special properties of the doorways here in the Highland Towers before doing so."

"What special properties?" I asked. As a delaying tactic, Beatrice was doing a wonderful job. I could only hope that Lady Gabriella wasn't slipping Roger and Rachel out the back somewhere while I was chatting up the help.

"All of the doorways to the suites of the Highland Towers are enchanted, sir. When the enchantment is active, there is an impenetrable field of magic in place over the door. It delivers a powerful jolt to any who try to cross the threshold, unless they already possess permission to enter or exit. When I open the door, sir, I would not wish for you to accidentally be injured by brushing against the barrier. It similarly affects those who try to force the door open if they do not have permission to do so."

I punched the door and received a semi-electric jolt for my trouble. Running up my arm, the electric hum set my teeth to vibrating and made my eyes sizzle. I gracelessly tumbled down the stairs, landing at the bottom, my left leg still jerking spasmodically. "Magic s-s-sucks," I said lying on my back. I stared up at the sky and watched some pretty convincing clouds pass by on the ceiling.

Warmth poured down from the sun as it came out from behind the clouds and I was consumed with envy for Gabby's enchanted ceiling. I hadn't felt the sun on my face for decades without bursting into flames—being a ghost didn't count—and it brought a tear of blood to my eye. I wiped the bloody tear off on the hem of my T-shirt and when my leg stopped jerking, I stood up.

"How much did it cost to get the ceiling done?" I called up the stairs. "And why do you keep calling me 'sir'? Shouldn't you call me 'Lord Eric' or something?" I walked back through the gate and picked up one of the chairs, testing its heft. Somebody could get really messed up with one of these things.

I heard the creak of the door opening, followed by the sound of high-heeled shoes on marble. Beatrice was wearing a green velvet dress that looked like it belonged in a Renaissance faire, except that it pushed everything up and to the middle with impressive results. Her bosom wasn't large, but the dress put what there was to good use.

Fiery red tresses cascaded in ringlets down to her shoulders. Her lips had the natural pouty look most women who get Botox injections are looking for and her eyes were a startling blue-gray, like storm clouds. "Please, do not break them, Highness. I have no doubt that you could, but the Lady, she would be so heartbroken. The Lord Winter, I doubt he would come back to redo them for her."

"Since you said 'please,'" I smiled, putting down the chair. "So, you belong to me now?"

"If you wish it, Highness."

"From sir to highness." I walked in her direction and ran my fingers through her hair. She tried to control herself, but she was terrified. It was like petting a skittish colt. Her nostrils flared and any sudden movement seemed likely to make her bolt. "That's a pretty good promotion. Your mistress must think I'm one huge misogynistic bastard. Which I guess is better than being taken for a pedophile."

"I'm certain no insult was intended." She let the words linger on her lips and it dawned on me that I'd been snowed again. She was a marvelous actress and she'd been giving me an Oscar winning performance. She wasn't scared at all. A lot of vamps get turned on by fear and she was trying to seduce me.

"You ever met a female vampire named Irene?" I asked.

"I don't believe so, Highness," she said, trembling. Boy, was she good.

"She was a good actress, too." I looked Beatrice in the eye. "She got even better when she died. Do you mind sitting over there?" I pointed to one of the chairs in the seating area.

"Of course not, sire."

"I'll be right back." I winked.

At the stairs, the door stood open, revealing a room that would have looked more at home in some palace in France a few hundred years ago. I'm certain it would have impressed Tabitha or Roger. It didn't impress me. I just wanted in.

"Okay, Gabby," I called into the room. "I really hope you aren't sleeping, because if you are, then I'm going to feel really stupid."

Windows. Doors. Walls. Magic protects the door, I said in my head, *but magic doesn't protect the ceiling. Does magic protect the walls?* I glanced over my shoulder at Beatrice. She sat obediently where I'd left her, observing me with a carefully indifferent eye. I walked to the window three feet to the left of the door. I held my hand over the glass, concentrating on breaking it open. Sure enough, my palm began to tingle. I did the same thing to the wall and grinned. Civilized vampires go in through doors, and maybe windows. Uncivilized vampires, who don't give a shit what others think of them, who could care less about their place in society, have more options. I punched the wall and my fist went right through it. Score one point for the Neanderthal!

✦ 28 ✦

ERIC:

LESS THAN NOBLESSE OBLIGE

Bits of plaster mixed with traces of blood on my knuckles as I forced my way through the wall. Beatrice choked out a *"Mon dieu!"* behind me, but I couldn't turn to look at her. This had to happen fast. In the movies, when a monster crashes through the side of a building, he gets to do it in one smooth motion. The wall explodes, creating a nice new half oval into which he steps, backlit so that the cloud of dust billowing up about him seems dramatic. No such luck for me. Punches turned to a combination of kicks and shoves with a healthy dose of claws at the end.

Inside, three servants opened fire with crossbows. The first bolt hit a two-by-four on the narrow side and stuck fast.

The other two went high and wide, one lancing into my open mouth as I flashed my fangs, then tearing through my left cheek and pinning me for a brief moment as I marveled at an all new pain. None of them got off a second shot before I was all the way in, and by that time it was too late. Their crossbows weren't made for speed loading.

Three humans versus a vampire.

Vampire wins.

Surprise, surprise.

I ran my fingers over the side of my face, but the jagged tear was gone, healed. I tore the third crossbow bolt out of my shoulder without wincing, then looked for Gabriella. "Knock. Knock." I found her in the bedroom, half dressed and moving sluggishly. Her skin smelled of strawberries and the scent was pleasant enough that I had to remind myself to stop being interested. I wasn't here on a date.

Part of what Beatrice said had been true. Gabriella didn't do so well during the daytime. Some vampires are like me. If something bad enough happens, we wake up and we're wide awake. The few times it happened to me, I didn't even go back to sleep. Other vamps just can't wake up at all until they rise the next night. Lady Gabriella was somewhere in between. Moving in stutters and starts, she reminded me of one of George Romero's zombies in *Night of the Living Dead*. If there had been a footrace between the two, I would've put my money on the zombie.

Another human servant sprang seemingly out of nowhere, firing at me with a revolver and screaming, "Get away from her!" He was blond and styled, a real pretty boy. I bounced him off the bedroom wall with a punch to the head and he sacked out like a good little lap dog.

"Esteban," Gabriella croaked.

"Hi, Gabby." Her bedroom was nice. All gold and red with a huge four-poster bed in the middle of it. Heat poured off the bed through some internal wiring system and it was accurate enough that I had to mentally acknowledge the achievement—it felt like body heat. There was the low steady thrum of a pulse, too.

"Don't hurt her." I turned at the sound of the voice, the familiar drawl, exaggerated more by the age of the speaker, the era in which he'd lived, rather than for purposeful effect. John Paul Courtney. "Don't hurt her," he repeated. His body coalesced between Gabriella and me, but this time his form was translucent, lit from within by a wavering amber light that cast an angelic hue upon his bobbleheaded self.

"I don't want to hurt her, you dumb ass," I snapped. "I just want some fucking answers."

"What answers?" Gabriella's voice was thick and slurred. Her face barely moved when she spoke, showing all the expressionlessness of a stroke victim, but on both sides of her pretty face. She stumbled forward, through the specter of my ghostly conscience. As usual, I was the only one who got the dubious benefit of perceiving His Judgmentalness.

Gabriella struggled to stand and I held out my hand rather than let her fall. I smelled more humans nearby. Several of them were women. Their scent was so strong I knew that they had been in the room when I was breaking through the wall. I could feel them in the house, all of those scared little hearts pounding away, all that blood. They had left their mistress struggling with her clothes on the floor and run. I wondered if she had told them to. I smelled two other scents as well: Roger and Rachel. Son of a bitch! They weren't here, but they'd been here last night, and they'd been together.

"So is anyone going to come out here and help you dress or are they all too chickenshit?" I asked.

She managed a brief shake of the head.

"Beatrice," I called over my shoulder. "If you're done catching your breath, get in here and help Gabby get dressed."

John Paul Courtney smiled.

"Oh, hurrah! I made the ghost happy." Once Beatrice took my place helping Gabriella, I stepped back. Her eyes followed me as I crossed the room. My hands traced the top of her dresser and I paused when I reached a set of porcelain horses. Her jaw tightened and her eyes were furious, but she said nothing, still working hard at getting the rest of her clothes on.

"Come on, son," John Paul drawled. "Leave her things alone."

"Get a grip, you nosy ass. I'm not going to break her keepsakes. Damn! You know why I came here. I didn't even know Roger and Rachel had been to the Highland Towers until I smelled them. All I wanted was the stupid magic rock from Lord What's-His-Hype . . ."

I noticed my audience. Bea and Gabby's joint dressing maneuver had slowed to a crawl while the two of them watched me arguing with someone they could neither see nor hear.

"Why can't they see you anyway?" I asked.

"I told you how it works. They ain't blood," Courtney told me, but there was a tremor when he said blood that reminded me of someone. The pain, the tenderness in his eyes when he looked at Gabriella.

"Wait. Wait. Wait." I pointed at Gabriella. She and Beatrice froze, but I gestured for them to continue. "Were you in love with her?"

"Maybe." His maybe sounded more like "meh-beh" and it was soft and sullen. I smiled. "What, you think I weren't living afore I was a haint?" Courtney asked. "We weren't never . . . Aw h—" He caught the *hell* that I saw coming and his cigar appeared in his hand.

"You almost said the h-word."

"I told you we was alike, you an' me. When I was young, my mouth weren't any cleaner than the outhouse behind the saloon, but I changed and so can you." He blew smoke rings at me and smiled, regaining his composure. "Tell you what. I'll tell you all about Gabby and me some time if you really want to know, but for now I'll put this in terms you can appreciate. Each time *El Alma Perdida* finds her way into the hands of my kin, each time certain conditions are met, I can fire her six times in the service of the Courtney line. I can do it, but I don't have to. You honor my request and I'll fire one of those shots on your behalf when you need it."

"What the hell kind of offer is that? I can fire the gun myself, you know."

"Not always," he drawled. "Even you need help from time

to time. If'n you was staked, maybe, or couldn't get to the gun in time . . . or if, say, someone else had aholt of it."

He had me there.

"Could you keep somebody else from firing the gun?"

"I could do either," he agreed.

"Wait," I said. "You said you could appear under certain conditions. What conditions?"

"I told you a few of them, too. You ain't ready to know yet, but the offer stands. Will you take it?"

"We'll see," I said. I should have said "meh-beh," but I didn't think of it in time.

When I turned back to Gabriella, she was clad in a high-collared dress that still showed ample cleavage.

"Better now?" I asked, once we were both seated in Gabriella's sitting room. Beatrice danced attendance on her, a mother hen, clearly worried about her "former" Mistress. Gabriella nodded awkwardly, but with more muscle control than before, a twitch that could have been an attempted smile flickering at the corner of her mouth.

Beatrice brought her a cup of warm blood in a delicate china cup and helped her drink it down carefully. "The blood is the life," Gabriella said artfully.

I was too busy counting doors to pay attention. There were four. Behind two of them I smelled men and metal. Six women cowered behind another door, the Lady's maids, I was guessing. The fourth door seemed devoid of life; it held my attention.

"Good." I leapt across the table and hefted her into the

air by her throat. Beatrice screamed. So did I. "Where the fuck are they?"

"Boy, if I could shoot you . . ." the ghost of Courtney snarled.

Why can't you? I wanted to ask, but Beatrice was already speaking. "Please, Master Eric, the rules . . . ," she begged.

"What rules?" I dropped Gabriella on the couch and looked at Beatrice.

"The Highland Towers has certain codes of conduct," Beatrice explained. "No vampire may assault another within any of the private rooms or on the grounds, or they face punishment at the hands of Lord Phillip. Of course, one is always allowed to defend one's self."

"Oh, well, that's fine then." I clapped my hands together. "I'm here to piss him off anyway." I leaned in so close we bumped noses. "I smell Roger here and I smell Rachel. Where are they?"

"I told you he is not here; neither is the woman," Gabriella said deliberately. "I have offered you my two most treasured handmaidens. I could offer you Esteban, my lover, but I understand he would be of little interest to you."

"This is the Gabby you don't want to hurt?" I asked John Paul Courtney, but he'd gone.

"Who are you talking to?" Beatrice asked.

"Jiminy Cricket," I answered. Esteban stirred, so I put him out with another blow to the head. That was going to smart. Gabby gritted her teeth. I suppose she didn't like seeing her entrée treated so roughly. It was time for another tactic.

I tried to clear my thoughts to calm down, but I was offended by the whole damn thing and it came out in a torrent. "Okay, I have to say this. Do all High Society vamps do this whole 'thralls are slaves to be passed around' crap? What the fuck is wrong with you people? I've got more thralls than I know what to do with already, but they aren't slaves. They are thralls by choice and if they want out, I'd be happy to let them go. I mean, I know that we're monsters and all and I eat people, but come on! You keep offering me people like they're objects. You tried to send me children for a snack. There's no way I'd ever hurt a kid. How do you not know that about me? And how many warm bodies do you think I need to run a bowling alley anyway?"

"Excuse me?" Gabriella's features were becoming more animated as the blood she was drinking did its best to overcome the effects of the daytime.

"You had people spying on me and they didn't tell you about the bowling alley? I'd fire somebody."

"Perhaps I shall. Even so, I am forced to return to the subject at hand. The one for whom you search is not here and has not been here for some time. He will not return until the game is over and the wager decided. If we lose, then he will not return at all. If you are planning to kill me, I ask that you don't. I cannot stop you; I'm too weak. My thralls mean nothing to you—"

"Game? Wager?" I stood up, couldn't stay still any longer, couldn't just sit there and listen to her talk.

"I told Roger that he never should have taken odds against him," Gabriella's voice faltered, then she continued, "but to beat Ebon Winter would have added respectability to his endeavors, legitimized his ascendance, and redeemed him after the Orchard Lake debacle."

"Does this game involve marbles?" I sat back down. Gabriella's eyes followed me warily, but if I wasn't misreading her, Beatrice was amused.

"Excuse me?" Lady Gabriella asked.

"Never mind, just something a guy in a jumpsuit told me the other day." I tapped Beatrice on the shoulder. "Now you see, that's funny. Sometimes I can't remember my own phone number, but I remember what some guy named Melvin was talking about. . . . No, shit, that would have been like four months ago. Wouldn't it?"

"Leave my apartments in peace and never return to them again uninvited," Gabriella said.

"Yeah, that'll work," I scoffed.

"You are a powerful being, Eric—I believe you prefer to be called by your given name only, without honorifics?" She flexed her hands as she spoke as if she were willing the blood she drank to flow into them.

"Yeah," I agreed. "Eric's fine."

"Keep the gifts I've given you. Do not give a thought to the damage you have done to my home, the threats you have made, or the insulting and demeaning way you have dealt with me. You have never dwelt amongst polite society; such lapses in judgment are to be expected, but please do not believe I will be so forgiving if you trifle with me a second time. You may be more powerful than I am, in person, but I assure you I will not be so exposed again." She stood, giving me the mother of all you-may-go-now looks.

"That's a nice offer," I admitted. "It really, really is." Rising to my feet, I gestured to Beatrice to pour me a cup of blood. She did so and I tossed it back in one swallow. "I even like the part where you threaten me. It's nice, makes you seem powerful. For the record, I apologize for busting in here the way I did, it was a bad idea."

"But?" she asked. Gabriella evaluated me, her eyes sizing me up like I was a horse or a side of beef.

Our gazes met and her eyes widened as she felt me slip inside the doorway to her soul just long enough to send a message: *You still haven't answered my question* and then withdraw. It flustered her and in that scant second, her mask of composure dropped and I saw a snapshot of the woman she must have been when John Paul Courtney knew her. Then she was back in control, the strange social vampire she'd become was back in force. Tabitha was right. She'd said the High Society vamps all became caricatures of themselves. The human that she'd been had felt nice, wholesome, virtuous, well-mannered. A lady that a guy like me or, if he'd really once been as much like me as he claimed, a guy like John Paul Courtney, could have pined after from afar . . . afraid that if we touched her, she'd be sullied.

"What time is it, Beatrice?" Lady Gabriella asked.

"Fifteen minutes until one, milady."

"You said you were going to steal something from Lord Phillip?"

I sighed. "Yeah, the Stone of Aorta or something. I'll probably have to kill him for it. He's the fat little bald fucker, right?"

Lady Gabriella had been drinking another sip of blood when I spoke. It shot out her nose, beginning a coughing fit I'd rarely seen a vampire experience. "He is, indeed, as you described," she said after regaining her composure. "That's . . . very industrious. May I ask why?"

"He fucked with my offspring without my permission. He's got something I want. It's Christmas in Void City and I want peace on Earth and ill will toward vampires. Pick a reason. And you still haven't answered my question."

"I'm not going to answer your question, Eric." She smiled when she said it. "So, you aren't interested in Roger?"

"Oh, no. I'm probably gonna kill him, too," I told her. "For one thing, he tried to sell me out to a demon . . ." I let my words trail off. A demon. If Rachel had demon sex magic, then she was supposed to be working for a demon, not for Roger. So why was she with him unless Roger and the demon were still working together?

"Yes?" Gabriella asked, snapping me out of my reverie.

"Since you're his mommy, I won't run down the whole list."

Gabriella looked smug. She'd been smug since Beatrice told her the time. "That is unfortunate. I cared very deeply for Roger. Still, he was an embarrassment for me. In some ways, it is for the best."

What did the time have to do with anything? I was still rolling around the idea of Roger, Rachel, and the demon. Which demon? Was it Jill? He wasn't a succubus, but that didn't mean he didn't have access to someone that could have taught Rachel the dark tantra. "I could make you tell me, you know."

"I don't think you could," Gabriella said. "You've too much of your—would he be your great-great grandfather?—in you. The righteous indignation, the posturing . . . it's all very useful when you're fighting werewolves, but not against vampires. He learned that the hard way. So will you. I have little doubt that you're capable of ending me without ever regretting it, but beating me, torturing me, forcing your way into my mind and stripping the answers from my brain . . . no." She touched my hand. "You could never do that."

She was right. If she'd been a man, I wouldn't have had any issues. Call me old-fashioned, but the idea of torturing a woman, of beating information out of her, made me want to vomit. I've sunk low since joining the ranks of the dead, but not that low.

"Come on, Beatrice," I said as I stood. "We've wasted enough of Gabby's time. She needs her beauty rest."

Beatrice hesitated, lingering at her mistress's side.

"I'm sorry, Beatrice," Gabriella told her. "But I did offer you to him and I'm afraid he has accepted. I'll have Esteban take your things . . . ?"

"To the Pollux," I answered, "across the street from where the Demon Heart was. But don't worry about that yet. I'll send somebody back for them."

We left, and as we walked down the stairs, I was greeted by the sight of thirty-seven thralls packed into the court-yard. One by one, they introduced themselves on behalf of some vampire or other and one by one they offered their assistance.

"What the hell?" I looked to Beatrice for an explanation.

"As far as they know, you broke through impenetrable wards just to question a Master. Combine that with your coming back from an explosion many were convinced would be the end of you and your recent destruction of Sweetheart Row and the vampire running it, I believe the inhabitants of the Highland Towers have sent their thralls around to make sure they aren't next in line for a visit."

I guess announcing myself to the entire building had been a bad idea, though it had certainly managed to stir up paranoia among the Highland Tower residents. A man walked past us carrying a toolbox like none I'd ever seen. He pushed his way through the crowd, opened his box, and began performing a magic ritual near Gabriella's door.

Gabriella stood in the doorway.

"I see, the trouble is right here. Looks like they fouled up the wards when you had the courtyard redone," the man said.

"Thank you for coming so quickly, Maurice."

He smiled at her in a cheerful handyman sort of way. "I get paid to hurry. You're top of the priorities list according to Lord Phillip, right under him.

"Huh, that's weird." He pulled a length of twisted hair from around the sill.

"What is that?" she asked.

"A gaff knot." He walked to the other window and felt around carefully, crossed both fingers, and withdrew a matching string. "It—"

"Fix it first, then explain it," she snapped.

Why the rush? I thought to myself. A thin sheen of

bloody sweat formed on Gabriella's upper lip. Why was she sweating?

"Melvin's a good mage, Lady Gabriella, it's not like him to be sloppy like this. A gaff knot is something magicians can use when they are working with a ward they didn't make. It holds the ward back so that they can do surface work, like painting, putting in new windows. He must have just left them up by mistake." He pulled another from around the door frame. "Maybe the wards were interfering with the paint they used on the wall. Was it an eternal mix?"

Melvin?

Gabriella nodded. "Yes, he said it would never need re-painting and would be self-repairing—"

As she spoke, the wall began doing just that. Bits of wood, paint, and plaster flowed up the wall like a videotape played in slow reverse.

"It is. All you had to do was pull the gaff knots. It's not like him to miss that, but anyone can make a mistake." He snapped the strings with his hands and gave them to Gabriella. He tilted his head at the same odd angle I'd often seen Magbidion use. "Yep. The wards are in place and the wall should be back to normal in ten or fifteen minutes. Anything else?"

"Will the ward hold even without the wall?"

"Sure," he answered. "It's only selectively permeable at the door, windows, and air vents."

"Air vents?"

"In case owners want to sneak into their own apartment

in animal forms," Maurice answered. Maurice . . . mages and their damn *M* names.

Gabriella smiled at me.

"I believe I will give you a partial answer to your question, Eric." She waited a beat. "One of the two people for whom you were looking?"

"Yeah?"

"She should make it back to the Pollux any time now."

Gabriella closed the door. Two seconds later I felt a terrible screaming in my mind. My new thrall sense told me that they were in pain. The Pollux was on fire. My children were burning and I could smell the smoke, feel their terror. I felt like Obi-Wan Kenobi when Alderaan was destroyed. I was thirty minutes away and that was about twenty-nine minutes too far. One by one the screams began to fade. Greta winked out last. Gabriella was right, though . . . now I knew where Rachel was.

❖ 29 ❖

TABITHA:

BURNING DOWN THE HOUSE

Flames. That's not what woke me up. I think it was the smoke, because the first thing I remember is choking, coughing so hard my lungs burned. Hot air. Too hot and thick to breathe, but I had to breathe. Why did I have to breathe?

"Eric?" I called out.

Heart pounding, I rolled out of the bed and onto the floor, because smoke rises and you're supposed to be able to breathe better on the floor. Blood coursed through my veins as if I were still human. I could even taste the smoke.

"Talbot?"

Whose bedroom was this? I couldn't remember. I didn't recognize it. There was a blond woman, cold and dead, lying on the bed. Greta. Right, Greta was a vampire—Eric's daughter or something. Someone was laughing. The fire was blue, not orange. Why blue fire? Natural gas?

In the doorway I got my explanation. Rachel was laughing, wreathed in flames, but untouched by them. "You should have stayed at the Highland Towers, sis."

"Rachel?" I still didn't know how she'd come back, but the gleam of hatred in her eyes . . . that I recognized. She'd looked at me with those same hate-filled eyes the last time I saw her in the hospital, two days before she died, when she'd begged me to find a way to save her. I'd been at her funeral. It had been open casket. I'd even gone back later to check the grave because my boyfriend was a vampire and I'd been totally scared that something weird would happen to her body. "Rachel! What are you doing?"

She smiled at me before turning away, closing the door behind her. Even over the sound of the flames I heard the lock. Eric had a dead bolt on the door that worked with a key on both sides. I dived for the door with all the vampiric speed I could muster, which was none at all. Sweat ran down my cheek, human sweat. I was stuck. I always had trouble using my vampire powers at their fullest when I'd been seeming human, but it had never been this bad before.

The clock on Eric's wall said it was just after one in the afternoon. I was awake during the day! I pounded on the door. My vampire strength was a no-show, too. I was practically human. Great, my coolest vampire gift was going to get me burned to a crisp!

"Shit!"

On top of everything else, I was so hungry I could barely stand, not blood hungry, either. My stomach growled more angrily than it had when I'd gone on the negative-calorie diet. By day seven, when I couldn't stand to eat any more cabbage soup, it was easier to starve myself.

Fire moved across the ceiling and the walls with a purpose. It curled and twisted, spreading slowly in some directions and more quickly in others as if driven by some sinister intelligence. God, it was hot.

I pulled myself up to my knees. On the bed, Greta's arm was on fire and she still wasn't waking up. I grabbed her foot and tugged her partway off the bed, took another breath, and pulled her the rest of the way down. Her head hit the hardwood floor with a sickening thud and I slapped at the eldritch fire on her arm with my hands.

"Wake up!" I screamed in her ear.

Greta slowly opened one eye, her mouth lolling open before she began to speak.

"What's burning?" she asked thickly.

"The Pollux is on fire!" I yelled at her.

Her head went limp and her left eye slowly started to close, so I slapped her as hard as I could. Pain lanced through my hand and I coughed out an "ow."

Greta opened both eyes and bared her fangs with deliberate threat. I tried to bare mine back, but nothing happened.

"I don't usually wake up so slow," Greta told me. Each word left her lips in a tangle, slurred like she was drunk. "Something's wrong. Is it daytime? So . . . tired."

She leaned back sharply and I shook her awake again. She was heavier than I thought she'd be.

In the distance I heard people screaming, like they were being burned alive.

"Holy shit!"

"Keep it away from me," Greta mumbled, "I'm allergic to holy stuff. Are there any cookies left? Could you eat one for me? I love to watch people eat cookies."

"Cookies?"

"Smells like cinnamon," she continued.

"We've got to get out of here," I told her. The Pollux was old and the wood was dry like kindling. I dropped Greta and crawled over to the door. After kicking it a couple of times to confirm that I wasn't strong enough to open it, I crawled back to Greta and pulled her to her feet. Tongues of fire engulfed the doorway and the smoke was so thick I could barely see standing up. Greta was beginning to doze off again, so I kicked her in the stomach. She snapped at me, but was too slow.

"You need to open that door, or we are both going to burn to ashes," I told her.

She looked at the door and then looked back at me without comprehension. "What door? That's a fireplace."

"What would Eric do?" I whispered to myself. "Eric would turn into something and knock down the door." Not an option for me at the moment. Okay, I wasn't strong enough and Greta wasn't awake enough. I tried to think it through and then the plan hit me. I got behind Greta and shoved her at the door as hard as I could. She hit it headfirst and flames ignited her hair. Hands pulling at her flaming tresses, Greta screamed.

I had never heard anybody scream like that before. Pure terror and agony were embodied in the sound that left her throat and all I could do was hope that she found the presence of mind to stop messing with her hair and knock down the door.

"Please, please, please," I muttered as I crouched down on the floor. Greta took off running in the wrong direction, blinded by pain. She crashed into the shower, rupturing the pipes. My eyes closed from the stinging smoke as the water washed over her. It was almost impossible to breathe and my body didn't seem too convinced that it no longer needed to perform that most basic of functions. Being stuck as a Living Doll was a pretty cruel trick. One, because I didn't want to be human right now and two, because seeming alive was going to get me killed. Coughs wracked my body and I couldn't talk anymore, couldn't stand, couldn't do anything but keep on coughing. A roar came from the shower, and I thought I heard Greta scream a single word. "Out." She charged across the room at the door, fangs bared, and claws extended. The door exploded outward unleashing Greta, screaming, into the hall.

On my hands and knees, I went after her. Outside of the bedroom things looked even worse; the floor was collapsing and the roof was on fire. All of it was glowing a sickening blue.

Greta plunged through a hole, flames trailing from her clothing, screaming all the way down to the first floor. She charged through the wall like a rhinoceros, still shrieking, still burning, heading for the parking deck. If I could get to the deck, then I would be safe from the fire. As for the sun, well, maybe we could stay low and to the middle. Or maybe, like this, so convincingly human, I could even fool the sun.

I looked down through the smoking jagged hole. Below, the flaming wreck of the floor stared up at me. Seeming human or not, I realized I was going to have to jump, as Greta had. Even as I fell, I saw a board sticking up at just the wrong angle and tried to twist out of the way.

Breathing no longer hurt because my breathing had stopped. I had stopped. I lay like a broken rag doll in the middle of the fire, with a two-by-four jutting out of my chest as tendrils of fire licked my body. I didn't catch fire the way Greta had, but my skin blistered and bubbled in the heat.

I'd been shot through the heart once, before the Demon Heart had blown up. Even that hadn't really hurt until the bolt had been pulled out, but being burned hurt a lot. The roaring crackle of the fire reminded me of the winters I'd spent with my grandfather in Vermont. I couldn't close my eyes, but the smoke was so thick I couldn't see anything, so it was easy to picture him in front of the fire, laughing and calling my name.

"Tabitha!" A voice that was not Grandpa's called out from behind me in the smoke. It sounded like Talbot's voice, but smaller. Little padded footsteps ran toward me as my back began to smolder. I was going to catch fire. I really didn't want to; Greta's screams had been, well, awful. Above me, the flooring began to creak dangerously. I was surprised to be so calm . . . must have been the wood in my heart.

Before I had too much time to think about burning to death, I was lifted up off of the plank and carried through the lobby, out through the hole in the wall and into the sun. I couldn't get enough air to scream. Just as quickly, we were in the shade of the parking deck, my clothes still smoldering. Talbot dropped me onto the cement and began patting me all over. "If Eric asks," he said, "I am only touching you to keep you from catching fire."

"Okay," I nodded. He looked around the parking deck and then back at the Pollux. His clothes looked awful. They were actually still smoldering in places. Greta had also made it to the parking deck. I saw her briefly, horribly burned, lying under a parked car.

"I don't suppose either of you thought to grab your cell phone?" Talbot chuckled exhaustedly. "I think mine is somewhere in the Pollux"—he patted his empty pockets—"next to my wallet, keys, Eric's thralls." Talbot sniffed the air. "Do you smell cinnamon?"

That was the last thing I heard before falling asleep.

✦ 30 ✦

ERIC:

REWIND

Roger just keeps blowing up my shit!" I grabbed the table in front of me and flung it into the ceiling where it stuck feetfirst like a crazy dart.

Several of the assembled humans didn't even flinch. A few even managed to compliment me on my accuracy. Others stared at me with patient wariness. *Is he going to kill us now?* I imagined them asking themselves. I'd already done a number on Gabriella's courtyard. Shards of broken magic glass lay scattered over the courtyard's meticulously tended grass. *I hear when he doesn't know what to do, he just grabs whoever is nearest and forces himself on them. I hope he eats Malloy, I'm so tired of listening to him whine about his master's inner turmoil.* Practiced neutral expressions surrounded me at every turn.

"Is there anything I can do to assist you, Highness?" asked a diminutive man in a cricket uniform. His jaunty little cap looked so funny and he wore it so seriously that I nearly laughed.

"Trouble at home," I told him.

A man from the back produced a bottle of wine that smelled like blood. "Blood wine, Sire?"

"Wine?" I asked.

"It's much like wine, Highness," a fetching young woman in a purple business suit offered, "but it's actually made of human blood, so it's completely compatible with your dietary restrictions. My mistress has also sent a bottle if you'd care to try it."

"Is that anything like blood booze?" I asked. My question was greeted with thunderous assent, that yes, it was, but far more expensive and with a taste that actually resembled wine.

"How many of you brought bottles of this blood wine?" I asked.

Soon seven bottles sat on the table and I wondered if getting drunk would really dull the pain of loss I was trying not to feel. If Tabitha was dead . . . if Greta was dead . . .

I closed my eyes to fight back the emotions and took long, deep breaths.

"Impressive, Highness," offered some dumb brunette, "and quite convincing."

I looked at Beatrice and my voice trembled when I spoke. "What do I say if I don't want to offend anybody, but I'd just as soon they all fucked off?"

No one even blinked as she turned to translate. "His Highness, the Lord Eric, wishes to convey his humble thanks for the gifts and offers of assistance." She fingered a strand of her own red hair, twisting it, the only outward sign of nervousness. "He gladly accepts your tokens of esteem and will be certain to relay more proper gratitude at another time. Unfortunately," she glanced up at the remains of the magic ceiling, the table I'd thrown obscuring the artistic sun overhead, "as the sun shines overhead, the eyelids of the immortal grow heavy and Lord Eric finds himself in need of rest.

"If you'd all leave your cards on the table," she gestured to a little white tea cart that had survived my wrath, "to ensure that the good intentions of your Masters and Mistresses are not forgotten and then file quickly and quietly out of the courtyard, it would be most appreciated."

She clasped her hands in front of her and smiled. Like magic, they filed past and vanished, leaving only little squares of paper and seven bottles of wine to mark their passing.

"Thanks, Bea. Do you mind if I call you Bea?"

"Anything you wish to call me would be—"

"None of that slave shit," I interrupted. "You're a person. What do you like to be called?"

Beatrice scoffed and her full pouting lips drew up into a very brief smile. "Well, my real name is Tina, but Lady Gabriella preferred Beatrice."

"Do you like Tina?" I asked.

She nodded, "But I'd rather keep Beatrice, if it's to your liking, Master. I said good-bye to Tina a long, long time ago."

"Then you're Beatrice. Do you want to go back to Gabby, Beatrice?"

"Sire?" Those beautiful gray eyes of hers lit up at that suggestion, but her expression changed to a more pensive one and she started twisting a lock of hair again, putting the tip of it on the corner of her mouth as she thought. "You wouldn't be offended?"

My laughter was a foreign bitter thing. "I think I'm going to get totally wasted and then act really stupid. If I make it through that okay, then you can come back to me if you want." I stood up and sent the chair in which I'd been sitting up into the ceiling to join the table. It didn't stick, falling back to the floor with a crash. "See, I'm not having the best luck lately. I mean, sure, I did come back from complete and utter obliteration recently, and now my car is a vampire, too, which is cool. It's pretty damn neat to watch him run over stuff . . . squirrels, armadillos . . . other vampires."

Beatrice's mouth fell open. My eyes locked onto a single strand of hair that stuck to her lips when the large lock fell free. "You have a vampire car?"

"It *could* be a zombie car, I guess. It eats meat, too . . . not just blood. Either way, it's definitely undead."

"Really?"

"And that ain't all of it," I said. "See, on top of that, I have to deal with all this trippy shit about me not really being a Vlad, but some legendary one-in-a-million, oh-no-we've-got-to-deal-with-one-of-these-crazy-sons-of-bitches type of vamp."

"Trippy shit?" Beatrice frowned.

"Oh, yeah, I've got trippy shit out the waz. You know how that Ebon Winter guy can turn into mist?"

She nodded. "It's very rare. He and Lord Phillip are the only vampires in the city who can do it."

"Well, I can turn into a fucking ghost, revenant, whatever, and the reason—you'll like this—the reason everybody fucks with me is because when I get really pissed off, I turn into some kind of uber vamp with purple eyes, leather wings, and the ability to control frickin' bats."

Beatrice took a hit off of the blood wine, wiped the top of the bottle and passed it across to me. I took a swig and shook my head. I've never liked wine, but it did taste different than blood and different is good. After another drink I continued, "Only now, one of my thralls, who isn't really my thrall, but some sort of thrall double agent, has been screwing around with me using some sort of sex magic."

I chugged the rest of the bottle. It's easier to do when you don't have to breathe. "Lord, this is nasty! Plus, you really don't want to get me drunk. The last time I got drunk, there was hockey and werewolves."

"You're the guy who killed the Void City Howlers?" she asked.

I opened a new bottle, wondering where my buzz was. "This shit doesn't have any kick at all," I complained.

"Let me see." Beatrice reached for the bottle, examining the label. "It's the cheap stuff." She went through the other bottles until she found one with some guy named Duke Gornsvalt's name on the label.

"Try this one. It's the real deal. Lady Gabriella buys a bottle of his champagne every year for New Year's Eve. When he's done with it, it doesn't even look like blood anymore."

"Really?"

"I heard that he once made a run of blood vodka for Lord Phillip. It took him thirty years to make five bottles."

I opened the bottle. It was a white wine. I hated white wine when I was alive, but the taste . . . it was very different from blood. It also had more kick to it than I remembered wine having. Another swallow and I remembered John Paul Courtney. "Oh, and I forgot . . . I've got a ghostly cowboy hanging around in my pistol." I reached into my jacket pocket and flashed her the gun butt.

"And you say you were obliterated?"

I nodded.

"How?" she asked.

"Blessed explosives."

"Then I'm coming with you." She took my arm and the warmth of her cut through my mood. Body heat will get a vampire every time. "I became a thrall because the world of the vampires was supposed to be mysterious and exciting and so far it's been mostly politics. This is as close as I've come to mysterious and exciting."

Great. Another groupie.

"One thing first, Bea." I held my hand out for the bottle and she slid it back to me. "You don't, like, want to hump me or anything, do you?"

She wrinkled her nose at me. "Um . . . no. Not to offend you, but ewww. You're dead and I'm not a necrophiliac. If I become a vampire someday, then maybe but—"

"Good," I interrupted. "Then you can come along." I stood up and thought about draining the bottle. I wanted to go charging across town to the Pollux, see if I could help, but didn't see the point. If they were gone, then they were gone. Grief welled up and I felt it die, cut off, like water from a spigot.

"Rachel's alive," I murmured.

"Hmmm?"

"Never mind." I put the bottle on the table and gestured at the hall. "I have to wake up Phil," I said tiredly. "If we're lucky, he'll just fucking kill me and put me out of my misery 'cause the Bend Over Festival is starting to wear very thin."

✦ 31 ✦

ERIC:
STONED

The grain of the wood ran from purple to black on Phillip's door; it was a beautiful piece of workmanship. Dennis came through the open doorway carrying an empty platter that smelled of burgers, fries, and orange soda. I got out of his way. Beatrice grabbed a chair in the lobby and waited for the excitement to begin.

"The children are safely ensconced within the Lady Tabitha's suite, Lord Eric. I have one of the Highland's day-care workers upstairs with them now to make certain they don't get into any trouble while their mother rests."

"Thanks." It's like thralls were stray dogs and I was every mutt's sucker.

"I see you've been admiring our door," he offered. "It's—"

"Brazilian rosewood, I know," I interrupted. "My parents had a bed veneered with it. It's still around somewhere, I'm just not sure what happened to it. Roger would know."

Dennis nodded. "How interesting. Is there anything else I can do for you before I retire? Lord Phillip's sleeping schedule is very erratic and I need to be rested when he awakens."

I grasped his shoulder. "How long is Ebony going to be like that?"

"I don't know." He shrugged. "Did you really break her thralldom by force?"

"Yeah," I said in an aggravated tone. "I guess that's what I did."

"I'll summon the nurse and have her take a look." Dennis headed for the door expecting me to release his shoulder, but I didn't comply. "Was there something else?" he asked.

"Get Phil's happy ass out of bed," I told him. His expression told me that there was no way in Hell he was going to obey that request. It wasn't a request. I knew that I was pushing everything and everyone too far, but I had nothing more to lose. If I stopped to think about everything, I was afraid I'd be paralyzed by my emotions. Maybe that was Roger's plan. Blow up the Pollux and hope I got myself killed when I rampaged through the Highland Towers . . . or maybe he just wanted me to feel like I had nothing left to lose. Marilyn was gone, everyone I knew and cared for had been eliminated . . . That didn't feel like a plan Roger would have come up with, it was too subtle, but a demon . . .

"Look, I know you don't want to and I know that he's going to be angry. You probably think you'd rather die or something, but I promise you"—my voice became a whisper—"if Phil doesn't get his ass in gear, then I'm going to kick in that door and take what I'm looking for."

"The wards here will cut you to ribbons," he told me.

Shoving past him, I walked up to the inner door and twisted the handle. A sensation similar to the one I'd felt upon entering the Highland Towers washed over me and I heard that same ghostly voice from before, the one that let me in the lobby door. "You are expected."

The door opened easily, no sign of a shock or any wards in place, and I stepped inside the room of someone who read way too many books. I smelled blood and death. Three bodies total, I was guessing, very likely the girls I'd seen earlier when I'd done the mental peeping tom thing.

"You may not—" was all Dennis got out before another voice cut him off.

"All is well, Dennis. Do not hinder that which cannot be hindered. I am awake," came a voice from behind a large velvet curtain. The bodies were behind that curtain, and the bed. "*Integer vitae scelerisque purus.* Heh, not exactly, but in a way, I suppose."

"Untouched by life and free of wickedness?" I said by way of translation. "Not exactly, but I really don't give a shit about your delusions. I'm just here for—"

Although he was fat and short, Phillip could move. He appeared before me grinning and in his dressing gown. The curtains didn't even rustle. His smile reminded me of

Scrooge's in that movie when he realizes that the ghosts have done their work all in one night and he still has time to make it all right before Tiny Tim gets dead. His whole appearance seemed false. He held a finger next to his nose and dashed across the room and around a corner.

"Aw, I really don't need this crap today, old man. I just . . . Jesus Christ!" A vampire in a glass case stared at me from across the room, a stake through his heart. He was supported by a human-size metal doll stand, only instead of clasping over his clothes like the ones Greta'd had for her Barbies, it snaked beneath the rear of his tweed jacket. The vamp's colorless eyes stared blankly through gold-rimmed spectacles with round lenses. They didn't move, but I felt like he was watching me . . . aware. His expression had been frozen in the midst of what was either a smirk or one of those you'll-never-change-will-you looks that I often get.

He'd become undead past his prime, but his good looks hadn't been eroded. The crow's-feet around his eyes made him look distinguished rather than old. I had him beat there, though. No wrinkles. He had to have been a good ten years or so older than me, physically. With the stake through his heart, there was no way I could tell how long he'd been a vampire. I hoped the bulk of it hadn't been spent in the case.

"My dear Percy, who serves as a remembrance to all that I do not bluff, I do not make empty threats, and there are indeed worse fates than death," I read aloud from the plaque at the base. "You are one twisted dude, Phil, but don't think that means that you can't—"

Phillip reappeared and pushed something into my hand, cupping both of his hands around mine. His earnest gaze met mine and he seemed both utterly at ease and pleased with himself. "The Stone of Aeternum? Yes? Here it is. I wanted to get this out of the way first thing so that we can enjoy our conversation. Would you like some wine? I believe you'll find I have a much better stock than Lady Gabriella. Ah, I almost forgot! How could I forget; I had it made just for you. I hope you'll like it."

He sped past me, through the open door, and out into the hallway. "Dennis! Go down to the cellar and bring up the special black case, the one from Duke Gornsvalt. Be very careful with it, it took him"—he looked me up and down—"fifteen years to manage it correctly. Oh! Oh! And have Brigitte prepare the special menu. Two for him and one for me. Oh, this will be marvelous."

Infectious as his excitement was, I still noticed the way Beatrice's breathing changed when he entered the hallway to speak with Dennis. Her heart rate sped up, not out of control, but different. I looked at Percy and wondered what the poor bastard had done to become a knickknack.

In my hand, I held a small black stone that might or might not really be the Stone of Aeternum. There was no label and it didn't seem very special. It didn't glow and it didn't hum; it just sat there like a rough lump of coal. It was an interesting dilemma; how would I know the real stone? Could I take this guy's word on it?

"So I'm just supposed to believe that you'd give me this powerful magic rock without a fight when guys like . . ." I struggled to remember the name properly, "J'iliol'lth would kill for it?"

Phillip walked back into the room and looked down at his dressing gown. "I haven't even dressed for dinner," he said with dismay. "Just a moment." Darting past me toward the bodies I'd smelled, he slipped behind a large burgundy-colored curtain that hung from floor to ceiling. Several minutes later he emerged dressed in a business suit that was so well tailored it made even him look a little dashing. "That's better. I do hope you'll pardon the delay. One makes preparations well in advance and then when the happy moment arrives, it's always rush, rush, rush. You were saying?"

"The Stone of Aeternum." I held it out to him. "How am I supposed to know it's the real deal?"

"That, I will leave to your own good judgment. Which, if you'll pardon my saying so, you are quite lacking. Good judgment, I mean, and therefore, hopefully you may rely on mine." Nearly floating as he walked, he moved to a large overstuffed chair and sat down. "By all means, be seated. Dennis should be here shortly with our order."

I sat down in the only other chair I saw, giving it a surreptitious kick to see if it was really an orange-scaled demon that was going to grab me. It smelled like Tabitha, though I knew she hadn't been here in days. "The Stone," I said, "seriously—"

"Come, come, Eric, my friend, if I wanted to give you a fake stone, I could have done so. I could have made it quite impressive, with an eerie glow and a subtle hum, a palpable sense of electricity gently pulsing through it, and fixed it up so that when you gazed into it you would have felt a sense of the infinite, the eternal. You would have known, just by looking at it, that eternity was confined within and you would have felt comforted by that fact. I chose, instead, to bestow upon you the actual item. Why should it be so hard to believe? I often bestow items of value upon interesting new vampires when we meet. Like the necklace I gave your . . . the one I gave Tabitha."

"The diamond necklace?" I asked.

"The very same. It has quite a history."

Yeah, I didn't like this guy. He seemed sincere enough, but it seems a lot of clever bastards use truths to tell their lies. Like the chair that still smelled like Tabitha. A guy like Phillip wouldn't have accidentally done that. He wanted to see how I'd react—more High Society bullshit.

32

TABITHA:

I'LL KILL HIM

Rough hands touched my shoulders while I slept. The nicest little dream I would never remember left my mind as I was rolled over. Gasoline and butane mixed together in a noxious chemical odor. I stretched and opened my eyes, expecting somehow to see Eric toweling off in the sink and griping about some new accident with his car. We'd make love and then . . . But the hands did not belong to Eric. A hard-looking mercenary in Void City Police Department SWAT gear crouched over me with one hand on my breast. My heart was still beating and I woke the rest of the way with a start.

"Get off of me!" I shouted, immediately attempting to change into a cat. Nothing happened. There was a barely perceptible tingle, almost as if the part of me that controlled my powers was asleep and trying to wake. . . . So I responded the old-fashioned way, with a knee to the groin. In most places it's not wise to assault a cop, but in The Void, you do what you need to do and if you're in the wrong, then you pay the Fang Fee and move along.

He fell back onto the concrete with a grunt and I pulled myself up and took in my surroundings. A large 3-B stenciled on the wall let me know that I was on the third level of the parking deck, but it didn't tell me where Talbot had run off to or why he'd left me here. Two more cops stood behind me. One had an assault rifle and the other had what looked like a flamethrower, not standard equipment for a task force that is usually cleaning up after vampires, not gunning for them. Both wore headsets and identical crew cuts, neither wore a helmet like the one the man I'd knocked down was wearing.

"Alpha-One to Big Top, we have a possible human bystander here." He paused, listening to someone on the other end, while the friend of his I'd kneed in the groin stood up slowly. He was wearing a headset, too. "She's got a heartbeat, Big Top." He sniffed the air loudly. "Plus the nose knows, you know?"

Didn't the blood on my shirt and the big hole in my chest clue these morons in? Then again, if they were real VCPD, they wouldn't assume. "Possible human" left room for the chance that I might be a shape-shifter. Living doesn't guarantee mundane, not in Void City. I touched my chest, then looked down. I had already healed. There was lots of blood, but it might have looked like I'd been attacked—if you were an idiot.

"Understood. Detaining subject for ID."

"Like Hell," I told them. I saw another three cops sweeping the uphill slope of the deck. The two groups I could see were organized into three-person teams: one man with a spear, another with an assault rifle, and a third with a flamethrower. One would run the spear under a car while the others would line up to shoot anything that came out from under it.

The other team was only one car away from the Le Baron Greta was under and I couldn't tell if there were more on other levels. Eric's parking deck was old school—narrow, circular parking levels wrapped around a central spiral for ascent and descent. Where the heck was Talbot? His powers had been working just fine the last time I'd seen him.

A gunshot would hurt, but fire could do worse, so I charged the one with the flamethrower first, much to the surprise of all three men. Did they think I was going to just stand there—even if I wasn't a vampire—while they called for backup?

On that note, I screamed, "Rape!" When I'd turned thirteen I'd gone from having almost no breasts at all to having the D-cups I have now. One of the first things my mother had done, almost before taking me to buy bras, was to enroll me in a self-defense class. My instructor had said to yell "Fire!" but I figured the fire was old news.

The one with the assault rifle dropped it with a curse and reached out to grab me, but I was already barreling at the man with the flamethrower. He also looked surprised and tried to hold up his hand to ward me off. I kept screaming "Rape!" and kicked him solidly in the knee. A loud snap let me know I'd done real damage and he went down to one knee.

I screamed "No!" and "Rape!" again, as I turned on the nearest man. He grabbed my left arm and I grabbed his right ear. My defense class instructor had told us that it only takes eight pounds of pressure to tear off the human ear. He was right.

Assault-Rifle-Guy grabbed the side of his head and screamed. Those self-defense classes were worthless against vampires, werewolves, and Talbot, but the basic principles worked just fine against humans.

"Fuck!" yelled the man with the spear. "What the hell is wrong with you, lady?"

The second team headed toward me and I went for the assault rifle. I had no idea how to fire it other than the point, aim, and pull the trigger lessons my dad had given me at age eight. I guess that was Dad's southern version of gun safety. My hand had just touched the butt of the gun when the man with the spear stomped my fingers and hit me in the temple with the butt of his spear hard enough to cross my eyes. I fell to my hands and knees, a boot on my back between my shoulders.

"Ma'am, we may be moonlighting, but we're still cops. Calm the fuck down. Nobody is raping anybody here."

"Bitch ripped off my ear!" the more injured cop yelled behind me. "I'm gonna kill her."

I heard him charge, his feet slapping the concrete as he ran. A scuffle started behind me between the guys who had run over to help and the cop who'd lost an ear. A third team headed our way, coming from a higher level. I flinched when they passed Greta's hiding place. "What the hell are you guys doing over here?" yelled one of the newcomers. "We ran into two civilians. Our team managed to deal with them without this kind of shit. Mirror test. Pulse. Move on. Mirror test. Pulse. Move on. How complicated is that for you assholes?"

"I woke up and one of them was on top of me," I said with as much false panic as I could muster. "He ripped up my top and he had his hands on my breasts. They were trying to shove something in my mouth to gag me. I don't know what's going on here and I don't want to know, just get them off of me! Don't let them hurt me anymore. I'll do what you want, just stop hurting me. You can have my wallet, my keys, you can even . . . h-have sex with me if you want, but . . . I don't want to die," I said as I sobbed convincingly.

"Shit!" said one of the other newcomers. The name on his vest was *Stacey* and he was older than the others, heavier set, but still in shape. He was bald, with a bushy brown mustache. "I knew it was a mistake to bring you in on this one, Baxter. If her memory needs adjusting, you're paying for it. I don't care how much it costs to put that kid of yours into the Ellery Academy, do you understand me?"

"She's lying, Captain," said the one with the boot on my back. I tried to pop my claws, but the only response was a sharp pain in my fingertips, a pinprick. "We took her pulse and found out she was human, but they wanted us to hold her for ID. Then she freaked out on us."

"Edwards," Captain Stacey snapped. "What the fuck happened? You're supposed to be keeping these new guys in line."

"Look, Captain, I had to take a piss," said the guy who had been holding the flamethrower. "When I came up, Baxter was on top of her with his hand up her shirt and she freaked out. What happened before that I don't know, but I didn't touch anybody any place." His voice trembled when he spoke, somewhere between fear and pain.

"Radio Big Top," Captain Stacey said to the man next to him. "I don't like talking to her."

He complied. "Big Top, this is Bravo-Two, Alpha group has a half-naked bleeding human up here who says they tried to physically assault her. What's your ETA?"

He waited, listening. I missed my vampire hearing. Why wasn't it working and why was I stuck seeing human? Was seeming human the only way I could wake up in daylight? It made sense. Ordinarily, I'd have slept through the whole thing . . . been burned up in the fire. My powers hadn't almost gotten me killed; they'd saved me the only way they could.

"Big Top's walking up the stairs now," said Bravo-Two.

Stacey shook his head. "You guys better hope your story checks out or you're going to wish that Miss Thang here had finished the job she started on you."

"He's hurting me," I complained weakly. "God, my chest . . . I can barely breathe." I started wheezing and choking. Whoever Big Top was, I didn't want to be here when she arrived.

"Baxter, get off of her and step back." Captain Stacey spit on the ground. "She's got two men with assault rifles aimed at her. She isn't going anywhere."

"She's lying," said the man with his boot on my back, but he did take his foot off of me. I scooted quickly away from them and put my back against the concrete riser at the outer edge of the deck. A small ray of sunshine was only inches from my foot. Could I seem human enough to fool the sun? If I couldn't, they'd sure as hell figure out I was a vampire when I caught fire.

I froze and then tucked my legs up against me, hugging them and began to rock back and forth. "Just let me go," I said over and over again, my head buried in my knees. "Just let me go. I won't tell anyone. I'll go straight home and I won't talk to anybody. I'll quit my job and I'll just move and you won't have to worry about me saying anything, just please don't kill me."

"Calm down, ma'am." Stacey frowned at me as he spoke and I wondered if I'd oversold my performance. "I know this doesn't make a whole lot of sense, but we're sweeping this deck for vampires."

"Feels weird working for a demon, though, Cap," Edwards whispered.

"His money spends just the same," Stacey snarled. "Now shut up."

High heels clicked on concrete and I heard the men step back for someone. I looked up and a woman in an obviously expensive green suit looked down at me. It was Rachel. Behind her, floating in some kind of mystic chains, was Talbot—alive, but gagged. It clicked. "Shit," I cursed angrily. Esteban had been delivering the Infernal Chains of Sarno Rayus to Rachel. They moved like snakes, twisting and altering anytime Talbot tried to shift, the gentle metallic tinkle as the links clinked together providing further proof they were the same chains that had been in Esteban's leather satchel.

"Like the chains?" Rachel teased. "Pretty cool, huh?"

"Shit," I cursed again.

"Did she pass the mirror test?" asked Rachel. She smiled knowingly at me as she asked, winking like this was a big joke.

"We didn't get past the pulse test," Alpha-One started.

"Idiots," Rachel hissed. "What am I paying you for? You always check the mirror first. No reflection means the target is a vampire! End of story. Pulse is second, because we don't want to murder any humans." Taking a deep breath, I exhaled and then stood up.

Captain Stacey hocked up a bit of phlegm and spit it on the concrete at Rachel's feet. "You aren't paying us for anything, witch." He took a step closer to her. "The demon is paying us to help you find and detain vampires along with the fee to clean up the mess from the fire you started next door."

"Don't get smart with me, Captain."

"Smart?" Captain Stacey walked over to the glowing chains restraining Talbot. He leaned in close, the light from the chains washing the color from his skin, lending him an

absurdly angelic glow, and he sniffed the air. "Smart would
be if you told me why you're detaining a mouser on a run
where we're being paid to gather up bloodsuckers."

"Jill will pay you the extra." Rachel pulled Talbot farther
away from him. "But don't worry; I assure you that this female is a vampire."

"Of course he will . . . it's still within the estimate." Stacey
spit on the ground again, turning to look at me. "You a Living Doll?" He grinned. "You must have been showing off to
the wrong people."

"Rachel." I looked past Captain Stacey. "Why are you
doing this?"

"Oh, don't act like you give a damn about me!" she yelled.
"You knew all about vampires. You'd read all those books.
You'd even already met some of them, found your way past
the veil hiding them from everyone. Damn it, Tabitha, you
had a passport to immortality in your handbag and you
didn't even try to plead my case. You let me die!"

"This is impossible," I mouthed voicelessly.

She touched my face. "Says the undead tramp," she
scoffed. "There are ways back, sis. They aren't pleasant," she
shuddered, "and they change you, but they're better than
the alternative. I do owe you some small debt of gratitude,
though. If you hadn't been Eric's little plaything, then J'iliol'lth
wouldn't have brought me back at all. He said it made me
the perfect bait. A man—a vampire like Eric—J'iliol'lth said
there was no way he could resist the wild younger sister.
Eric was inside me before we even got back to the Pollux.
Easy-peasy."

One of the cops let out a low whistle at that. Another said, "Shit" and looked away.

"Pardon?" I said softly.

"You don't understand where I was or what they do to little witch wannabes down there. I thought it would be tough, sleeping with him, doing this to you, but it wasn't as bad as I thought. He's a very good lover. The power he gives off is intoxicating by itself, but the way he moves—well, you already know about that," Rachel said as she conjured a blue flame in the palm of her hand. It changed from blue to red to green and back again, then settled on purple. "And of course, the deal came with magic, real magic. Do you know how much I dreamed of real magic?"

She always had been more into witchcraft than vampires.

"I do," said a voice from behind her. Magbidion stepped out of the stairwell. He was washed, shaved, and wearing new clothes. It took ten years off his age.

Stacey nodded to one of his men and one of the assault rifles shifted to point at Magbidion. "I only want to talk." Magbidion held up his hands. "I sold my soul for magic, just to taste it, for one real moment. Eric is going to get me out of that deal. He's killed more demons than you've ever met. Let him take care of your problem, too."

The cops exchanged looks. I think things were getting more complicated than they'd been led to believe. Stacey turned to say something to Rachel, but she stepped around him. "I didn't have to give up my soul, old man." She laughed and ran a hand down the outside curve of her body. "Seduce Eric; get him ready for what my employer has in mind for him.

And then, when the time was right, use a little bit of borrowed pyromancy to destroy the Pollux. After that, I show up at the appointed place and time, watch the fireworks, and collect my check. I'm free and clear, though I'll still be on retainer."

"Really?" asked Magbidion. "Now, see, that's a lot better than the deal I got."

"You don't know how to negotiate." She chuckled. Six more policemen filed out of the door behind Magbidion. Two of them leveled their guns at him.

"The rest of the deck is clear, Cap," one of them yelled to Stacey.

"Kill the mage," Rachel ordered.

Captain Stacey drew his sidearm with speed that had to be more than mortal, placing it in one smooth motion against Rachel's temple. "You're past your spending limit, witch. Adding the fee for the mouser took you right to the edge of the agreed-upon estimate. We aren't taking on anything extra on credit."

"Damn it, Stacey." Rachel spoke softly, not willing to give him an excuse.

"Your boss could have given you a bigger credit line," Captain Stacey said, "but he didn't. So we're out. We swept the deck. We found your vampire and your mouser and I have a helicopter waiting for me and my men on the roof."

"Jill will—"

"Fuck Jill," Stacey said. "He's a demon. If he didn't like the contract, then he of all people should have known better than to sign it."

"Captain," I said, "take me with you."

"Do you have four hundred and seventy-five thousand dollars in cash?" Stacey asked.

I shook my head.

"Then we ain't your cavalry." His eyes flicked, showing slit pupils. "See you around, Highness." He patted Talbot's chained form as he and his men strode past, the men in the rear keeping their guns leveled in our direction.

"Just us, now." Magbidion made a gesture with his right hand. Rachel did the reverse with her left. Nothing happened that I could see, but Magbidion sighed. "I really should have stayed in the RV."

None of them had my attention. Eric had cheated on me before. It wasn't even really cheating because I'd known about it from the start. I was his, but he'd always needed more than one woman. I had believed it. I'd bought into it. He had lots of women, but I was the special one, I was the one that was his actual girlfriend. I knew he'd been sleeping with Rachel . . . I was even mostly okay with it.

But something else had clicked. "You're the girl," I said. "The one he wanted to pick for a threesome?" It was an offer I'd made him once he'd turned me, before I knew about my ability to seem human, to turn on my body heat, my heartbeat. I'd told him he could pick any one human to join us in our bed. Rachel damned Eric with a smile and my heart stopped beating. For him to sleep with her was one thing. For him to expect me to sleep with her . . . to have even considered it . . . "I'll kill him."

And then I felt them. My powers, like a slumbering beast, a tiger waking from a drugged sleep . . . the tingling numbness was gone. My jaw popped as my fangs slid firmly into place and I relished the pain when they tore through my gums.

I was awake. All of me. Anger was the key.

✦ 33 ✦

ERIC:

AN EXCESS OF INFAMY

The tantalizing odor of well-grilled beef filled the elevator shaft. Even through the two intervening doors the scent was clear and tempting. Strong food smells still made me salivate on occasion and I carefully closed my mouth and swallowed. A light *ting* announced the arrival of the elevator and when the doors opened, the aroma overcame all other smells. Phillip tapped his fingers together in guileless anticipation. I stood up to go for the door and the older vampire shooed me back into my chair.

"Let it come to you." He licked his lips, leaving a smear of blood on them. "Anticipation is a part of it. Deny yourself the expectation and you will have squandered a portion of the experience. Savor it and you will have realized the potential of the moment. The eternal must maximize all of their experiences to the utmost capacity while simultaneously leaving room for minor improvements, perhaps even arranging flaws. One does not wish to create an experience that cannot be rivaled, for fear that all future entertainments of a similar breed will—"

Beatrice opened the door for Dennis, who carried in a tray with three covered metal plates on it. Behind him, a girl who couldn't have been older than fourteen brought in a cooler and set it down. She opened a concealed closet and withdrew a small table that she placed between Phillip and myself. Dennis set the tray on the table and crossed back to the door. "Will there be anything else?" he asked.

"Thank you, Dennis," said Phillip. "Now out with you." Dennis did as instructed. "You didn't look at the girl," Phillip observed as the door closed.

"She's what, fourteen?" I said, lifting the lid off of the plate closest to me.

"Eleven." Phillip laughed. "Though everyone does guess high. She'll be astonishing when she reaches maturity."

"Yeah, maybe so, but I don't look at them until they are a bit older, you know? Like, oh, out of high school."

"I've offended you," Phillip stated.

"Don't take it personally, most undead do. That's why I have a habit of killing them. So . . . Now what, we stare at steak and talk about preteen hotties? Because if that's your idea of a good time, then I'm getting the hell out of Dodge."

"You may go, if you wish," he said sadly. "Take the Stone of Aeternum and do with it what you will. Give it to J'iliol'lth. Keep it. It is of little consequence. It will find its way back to me in time for my ascension. I have foreseen as much."

"You've foreseen it?" I asked. "What're you . . . psychic, too?"

Phillip sighed. "I had great hopes for our meeting. I've prepared for it and planned it; I was just wrong about it. It doesn't often happen to me, being wrong. You might as well take your steaks; I won't enjoy mine without you. When I was preparing their enchantment, every thought I spared to them was of my meeting with you when we could dine on them together. I had forgotten your comparative youth and your flightiness. A result of your unusual circumstance, I have no doubt."

"Unusual circumstance?"

Phillip, who had risen and crossed to the cooler, stopped moving. I didn't need to see his face; I could hear the grin.

"I suppose we could discuss it, but perhaps while we eat?"

"Eat?" I asked. "As in chew, chew, swallow?"

He removed a pair of small brown bottles from the cooler. "The Disinclined Vintage: each bottle lovelessly prepared by Duke Gornsvalt at considerable expense and with unwilling hands." Phillip read aloud the inscription on the yellow label and chuckled. "Duke Gornsvalt was quite wroth with me until I sent him one of those steaks. Shall we try ours? They are growing cold."

I looked back at the steak. "How?"

"I rarely answer 'how' questions," he said as he returned to the table. "I will do so this once because the answer is quite plain: it's magic. What good is magic, to what purpose alchemy, if it cannot ease our burdens, imagined or otherwise?"

On the left side of the plate, there was a fork, on the right, a steak knife. I cut a piece of steak and as I brought it to my mouth, my fangs extended. After a few tries, I got them to retract so I could take a proper bite. It was overcooked, barely pink through the middle, but it tasted like heaven to me. Swallowing was a problem, though; I couldn't seem to get the entire piece of meat down my throat and I gagged.

"You're not chewing it thoroughly enough." Phillip demonstrated, cutting himself a much smaller piece. He put it into his mouth and winced when he bit his tongue.

We got the hang of it, though. My fangs remained a problem off and on throughout the meal; the texture of solid food, the excitement of it, brought out vampiric instincts that I'd cultivated for years. Chewing food is not like riding a bike. After a decade or two, you forget how.

"At the end of this meal, do I get presented with a bill?" I asked.

"Why bother?" Phillip set one bottle of the Disinclined Vintage next to my plate and the other next to his own. "I know you couldn't pay it. The cosmos is insistent on certain things and this is one of them. Vampires cannot eat—not like humans. To turn the laws of our breed upside down in this fashion requires an obscene expenditure of resources.

The beer was a bit easier. I could have brought in a more plebian blood brew, but I had Duke Gornsvalt do it because he has a certain talent for exotic beverages and I wanted it to taste like you remember. He did warn me it may cause us to urinate, however, so be prepared."

"Real pee or blood?" I asked.

"I didn't ask." Phillip coughed. "It never even occurred to me. I like surprises."

He watched as I removed the cap and tasted the beer. I'd expected it to taste like blood. I'd had "blood brew" before— fermented blood that packed the same kick as real alcohol. This did not taste the same. "It tastes like camel piss."

"Isn't it supposed to?" Phillip asked in midmouthful.

"Pretty much," I acknowledged.

"This is much more as I had foreseen," Phillip said as he patted the table. "Thank you for fulfilling my expectations."

"Uh-huh," I answered. The beer had more kick than it should have had and the buzz I wanted moved in, taking the edge off. We chewed in silence. I cut the second steak in half, putting the larger piece on Phillip's plate. He was the founder of the feast; I figured that he deserved it.

"But I ordered that steak for you," he said.

"There is no way I'm eating a second steak in front of you, while you have an empty plate," I told him. "Just eat it."

He bristled slightly, but did as I instructed.

When we were done, both our jaws hurt from all the chewing and we sat there in a state of pained, yet satisfactory, fullness. "Tell me what you meant before about my circumstance," I said, breaking the silence.

"I will answer, to the best of my ability, any one question on any subject," he said with a casual wave of his arm.

"Okay, but you have to answer the question I'm trying to ask and not screw me over if I get the words wrong. What I want to know is, what special circumstance? You were talking about the whole uber vamp thing, right? Or maybe the reason my eyes are still blue?"

He took a long pull of beer and finished his bottle. "I was."

"Then tell me."

"It's all in the timing," Phillip began. "With you, everything had to go in a very strict progression. You were murdered. After the crash, you lay there in the dirt. Roger stood there and watched you die before calling the paramedics. He taunted you. You struggled to rise, enraged at your own murder. Given time and opportunity, had you been a normal human, you would have risen as a revenant and Roger's unlife would have become most unpleasant. In time, I feel confident that you would have managed to master your powers enough to eventually catch and end him. I'm not sure his hired mages could have moved you along. Even as you lay there, I could feel your power growing."

"Feel it?" I asked.

"Oh, yes, after all, you were and are a Courtney."

At those words John Paul Courtney manifested behind Phillip's back. His face was twisted with rage. Fangs lowered from his upper jaws—curved fangs, not straight like mine. His mouth opened wider than humanly or vampiricly possible, unhinging like a snake. His fists clenched at his side. He let loose a single angry hiss, forked tongue darting past his fangs, but then gained control of himself, vanishing without another sound. My eyes widened. "Holy shit."

"Yes," he said. "I know all about your family, more than you do."

Really, I thought, *did you know my great grandpaw was a weresnake?*

"You see, even in life I was a wizard, a sorcerer, a magician, an alchemist. It is enough to say that I was gifted with true mystic flair. I have the dubious honor of being the reason why mages who become vampires are hunted down and destroyed by their former allies. They will allow no more like me."

"You upset the apple cart," I said with a grunt of admiration. I like people who disturb the status quo—any status quo but mine, that is. "You're probably the reason guild mages are so touchy about working with vamps in general, too."

"Precisely so." He rubbed his hands together as he spoke, repeatedly flashing that devil's grin he favored so much. "Any being as powerful as you comes to my notice instantly through the web and weave of my magical influence, your peculiar situation notwithstanding. Void City is my domain. If I'm to be completely truthful, I had expected your creation, sensed it, foreseen it, and I had taken several days to prepare."

"My problem was twofold: how to slow your development while simultaneously ensuring your survival? Were you to rise at full strength, your powers intact, you would have realized your potential too quickly to be of use to me—too swiftly to be interesting as well. The timing was dreadful. There wasn't enough, you see."

"Wait." I leaned toward him. *El Alma Perdida* pulled against my jeans as I moved. "So you stole my body?"

"I had no need. It was quite simple to follow your body to the morgue and deal with you there."

"What did you do? Are you trying to tell me you're my sire? 'Cause no offense, but Darth Vader, you ain't."

Shock is the only word I can think of to describe the look on Phillip's face at the suggestion. "Of course not, my boy. No, no, no. Heaven forbid. No, I had you embalmed with a little alchemical concoction which, when applied, destabilized the—shall we call it judgment—under which you found yourself."

"Judgment?"

"Curse, then."

"What curse?"

"The Courtney family curse is a transmuted judgment of sorts. Sins of the father, that sort of thing, very Old Testament. My alchemical concoction delayed the full effects, allowed it to work its will upon you, to bring you back, but prevented the complete attainment of your vampiric nature and hid you from your sire. I'd expected it to last another decade or more, but there was no way I could have foreseen your flurry of activity, the many times you've been reduced to ash. Each time you re-formed, you came closer to your true potential."

"So you're behind *everything* then."

Phillip seemed to think that was really funny; he shook

his head as he laughed. "No, my boy. That is another kettle of fish. Trust me when I say you'll figure it all out if you don't get ahead of yourself."

He floated out of his chair and landed in front of the fireplace, the edges of his outline were blurred by wisps of vapor as he moved. His control reminded me of Winter. He took a small box from the mantel. It looked like steel, a very sturdy thing, without decoration. "I want to ascend further and I need your help to do it. Here, take this as another gesture of my goodwill . . ."

He opened the box. Inside, a small journal, burned around the edges, sat silent and alone. The cover read, *Le Coeur du Démon*.

"This is different than the stained-glass thing downstairs."

"I hadn't noticed." Phillip beamed. Before I could ask him to elaborate, he was blabbing again. "If I had left you as you were, you would likely have already confronted your sire. She would have destroyed you or you would have destroyed her and I would be pursuing less amusing roads to victory. Now, she has only just sensed you for the first time. You've created a *memento mori* and she cannot but have sensed its creation. Her mind quests for your mind, but the remnants of my potion make that quite difficult."

"I haven't felt anything. Wait . . . my sire's a *she?*"

"You will and she is. Your sire is unimaginably boring, yet she does represent a singularly rare vampiric accomplishment, one that I can use. I could technically use you, of course, but I never murder interesting people."

"So she, my sire. She just happened to be standing on the side of the road when I was murdered?"

"No, my boy, Lisette hasn't left France in over a century."

"So . . . what . . . I'm the vampire equivalent of artificial insemination?" I shook my head. "Did she use a magic turkey baster?"

"She turned another Courtney into a vampire, a Courtney who begged to be forgiven, to be saved, and he was, but in exchange, the next seven generations of his family had to serve"—he paused, gesturing to the ceiling—"Him."

"You're shitting me."

"I assure you that I am not," Phillip said.

"No wonder Dad was so upset when I dropped out of seminary and enlisted during the war."

"You were the last Courtney male who could have been affected by the curse."

"I think I've heard enough."

"Surely you're curious."

"No, I'm usually not. There are whole worlds of information folks think I ought to be curious about."

Phillip spun in a small circle and jumped back to his chair, where, standing in the seat, he addressed me. "Come, my boy, what could it hurt?" He held out the box containing the journal.

"Shit," I said. It would be stupid to refuse. If Vamp Mom was going to come after me anyway and she was as powerful as all that . . . I considered refusing just to be obstinate. In the end, I reached out and took the box.

"The journal is in French. Do any of your thralls speak the language, or should I provide an interpreter?" Phillip smiled.

"I'm good." I walked to the door. "One last thing," I asked. "You said I'd created a *memento mori*. That means 'remember your death.' I'm guessing that you mean Fang, my Mustang, but what the hell is it?"

"Latin is a magnificent language, my boy, and like so many languages, its phrases may have subtly different meanings based solely on their context. When you think of an Emperor's *memento mori*, it is more accurate to say that the name means 'remember that you are mortal.'

"To achieve their true potential, an Emperor must do two things: create a *memento mori*, a repository to contain the portion of his darkness that he cannot completely control. Usually it's a small item, a necklace, a ring, a pair of spectacles . . . something that can be kept close, because once it is created, the Emperor's powers are tied to it.

"Until an Emperor creates a *memento mori*, his powers are often unreliable. *Memento mori* are also a weakness. Until you created Fang, you could not truly be destroyed."

"And now?"

"Now, if someone were to destroy Fang and to destroy you, then you would no longer be a vampire at all. You would be a revenant and nothing more."

"Good to know." I sighed. "What's the second thing?"

"Postmortem stress syndrome. You still think with your brain and see with your eyes. Even your Tabitha no longer does that. She may not yet have realized it, but she 'sees' with the essence of her being. Flesh is simply a convenient interface."

I said, "Thanks, Yoda," and stepped out into the hall, where I grabbed Beatrice by the arm to ask a very important question: "Do you really speak French?"

✦ 34 ✦

ERIC:
ONCE UPON A TIME

We sat out in Lord Phillip's waiting room while Beatrice read me the brief journal, translating as she went. I wasn't certain how much it helped. It was basically a re-telling of the mural I'd seen downstairs, only this copy had the names filled in. The female vamp's name was Lisette, also referred to as *Démon Coeur*, the Demon Heart. The irony that I'd named my strip club just that did not escape me.

The Knight had a similar name, apparently because he was part of a group of knights called *Le Coeur du Démon*. The Heart of the Demon. They'd named themselves after the monster they wanted to kill. They would stop at nothing less than tearing the Demon's heart from her chest.

They failed. The journal told the story of the last of the knights . . . the one who'd temporarily been a vampire. I couldn't pay attention to all of it; the beer and the food made me sleepy and full in a way that I hadn't been in fifty years. For reasons undetailed in the text, the Knight had given up the quest, moved to America, and changed his last name to Courtney. But I thought I knew why. He'd been afraid either for himself or someone he loved and he ran. On the final page, the author promised to pick up the tale in a new volume documenting the next generation of the Courtney line. The last entry was signed with a single letter—the only indication of authorship throughout the entire work—simply, *P*.

"C'mon, Beatrice." We left and headed toward the Gryphon Suite. "Did Lady Gabriella get all of that?" I asked her.

"Excuse me?" she said.

"She's given you to me, but you're still her thrall, correct? She seems to have a lot of spies, so I'm guessing she could see what happened in there, and she heard what you read?"

"She did see, yes," Beatrice admitted.

"Good. If someone kills you maybe I can bargain with her for the information later. I have terrible memory problems. I may need you to tell me the whole thing again, maybe more than once."

I didn't want Gabby spying on me all the time, though. I also didn't want to rip Bea from her by force as I'd done with Ebony. Was there a third choice? I thought back to the yellow notebook pages Magbidion had given me about thralls. Yep, a thrall could be released by a master or mistress willingly. It was a matter of willpower and saying the correct phrases.

"Is she watching us now?" I asked, stepping into an elevator that was, for once, without a human operator. As the doors closed behind us, Beatrice nodded. "Where are you marked?" Beatrice pulled her top open at the neck and bent over so that I could see the rose on her left breast.

"Release her, Lady Gabriella. You gave her to me and I have accepted."

The rose flashed brightly, then faded. Beatrice grimaced and began to change. Crow's-feet appeared at the corners of her eyes. "Please. If you're going to enthrall me, do it quickly," she said. Her cheeks began to sag and wrinkle as streaks of gray flowed into her hair. I did the deed and watched as the ravages of time faded with only slightly less speed than that with which they had arrived.

I must be better at the whole turning-back-the-clock thing than Gabby, I thought as I studied Bea with a critical eye. Her appearance seemed a bit younger than it had when I'd first seen her—maybe early twenties or late teens. It made sense. Gabby was just a Master and I was a Vlad . . . or whatever.

"How?" Beatrice took two steps away from me, studying her reflection in the metal of the elevator's interior doors. "I'm younger than I was before I became a thrall. How did you do that?"

"Comes from making a whole lotta thralls in two days, I guess," I lied.

The elevator doors opened and we walked through Tabitha's waiting area into the apartment. Ebony's kids didn't look up from the board game they were playing with the Highland Towers' child care guy.

Ignoring them, I pulled Beatrice into the bedroom and closed the door. Asleep on the only bed, Ebony stirred but remained unconscious.

"Excuse me, Highness?" Beatrice said. "Many male vampires like to seal the deal, as it were, with their new thralls." I listened to the sounds of Ebony's kids rolling the dice, moving their pawns along a candy-colored path.

"I thought," I looked at my feet uncomfortably and then looked back at her, "you know . . . ewww."

"That was when I was still in Lady Gabriella's service." Beatrice spoke carefully. She looked at the bed and blushed. "It's been a while since I've been exposed to a Vlad's pheromones without the protection of being a thrall. It shields you, but not from your own master. If your master is sexually compatible, then it is enhanced."

Sitting down on the bed, I patted Ebony's leg casually. "That certainly explains a lot." No wonder all my thralls wanted to hump me.

"And some vampires give off a more powerful . . . compulsion than others. Yours is very . . . intense. I think it should have built up more gradually. You can will certain people not to be affected, if you want."

Unsure of how to do what she was asking, I concentrated on her and thought really hard about her not being attracted to me. "You'll have to tell me when it works."

"That's better," she said after a moment.

"*Cui bono,*" I said, turning back to the problem at hand. "We've got to go to the Pollux to see if anyone is still alive. Do you have a car?"

She nodded.

"How big is the trunk?"

◆ 35 ◆

TABITHA:

AN UNEXPECTED RESCUE

In the parking deck near the Pollux, I found myself in the middle of a fight between two mages. Magbidion was on my side, Talbot was chained up, and Greta was nowhere to be seen. The sun was shining brightly overhead, but the structure provided ample shade. Rachel had underestimated me, the way everyone always does. I'm not weak.

I wasn't weak when I was pretending to be human and now that my vampire abilities were back, I was truly a force to be reckoned with. Eric was going to find that out when I got my hands on him. What kind of a man expects a woman to have sex with her own sister for his amusement? I understood the thought, the fantasy, but Eric had gone beyond that and my fury drove me much in the same way his had often driven him.

Eric's leather bat wings and black skin weren't in my arsenal, but my own speed, strength, and claws were more than enough. Rachel dueled with Magbidion, the two spell slingers made gestures in the air, spat magic words, and matched each other spell for spell. She could have killed Magbidion any time she wanted to. I could tell from the pouty little half smirk she always got when she thought she'd already won but wanted to run up the score. I crouched, preparing myself to charge. Despite all the things she'd said and done, it was hard to attack. Family is family. I gritted my fangs and charged with a growl. Rachel stopped playing with Magbidion and an arc of electricity struck him from the light over his head. He fell in utter silence and lay still, barely breathing. I slashed at her with my claws and she whipped past me, her feet floating above the ground.

"You're actually gonna fight me, sis." Her eyes widened and went red, the eyes of an angry vampire, and then they went purple—Eric's uber vamp eyes. "How cool is that?" Skin darkening to pitch black, she flexed long talons at me.

"What the hell?" I blinked at her, my mouth agape.

"Every time I make him feel alive." Wings ripped through the back of Rachel's suit, leathery wings—Eric's wings. "I siphon off a little bit of his power." My little sister stared at me across the parking deck, the female image of my boyfriend at his baddest and blew me a kiss.

"Yeah, but how long does it last?" Changing her body was a mistake. I could see her as an enemy. She didn't look like my sister anymore, more like a crude parody. We exchanged blows. I opened a long gash in her suit jacket, exposing the coal-black flesh of her stomach. She moved with the blow going past me, tearing my back, ribbons of my flesh clinging to her talons.

"Long enough to handle you." She clipped my head with a kick and it spun me around, breaking the skin on my forehead.

"That's the only thing bad about this job," Rachel said. I snagged her shoulder, catching cloth from her torn jacket, missing the meat. She backhanded me into the Le Baron. I struck the rear tire, knocking it loose and bending the axle. For a half a second I stared at the spot where Greta had lain prone, but she was gone. "When I'm done—no more Eric."

"What do you mean?" I rolled to my feet, dodged a claw that she'd leveled at my head, and struck her in the head with my elbow. Rachel swatted me with her wings and I slammed into the concrete column at the center of the deck where the spiral allowed cars access between the levels.

"I'll never be this powerful again." She paused as she flapped her wings hard enough to lift herself off of the floor, but the ceiling was too low to allow her much maneuvering room. "Not unless I can find another Emperor-class vampire just lying around. I mean, there are seven, and I even know where to find one of them, but as far as I know, she's straight."

I let her talk, allowing my vampiric metabolism to heal me and hopefully letting her run down the clock on her uber vamp power.

"Then why give up the magic if it's so important to you?" My head wound was gone already, the skin smooth under my fingers. No more wince-producing twinges came from my back when I moved my shoulders.

"Don't get me wrong; I'll still have pyromancy from the demon when I'm free, but it's more of a channeling thing. I need both the demon and the Emperor vampire to mainline this kind of magic."

Blue flames coursed along her outstretched talons and I flinched. *Please don't let me be set on fire again.*

"All healed up?" she asked mockingly. I lunged for her, but she spiraled away through the air and over the deck wall. In the sunlight, she turned to face me, her skin returning to normal, fangs receding. Out of uber vamp juice, or preserving it. Hovering in the air, with her tattered jacket and the backless top she wore underneath, Rachel was more beautiful than I'd ever seen her look, a ragged angel, hair backlit by the sun.

It was one more cruel reminder how much Rachel had paid to cling to life. I'd heard her claim that she hadn't sold her soul, but she was fooling herself. Even so, damnation agreed with her.

"Come and get me, sis." She tossed her hair with a shake of her head. "I'll wait right here."

Talbot floated after her against his will, pulled by the enchanted chains.

"No," I mouthed. I didn't love him or anything, but he had come running into a burning building to rescue me. I didn't want him to die.

"Why do you want Talbot?" I yelled. "I thought you were here to kill vampires."

"There you go, thinking again." Rachel clucked her tongue and shook her finger at me. "Maybe I just want to have sex with him later."

"You're such a whore."

"No, but I do like sex, always have . . . and now I get power from it. Although, technically I didn't have to sleep with Eric. I could have done it with joint meditation or massage therapy; it was just an option I exercised, because let's face it, sex is a hell of a lot more fun. That makes me an *escort*. But you, you shacked up with an ancient perverted old Vlad that disgusted you, just so you'd have a nice place to stay. You fucked him because you wanted what he could give you. So if there's a whore here . . . it's you."

"You're kidding yourself. Phillip was a bad choice, but once I got to know the real him, I told him to fuck himself and left. But you, you can't just quit or your demon pimp will send you back to Hell."

A wave of fire washed through the level of the parking deck that I was on. Rachel's voice called out above the roar. "I was going to let you live, but you talk too much—"

I ran. Flames licked the back of my head, but I didn't stop running. Patting my hair out as I went, I ran down, down, down, and down. What I was going to do when I got to the bottom level, I didn't know, but I hoped I'd think of something.

On the ground level I spied Magbidion's RV and Eric's Mustang. The RV provided the best cover, but there was no way I could outrun Rachel in it. I just hoped Eric's keys were in his car. The door was unlocked. I opened the driver's-side door, still trying to guesstimate how long I could last in partial sun. Maybe I could duck down . . . drive with one hand at the bottom of the wheel or something.

"Where ya going, sis?"

Rachel floated down, lifting over the little concrete barrier at the edge of the parking area and landing gently on the concrete. Not bothering to glide anymore, she stalked in my direction, her head tilted slightly to the left as if she were listening to someone else. "The puppet danced just like he was supposed to," she said. "Eric's not coming to save you. He's been kept busy at the Highland Towers. He might be the best lay I've ever had, but mentally he's thick like brick, you know? There's an animal-like craftiness, but he's a total retard."

There were no keys in the Mustang. Frustrated, I punched the steering wheel . . . and things got weird. The radio turned on all by itself. A heavy metal guitar riff rang out over the speakers, imitating a race car engine throttling up. All of the interior lights in the deck blinked out at once, leaving Rachel illuminated only by the high beams of Eric's Mustang.

"What the fuck?" Rachel and I echoed each other.

The bright white of the car's headlights turned to crimson, casting Rachel in a blood-tinted hue.

"*Memento mori.*" She said the words like a curse, as if they were a stand-in for *motherfucker*. "He cares about her enough for his darkness to intercede?" The last bit I heard only because my vamp senses were back to full, but she sounded hurt.

The Mustang's tires squealed as they turned in place, leaving a layer of smoking rubber on the concrete. It was Rachel's turn to run.

I recognized the song on the radio when the car took off after her. It was "Fuel" by Metallica. Eric's car had his taste in music. Or maybe . . . "Eric, are you doing this?"

Nobody answered, but it felt like him, the angry him, the tall, dark, and purple-eyed him. Rachel leapt out into the sun, hovering just above the concrete barrier. She spun in the air, fingers twisting deftly at the start of what I assumed was the spell that would incinerate me and the car.

The car had other plans. It accelerated, straight for the concrete wall of the deck, bursting through it, clipping Rachel. Sunlight hit the car, but it didn't burn. Flamelike detailing swirled up the hood, along the sides, and the windows darkened from clear to almost black.

The rest I heard rather than felt. A series of crashes and more tire-squealing, punctuated by several explosions that rocked the car, were my best indicators that Rachel was still alive. As the Mustang kept trying to catch her, as its ire grew, I felt Eric again, very muffled and far away, but he was coming. At that instant everything went quiet. We drove for a few more feet before the windows went clear. The Mustang and I were safely within the shadows of the parking deck.

I didn't see Rachel anywhere, but I did see Magbidion, so

I hopped out of the car to check on him. The car followed me, rolling over the blood that spattered the deck, leaving nothing but clean concrete in its wake.

Mags was unconscious, but seemed to be otherwise okay. On a hunch, I took his keys and checked his RV. Greta was in there—she'd been cleaned up a bit and carefully arranged on the fold-out bed, covered in a garish orange and pink floral throw blanket. She was badly singed, but I had no idea whether that had been from the burning of the Pollux, one of the creeps' flamethrowers, or one of Rachel's spells. I had a few seconds to wonder who'd gotten her off the third level and how they'd done it without being spotted by me or by Rachel before I heard sirens blaring. The Void City Fire Department had finally decided to give the Pollux their attention. I wondered if Captain Stacey would be with them.

Waiting for dark by myself was pure agony. Magic, tension, or something kept me awake, which was better for security but not good on my nerves. I hauled Magbidion and then Greta over to Eric's Mustang and stowed them inside, then climbed inside myself. I figured we'd be safest there if Rachel came back. I put Greta in the front seat and pulled Magbidion into the back next to me, for warmth. After that I stared at the ceiling and pondered why I wasn't falling asleep.

"That was really Rachel." I tested the idea and the words together. Would I have done what she did to avoid dying? In a way, hadn't I sold out by letting myself be changed? Maybe not the way she'd changed, but just as monstrously . . .

She'd sold her services for magic and a second chance and I'd traded my life for a shot at a different kind of life. I understood the desire, but I didn't want to identify with her. Dead and buried, she'd been easier to love.

Thinking about my sister, I finally fell asleep. When I woke, it was to Eric's hand on my arm as he knelt over me. "Tabitha? Baby? Are you okay?"

I was hungry, angry, and depressed. He had bad timing . . . or worse, it had all been planned and I was just as stupid as he was for letting myself be used. Greta was still unconscious. Magbidion was no longer next to me and Eric had brought yet another new girl with him.

Red-eyed and screeching, I tore into him. "Bastard! You've been gone for what? An hour? And you're already fucking somebody else?" He didn't block my claws as they cut his chest.

"I didn't have sex with Beatrice," Eric said, but I wasn't listening. I raked his stomach and it burst open, little bits of meat and blood rolling down his pants and onto my chest. "I didn't have sex with anybody." One strong push sent him into the air. His head hit the concrete ceiling, but he caught himself as he fell and landed on his feet at the back of the RV.

"Tab, listen. Calm down. There has been some really strange stuff going on, and you've got to—"

His eyes were so open, so clear, so intelligent. He didn't even sound like himself.

"Shut up!" I screamed. "You'd fuck anybody! You were fucking Rachel and worse, you wanted me to!"

"I'll admit I did have the thought, but"—he shrugged—"I am a guy."

I leapt up, but my feet slid in the blood and I went back down, catching myself on the side of Magbidion's RV. I came up fast, with a hint of my vampire speed, but not enough to stop myself from slipping and falling again.

"My little sister! I know you don't want to talk about it, but she's back from the dead and working for Roger! And she almost killed us . . . would have killed us if it hadn't been for your car. Where were you, you asshole?"

"I was being blocked. I thought everyone here was dead." He shrugged. "So I handled some other business before coming here to try to trap . . . Wait. Did you say that your sister is *back* from the dead? When did she die?"

Something was slowing him down. He wasn't as nimble as he had been, even after things had gotten screwy. Maybe Rachel was draining him, recharging. On a good day I was faster than him. But with him moving as slowly as he was, it was a massacre. Twice he tried to lock gazes with me, but I'm not stupid—he'd done that to me at the entrance to the Artiste Unknown and I'd had to go through with a really horrible evening just to fulfill the compulsion, going through the movements of having fun, while Eric had gone home with my little sister, with Rachel!

"You bastard! I thought you loved me. I'm so stupid. I really thought you loved me."

"I never said that, Tabitha, but listen—"

Flipping over and behind him, I caught him by the neck as I'd seen him grab so many others. I seized his neck with one hand and his shoulder with the other. It was easy, like snapping beans in the backyard with my momma when I was little.

"Moist! Warm! Tightness!" It was all I could think of to say as I ripped off his head. He started rotting even before I let go of him and I stumbled back. Pulling his head off shouldn't have killed him. The woman with him opened and closed her mouth without saying anything, like the words just wouldn't come.

"You did great, sis!" said a familiar voice behind me. Rachel hovered in the sunlight just beyond the edge of the deck. With a simple gesture, she threw a tire iron at my head. I got out of the way, but as I did so, the tire iron altered direction and instead of striking me, it angled toward the Mustang, smashing straight through the engine block.

A second gesture and Talbot drifted back into view, the chain which bound him slithering across the concrete. As I watched, the links separated and reattached themselves to both imprison Greta and bind Eric's remains. "You see, Tab," Rachel told me casually, "once we had him where we wanted him, we needed someone who could subdue him. Sure, I probably could have done it, but there was always the outside chance that he'd find a way to kill me or stop me. He's really good at that. But once I realized how much he cared for you . . . well, I knew he wouldn't kill you, no matter what you did, especially after losing Marilyn."

"Please let me go," said the woman that had shown up with Eric. "He was going to eat me."

"Get out of here," Rachel told her scornfully. The woman

fled and Rachel had us all in her grip. One question I wanted to ask burned brightly in my mind. She'd said subdue . . . Did that mean that I hadn't really killed him? Now that I thought about it, I was sure Eric would survive having his head ripped off. He'd survived holy water, stakes, explosives . . . yup, he'd be fine. Chances were Rachel was telling the truth.

She'd also said he cared for me.

✦ 36 ✦

ERIC:

DECAPITATED

Okay, I admit it. I knew decapitation wasn't going to kill me. It had never happened to me before, but I'd come back from having no remains at all. The way I saw it, being headless couldn't be all that bad. I hadn't even tried to dodge Tabitha.

I used to think that the removal of the head was a reliable way to off a vampire. Of course, I also thought that having Roger eaten by werewolves was going to get rid of him for good. I guess some things just don't work when you're dealing with the high-end bad guys. You see, the idea was to let Tabitha blow off a little steam. I hadn't counted on getting jobbed by Rachel in the meantime.

Rachel loaded us all up into a moving van, my body went into one box (I didn't see what kind) and my head went into a red-and-white plastic cooler. In the box, I considered my options. I couldn't feel my body and, try as I might, I was incapable of speech. Similar to being staked through the heart, decapitation apparently completely paralyzed those that it did not kill . . . Or maybe since I hadn't been through postmortem syndrome, I still thought too much like a human and couldn't wrap my brain around moving something to which I was no longer attached. Either way, I would not be busting my body out of its box and reclaiming my own head. I tried.

When the box reopened and Rachel pulled me out, I looked around as well as I could. We were on the top floor of the Lovett Building. I recognized the big golden dome even from within. From the inside, the dome was semitransparent and the stars shone brighter than they appeared from downtown. The rest of me was already chained up in the center of an elaborate ritual setup. An oddly shaped metal tree held my body upright while one of its branches bore a sharpened piece of wood that pierced my heart. That particular branch was hinged so that it could be folded in or out, removing the stake and then shoving it back in.

A circle of white powder and cat's-eye marbles surrounded the tree. A golden pentagram had been etched into the floor so that the circle of marbles was in the middle. Five little black candles with blue flames decorated the points of the pentagram.

A series of raised bleachers had been arranged around the edges of the dome. They were empty except for the left side of the first few rows. On those rows sat an audience, mostly vampires that I'd seen before in The Velvet. In front of the bleachers was a small folding table with four chairs. J'iliol'lth sat in the left-most chair with two empty chairs to his right. The fourth chair held Ebon Winter.

Winter waved at me and strode over to my head. "Just so you know, I'm here on behalf of my sire to ensure that J'iliol'lth adheres to the rules. As are these," he gestured to the folks in the bleachers, but they didn't even look at him, eyes focused on J'iliol'lth, "fine people. I must say that I'm dreadfully disappointed in you. I abhor losing, especially after all I've done to aid you. You've still time to redeem yourself, however. The ritual doesn't start for a few minutes."

Looking over Winter's shoulder, I saw the bastard who'd been behind everything standing at a podium at the tip of the pentagram. If I'd still been connected to my body, I would have charged him without thinking.

Roger smiled at me from behind his book, a huge cliché of a volume—it might as well have had *Evil Book of Spells* embossed in gold on the cover—and gestured for Rachel to bring me closer. Roger had always been older than me and his vampiric embrace made him look older still. He wore thin reading glasses even though he no longer needed them. As affectations went, it just made him seem more bookish.

"Hey." He removed his glasses and rubbed his eyes. "You almost got me with the werewolf thing. I have to hand it to you, I never thought you'd have the brains to use backup. I always said all you had to do to rule the world was control your temper, your lust, and your tongue. When your abilities become mine, everyone will see how true that statement was."

He looked back at the book and then at my body. "Put his head on his body, Rachel. If I've correctly deciphered your notes, he'll need to be intact for the ritual. It should also help with the smell."

Rachel floated over the circle and placed my head upon my neck. She held my head in place with one hand and raised the hinged limb that held the stake in my heart. My transformation from separate to whole was almost instantaneous. Even my T-shirt was restored. Rachel drove the stake home again and my consciousness blurred, the buzz of the beer and the wine I'd had dropped me directly into the enlightened state of drunkenness where everything seems to make sense even when it really doesn't. Marilyn. Roger. Melvin. J'iliol'lth. Rachel. Ebon Winter. They all danced around in my head.

The cat's-eye marbles were soul prisons. I knew that because Melvin told me . . . Melvin who'd made sure that when I punched through the wall at Lady Gabriella's, there'd be a hole in the wards right where I needed it to be. Melvin who worked for Winter, who'd bet that I could win. I wondered what else Winter had done behind the scenes.

"Check his enchantment." Roger's voice rose in pitch, nearly to a squeak. "Make sure your anger-management spell is in place."

Familiar and friendly, Rachel's cinnamon magic washed over me. "He's fine," she said, then chuckled. "I even put in a little extra buzz. He's feeling no pain."

She walked away and came back out with Talbot, Greta, and Tabitha. They were bound by magic chains that moved across the floor in a serpentine manner. Greta and Tabitha had been staked. Rachel gestured, and the chains released the girls. Rachel propped them against the dome so they would have a good view of my death. The chain extended itself up along the dome as well, hanging Talbot next to them in the air.

My thoughts were slow, but smooth. I ran through my options with no sense of urgency or concern. I had all the time in the world to figure this out. Two minutes was an eternity. I had to find a way to kill Roger that didn't involve moving. I had to save Greta, Tabitha, and Talbot in the process. Then, I needed to kill J'iliol'lth. If I couldn't do any of those things, I still had to make sure that Roger lost.

He'd burned the Pollux and the Demon Heart. He'd been raping Marilyn; he'd made her his thrall so that she couldn't tell me about it. He'd used Rachel to get at me. Rachel. My partial thrall. That gave me an idea. When I'd made Rachel my thrall—or attempted to—the ritual had only worked partway because I didn't make a blood tattoo or say the ritual words. Is there a time restriction on completing the ritual? I asked myself. Or did I just have to . . .

Of course, they'd have to unstake me first or none of it would matter. The way I figured it, the entire reason everything had been so complicated was that Roger had wanted to be certain that I couldn't go Grape Ape on him, lose my temper, and turn into the uber vamp.

"Unstake him," Roger ordered. "He has to be intact for the spell to work. A hole in his chest might be a problem."

Rachel pretended to be aghast. "But Master, he could turn into a revenant and escape." This time, I could tell she was faking it and I think she meant for me to know. Rachel glanced pointedly toward the marbles. Cat's-eye marbles. Soul prisons. With a memory like mine, it's a miracle that I remembered. Maybe it was because Melvin looked like Dan Aykroyd or maybe it was the way he had geeked out over my revenant form, but the words Melvin had said stuck with me, word for word: *"When they come at you next, they'll try the soul prison route, but I can guarantee you they'll get nonguild labor to put it together. It'll look like a cat's-eye marble. They're wicked powerful, but they'll shatter like glass if you hit them with a rock. Good luck."*

My plan didn't require a rock, but it did hinge on someone whose name began with the letter *R*.

"It's a risk we'll have to take," Roger ordered.

Rachel did as he asked, darting out of my reach, stopping just past the boundary created by the circle of stones. Did Roger think I was that stupid? Even without the info Melvin had laid on me, if I could go noncorporeal and escape, then all Roger's preparations made no sense. Unless he needed me to go noncorporeal . . . so that I would be a revenant so that his little ring of soul prisons could trap my ass. All I would have had to do was go ghost-mode and I would have been all Roger's.

For a split second, my rage broke through Rachel's spell

and when it did, I saw Fang being unhooked from a tow truck, saw Beatrice pulling a tire iron out of his engine block. I heard the creak of metal as his inner workings slid back together and he repaired himself. In that instant, I knew what Fang was. When I had rage blackouts, the part of me that made decisions when I was so angry that I acted on instinct . . . that part of me was Fang. Somehow, when I'd come back, I'd come back in two pieces. And neither one of me was going to play along with Roger's undead makeover.

Roger. They must have taken the Stone of Aeternum out of my pants pocket before hanging me up on the tree, because Roger held it in his hands over the book. He looked smug. And a smug Roger is a stupid Roger. I needed time for my backup to arrive. Fang felt close, but I couldn't tell exactly how close. Still, stalling wasn't the problem. The real problem was Rachel. I needed her to be closer. Much closer. How could I get Roger to send her over here?

The answer was simple: act like me. As Roger saw me, I was a loud obnoxious dickhead with a soft spot for his friends, a hopeless romantic with no real sense of romance, a guy who'd make life-altering decisions on a whim, a guy who doesn't hold anything back. Fine.

"So," I asked, "Roger—how's it feel to be a fuckup?"

"Excuse me?" he asked.

"I'm supposed to turn into my ghost form—a revenant or whatever—and come flying at you, is that it? It's a good plan, but it's sloppy, just like you. And it ain't gonna happen. You can't just use the Stone of Aeternum on me and get it over with, can you?"

"Eric, Eric, Eric," Roger tut-tutted, "I have no idea what you mean."

"You really do think I'm that stupid, don't you? Look. This may surprise you, Roger, but I really don't care what happens to me. I'll do what you want, but you have to agree to let Talbot, Tabitha, and Greta go. You have to agree not to act against them unless they physically assault you and I mean no egging them on. No bothering them. No sending other people after them. You also have to reimburse Greta for the cash she paid to buy back my buildings and my stuff. Oh, and you also have to let Tabitha keep the suite at the Highland Towers."

Roger licked his lips, leaving a thin trail of red behind. "She'll have to agree to stay out of my way."

"Fine."

He said, "Done. Witnessed by Ebon Winter, J'iliol'lth, and the others present. Turn into your ghost form and fly toward me."

"One last thing," I said.

"What?" he asked.

"I want to kiss Rachel good-bye."

"I don't know," Roger said carefully. "You might try to kill her."

"Do you need her for the ritual?" I asked.

He bit his lip, removed his glasses, and rubbed his eyes again before putting them back on. "No."

"Then what? You're afraid of me? I'm chained to a magic post here. What the fuck am I gonna do? God, you're such a coward."

"Don't call me that."

"Yes, why call a spade a spade?" Winter laughed. Roger glared at him. "Oh, don't mind me," Winter continued, placing a hand to his chest. "Do what you will. I'm not the one who'll have to live it down. Rabbit Roger, the Yellow Vlad of Void City. It has a certain poetry to it, don't you think?" The audience in the bleachers went off like a laugh track, right on cue to push Roger over the edge. Looking across the room, I noticed Beatrice had slipped into the room unnoticed. She took a seat near some of the others and laughed inconspicuously on cue.

Roger cursed. "Do it," he told Rachel.

"I agree to kiss him and then we're straight? I'm free to go, but on retainer?" Rachel asked. And then I saw Rachel's plan, too, because we both had the same plan. She'd played her part to the hilt trying to make sure that I had enough info to figure it out.

Roger nodded, but she wasn't looking at him. She was looking at J'iliol'lth. The demon nodded, too. He withdrew a thick stack of papers from a metal briefcase and turned to the last page. The vampires around him strained to get a look at it. J'iliol'lth cut his finger letting viscous brown nonblood drip onto a signet ring. He held it poised over the paper.

"The moment you kiss him," J'iliol'lth assured her, "I'll mark your contract fulfilled. The mortgage on your soul will be paid in full and you will be free."

Rachel floated toward me, barely suppressing a smile, and I had butterflies in my stomach. *I can't tell you what to do,* her voice whispered in my head, *but please tell me you've figured it out.* It could have been what remained of the steak and the beer, or it could have been that I was about to bet my unlife on a mouthful of blood, my ability to force Roger out of Rachel's head, and one undead Mustang convertible circa 1964. I normally worry about tests, but I'd already done a practice run on this one, pushing Roger's own sire out of Ebony's head and my faith in Fang was unwavering. After all, if you can't trust yourself . . . ?

◆ 37 ◆

ERIC:
THE POWER OF SPIT

When you become a vampire, one of the first things you notice, aside from the hunger, is how gross everything can be. You have to be careful licking your lips or you'll leave a trail of blood. Roger did that all the time; it was a basically disgusting habit.

All your bodily fluids are replaced with blood. When your mouth waters, you have to be very fastidious about drool. Bloodstains are hard to get out and drooling blood on your date can be a total deal breaker. When Rachel walked toward me, my mouth filled with what passed for saliva and I let it pool.

She had conditioned me to find her attractive and I did. Her presence was intoxicating and standing in the same room with her was all it took to make me crave her touch, her taste. Floating over the white powder into the circle, she touched my cheek and smiled.

"It's a shame it has to be this way," she said with apparently genuine regret. "You're the best lover I've ever had and I really do like you."

Leaning in for the kiss, she touched the back of my head, ran her fingers through my hair. Her lips parted. Her eyes closed and I spat a mouthful of blood onto her cheek. Shrieking involuntarily, she drew back and slapped my face.

Please, please, please, her thoughts hit me.

I concentrated on the blood, willing it to move according to my wishes. It slid across her left cheek, changing colors, taking the shape I desired: a butterfly. She wiped her hand across her face in disgust. When it came away clean, her eyes widened and she stared at her hand without comprehension until I started saying the words. It was the best acting job I'd ever seen.

"I mark thee and bind thee," I incanted quickly, "Master to servant. Servant to master. You are mine until I set you free. You are mine. So mote it be."

As before, I felt pain, but this time it was a pleasure. Across the room, Roger glared at me. Our eyes met. My mind touched his. *I said you were a fuck-up.*

Roger's thoughts were as slippery as he was. I forced him from Rachel's psyche, trying to keep a grip on his mind with mine. He wriggled free once, but I caught him again and hung on. "Rachel!" I hissed between gritted teeth, "Release me."

It has to be an order, she thought at me. Mentally, I made it a command.

Roger's mouth opened and closed like a fish animated by Art Babbitt. Out of the corner of my eye, I saw Rachel glance at J'iliol'lth, saw her smile when she confirmed that he'd already made his mark on her contract. A single word from her unlocked the shackles, dropping them and me. I slid down the metal tree onto my knees.

"I think you probably need to be mad now," she said and I felt the artificial calm that had been plaguing me drop away. Her soft caress brought my anger roiling back and with it, I saw a vision of Fang, driving up the wall of the Lovett Building.

"Now sic 'em!" I spat. I made that an order, too. . . . Just in case. Rachel giggled and turned on our audience, blue fire at her fingertips.

"He thought his way out of it," Winter told J'iliol'lth with glee. "I win again! Isn't it marvelous?"

Roger's mind was slippery on the surface, strong and ordered beneath. Mine was absolutely chaotic, but I had fought several vampires mind to mind, I'd gone through the thralldom ritual, the real one, more than once, and from the feel of things, Marilyn may have been his only thrall. It gave me power, perspective. Besides, he had it coming from way back.

Roger's fingers involuntarily relaxed and the Stone of Aeternum rolled across the floor. J'iliol'lth dived over the table to get the stone. Beatrice beat him to it. The rest of the audience ran like hell, and a communal scream went up among them as Fang crashed through the dome of the Lovett Building and landed on the middle of the group. Shards of gold-tinted glass rained down on the crowd as "Bodies" by Drowning Pool blared from the Mustang's speakers.

The half-dozen vamps beneath Fang's undercarriage pushed against him as one, only to shriek even louder when the flesh on their hands and forearms ripped free with the sound of tearing fabric. It flattened against Fang and sank into the metal. Inch by rapid inch, they were taken, stripped, shucked, and digested by my *memento mori*.

The ones he missed, Rachel nailed with dots of blue flame that caught and spread. They burned one by one, each adding to the blaze like a book of lit matches.

In the soft blue light, Winter pulled the stake out of Tabitha and pointed her toward Greta. He touched Talbot's chain and gave an unintelligible command. Instantly the chains fell away, rapidly slithering into a neat coil at Winter's feet. Once Tabitha freed Greta, I stopped watching the world outside my mind's eye and turned all my attention on my ex–best friend Roger.

"You can't fight me this way, Eric. You can barely think! You're little more than an animal," Roger said, lashing out at me mentally. I made no effort to defend myself, continuing my charge deep into his psyche. If he wanted to tear holes in my mind, he was welcome to it, so long as I got him, too.

"I let you go the first time. After everything you did, I tried to let you go," I roared. "I would have let you go this time, too. But I had to watch Marilyn burn, not just her body, her soul. I could have made her young again if she'd been my thrall. We could have been together this whole fucking time!"

"You didn't deserve her," he shouted back. "She never even loved you." He was a quick study. Shields popped up around his mind and I battered them down. His mental self manifested armor, a sword, and a shield. My mental self just looked like me. He cut deeply with the psychic sword and blood gushed from my image.

"Didn't deserve her?" I concentrated on what it was like to be the uber vamp, focused on my rage, and sent it at Roger with a roar. Mental-me grew wings and black skin. In my head, I was the uber vamp. Roger shit himself. I guess in his head, his mental version of himself, he was still human.

"The stones, the ones in the circle, are called spirit wardens. I could have trapped you and then elevated myself to Vladhood. Then I could have used your spirit to become what you are."

"Except that you can only ascend once every century," Tabitha snarled, "If you'd ever asked Phillip, he could have told you that."

I blinked and glanced about. I hadn't realized that we were also speaking aloud.

Roger looked angrily at J'iliol'lth and I charged across the pentagram toward him in the physical world, trying to do the same in his mind. He threw himself backward in an awkward flip, but he wasn't close to fast enough once I hit top speed. I felt like a coke-head mainlining for the first time.

The rush rattled my teeth and numbed my tongue. Mint assailed my nostrils and I lashed out at the source without taking my eyes off Roger. J'iliol'lth screamed to my left and my hand came back covered in brown goop.

"Wanna know something really scary, Roger?" I shouted. "I'm not even going to kill you!"

I caught him by the neck and snapped his spine, my actions echoing from the physical world into the mental battleground in which we fought.

"You raped my fiancée, murdered her, and sold her soul to a demon!" I reached down, grabbed a fistful of crotch and tore off everything I'd seized. Roger desperately clawed and slashed at me, leaving long bloody wounds on my chest and shoulders.

"You should have stayed dead!" Plunging my fist through his sternum, I wrapped my fingers around his heart. He turned into a frog and squirmed free of my grasp. As he leapt free, he became human again and then went from human to bat, flying for the hole in the dome, flapping toward freedom. "Come back here, you sonovabitch!" I swore, just as a shot rang out from across the room.

Roger burst into flames to the sound of John Paul Courtney's laughter. "Ain't no way I'm gonna sit through another fight with that one." Courtney's ghost blew across the barrel of *El Alma Perdida* and met my eyes. "That's yore one shot. Now git it done."

I dragged the flaming shape-locked bat that was Roger into the pentagram next to the ring of spirit wardens, ignoring the flames that coursed from him to me. His tiny heart popped with all the resistance of a crack whore's virtue. I tore off his head and let it burn. As his body did the same, one of the spirit wardens shone a vibrant green. Roger's remains crumbled into powder. The flames vanished with him.

I picked up the spirit warden and inside, barely visible to the naked eye, a miniature Roger, humanoid, screamed and pounded on the walls of his tiny mystic prison, spectral flames blazing brightly on his back.

Rachel looked over my shoulder and laughed. "Oh my God. I didn't know they worked that way. That is so cool! We should kill J'iliol'lth over one of these, too. That way he can't mess with my—"

"No."

The disgusting demon stood at the top of the ruined bleachers, back to the gaping hole Fang had left there. Beatrice was sitting in Fang's passenger seat. A menacing engine rev made J'iliol'lth twitch, but he stayed put.

"Eric," J'iliol'lth crooned, "you won! Now we can make you a true immortal—"

"No," I said again. "You think I don't know that you did all this? You put Roger out front, your little red flag to make the bull charge, but he couldn't have done this without your help. Him I understand. He hated me. But you did all this for a magic rock."

"I *am* a demon," J'iliol'lth said.

"You get eaten."

J'iliol'lth leapt backward, turning in one smooth motion as filthy, bracken-covered wings erupted from his jacket. I ran after him, the transformation to uber vamp effortless.

"He's getting away," Tabitha shouted.

"Not today." I grabbed Talbot under his arms and took him with me, the two of us shooting through the hole in the Lovett Building's golden dome in hot pursuit of the demon, the cold air of the December evening chilling my flesh, seeping into my bones. It felt like old times.

38

ERIC:

DEMONS DON'T GET DO-OVERS

I didn't see him. "Where'd he go?" I shouted. I'd spent more time flying as a bat than as the uber vamp and the uber vamp didn't have radar. The long leathery wings sported by my vampiric form fell somewhere between the wings I sported as a normal-size chiroptera and the wings of a seagull—the membrane didn't stretch and flex the same. My ghost time hadn't provided me any useful practice, either.

"Three o'clock," Talbot answered.

"Where?"

Jill blended in against the cityscape, the dark office buildings in their power-saver modes.

"Now two o'clock," Talbot yelled.

I saw him, a flash of demon backlit by the lights of the Void City Metro Bank building—its windows decorated for Christmas, tinted to make patterns: a candy cane on one side, a narrow Christmas tree on the other. Jill flittered mothlike past the alternating red and white, whipping past the corner of the building. He was too fast, too used to flying.

"Damn it!"

Talbot slapped my bicep. "You've got to get him before he makes it to another locus point."

"A what?"

"J'iliol'lth is a lesser lord," Talbot said. "A Nefario. He can only transition between this plane and his own at mystical loci, like the Lovett Building."

"But we just left there."

"Your car broke the dome. Some loci have to be amplified to function. The dome has to be in perfect condition or it won't work."

"Go team!"

We cut around the bank, swinging too wide as Talbot's weight threw me off and I lost J'iliol'lth. Increasing my wing-beat cycle, I angled upward, giving myself a better view. Void City stretched out beneath us, a city in denial—its lights never bright enough to pierce the shadows of magic that concealed its supernatural inhabitants from their mundane neighbors—the lone city in America where creatures of the night could roam unremembered.

"I've lost him," Talbot snarled.

"Name another place he can escape from."

"The Highland Towers, the . . ." Talbot's words were lost in the wind as I shot toward the Highland Towers, buildings passing beneath me, cars moving along the street completely unaware of the struggle going on above their heads.

"Do you see him?"

"Six o'clock!" Talbot pointed and I spotted the demon and dived. He was making for Lord Phil's snooty-ass home for the tragically upper crust, but he wheeled away as I flew at him, flying higher as he all but vanished against the night sky.

All I had to do was get Talbot close enough to claw and bite, but J'iliol'lth knew that just as well as I did. We flew up until Void City diminished beneath us. J'iliol'lth darted into a bank of dark moisture-rich clouds and I followed, plunging blind into the billowy gray of what might soon be a storm. Maybe it meant we'd have a white Christmas, but if I couldn't catch Jill, I wouldn't be celebrating.

Through a gauzy skein of clouds, I saw Void City as I'd never before seen her—all sparkling lights and wonder, from the newly refinished halls of the Ellery Academy to the condemned church that sat vacant in downtown, more castle than steepled edifice of worship. The spotlights from the Iversonian lit J'iliol'lth for one second in the sky, the light rendering him translucent. I strained up, kicking backward in the sky, raised Talbot over my head . . . and threw him at the demon.

I missed.

Talbot plunged through the night sky in an unerring arc toward the ground. He didn't scream. Arms and legs spread to catch the winds and slow his progress, Talbot looked over his shoulder. "You better catch my ass, Eric."

J'iliol'lth's laughter rang out, that same unpleasant rattle of crunching bass and high-pitched whinny. He followed me down, lighting upon the decorative cornice of a high-rise apartment building to watch. I could have gone after him then, surprised him, and let Talbot fall, but I don't abandon my friends.

"Try to land on your feet, mouser," Jill crowed.

With a muttered curse (I don't remember which one, maybe it was several), I pushed myself as far as I could go, finding the optimum rhythm to the uber vamp's unfamiliar wingbeat cycles, getting maximum positive and negative pressure. In my head, I pictured Talbot as Greta's popsicle star and J'iliol'lth as my Christmas tree. I zipped through the air, seizing Talbot with my legs, carrying him at an angle to slow his fall, then angling up again in an arc. It would have been much easier with bat senses.

The demon moved at the last instant, forcing me to skew to the left or plunge Talbot directly into the concrete that had previously served as J'iliol'lth's perch.

"You really suck at this, Eric," Talbot shouted.

"You want me to throw you at him again?"

"No!"

I did it anyway, twirling him in the air as if I were one of those big East German chicks competing in the hammer toss back in the '64 Olympics. Talbot screamed that time, but it wasn't a curse or a cry of terror, it was one name: mine. I still think he could have snagged J'iliol'lth if he'd have only reached a little harder. I went after Talbot and J'iliol'lth slowed to watch.

Hurtling toward the ground, I caught Talbot again, moving faster. J'iliol'lth didn't wait to see what I would do, winging it for the Highland Towers. I was accelerating again, but the demon had a head start.

"Do. Not. Throw. Me."

"Just one last time."

"No!"

"Fine."

I flew at a downward angle, letting gravity help to increase my speed. Concentrating on the feel of my wings, the ways they pushed and pulled against the air, I searched for the familiar feeling, the optimum wingbeat cycle I'd managed the first time I caught Talbot . . . then I was in the zone. Flying is like jazz. It has a rhythm, a beat, it changes, but when it's done right, even the improvisations sound like they belong. In a race between a moth and a bat, the bat wins. It's simple aerodynamics: bats are faster, more maneuverable, even more efficient.

Realizing he could no longer outrun me, Jill began hugging the buildings, trying to shake me off, but I was used to carrying Talbot and being undead meant my stamina was not a problem.

"Why doesn't he set me on fire or something?" I asked Talbot.

"He can't. Nefarios can channel power into others, but they don't have much of their own."

"He should have carried a gun," I said.

"Huh?"

"It wouldn't have hurt me much or very long, but he could have put a couple of holes in my wings . . ."

We both got quiet, paranoid that having spoken of the possibility would bring it to pass.

J'iliol'lth made it as far as the parking deck across the street from the Highland Towers before I crashed into him at full speed. Three of us—demon, vampire, and mouser— tumbled across the upper deck. Jill came up first, turning to fly when Talbot landed on him in a flash of white. Fully transformed, Talbot stood only an inch or two shorter than the uber vamp. A silver mane, matching the shock of fur at the tip of his tail, stood out in stark contrast against the thick sable fur covering the body of an anthropomorphized lion. The silver hair shimmered, casting a faint light that blended with the ambient glow emitted by Talbot's star emerald eyes.

J'iliol'lth screamed in pain, clutching at the now flaming shoulder into which Talbot had sunk his claws (also silver), the tips sinking down into the bone. Talbot growled, baring fangs that matched his claws, pearlescent luminance escaping his mouth.

"Please," Jill shouted, imploring me, not Talbot. "I'll do anything."

"I already told you, Jill." I took a step forward as Talbot ripped the wings from the demon's back with one casual jerk of his left hand. "You get eaten." I watched as Talbot devoured sizzling pieces of demon. I listened to the screams.

"How did he taste?" I asked.

"Like chicken," Talbot answered, his mouth full.

In spite of everything, I laughed.

John Paul Courtney's ghost manifested on the deck, leaning against a BMW. "Good job, son. You shouldn't 'a made no deal with it in the first place, but you did right in the end." He tipped his hat to me and faded away. *El Alma Perdida* lay on the hood of the BMW next to a western-style gun belt. "Don't forget that I fired that bullet at Roger on good faith, son." His voice echoed in the open air. "You remember the price."

"Ghosts." Talbot shook his head, then went back to licking the flecks of demon from his fur.

"What about your other five shots?" I asked my ancestor.

"One at a time, son. Just remember the price for this one."

Yeah, I remembered the price: no killing Gabriella. Just as well . . . I didn't want to kill her anyway. Lord Phillip had messed with her enough that as long as she left my crew alone, I had no reason to start a fight.

The squeal of tires preceded Fang's arrival. By the time Tabitha, Rachel, and Beatrice had climbed out of the car, Talbot had reverted to normal, bits of J'iliol'lth still trailing from his mouth. There wasn't much left. He slurped up the last few shreds and forced himself to swallow.

"Damn it," Rachel snarled. "You fucking cat, if we could have imprisoned him, I might have been able to keep the pyromancy. Now, I'll be lucky if I can light a goddam match!"

"Good," I whispered.

"I knew there was a reason cats freaked me out," Rachel said, shuddering.

"I didn't know how else to kill him," Talbot explained. "It was the only way to be sure." And that was why I'd kept Talbot with me ever since El Segundo. Oni won't eat other demons. They have a code. They won't even fight them. But if you have a demon that you just can't kill, if you have to be one hundred percent sure that it's dead and gone, a mouser is the only way to go.

Beatrice handed me the Stone of Aeternum. Rachel picked up the gun belt and slid it around my waist. Beatrice handed me the pistol and as I holstered it, Tabitha sighed and turned away. She looked hurt, angry, unable to even meet my gaze. We had a lot to talk about and I sure as hell had things to answer for, but first I had a little unfinished business.

◆ 39 ◆

ERIC:

BACK AT THE HIGHLAND

Nobody bugged me when I walked into the Highland Towers. Maybe they all knew what had happened. Someone with access to the Lovett Building must have had hidden cameras on the roof, a spy, a crystal ball, even if it was just to let them know that they could rent out J'iliol'lth's office space to some other demon. Then again, there had also been Winter's audience. Those guys were probably tearing up the phone lines yapping, at least, the few that survived Fang's assault and Rachel's flambé action. I stopped off at the Rose Suite and rang the bell to be nice. Esteban answered the door, the bruises around his dark blue eyes eminently recognizable through the door slot.

"Well, you sure heal slowly for a thrall."

"It seems that since my injuries were caused by an Emperor, my mistress's healing gifts—"

"I don't really care, I was just being polite. I'm done now, at least when it comes to you. Where's Gabriella?"

"Lady Gabriella is indisposed at the—"

I took a deep breath and spoke to him in a language I knew he'd understand: bullshit. "Tell the Lady that His Highness Eric of Void City would greatly appreciate a moment of her time. She needn't come outside. We may even converse through the door if she so desires, but I have news of the utmost gravity and I want her to hear it from me."

Esteban retreated and twenty-seven seconds later, Gabriella opened the spy slot at the top of the door. "You sounded almost cordial."

"Yeah, I guess." I cleared my throat. "Roger lost. He's dead and this needs to be the end of it. Come after me or mine . . . threat, threat, threat . . . You get the idea. Stay out of my way, let it go, and I'll try to steer clear of your business. You lost a son, but he screwed my fiancée, murdered her, and sold her soul to a demon. He destroyed my club and my movie palace, wrecked my Mustang, and tried to suck out my soul. By vampire rules, I ought to come after you, because you knew about it and because you're his sire, but I'm willing to let bygones be bygones if you are. So— are you?"

While she thought it over, I popped my knuckles one at a time and stared at the ceiling. "It will be as you wish, Highness."

"Fuckin' A," I told her. "I didn't want to kill you anyway. It would have made a cowboy I know very unhappy." She coughed and I headed up to Phillip's place before she could say another word.

Phillip's door was already open and I walked right in. The old schemer was sitting at his desk writing in a journal. His pen moved with great speed upon the page, covering the blank white expanse with odd symbols and cryptic notes. He held up a finger, finished his sentence, and met my gaze. "*Acta est fabula, plaudite.*"

"No, thanks, I'll leave the applause to others." I reached into my pocket and pulled out the Stone of Aeternum.

"I thought you would bring this back to me." He rose, retrieved a black case, and opened it to reveal a bunch of other little trinkets.

"I'm not sure I'm giving it back to you," I said.

For the first time I got to see Phillip's eyes glow red. It was a quick flash, but I'd seen it. Nice to know I could rattle his cage.

"Can this thing really be used to make me immortal?" I asked.

"It could." He still sounded huffy. "You would need to place it inside your heart."

"Sounds easy."

"And then cure your vampirism while it was contained within."

"How do you suggest I do that?" I asked.

"Violently," Phillip purred, "the same way you do everything."

"I supposed I deserved that. Are we going to have a problem if I want to give it a try?"

"If you haven't accomplished your goal by the time I need the Stone returned to me—"

"I'll give it back to you. You have my word."

"May I do the honors?" he asked. I turned it over in my hand before passing it off to him. "*Ad vitam aeternam, mi amice. Alea iacta est.*" He drove his hand toward my chest, pushing the stone into place without breaking the skin. You've gotta love magic.

"That was easier than the way I had planned on doing it," I told him. "What was it you said?"

"To eternal life, my friend," Phillip repeated, "the die has been cast." He winked at me. "I thought you spoke Latin."

"Not as well as you."

Phillip clapped me on the arm. "It went well, then?" he asked. "The confrontation?"

"I'm still the walking dead," I answered with a shrug. "I still have girl trouble, not to mention an undead car. And I'm still broke."

"Not exactly," Phillip chuckled. "I've arranged for your identity to be reinstated. Your accounts have been reopened. I have people trying to reclaim the most sentimental of your possessions. It may take some time."

"Thanks."

"Think nothing of it. In addition, Roger's possessions and monetary resources are to be transferred to you. I did take a small percentage of the total as a handler's fee, but the bulk of the fortune remains."

"How much of a handler's fee?" I asked.

"Thirty-three and one-third percent," he said, looking me over.

"You're a crook," I said with a trace of amusement, "but I'll take it."

"I thought you might." He nodded. "I've also arranged for an additional suite of rooms here to be converted to your use. It's the least we, the residents of Highland Towers, can do, based on the inexcusable behavior of our fellow tenant. Your Ebony is already upstairs with the children. She has awakened. I've sent someone to show Beatrice, Rachel, Tabitha, Magbidion and . . . Talbot the way to them as well."

"I'll probably only stay until I rebuild the Pollux," I told him.

"What about your exotic dance hall?" he asked. "I always meant to go and see it."

Shaking my head, I withdrew the spirit warden containing Roger's soul. "Haven't you heard? I've decided to open a bowling alley instead. Seriously, I have enough girl problems without that place. Besides, Marilyn died there . . . it'd be too weird."

Phillip's eyes followed the glowing green sphere in my hand, watching Roger's impotent rage. "And that?" Phillip asked.

I tossed it to him. "A souvenir. If I keep it, he'll probably get loose or something. Someone will break it or one of Ebony's kids will swallow it . . . I thought you could put it in a little case next to Percy's. It could read *Exhibit B*."

Staring deep into the spirit warden, Phillip shook it vigorously and watched the perpetually burning Roger within dissipate and re-form. "Priceless. I adore it. I'll send up something your young lady will like, a peace offering for you to give to her. We'll speak about the other matter in a few days' time, after you've settled in."

"What other matter?" I asked.

"Your trip to Paris," he said.

"I'm going to Paris?"

Phillip clutched his hands together. "I hope I'm not speaking out of turn, but it does make quite a romantic spot for a honeymoon."

"And who's getting married?"

"Unless I miss my guess, you are, to your young Queen, Lady Tabitha. It's also where your sire now lives. Am I right in assuming that during your fight with Roger, you experienced no difficulties in accessing your vampiric abilities?"

I kicked in the speed, dropped it, kicked it again. "Well, I'll be damned," I swore.

"No, you won't," John Paul's voice echoed.

Phillip glanced about the room. "What was that?"

"My conscience," I told him.

"That's what one gets for asking," he said. "The increasing reliability of your powers signifies a decline in the enchantment that shielded you from your sire, as well as the nearness of your *memento mori*. You'll need to think carefully about whether or not to take the car with you when you go to Paris. The further you are from it, the greater the likelihood that you'll begin to experience a certain amount of unreliability once more."

"Wait. You think I'm just going to go running after my sire just because you told me where she is?"

"To thine own self be true." He gazed up at me, fluttering his eyelashes. "And besides, you are a Courtney."

"You suck," I told him. Phillip nodded, turning back to the little marble in his hand, and I left him happily torment-ing Roger. At the very least, I figured that Percy might feel better, knowing there were fates not only worse than death, but worse than his. Phillip would torture Roger in ways I'd never conceived of, and he'd do it consistently until he'd run out of new and inventive ways to make his existence hell. If I'd taken Roger home with me, I would have forgotten about him in a week or two. Roger deserved worse than that.

Dennis met me in the elevator and showed me to my rooms. Bea was up there running interference between Ra-chel and Tabitha. Talbot sat on an overstuffed ottoman, try-ing to stay out of it. If I could have done the same, I would have. Magbidion walked in from one of the bedrooms. I thanked him and told him that Beatrice was in charge while Tabitha and I were gone. I made sure Rachel heard me and I took Tabitha by the arm. "Can we go for a ride and talk?" I asked.

"Are you sure you wouldn't like to take Rachel?" It was just more of Tabitha's shit, but I took it because during the last few days when all the bad stuff happened, even when she'd been ripping off my head, I'd come to understand the truth: I'd never love anyone the way I loved Marilyn, but Tabitha was the only girlfriend I'd had since I died that I missed when she walked away, that I worried about. Maybe what I feel for her isn't love, but then again, maybe it's as close as an old dead man like me is ever likely to get.

"I'm sure." I reached out with my mind and felt Greta in another room nearby, watching the news on television. Ebony was in there with her, groggy, but awake. It even felt like the lights were starting to come back on inside her mind. "Come on," I told Tabitha. "Let's get out of here. Are you hungry? I thought maybe we could hunt?"

"I suppose," she said with reluctance.

40

TABITHA:

NOT A ROMANTIC BONE

Eric took us out in his Mustang, which he introduced to me, finally, as Fang. While Eric was opening the door for me, I gave the 'Stang a surreptitious little pat on the hood, still grateful for its help in the parking deck fight.

Eric and I hunted through the city streets, two predators, a mated pair. I was still angry at him, but he was so sorry, like a little puppy dog, that it was hard to stay mad. Eric had taken me hunting. He never took anyone hunting with him, not even Greta. Would Eric have taken a "moist warm tightness" hunting? I think not. The moon was hidden behind the clouds above us and it felt like it might rain.

After picking up two late-night shoppers, we drove

Fang over to the ruins of the Pollux and the Demon Heart. Christmas lights dotted downtown right up to the edge of Eric's property. The last sign of yuletide cheer was a blinking stocking hung over the enclosed bus stop. Not the most romantic setting. I told him as much.

"Not exactly what I'd planned," he admitted. "I meant to be driving out to the old Eighth Street church, to look at the Christmas lights and the nativity scene. Fang wanted to come here, instead."

"We can drive out there later, if you want," I offered. "I understand if you want to look at the Pollux for a while." I wasn't entirely sure if I was talking to Eric or Fang.

Eric hopped out of the car. "Son of a bitch!" he shouted. He ran for the theater, transforming into the uber vamp as he ran, exchanging strides for flaps of his massive wings, flying across the rubble, burrowing deep into the ashes.

Heartbeats.

I got out of the car. Three sets of heartbeats.

He pulled three of his whores out of the wreckage: Gladys, Erin, and Cheryl. They looked badly burned, but the burns were healing. Rachel had set them on fire and left them for dead. Sally and Jodi hadn't fared as well. They were gone.

Watching him fuss over them made me realize something about him. He really does care, not just about me, but about things, people. I don't think I've ever met another vampire who cared about someone they just met, especially humans. Even I don't and I haven't been a vampire long.

"Anything I can do to help?" I asked.

"Testing a theory," he said. He cut through his forearm with his claws, spraying the still cooling blood of the night's kill on his trollops. The effect was impressive, but not impressive enough for him. I could see his disappointment. I think he wanted them to be good as new when the first drop of blood touched their skin. "I don't know why I didn't sense them before," he told me. "I mean, my thrall sense got kinda shorted out when the fire started and everyone started burning, but damn. And the firefighters just left them here . . . fucking enchantment on the stupid fucking city . . . probably didn't even see them."

Or Stacey was there and he didn't care, because he knew you were broke, I thought.

We loaded them into Fang's backseat and sat down on the bench at the bus stop under the blinking light of the lone illuminated stocking. "Damn it," he swore.

"They'll be okay, Eric. Won't they? It seems like they'll be okay." I sat next to him on the bench and put my head on his shoulder. He shrank back to normal size.

"I think they'll be fine," he sighed. "It isn't that."

"What is it?"

"I thought we could do something a little different, tonight."

"Different how?" I asked. Eric put his hand on my thigh and looked at me, really looked at me.

"I needed to do something important tonight." He took his hand off my thigh. I slowly cranked up my body heat; unthinkingly, he put his hand back down. Storm clouds gathered in his eyes and the blue of his irises waxed brighter until they were a deep luminous purple.

"I've only ever done this once before and for all the other ways in which I'm a modern man, I think that I wanted this to stay old-fashioned," his attention shifted to Fang, "if that's okay with you."

My heart stirred within my breast and I closed my eyes and squelched it with all my might. "It's kind of sweet, I guess."

He reached into his pocket and handed me a diamond solitaire. It still smelled like the woman he'd taken it off of, the late-night shopper. She'd been about my size.

"That's your idea of a proposal?" I asked. It was what I wanted, but not the way I wanted it. The little voice in my head was screaming for me to shut up and just be happy, but one thing I'd learned since becoming a vampire is that I'm special. Could I go through eternity with someone who thought handing me a dead woman's ring at a bus stop was romantic? Eric took me for granted and I was tired of it, as much as I loved him.

"I . . . yes." He checked the car again, worried about his thralls. I turned his face back to me with a gentle touch.

"Look at me, Eric. You made me a vampire and then you tried to get rid of me because it made you uncomfortable. Is that going to happen again? Do you really love me or are you just saying that because you lost Marilyn and you need someone to cling to?" As I was talking, my brain kept screaming for my mouth to shut up and my lungs kept trying to start working again. My heart wanted to beat, my blood wanted to pump; I was having a hard time keeping a lid on everything.

"It's not the same love I felt for her, Tabitha. I won't lie about that, but, what I do feel for you—I think it's love, too."

He took my hand when he said it and squeezed it tight. "I thought you were dead. When the Pollux was on fire and I felt Greta burning, I thought you were both dead. That's when I knew. I didn't really love Marilyn anymore. I miss her, but only because we were close, familiar. I must have stopped loving her so long ago that I can't remember what it was like."

"I love you, Eric. I love you so much I'm stupid about it. Whatever you want to do, in or out of the bedroom, I want to say yes, just because you want to do it, but I can't let you treat me this way." My lips trembled and a tear ran down my face. From the smell I could tell it was a real tear, a human tear, not blood, and I felt more relieved than I can say. "If we stay together, you can't go screwing around on me."

"Tabitha." He put a hand on my shoulder. "It's like this, when I'm thinking straight, that's fine, but I don't always think straight. Some demon is always using some spell on me. There is always some evil plot. Roger's gone and Jill's destroyed, but Phillip says that I have a sire to worry about, a sire who is as powerful as I am and will definitely want to screw things up for me."

"You just want a loophole so that you can sleep with Rachel." I pouted.

"She's something else that we have to talk about." He sighed. "I know that she did some terrible things, but she did them to get herself out of Hell, to get her life back, and when push came to shove, she did what she could to make sure I figured out how to defeat Roger and that J'iliol'lth was behind it all."

"I know." I chewed my lip. Eric opened his mouth to say something else, but I spoke first. "You don't get to sleep with her," I blurted.

"I know."

"And no three-ways . . . at least not with her."

He grinned and I either had to slap him or kiss him.

We kissed and Eric's hands roamed over my torso in a way that I'd missed since joining the ranks of the undead. We necked the way only vampires can and our clothes made their way to the concrete next to the bench one article at a time.

"We're in a bus stop," I complained.

"I thought you said you wanted to do anything I wanted to do." He laid me down on the pile of our clothes, the corners of my mouth drawn involuntarily into a smirk. I had said that.

"I still want a ring," I said as he entered me.

"I got you a ring."

"A ring of my own." I bit him gently on the ear.

"You'll get one," he promised. "A big one."

"And a church wedding," I added.

"Okay, sure, we'll figure it out."

As we neared climax, I couldn't resist: "Where do you want to go on our honeymoon?"

"Paris," he said breathlessly.

"Why?" I asked.

"So that we'll always have it," he answered.

It was the right answer. "I love you," I told him.

"Thanks," he said. It wasn't what I wanted to hear, but it was enough.

✦ 41 ✦

ERIC:
LOOSE ENDS

About an hour before bedtime, Phillip delivered on his promise. He sent up a new wardrobe of various fashions for Tabitha. Three weeks' worth of clothes, underwear, and lingerie, all enchanted to do this funky color-changing thing. He'd even had everything all wrapped up for Christmas. She loved it and when I tucked her into bed, she was wearing one of her new nighties.

The headboard and footboard were paneled in Brazilian rosewood; it had been my parents' bed. I'd wondered what had happened to it when Dad died. Now I knew. Like so many other things, Roger had helped himself to it. I held Tabitha as she settled in and once she was asleep, I climbed out of bed, went to the phone, and dialed room service.

"Room service," said a sultry female voice.

"I need you to get Dennis on the phone."

"I can't, Sire," she apologized. "He won't arise until tomorrow evening. When he does, I'd be happy to deliver a message for you."

"Arise?" I asked.

"He was selected during the night, fifty or sixty minutes ago. Lord Phillip was very pleased with him."

"I'll bet," I observed. "He'll be missed. So are you the new girl?"

"I might be the favorite for the next round," she admitted. "My name's Wendy."

"What happens to the applicants who fail, Wendy?"

"They are presented to the chosen one as gifts to do with as he or she pleases."

"So Dennis won the guy round and you're hoping to win the girl round, huh?"

"Yes, milord."

"Maybe you can help me after all, Wendy. Is Lord Phillip still awake?"

"One moment and I'll check." She put me on hold and I listened to Prokofiev's *Peter and the Wolf* while I waited.

"He is, Lord Eric," she said when she came back. "I'll connect you."

"Eric, my boy," Phillip said, "what can I do for you?"

"I wanted to call and thank you for the clothes," I told him. "I especially like the way you had Dennis claim he was delivering something I'd ordered months ago. It was a nice touch. I couldn't tell he was lying."

"He's an accomplished liar, that one," Phillip agreed. "He'll make a fine friend and then, after a while, he'll make an even better enemy."

"That he will," I concurred.

"What else can I do for you?" he asked.

"Nothing," I told him. "That's really all I wanted." I didn't sound convincing, but I hung up anyway.

I watched Tabitha breathe for an hour before I slipped out of her room and across the hall to my new suite. Beatrice was watching a cooking show with the volume off and the subtitles set to French, while Gladys, Cheryl, and Erin slept off their wounds on one of the king-size beds. Phil had outdone himself with the suite he'd provided. Five bedrooms, two dens, a kitchen, and three and a half baths were more than I was used to having. There was even an office that looked enough like mine to make me paranoid.

Rachel walked out of the bathroom wearing nothing but an evil grin. She looked kind of weird with the butterfly on her cheek, but she still exuded sex. "I want to be in charge of your bachelor party," she said, running her hands down her body.

Cinnamon hit my nostrils, and from the smell, it wasn't just affecting me. Beatrice was getting interested, despite herself.

"I think Talbot might be a better choice," I told her.

"You think so?" She tugged on the hoops piercing her nipples. "Why don't you let me show you a preliminary outline." Her hands glided down her smooth taut skin to her navel piercing. Shit.

"Put some clothes on," I told her before her hands could go any lower.

"She'd never know." Rachel pouted.

"Not until you told her," I said.

Rachel laughed, sliding into some panties and a baby doll nightie. Not my idea of clothes, but it fit the letter of the law if not the spirit of the request. "Why don't Bea and I put on a show for you." She smiled.

"It's tempting, but no. I do need your help with something, though."

"What?" she asked eagerly.

"I need to find a good jewelry store. I promised your sister a ring." I turned to Beatrice. "You're coming along, too."

Rachel put on some real clothes and we drove out of town toward a twenty-four-hour jeweler Beatrice said all the society vampires used.

As we passed by the city limits I noticed a large billboard in the rearview mirror. It read, *Welcome to the Void.* Beneath it, *City Music Festival* had been painted out. Over that, in red spray paint, someone had scrawled, *We suck.* I wondered if the author was just being vulgar or if he had any idea how true that statement really was. I made a mental note to have Talbot get me a good digital picture before the city had it painted over.

"I want to ask you both something," I said. "Something that's been bouncing around the back of my head for a while now. Normally I don't want to know these things, but this evening . . ."

"What is it?" Beatrice asked.

"Roger made Marilyn his thrall over forty years ago . . ." I paused.

"You don't want to know," Rachel offered.

". . . but Roger was a Master, so she should have stopped aging . . ."

"How much more slowly than normal did she age?" Beatrice asked.

"He doesn't need to know," Rachel said emphatically.

She was right, but this was Marilyn and I was going to know, even if I forgot it, even if it changed nothing. I owed her that.

"I didn't notice any slowdown in her aging process at all."

"Then she was fighting him," Beatrice whispered. "When you fight your master's will, you age. If she aged normally, then—"

"Then she fought him, every day, all day," I said. "That's my girl." Something cold and wet hit my cheeks and when I wiped at it my hands came away red.

Fang swerved slightly to pass over some bit of roadkill. The eerily soft clatter of tiny bones rained down on the pile of Fang's other meals in the trunk, like a morbid rainstick. Thinking of rain made me think of dripping water, which made me think of . . . "Shit!"

"What is it?" both women asked.

"My sword!" Fang hung a U-turn in the middle of the highway, scattering cars and eliciting honks from other drivers.

"What sword?" Beatrice asked me.

"My magic ice sword! I left it in the closet. If some damn fireman stole my magic sword, I'm gonna be so fucking pissed off!"

Red and blue lights flared in my rearview mirror. Just what I needed—cops. Fang's excitement coursed out through the steering wheel, like a horse eager to gallop.

Laughter rang out from the backseat. "Don't you think you ought to stop for the police?" Rachel asked. "Just accept the ticket and let Phillip fix it for you later."

That would have been the smart thing to do, but I didn't want to do the smart thing, and it wasn't just me; Fang didn't want to stop, either. I took my foot off the brake. The accelerator dropped to the floor, my foot still hovering in the air above it.

Fang wanted to keep on going, to tear ass through the city until we lost them. He didn't care about morals or laws. Fang just cared about using his power, having a blast, getting fed. Greta had better take good care of him while I was in Paris. I was going to miss Fang.

"Fine," I told the car. "Go for it."

Fang kicked in the speed and Beatrice let out a loud whoop. I supposed she'd finally found the exciting life. "I forgot to tell you something," she shouted over the wind, the engine, and the radio.

"What?"

"You got a note from Ebon Winter."

I laughed. "A Christmas card?"

"Sort of." She smiled. "It was a gift certificate good for him to redo the interior of the Pollux when you rebuild it."

"That's awful nice of him." He'd done the courtyard outside Lady Gabriella's; there was no telling what he could do
for the Pollux.

"He also sent a note." She handed it over the seat to me
and I took my hands off the wheel, let Fang drive himself.

It read:

> My Dearest Eric,
> I hope this missive finds you well. Thank you
> ever so much for all the fun you've provided me
> over the last few months. For that I feel I owe
> you many thanks as well as the following warn-
> ing: I've bet against you in Paris.
>
> Happy Holidays,
> Winter

Months? That meant Winter had already been betting on
me when I ran up against William and the other werewolves
out at Orchard Lake.

Well, Merry Christmas to you, too, you son of a bitch. Fine, you
know what, let him bring it. Let them all bring it. Because
when it comes right down to it, I'm a badass vampire and I
can take it.